A MAN
WITHOUT BREATH

Also by Philip Kerr

THE BERNIE GUNTHER BOOKS
The Berlin Noir Trilogy:
March Violets
The Pale Criminal
A German Requiem

·

The One from the Other
A Quiet Flame
If the Dead Rise Not
Field Gray
Prague Fatale

OTHER WORKS
A Philosophical Investigation
Dead Meat
The Grid
Esau
The Five-Year Plan
The Second Angel
The Shot
Dark Matter: The Private Life of Sir Isaac Newton
Hitler's Peace

FOR CHILDREN
Children of the Lamp:
The Akhenaten Adventure
The Blue Djinn of Babylon
The Cobra King of Kathmandu
The Day of the Djinn Warriors
The Eye of the Forest
The Five Fakirs of Faizabad
The Grave Robbers of Genghis Khan

·

One Small Step

A MAN
WITHOUT BREATH

A BERNIE GUNTHER NOVEL

Philip Kerr

A MARIAN WOOD BOOK

Published by G. P. Putnam's Sons
a member of Penguin Group (USA) Inc.
New York

A Marian Wood Book
Published by G. P. Putnam's Sons
Publishers Since 1838
Published by the Penguin Group
Penguin Group (USA) Inc., 375 Hudson Street,
New York, New York 10014, USA

USA · Canada · UK · Ireland · Australia
New Zealand · India · South Africa · China

Penguin Books Ltd, Registered Offices:
80 Strand, London WC2R 0RL, England
For more information about the Penguin Group visit penguin.com

Copyright © 2013 by Thynker Ltd.

Library of Congress Cataloging-in-Publication Data

Kerr, Philip.
A man without breath : a Bernie Gunther novel / Philip Kerr.
p.   cm
"A Marian Wood book."
ISBN 978-0-399-16079-0
1. Gunther, Bernhard (Fictitious character)—Fiction.   2. Private investigators—
Germany—Fiction.   3. Mystery fiction.   4. Historical fiction.   I. Title.
PR6061.E784M35   2013   2012050227
823'.914—dc23

Printed in the United States of America
1   3   5   7   9   10   8   6   4   2

BOOK DESIGN BY AMANDA DEWEY

*This novel is a small token of thanks
to Tony Lacey for getting me started,
and to Marian Wood for keeping me going.*

A nation without a religion—that is like a man without breath.

—JOSEPH GOEBBELS, from his only published novel, *Michael*

PART ONE

Franz Meyer stood up at the head of the table, glanced down, touched the cloth, and awaited our silence. With his fair hair, blue eyes, and neoclassical features that looked as if they'd been carved by Arno Breker, Hitler's official state sculptor, he was no one's idea of a Jew. Half of the SS and SD were more obviously Semitic. Meyer took a deep, almost euphoric breath, gave a broad grin that was part relief and part joie de vivre, and raised his glass to each of the four women seated around the table. None were Jewish and yet, by the racial stereotypes beloved of the Propaganda Ministry, they might have been; all were Germans with strong noses, dark eyes, and even darker hair. For a moment Meyer seemed choked with emotion, and when at last he was able to speak, there were tears in his eyes.

"I'd like to thank my wife and her sisters for your efforts on my behalf," he said. "To do what you did took great courage, and I can't tell you what it meant to those of us who were imprisoned in the Jewish Welfare Office to know that there were so many people on the outside who cared enough to come and demonstrate on our behalf."

"I still can't believe they haven't arrested us," said Meyer's wife, Siv.

"They're so used to people just doing what they're told," said his sister-in-law, Klara, "that they don't know what to do."

"We'll go back to Rosenstrasse tomorrow," insisted Siv. "We won't stop until everyone in there is released. All two thousand of them. We've shown what we can do when public opinion is mobilized. We have to keep the pressure up."

"Yes," said Meyer. "And we will. We will. But right now I'd like to propose a toast. To our new friend Bernie Gunther. But for him and his colleagues at the War Crimes Bureau, I'd probably still be imprisoned in the Jewish Welfare Office. And who knows where after that?" He smiled. "To Bernie."

There were six of us in the cozy little dining room in the Meyers' apartment in Lützowerstrasse. As four of them stood up and toasted me silently, I shook my head. I wasn't sure I deserved Franz Meyer's thanks, and besides, the wine we were drinking was a decent German red—a Spätburgunder from long before the war that he and his wife would have done better to have traded for some food instead of wasting it on me. Any wine—let alone a good German red—was almost impossible to come by in Berlin.

Politely I waited for them to drink to my health before standing up to contradict my host. "I'm not sure I can claim to have had much influence on the SS," I explained. "I spoke to a couple of cops I know who were policing your demonstration and they told me there's a strong rumor doing the rounds that most of the prisoners arrested on Saturday as part of the factory action will probably be released in a few days."

"That's incredible," said Klara. "But what does it mean, Bernie? Do you think the authorities are actually going soft on deportations?"

Before I could offer my opinion the air raid warning siren sounded. We all looked at each other in surprise; it had been almost two years since the last air raid by the Royal Air Force.

"We should go to the shelter," I said. "Or the basement, perhaps."

Meyer nodded. "Yes, you're right," he said firmly. "You should all go. Just in case it's for real."

I fetched my coat and hat off the stand and turned back to Meyer.

"But you're coming, too, aren't you?" I said.

"Jews aren't permitted in the shelters. Perhaps you didn't notice it before. Well, there's no reason why you should have. I don't think there's been an air raid since we started to wear the yellow star."

I shook my head. "No, I didn't." I shrugged. "So, where are Jews supposed to go?"

"To hell, of course. At least that's what they hope." This time Meyer's grin was sardonic. "Besides, people know this is a Jewish apartment, and since the law requires that homes be left with their doors and windows open, to minimize the effect of a pressure wave from a bomb blast, that's also an invitation to some local thief to come and steal from us." He shook his head. "So I shall stay here."

I glanced out the window; in the street below, hundreds of people were already being herded toward the local shelter by uniformed police. There wasn't much time to lose.

"Franz," said Siv. "We're not going there without you. Just leave your coat. If they can't see your star, they'll have to assume you're German. You can carry me in and say I fainted, and if I show my pass and say I'm your wife then no one will be any the wiser."

"She's right," I said.

"And if I'm arrested, what then? I've only just been released." Meyer shook his head and laughed. "Besides, it's probably a false alarm. Hasn't Fat Hermann promised us that this is the best-defended city in Europe?"

The siren continued to wail outside like some dreadful mechanical clarion announcing the end of a night shift in the smoking factories of hell.

Siv Meyer sat down at the table and clasped her hands tight. "If you're not going, then I'm not going."

"Neither am I," Klara said, sitting down beside her.

"There's no time to argue about this," said Meyer. "You should go. All of you."

"He's right," I said, more urgently now as already we could hear the drone of the bombers in the distance; it was obvious this was no false alarm. I opened the door and waved the four women toward me. "Come on," I said.

"No," said Siv. "We're staying."

The two other sisters glanced at each other and then sat down alongside their Jewish brother-in-law. This left me on my feet with a coat in my hand and a nervous look on my face. After all, I'd seen what our own bombers had done to Minsk and parts of France. I put on the coat and shoved my hands in the pockets so as to conceal the fact that they were shaking.

"I don't think they're coming to drop propaganda leaflets," I said. "Not this time."

"Yes, but it's not civilians like us they're after, surely," said Siv. "It's the government district. They'll know there's a hospital near here. The RAF won't want to risk hitting the Catholic Hospital, will they? The English aren't like that. It's the Wilhelmstrasse they'll be after."

"How will they know from two thousand feet up in the air?" I heard myself utter weakly.

"She's right," said Meyer. "It's not the west of Berlin they're targeting. It's the east. Which means it's probably just as well we're none of us in Rosenstrasse tonight." He smiled at me. "You should go, Bernie. We'll be all right. You'll see."

"I expect you're right," I said and, deciding to ignore the air raid siren like the others, I started to take off my coat. "All the same, I can hardly leave you all here."

"Why not?" asked Klara.

I shrugged, but what it really came down to was this: I could hardly leave and still manage to look good in Klara's lovely brown eyes, and I was quite keen that she should have a good impression of me; but I didn't feel I could say this to her, not yet.

For a moment I felt my chest tighten as my nerves continued to get the better of me. Then I heard some bombs explode in the distance and breathed a sigh of relief. Back in the trenches, during the Great War, when you could hear the shells exploding somewhere else, it usually meant you were safe because it was commonly held that you never heard the one that killed you.

"Sounds like it's north Berlin that's getting it," I said, leaning in the doorway. "The petroleum refinery on Thalerstrasse, probably. It's the only real target around here. But I think we should at least get under the table. Just in case a stray bomb—"

I think that was the last thing I said and probably it was the fact that I was standing in the doorway that saved my life because just then the glass in the nearest window frame seemed to melt into a thousand drops of light. Some of these old Berlin apartment buildings were made to last, and I later learned that the bomb that blew up the one we were in—not to mention the hospital on Lützowstrasse— and flattened it in a split second would certainly have killed me had not the lintel above my head and the stout oak door that was hanging inside it resisted the weight of the roof's metal joist, for this is what killed Siv Meyer and her three sisters.

After that there was darkness and silence, except for the sound of a kettle on a gas plate whistling as it came slowly to the boil, although this was probably just the sensation in my battered eardrums. It was as if someone had switched off an electric light and then pulled away the floorboards on which I had been standing, and the effect of the world disappearing from underneath my feet might have been similar to the sensation of being hooded and hanged on a gallows. I don't know. All I really remember of what happened is that I was upside down lying on a pile of rubble when I recovered consciousness and there was a door on top of my face which, for several minutes until I recovered enough breath in my bomb-blasted lungs to moan for help, I was convinced was the lid of my own damned coffin.

I HAD LEFT KRIPO IN THE SUMMER of 1942 and joined the Wehrmacht War Crimes Bureau with the connivance of my old colleague Arthur Nebe. As the commander of Special Action Group B, which was headquartered in Smolensk, where tens of thousands of Russian Jews had been murdered, Nebe knew a thing or two about war crimes himself; I'm certain it appealed to his Berliner's black humor that I should find myself attached to an organization of old Prussian judges, most of whom were staunchly anti-Nazi. Dedicated to the military ideals as laid down in the Geneva Convention of 1929, they believed there was a proper and honorable way for the army—any army—to fight a war. Nebe must have thought it very funny that there existed a judicial body within the German High Command that not only resisted having Party members in its distinguished ranks but was also quite prepared to devote its considerable resources to the investigation and prosecution of crimes committed by and against German soldiers: theft, looting, rape, and murder could all be the subject of lengthy and serious inquiries—sometimes earning their perpetrators a death sentence. I thought it was kind of funny myself but then, like Nebe, I'm also from Berlin and it's known that we have a strange sense of humor. By the winter of 1943, you found your laughs where you could, and I don't know how else to describe a situation in which you can have an army corporal hanged for the rape and murder of a Russian peasant girl in one village that's only a few kilometers from another village where an SS special action group has just murdered twenty-five thousand men, women, and children. I expect the Greeks have a word for that kind of comedy, and if I'd paid a little more attention to my classics master at school I might have known what that word was.

The judges—they were nearly all judges—who worked for the

bureau were not hypocrites any more than they were Nazis, and they saw no reason why their moral standards should decline just because the government of Germany had no moral standards at all. The Greeks certainly had a word for that, all right, and I even knew what it was, although it's fair to say I'd had to learn how to spell it again; they called that kind of behavior *ethics*, and my being concerned with rightness and wrongness felt good since it helped to restore in me a sense of pride in who and what I was. At least for a while, anyway.

Most of the time I assisted the bureau's judges—several of whom I'd known during the Weimar Republic—in taking depositions from witnesses or finding new cases for the bureau to investigate. That was how I first met Siv Meyer. She was a friend of a girl called Renata Matter, who was a good friend of mine and who worked at the Hotel Adlon; Siv played the piano in the orchestra at the Adlon.

I met her at the hotel on Sunday, February 28, which was the day after Berlin's last Jews—some ten thousand people—had been arrested for deportation to ghettos in the east. Franz Meyer was a worker at the Osram electric lightbulb factory in Wilmersdorf, which was where he was arrested, but before this he had been a doctor, and this was how he came to find himself working as a medical orderly on a German hospital ship that had been attacked and sunk by a British submarine off the coast of Norway in August 1941. My boss and the bureau chief, Johannes Goldsche, had tried to investigate the case but, at the time, it was thought that there had been no survivors. So when Renata Matter told me Franz Meyer's story, I went to see his wife at their apartment in Lützowerstrasse.

It was a short walk from my own apartment on Fasanenstrasse, with a view of the canal and the local town hall, and only a short walk from the Schulstrasse synagogue, where many of Berlin's Jews had been held in transit on their way to an unknown fate in the east. Meyer had only escaped arrest himself because he was a *Mischling*— a Jew who was married to a German.

From the wedding photograph on the Biedermeier sideboard it was easy to see what they saw in each other. Franz Meyer was absurdly handsome and very like Franchot Tone, the movie actor who was once married to Joan Crawford; Siv was just beautiful and there's nothing absurd about that; more importantly, so were her three sisters, Klara, Frieda, and Hedwig, all of whom were present when I met their sister for the first time.

"Why didn't your husband come forward before?" I asked Siv Meyer over a cup of ersatz coffee, which was the only kind of coffee anyone had now. "This incident took place on August thirtieth, 1941. Why is he only willing to speak about it now?"

"Clearly you don't know very much about what it's like to be a Jew in Berlin," she said.

"You're right. I don't."

"No Jew wants to draw attention to himself by being a part of any inquiry in Germany. Even if it is a good cause."

I shrugged. "I can understand that," I said. "A witness for the bureau one day and a prisoner of the Gestapo the next. On the other hand, I do know what it's like to be a Jew in the east, and if you want to prevent your husband from ending up there, I hope you're telling the truth about all this. At the War Crimes Bureau we get lots of people who try to waste our time."

"You were in the east?"

"Minsk," I said simply. "They sent me back here to Berlin and the War Crimes Bureau for questioning my orders."

"What's happening out there? In the ghettos? In the concentration camps? One hears so many different stories about what resettlement amounts to."

I shrugged. "I don't think the stories even get close to the horror of what's happening in the eastern ghettos. And by the way, there is no resettlement. There's just starvation and death."

Siv Meyer let out a sigh and then exchanged a glance with her sisters. I was fond of looking at her three sisters myself. It made a very pleasant change to take a deposition from an attractive and well-spoken woman instead of an injured soldier.

"Thank you for being honest, Herr Gunther," she said. "As well as the stories, one hears so many lies." She nodded. "Since you've been so honest, let me be honest, too. The main reason my husband hasn't talked before about the sinking of the SS *Hrotsvitha von Gandersheim* is because he hardly wanted to make a gift of some useful anti-British propaganda to Dr. Goebbels. Of course, now that he's been arrested it seems that this might be his only chance of staying out of a concentration camp."

"We don't have much to do with the Propaganda Ministry, Frau Meyer. Not if we can help it. Perhaps it's them you should be speaking to."

"I don't doubt you mean what you say, Herr Gunther," said Siv Meyer. "Nevertheless, British war crimes against defenseless German hospital ships make good propaganda."

"That's just the kind of story which is especially useful now," added Klara. "After Stalingrad."

I had to admit she was probably right. The surrender of the German Sixth Army in Stalingrad on February 2 had been the greatest disaster suffered by the Nazis since their coming to power; and Goebbels's speech on the eighteenth urging total war on the German people certainly needed incidents like the sinking of a hospital ship to prove that there was no way back for us now; that it was victory or nothing.

"Look," I said, "I can't promise anything, but if you tell me where they're holding your husband, I'll go there right now and see him, Frau Meyer. If I think there's something in his story, I'll contact my superiors and see if we can get him released as a key witness for an inquiry."

"He's being detained at the Jewish Welfare Office, on Rosenstrasse," said Siv. "We'll come with you, if you like."

I shook my head. "That's quite all right. I know where it is."

"You don't understand," said Klara. "We're all going there anyway. To protest against Franz's detention."

"I don't think that's a very good idea," I said. "You'll be arrested."

"There are lots of wives who are going," said Siv. "They can't arrest us all."

"Why not?" I asked. "In case you haven't noticed, they've arrested all of the Jews."

HEARING FOOTSTEPS NEAR MY HEAD, I tried to push the heavy wooden door off my face but my left hand was trapped and the right too painful to use. Someone shouted something and a minute or two later I felt myself slide a little as the rubble on which I lay shifted like the scree on a steep mountainside, and then the door was lifted away to reveal my rescuers. The apartment building was almost completely gone and all that remained in the cold moonlight was one high chimney containing an ascending series of fireplaces. Several hands placed me onto a stretcher and I was carried off the tangled, smoking heap of bricks, concrete, leaking water pipes, and wooden planks and laid in the middle of the road, where I enjoyed a perfect view of a building burning in the distance and then the beams from Berlin's defense searchlights as they continued to search the sky for enemy planes; but the siren was sounding the all clear and I could hear the footsteps of people already coming up from the shelters to look for what was left of their homes. I wondered if my own home in Fasanenstrasse was all right. Not that there was very much in it. Nearly everything of value had been sold or traded on the black market.

Gradually I began to move my head, one way and the other, until I felt able to push myself up on one elbow to look around. But I could hardly breathe; my chest was still full of dust and smoke and the exertion provoked a fit of coughing that was only alleviated when a man I half recognized helped me to a drink of water and laid a blanket on top of me.

About a minute later there was a loud shout and the chimney came down on top of the spot where I'd been lying. The dust from its collapse covered me so I was moved farther down the street and set down next to some others who were awaiting medical attention. Klara was lying beside me now at less than an arm's length; her dress was hardly torn, her eyes were open, and her body was quite unmarked; I called her name several times before it finally dawned on me that she was dead. It was as if her life had just stopped like a clock, and it hardly seemed possible that so much of her future—she couldn't have been older than thirty—had disappeared in the space of a few seconds.

Other corpses were laid out in the street next to her. I couldn't see how many. I sat up to look for Franz Meyer and the others but the effort was too much and I fell back and closed my eyes. And fainted, I suppose.

"Give us back our men."

You could hear them three streets away—a large and angry crowd of women—and as we turned the corner of Rosenstrasse I felt my jaw slacken. I hadn't seen anything like this on the streets of Berlin since before Hitler came to power. And whoever would have thought that wearing a nice hat and carrying a handbag was the best way to dress when you were opposing the Nazis?

"Release our husbands," shouted the mob of women as we pushed our way along the street. "Release our husbands now."

There were many more of them than I had been expecting—perhaps several hundred. Even Klara looked surprised, but not as surprised as the cops and SS who were guarding the Jewish Welfare Office. They gripped their machine pistols and rifles and muttered curses and abuse at the women standing nearest to the door and looked horrified to find themselves ignored or even roundly cursed back. This wasn't how it was supposed to be: if you had a gun, then people were supposed to do what they were told. That's page one of how to be a Nazi.

The welfare office on Rosenstrasse near Berlin's Alexanderplatz was a gray granite Wilhelmine building with a saddle roof next to a synagogue—formerly the oldest in Berlin—partly destroyed by the Nazis in November 1938, and within spitting distance of the Police Praesidium, where I had spent most of my adult working life. I might no longer have been working for Kripo but I'd managed to keep my beer token—the brass identity disk that commanded such craven respect in most German citizens.

"We're decent German women," shouted one woman. "Loyal to the Leader and to the Fatherland. You can't speak to us like that, you cheeky young bastard."

"I can speak to anyone like that who's misguided enough to be married to a Jew," I heard one of the uniformed cops—a corporal— say to her. "Go home, lady, or you'll be shot."

"You need a good spanking, you little pip," said another woman. "Does your mother know you're such an arrogant whelp?"

"You see?" said Klara, triumphantly. "They can't shoot us all."

"Can't we?" sneered the corporal. "When we have the orders to shoot, I can promise you'll get it first, Granny."

"Take it easy, Corporal," I said, and flashed my beer token in front of his face. "There's really no need to be rude to these ladies. Especially on a Sunday afternoon."

"Yes, sir," he said smartly. "Sorry, sir." He nodded back over his shoulder. "Are you going in there, sir?"

"Yes," I said. I turned to Klara and Siv. "I'll try to be as quick as I can."

"Then if you would be so kind," said the corporal, "we need orders, sir. No one's told us what to do. Just to stay here and stop people from going in. Perhaps you might mention that, sir."

I shrugged. "Sure, Corporal. But from what I can see, you're already doing a grand job."

"We are?"

"You're keeping the peace, aren't you?"

"Yes, sir."

"You can't keep the peace if you start shooting at all these ladies, now can you?" I smiled at him and then patted his shoulder. "In my experience, Corporal, the best police work looks like nothing at all and is always soon forgotten."

I was unprepared for the scene that met me inside, where the smell was already intolerable: a welfare office is not designed to be a transit camp for two thousand prisoners. Men and women with identity tags on strings around their necks like traveling children were lined up to use a lavatory that had no door, while others were crammed fifty or sixty to an office where it was standing room only. Welfare parcels—many of them brought by the women outside—filled another room where they had been tossed but no one was complaining; things were quiet; after almost a decade of Nazi rule, Jews knew better than to complain. It was only the police sergeant in charge of these people who seemed inclined to bemoan his lot, and as he searched a clipboard for Franz Meyer's name and then led me to the second-floor office where the man was being held, he began to unroll the barbed S-wire of his sharp complaint:

"I don't know what I'm supposed to do with all these people. No one's told me a damned thing. How long they're going to be here. How to make them comfortable. How to answer all of these bloody women who are demanding answers. It's not so easy, I can tell you. All I've got is what was in this office building when we turned up yesterday. Toilet paper ran out within an hour of us being here. And Christ only knows how I'm going to feed them. There's nothing open on a Sunday."

"Why don't you open those food parcels and give them that?" I asked.

The sergeant looked incredulous. "I couldn't do that," he said. "Those are private parcels."

"I shouldn't think that the people they belong to will mind," I said. "Just as long as they get something to eat."

We found Franz Meyer seated in one of the larger offices where almost a hundred men were waiting patiently for something to happen. The sergeant called Meyer out and, still grumbling, went off to think about what I'd suggested about the parcels, while I spoke to my potential war crimes witness in the comparative privacy of the corridor.

I told him that I worked for the War Crimes Bureau and why I was there. Meanwhile, outside the building, the women's protest seemed to be getting louder.

"Your wife and sisters-in-law are outside," I told him. "It's them who put me up to this."

"Please tell them to go home," said Meyer. "It's safer in here than out there, I think."

"I agree. But they're not about to listen to me."

Meyer grinned. "Yes, I can imagine."

"The sooner you tell me about what happened on the SS *Hrotsvitha von Gandersheim*, the sooner I can speak to my boss and see about getting you out of here, and the sooner we can get them all out of harm's way." I paused. "That is, if you're prepared to give me a deposition."

"It's my only chance of avoiding a concentration camp, I think."

"Or worse," I added, by way of extra incentive.

"Well, that's honest, I suppose." He shrugged.

"I'll take that as a yes, shall I?"

He nodded and we spent the next thirty minutes writing out his statement about what had happened off the coast of Norway in August 1941. When he'd signed it, I wagged my finger at him.

"Coming here like this I'm sticking my neck out for you," I told him. "So you'd better not let me down. If I so much as get a whiff of you changing your story, I'll wash my hands of you. Got that?"

He nodded. "So why are you sticking your neck out?"

It was a good question and probably it deserved an answer but I hardly wanted to go into how a friend of a friend had asked me to help, which is how these things usually got fixed in Germany; and I certainly didn't want to mention how attractive I found his sister-in-law Klara, or that I was making up for some lost time when it came to helping Jews; and maybe a bit more than only lost time.

"Let's just say I don't like the Tommies very much and leave it at that, shall we?" I shook my head. "Besides, I'm not promising anything. It's up to my boss, Judge Goldsche. If he thinks your deposi-·tion can start an inquiry into a British war crime, he's the one who'll have to persuade the Foreign Office that this is worth a white book, not me."

"What's a white book?"

"An official publication that's intended to present the German side of an incident that might amount to a violation of the laws of war. It's the bureau that does all the legwork, but it's the Foreign Office that publishes the report."

"That sounds as if it might take a while."

I shook my head. "Fortunately for you, the bureau and the judge have a great deal of power. Even in Nazi Germany. If the judge buys your story, we'll have you home tomorrow."

2

They took me to the state hospital in Friedrichshain. I was suffering from a concussion and smoke inhalation; the smoke inhalation was nothing new, but as a result of the concussion the doctor advised me to stay in bed for a couple of days. I've always disliked hospitals. They sell just a little too much reality for my taste. But I did feel tired. Being bombed by the RAF will do that to you. So the advice of this fresh-faced aspirin Jesus suited me very well. I thought I was due a bit of time with my feet up and my mouth in traction. Besides, I was a lot better off in the hospital than in my apartment; they were still feeding patients in the state hospital, which was more than I could say about home, where the pot was empty.

From my window I had a nice view of the St. George's cemetery but I didn't mind that: the state hospital faces the Böhmisches Brewery on the other side of Landsberger Allee, which means there's always a strong smell of hops in the air. I can't think of a better way to encourage a Berliner's recovery than the smell of German beer. Not that we saw much of it in the city's bars: most of the beer brewed in Berlin went straight to our brave boys on the Russian front. But I can't say that I begrudged them a couple of brews. After Stalingrad I expect they needed a taste of home to keep their spirits up. There wasn't a great deal else to keep a man's spirits up in the winter of 1943.

Either way, I was better off than Siv Meyer and her sisters, who were all dead. The only survivors of that night were me and Franz, who was in the Jewish Hospital. Where else? The bigger surprise was that there was a Jewish hospital in the first place.

I was not without visitors. Renata Matter came to see me. It was Renata who told me my own home was undamaged and who gave me the news about the Meyer sisters. She was pretty upset about it, too, and being a good Roman Catholic she had already spent the morning praying for their souls. She seemed just as upset by the news that the priest of St. Hedwig's, Bernhard Lichtenberg, had been put in prison and seemed likely to be sent to Dachau, where—according to her—"more than two thousand priests" were already incarcerated. Two thousand priests in Dachau was a depressing thought. That's the thing about hospital visitors: sometimes you wish they simply hadn't bothered to come along to try to cheer you up.

This was certainly how I felt about my other visitor, a commissar from the Gestapo called Werner Sachse. I knew Sachse from the Alex, and in truth he wasn't a bad fellow for a Gestapo officer but I knew he wasn't there to bring me the gift of a stollen and an encouraging word. He wore hair as neat as the lines in a carpenter's notebook, a black leather coat that creaked like snow under your feet when he moved, and a black hat and black tie that made me uncomfortable.

"I'll have the brass handles and the satin lining, please," I said. "And an open casket, I think."

Sachse's face looked puzzled.

"I guess your pay grade doesn't run to black humor. Just black ties and coats."

"You'd be surprised." He shrugged. "We have our jokes in the Gestapo."

"Sure you do. Only they're called evidence for the People's Court in Moabit."

"I like you, Gunther. So you won't mind if I warn you about making jokes like that. Especially after Stalingrad. These days it's called 'undermining defensive strength.' And they cut your head off for it. Last year they beheaded three people a day for making jokes like that."

"Haven't you heard? I'm sick. I've got a concussion. I can hardly breathe. I'm not myself. If they cut my head off, I probably wouldn't notice anyway. That's my defense if this comes to court. What is your pay grade anyway, Werner?"

"A3. Why do you ask?"

"I was just wondering why a man who makes six hundred marks a week would come all this way to warn me about undermining our defensive strength—assuming such a thing actually exists after Stalingrad."

"It was just a friendly warning. In passing. But that's not why I'm here, Gunther."

"I can't imagine you're here to confess to a war crime, Werner. Not yet, anyway."

"You'd like that, wouldn't you?"

"I wonder how far we could get with that before they cut off both our heads?"

"Tell me about Franz Meyer."

"He's sick, too."

"Yes, I know. I just came from the Jewish Hospital."

"How is he?"

Sachse shook his head. "Doing really well. He's in a coma."

"You see? I was right. Your pay grade doesn't run to humor. These days you need to be at least a Kriminalrat before they allow you to make jokes that are actually funny."

"The Meyers were under surveillance, did you know that?"

"No. I wasn't there long enough to notice. Not with Klara around. She was a real beauty."

"Yes, it's too bad about *her*, I agree." He paused. "You were in their apartment, twice. On the Sunday and then the Monday evening."

"That's correct. Hey, I don't suppose the V-men who were watching the Meyers got killed, too?"

"No. They're still alive."

"Pity."

"But who says they were V-men? This wasn't an undercover operation. I expect the Meyers knew they were being watched, even if you were too dumb to notice."

He lit a couple of cigarettes and put one in my mouth.

"Thanks, Werner."

"Look, you big dumb ugly bastard, you might as well know it was me and some of the other lads from the Gestapo who found you and pulled you off that pile of rubble before the chimney came down. It was the Gestapo who saved your life, Gunther. So you see, we must have a sense of humor. The sensible thing would probably have been to have left you there to get crushed."

"Straight?"

"Straight."

"Then thanks. I owe you one."

"That's what I figured. It's why I'm here asking about Franz Meyer."

"All right. I'm listening. Get your klieg light and switch it on."

"Some honest answers. You owe me that much at least."

I took a short drag on my cigarette—just to get my breath—and then nodded. "That and this smoke. It actually tastes like a proper nail."

"What were you doing in Lützowerstrasse? And don't say 'just visiting.' "

"When Franz Meyer got picked up by the Gestapo in the factory action, his missus figured on the War Crimes Bureau pulling his coal out of the fire. He was the only surviving witness to a war crime when a Tommy submarine torpedoed a hospital ship off the coast of Norway in 1941. The SS *Hrotsvitha von Gandersheim*. I took his deposition and then persuaded my boss to sign an order for his release."

"And what was in this for you?"

"That's my job, Werner. They point my suit at a possible crime and I try to check it out. Look, I won't deny that the Meyers were very grateful. They invited me to dinner and opened their last bottle of Spätburgunder in celebration of Meyer's release from the Jewish Welfare Office on Rosenstrasse. We were raising a glass when the bomb hit. But I can't deny that I had a certain satisfaction in sticking one on the Tommies. Sanctimonious bastards. According to them, the *Hrotsvitha von Gandersheim* was just a troop-carrying convoy and not a hospital ship at all. Twelve hundred men drowned. Troops, perhaps, but injured troops who were returning home to Germany. His deposition is with my boss, Judge Goldsche. You can read it for yourself and see if I'm telling the truth."

"Yes, I checked. But why didn't you all go to the shelter with everyone else?"

"Meyer's a Jew. He's not allowed in the shelter."

"All right, but what about the rest of you? The wife, her sisters—none of them was a Jew. You must admit that's a bit suspicious."

"We didn't think the air raid was for real. So we decided to stick it out."

"Fair enough." Sachse sighed. "None of us will make that mistake again, I suppose. Berlin is a ruin. Saint Hedwig's is burned out, Prager Platz is just rubble, and the hospital on Lützowerstrasse was completely destroyed. The RAF dropped more than a thousand tons of bombs. On civilian targets. Now, that's what I call a fucking war crime. While you're at it, investigate that, will you?"

I nodded. "Yes."

"Did the Meyers make any mention of any foreign currency? Swiss francs, perhaps?"

"You mean for me?" I shook my head. "No. I wasn't even offered a lousy packet of cigarettes." I frowned. "Are you saying those bastards had money?"

Sachse nodded.

"Well, they never offered me any."

"Any mention of a man called Wilhelm Schmidhuber?"

"No."

"Friedrich Arnold? Julius Fliess?"

I shook my head.

"Operation Seven, perhaps?"

"Never heard of it."

"Dietrich Bonhoeffer?"

"The pastor?"

Sachse nodded.

"No. I'd have remembered his name. What's this all about, Werner?"

Sachse took a pull on his cigarette, glanced at the man in the next bed, and drew his chair closer to me—close enough to smell his Klar Klassik shaving water; even on the Gestapo it made a pleasant change from stale bandages, piss on the windowpanes, and forgotten bedpans.

"Operation Seven was a plan to help seven Jews escape from Germany to Switzerland."

"Seven important Jews?"

"No such thing. Not anymore. All of the important Jews have left Germany or are— Well, they've left. No, these were just seven ordinary Jews."

"I see."

"Of course, the Swiss are every bit as anti-Semitic as we are and won't do anything unless it's for money. We believe the conspirators were obliged to raise a large sum of money in order to ensure that these Jews could pay their own way and not constitute a burden on the Swiss state. This money was smuggled into Switzerland. Operation Seven was originally Operation Eight, however, and included Franz Meyer. We had them under surveillance in the hope that they might lead us to the other conspirators."

"That's too bad."

Werner Sachse nodded slowly. "I believe your story," he said.

"Thanks, Werner. I appreciate it. All the same, I assume you still searched my pockets for Swiss francs when I was lying on the street."

"Of course. When you turned up I thought we'd hit pay dirt. You can see how very sad I was to discover you were probably on the level."

"It's like I always say, Werner. There's nothing quite as disappointing as the discovery that our friends and neighbors are no more dishonest than we are ourselves."

FRIDAY, MARCH 5, 1943

A couple of days later the doctor gave me some more aspirin, advised me to get plenty of fresh air to help with my breathing, and told me I could go home. Berlin was rightly famous for its air, but it wasn't always so fresh—not since the Nazis had taken over.

Coincidentally, it was the same day the authorities told the Jews still held in the welfare office that they could go home, too. I couldn't believe it when I heard, and I imagine that the men and women who were released could believe it even less than me. The authorities had gone so far as to track down some Jews who'd already been deported and had them sent back to Berlin and released, like the others.

What was happening here? What was in the minds of the government? Was it possible that after the huge defeat at Stalingrad the Nazis were losing their grip? Or had the Nazis really listened to the protests of a thousand determined German women? It was hard to tell but it seemed the only possible conclusion. There were ten thousand Jews who had been arrested on the twenty-seventh of February and of these, fewer than two thousand had gone to Rosenstrasse; some had been remanded to the Clou Concert Hall on Mauerstrasse, others to the stables of a barracks on Rathenower Strasse, and still more to a synagogue on Levetzowstrasse in Moabit; but it was only at the Rosenstrasse, where Jews married to Germans were detained, that a protest had taken place and it was only there that any Jews were released. The way I heard it later, all of the Jews from the other sites were deported to the east. But if the protest really had succeeded, it begged the question, what might have been achieved if mass protests had taken place before? It was a sobering thought that the first organized opposition to the Nazis in ten years had probably succeeded.

That was one sobering thought; another was that if I hadn't helped Franz Meyer, he would certainly have stayed in the welfare office in Rosenstrasse and his wife and sisters would probably have remained with the rest of the women outside, in which case all of them would still live. Homeless, perhaps. But alive, yes, that was quite conceivable. There's no amount of aspirin you can swallow that will take away that kind of toothache.

I left the state hospital but I didn't go home. At least not right away. I took a Ringbahn train northwest, to Gesundbrunnen. To begin work again.

The Jewish Hospital in Wedding was about six or seven modern buildings on the corner of Schulstrasse and Exerzierstrasse, and next to St. George's Hospital. As surprising as the fact that such a thing as a Jewish hospital even existed in Berlin was the discovery that the place was modern, relatively well equipped, and full of doctors, nurses, and patients. Since all of them were Jews, the place was also guarded by a small detachment of SS. Almost as soon as I identified myself at the front desk I discovered that the hospital even had its own branch of Gestapo, one of whose officers was summoned at the same time as the hospital director, Dr. Walter Lustig.

Lustig arrived first and it turned out we'd met several times before: a hard-arsed Silesian—they always make the most unpleasant Prussians—Lustig had been head of the medical department in the Police Praesidium at the Alex and we'd always disliked each other.

I disliked him because I don't much care for pompous men with the bearing if not the height of a senior Prussian officer; he probably thought I disliked him because he was a Jew. But in truth, seeing him at the hospital was the first time I realized he was Jewish—the yellow star on his white coat left me in no doubt about that. He disliked me because he was the type who seemed to dislike nearly everyone who was in a subordinate position to him or ill educated by his elevated academic standards. At the Alex we'd called him Doctor Doctor because he had university degrees in both philosophy and medicine, and never failed to remind people of this distinction.

Now he clicked his heels and bowed stiffly as if he'd just marched off the parade ground at the Prussian military academy.

"Herr Gunther," he said. "After all these long years we meet again. To what do we owe this dubious pleasure?"

It certainly didn't seem as if his new lower status as a member of a pariah race had affected his attitude in any way. I could almost see the wax on the eagle with which he'd decorated his top lip. I hadn't forgotten his pomposity but it seemed I had forgotten his breath, which required a good half meter at least for a man with a heavy cold to feel properly safe in his company.

"Good to see you, too, Dr. Lustig. So this is where you've been keeping yourself. I always wondered what happened to you."

"I can't imagine it kept you awake at night."

"No. Not in the least. These days I sleep like a dog without dreams. All the same, I'm pleased to see you well." I glanced around. There were some Hebraic-looking design details on the wall but no sign of the kind of angular, astronomical artwork the Nazis were fond of adding to anything owned or used by Jews. "Nice place you've got here, Doc."

Lustig bowed again and then glanced ostentatiously at his pocket watch. "Yes, yes, but you know, *tempus fugit*."

"You have a patient, Franz Meyer, who was brought here on

Monday night or perhaps the early hours of Tuesday morning. He's the key witness in a war crimes inquiry I'm carrying out for the Wehrmacht. I'd like to see him, if I may."

"You're no longer with the police?"

"No, sir." I handed him my business card.

"Then it seems we have something in common. Whoever would have thought such a thing?"

"Life springs all sorts of surprises on the living."

"That's especially true in here, Herr Gunther. Address?"

"Mine, or Herr Meyer's?"

"Herr Meyer's, of course."

"Apartment three, Ten Lützowerstrasse, Berlin Charlottenburg."

Curtly, Lustig repeated the name and address to the attractive nurse now accompanying him. Immediately and without being told, she went into the office behind the front desk and searched a large filing cabinet for the patient's notes. Somehow I sensed Lustig was used to always having the first plate at dinner.

He was already snapping his fat fingers at her. "Come on, come on, I haven't got all day."

"I can see you're as busy as ever, Herr Doctor," I said, as the nurse returned to his side and handed over the file.

"There is some sanctuary in that, at least," he murmured, glancing over the notes. "Yes, I remember him now, poor fellow. Half his head is missing. How he's still alive is beyond my medical understanding. He's been in a coma since he got here. Do you still wish to see him? Perhaps wasting time is an institutional habit in the War Crimes Bureau, just as much as it was in Kripo?"

"You know? I'd like to see him. I just want to check he's not as scared of you as she is, Doc." I smiled at his nurse. In my experience nurses—even the pretty ones—are always worth a smile.

"Very well." Lustig uttered a weary sigh that was part groan and walked quickly along the corridor. "Come along, Herr Gunther," he yelled, "you must pursue me, you must pursue me. We need to hurry if we are to find Herr Meyer capable of uttering the one all-important word that may provide the vital assistance for your inquiry. Evidently my own word counts for very little these days."

A few seconds later we met a man with a largish scar under his ill-tempered mouth that looked like a third lip.

"And this is why that is," added the doctor. "Criminal Commissar Dobberke. Dobberke is head of the Gestapo office in this hospital. A very important position that ensures our enduring safety and loyal service to the elected government."

Lustig handed the Gestapo man my card.

"Dobberke, this is Herr Gunther, formerly of the Alex and now with the Bureau of War Crimes in the Wehrmacht's legal department. He wishes to see if one of our patients is capable of providing the vital testimony that will change the course of military jurisprudence."

Quickly I walked after Lustig; so did Dobberke. After several days in bed, I figured such violent exercise could only do me good.

We went into a ward full of men in various states of ill health. It hardly seemed necessary but all of these patients wore a yellow star on their pajamas and dressing gowns. They looked undernourished but that was hardly unusual by Berlin standards; there wasn't one of us in the city—Jew or German—who couldn't have used a square meal. Some were smoking, some were talking, and some were playing chess; none of them paid us much regard.

Meyer was behind a screen, in the last bed under a tall window with a view of a fine lawn and a circular ornamental pond. Not that Meyer seemed likely to avail himself of the view; his eyes were closed and there was a bandage around a no longer completely round head, which reminded me of a partly deflated football. But even badly injured he was still startlingly handsome, like some ruined marble Greek statue on the Pergamon Altar.

Lustig went through the motions, checking the unconscious man's pulse and taking his temperature with one eye on the nurse, and only glancing cursorily at his chart before tutting loudly and shaking his head. It was the kind of bedside manner that would have embarrassed Victor Frankenstein.

"I thought so," he said firmly. "A vegetable. That's my prognosis." He smiled brightly. "But go ahead, Herr Gunther. Be my guest. You may question this patient for as long as you see fit. Just don't expect any answers." He laughed. "Especially with Commissar Dobberke at your side."

And then he was gone, leaving me alone with Dobberke.

"That was a touching reunion." By way of explanation I added: "Formerly he and I were colleagues at the Police Praesidium." I shook my head. "I can't say time or circumstances have mellowed him any."

"He's not such a bad fellow," Dobberke said generously. "For a Jew, I mean. But for him, this place would never keep going."

I sat down on the edge of Franz Meyer's bed and sighed.

"I don't see this fellow talking to anyone soon, except Saint Peter," I said. "I haven't seen a man with a head injury like that since 1918. It's like someone took a hammer to a coconut."

"That's quite a lump you have on your own head," said Dobberke.

I touched my head self-consciously. "I'm all right." I shrugged. "Why *does* it keep going? The hospital?"

"It's a garbage can for misfits," he said. "A collection camp. You see, the Jews here are an odd lot. They're orphans of uncertain parentage, some collaborators, a few pet Jews who are under the protection of one bigwig or another, several attempted suicides—"

Dobberke caught the look of surprise on my face and shrugged.

"Yes, suicides," he said. "Well, you can't make someone who's half dead walk on and off a deportation train, can you? That's just more trouble than it's worth. So they send those yids here, nurse them back to health and then, when they're well again, put them on the next train east. That's what'll happen to this poor bastard if ever he comes round."

"So not everyone in here is actually sick?"

"Lord, no." He lit a cigarette. "I expect they'll close it down soon enough. Word is that Kaltenbrunner has his eye on owning this hospital."

"That ought to come in handy. Nice place like this? Make a nice suite of offices."

Following the death of my old boss, Reinhard Heydrich, Ernst Kaltenbrunner was the new head of the RSHA, but quite what he wanted with his own Jewish hospital was anyone's guess. His own drying-out clinic, perhaps, but I managed to keep that particular thought to myself; Werner Sachse's advice to watch my mouth had been wearing red intelligence stripes; after Stalingrad everyone—but more especially Berliners, like me, for whom black humor was a religious calling—was probably well advised to keep a zip on the lip.

"Will he get it? Kaltenbrunner?"

"I haven't the faintest idea."

Because I wanted to look at anything other than poor Franz Meyer's badly damaged head, I went to the window, which was when I noticed the flower arrangement on his bedside table.

"That's interesting," I said, looking at the card next to the vase, which was unsigned.

"What is?"

"The daffodils," I said. "I've just come out of the hospital and no one sent me any flowers. And yet this fellow has fresh flowers and from Theodor Hübner's shop on Prinzenstrasse, no less."

"So?"

"In Kreuzberg."

"I still don't—"

"It used to be a florist's by royal appointment. Still is, for all I know. Which means they're expensive. Very expensive." I frowned. "What I mean to say is, I doubt there are many people in here who get fresh flowers from Hübner's. In here or anywhere else, for that matter."

Dobberke shrugged. "His family must have sent them. The Jews still have plenty of money hidden under their mattresses. Everyone knows that. I was out east, in Riga, and you should have seen what these bastards had in their underwear. Gold, silver, diamonds, you name it."

I smiled patiently, avoiding the obvious question exactly how it was that Dobberke came to be looking for valuables in someone else's underwear.

"Meyer's family were Germans," I said. "And besides, they're all dead. Killed by the same bomb that gave him the center parting in his hair. No, this must have been someone else who sent these flowers. Someone German—someone with money and taste. Someone who only has the best."

"Well, he's not saying who they're from," observed Dobberke.

"No," I said. "He's not saying anything, is he? Dr. Lustig was right about that, at least."

"I could look into it if you thought it was important. Perhaps one of the nurses could tell you who sent them."

"No," I said firmly. "Forget about it. It's an old habit of mine, being a detective. Some people collect stamps, others like postcards or autographs. Me, I collect trivial questions. Why this? Why that? Of course, any fool can start a collection like that and it goes without saying that it's the answers to the questions that are really valuable, because the answers are a lot harder to track down."

I took another long hard look at Franz Meyer and realized it could just as easily have been me lying in that bed with half a head, and for the first time in a long time I suppose I felt lucky. I don't know what else you call it when an RAF bomb kills four, maims one, and leaves you with nothing more than a bump on the head. But just the idea of me being lucky again made me smile. Perhaps I'd turned some sort of a corner in my life. It was that and maybe also the apparent success of the women's protest in Rosenstrasse and the other good luck I'd had not to have been part of the Sixth Army in Stalingrad.

"What's amusing?" asked Dobberke.

I shook my head. "I was just thinking that the important thing in life—the really important thing after all is said and done—is just to stay alive."

"Is that one of the answers?" asked Dobberke.

I nodded. "I think perhaps it's the most important answer of all, don't you think?"

It was a twelve-minute walk to work depending on the weather. When it was cold, the streets froze hard and you had to walk slowly or risk a broken arm. When it thawed, you only had to beware of falling icicles. At the beginning of March, it was still very cold at night but getting warmer during the day, and at last I felt able to remove the layers of newspaper that had helped to insulate the inside of my boots against a freezing Berlin winter. That made walking easier, too.

The Wehrmacht High Command (OKW) was housed in perhaps the largest office complex in Berlin: a five-story building of gray granite on the north side of the Landwehr Canal, it occupied the whole corner of Bendlerstrasse and Tirpitzufer. Formerly the head-quarters of the Imperial German Navy, it was better known as the Bendlerblock. The bureau's offices, at Blumeshof 17, looked onto the back of this building and a rose garden that, in summer, filled the air with such a strong smell of roses some of us who worked there called it the flower house. In my office under the eaves of the high red saddle roof, I had a desk, a filing cabinet, a rug on the wooden floor, and an armchair—I even had a painting and a little piece of bronze from the government's own collection of art. I did not have a portrait of the Leader. Few people who worked at the OKW did.

Usually I got to work early and stayed late but this had very little to do with loyalty or professional zeal; the heating system in the flower house was so efficient that the cold windowpanes were always covered in condensation so that you had to wipe them before you could look outside; there were even uniformed orderlies who went around building up the coal fires in the individual offices; this was just as well, as these were enormous. All of this meant that life was much more comfortable at the office than it was at home—especially when one considered the generosity of the OKW's canteen, which was always open. Mostly the food was just stodge—potatoes, pasta, and bread—but there was plenty of it. There was even soap and toilet paper in the washrooms, and newspapers in the mess.

The War Crimes Bureau was part of the Wehrmacht legal department's international section, whose chief was the ailing Maximilian Wagner. Reporting to him was my boss, Judge Johannes Goldsche. He had headed the bureau from its inception in 1939. He was about sixty, with fair hair and a small mustache, a hooked nose, largish ears, a forehead as high as the roof on the flower house, and an Olympian disdain for the Nazis that stemmed from many years in private practice as a lawyer and judge during the Weimar Republic. His appointment to the bureau owed nothing to his politics and everything to his previous experience of war crimes investigations, having been deputy director of a similar Prussian bureau during the Great War. By state law the Wehrmacht was not supposed to be interested in politics and it took this independence very seriously indeed. In the Wehrmacht's legal office none of the six jurists charged with the regulation of the various military services were Party members. This is why—although I was not a lawyer—I fitted in very well. I think Goldsche regarded a Berlin detective as a useful blunt object in an arsenal that was filled with more subtle weapons, and he frequently used me to investigate cases where a more robust method of inquiry was required than just the taking of depositions. Few of the judges who worked for the bureau were capable of treating the shirking pigs and lying Fritzes that made up the modern German Army—especially the ones who had committed war crimes themselves—as roughly as they sometimes deserved. What none of these invariably Prussian judges perceived was that there were benefits attached to being a witness in a war crimes inquiry: a leave of absence from active service being the main one; as much as possible, we tried to interview men in the field but it wasn't every judge who wanted to spend days traveling to the Russian front; and one or two of the younger judges who did—Karl Hofmann, for one—found themselves posted to active service. Those who had tried the experience were very nervous about flying to the front and, it's fair to say, so was I. There are better ways to spend your day than bouncing around inside the freezing fuselage of an Iron Annie in winter. Even Hermann Göring preferred the train. But the train was slow and coal shortages often meant that locomotives were stranded for hours—often days—on end. If you were a judge with the bureau, the best thing was to avoid the front altogether, to stay warm at home in Berlin and send someone else to the field; someone like me.

When I arrived at my desk I found a handwritten note summoning me to Goldsche's office, so I took off my coat and belts, grabbed a notebook and a pencil, and went down to the second floor. It was a lot colder there on account of the fact that several of the windows had been blown out by the recent bombing and were being replaced by some whistling Russians—part of a POW battalion of glaziers, carpenters, and roofers that had come into being in order to make up for the shortage of German workmen. The Russians seemed happy enough. Replacing windows was a better job than disposing of unexploded RAF bombs. And probably anything was better than the Russian front, especially if you were a Russian, where their casualty rate was ten times worse than ours. Unfortunately that didn't look like it was going to stop them from winning.

I knocked on Goldsche's door and then entered to find him sitting by the fire wreathed like Zeus in a cloud of pipe smoke, drinking coffee—it must have been his birthday—and facing a thin, bespectacled, almost delicate man of about forty, who had a face as long and pale as a rasher of streaky bacon, and about as devoid of expression. Like most of the men I saw at the bureau, neither of them looked as if they belonged in uniform. I'd seen more convincing soldiers inside a toy box. I didn't feel particularly comfortable wearing a uniform myself, especially as mine had a little black SD triangle on the left sleeve. (That was another reason Goldsche liked me working there; being SD gave me a certain clout in the field that wasn't available to the army.) But their lack of obvious martial aptitude was more easily explained than my own: as civil servants within the armed forces, men like Goldsche and his unknown colleague had administrative or legal titles but not ranks and wore uniforms with distinctive silver braid shoulder boards to denote their special status as non-military soldiers. It was all very confusing, although I daresay it was much more confusing to people in the OKW how an SD officer like me came to be working for the bureau, and sometimes the SD triangle earned me some suspicious looks in the canteen. But I was used to feeling out of place in Nazi Germany. Besides, Johannes Goldsche knew very well I wasn't a Party member—that, as a member of Kripo, I hadn't had much choice in the matter of my uniform—and this was really all that mattered in the old Prussian's republican book; this and the fact that I disliked the Nazis almost as much as he did.

I came to attention beside Goldsche's chair and glanced over the pictures on the wall while I waited for the judge to address me. Goldsche was a keen musician and in most of the pictures he was part of a piano trio that included a famous German actor called Otto Gebühr.

I hadn't heard the trio play but I had seen Gebühr's performance as Frederick the Great in more films than seemed altogether necessary. The judge had music on the radio, although that was nothing to do with his love of music; Goldsche always turned on the radio when he wanted to have a private conversation, just in case anyone from the Research Office—which remained under Göring's control—was eavesdropping.

"Hans, this is the fellow I was telling you about," said Goldsche. "Captain Bernhard Gunther, formerly a commissar with Kripo at the Police Praesidium on Alexanderplatz, and now attached to the bureau."

I clicked my heels, like a good Prussian, and the man waved a silent greeting with his cigarette holder.

"Gunther, this is Military Court Official von Dohnanyi, formerly of the Reich Ministry of Justice and the Imperial Court but these days he's deputy head of the Abwehr's central section."

All of which meant, of course, that the special shoulder boards and distinctive collar patches and civil servant titles were really quite unnecessary; von Dohnanyi was a baron, and in the OKW this was the only kind of rank that ever really mattered.

"Pleased to meet you, Gunther." Dohnanyi was softly spoken like a lot of Berlin lawyers, although perhaps not as slippery as some I'd known. I figured him for one of those lawyers who were more interested in making law than in using it to turn a quick mark.

"Don't be fooled by that witchcraft badge he's wearing on his sleeve," added Goldsche. "Gunther was a loyal servant of the republic for many years. And a damned good policeman. For a while he was quite a thorn in the side of our new masters, weren't you, Gunther?"

"That's not for me to say. But I'll take the compliment." I glanced at the silver tray on the table between them. "And some of that coffee, perhaps."

Goldsche grinned. "Of course. Please. Sit down."

I sat down and Goldsche helped me to some coffee.

"I don't know where the *Putzer* got this," said Goldsche, "but it's actually very good. As a lawyer I should probably have my suspicions about his being a blackie."

"Yes, you probably should," I remarked. The coffee was delicious. "At two hundred marks for a half kilo that's quite an orderly you have there. I'd hang on to him if I were you and learn to look the other way like everyone else does in this city."

"Oh dear." Von Dohnanyi smiled very faintly. "I suppose I should confess that the coffee came from me," he said. "My father gets it whenever he plays a concert in Budapest or Vienna. I was going to mention it before but I hardly wanted to diminish your good opinion of the *Putzer*, Johannes. Now it seems I might get him into trouble. The coffee was a gift from me."

"My dear fellow, you're too kind." Goldsche glanced my way. "Von Dohnanyi's father is the great conductor and composer Ernst von Dohnanyi." Goldsche was a tremendous snob about classical music.

"Do you like music, Captain Gunther?"

Dohnanyi's inquiry was scrupulously polite; behind his round, frameless glasses the eyes didn't care if I liked music or not; but then, neither did I, and without the *von* in front of my name I certainly wasn't nearly as scrupulous as he was about what I used to fill my ears.

"I like a good melody if it's sung by a pretty girl with a good pair of lungs, especially when the lyric is a vulgar one and the lungs are really noticeable. And I can't tell an arpeggio from an archipelago. But life's too short for Wagner, I do know that much."

Goldsche grinned enthusiastically. He always seemed to take a vicarious delight in my capacity for blunt talking, which I enjoyed playing up to. "What else do you know?" he inquired.

"I whistle when I'm in the bath, which isn't as often as I'd like," I added, lighting a cigarette. That was the other good thing about working for the OKW, there was always a plentiful supply of quite decent cigarettes. "Talking of which, it seems the Russians are here already."

"What do you mean?" asked von Dohnanyi, momentarily alarmed.

"Those fellows whistling in the corridor outside the door," I said. "The skilled German craftsmen from the local glaziers' guild who are repairing the flower house windows. They're Russians."

"Good Lord," said Goldsche. "Here? In the OKW. That hardly seems like a good idea. What about security?"

"Someone's got to repair the windows," I said. "It's cold outside. There's no secret about that. I just hope the glass is more durable than the Luftwaffe, because I've got the feeling the RAF is planning a return visit."

Von Dohnanyi allowed himself a thin smile and then an even thinner puff of his cigarette. I'd seen children smoke with more gusto.

"How are you feeling, anyway?" Goldsche looked at the other lawyer and explained. "Gunther was in a house in Lützow that was bombed while he was taking a deposition from a potential witness. He's lucky to be here at all."

"That's certainly the way I feel about it." I tapped my chest. "And I'm much better, thanks."

"Fit for work?"

"Chest is still a bit tight, but otherwise I'm more or less back to normal."

"And the witness? Herr Meyer?"

"He's alive, but I'm afraid the only evidence he's going to give anytime soon is in the court of heaven."

"You've seen him?" asked von Dohnanyi. "In the Jewish Hospital?"

"Yes, poor fellow. A large part of his brain seems to have gone missing. Not that anyone notices that kind of thing very much nowadays. But he's no use to us now, I'm afraid."

"Pity," said Goldsche. "He was going to be an important witness in a case we were preparing against the Royal Navy," he told von Dohnanyi. "The British Navy really does think it can get away with murder. Unlike the American Navy, which recognizes all our hospital ships, the Royal Navy recognizes the larger tonnage hospital ships but not the smaller ones."

"Because the smaller ones are picking up our unwounded air crews?" asked von Dohnanyi.

"That's right. It's a great pity this case collapsed before it even got started. Then again, it does make life a little simpler for us. Not to mention more palatable. Goebbels was interested in putting Franz Meyer on the radio. That wouldn't have done at all."

"It's not just the Ministry of Propaganda who were interested in Franz Meyer," I said. "The Gestapo came to see me while I was in the state hospital, asking questions about Meyer."

"Did they?" murmured von Dohnanyi.

"What sort of questions?" asked Goldsche.

I shrugged. "Who his friends were, that kind of thing. They seemed to think Meyer might have been mixed up in some sort of currency smuggling racket in order to help persuade the Swiss to offer asylum to a group of Jews."

Goldsche looked puzzled.

"Money for refugees," I added. "Well, you know how big-hearted the Swiss are. They make all that lovely white chocolate just to help sugar the lie that they're peace-loving and kind. Of course, they're not. Never were. Even the German Army was in the habit of recruiting Swiss mercenaries. The Italians used to call it a bad war when Swiss pikemen were involved because their kind of fighting was so vicious."

"What did you tell them?" asked Goldsche. "The Gestapo?"

"I didn't tell them anything." I shrugged. "I don't know about a currency racket. The Gestapo mentioned a few names. But I certainly hadn't heard of them. Anyway, the commissar who came to see me—I know him. He's not bad as Gestapo officers go. Fellow by the name of Werner Sachse. I'm not sure if he's a Party member but I wouldn't be surprised if he wasn't."

"I don't like the Gestapo involving themselves with our inquiries," said Goldsche. "I don't like it at all. Our judicial independence is always under threat from Himmler and his thugs."

I shook my head. "The Gestapo are like dogs. You have to let them lick the bone for a while or they become savage. Take my word for it. This was a routine inquiry. The commissar licked the bone, let me fold his ears, and then he slunk away. Simple as that. And there's no need for alarm. I don't see anyone winding up this department because seven Jews went skiing in Switzerland without permission."

Von Dohnanyi shrugged. "Captain Gunther is probably right," he said. "This commissar was just going through the motions, that's all."

I smiled patiently, sipped my coffee, checked my own natural curiosity about exactly how it was that von Dohnanyi had known Meyer was in the Jewish Hospital, and tried to bring the meeting to order. "What did you want to see me about, sir?"

"Oh yes." Goldsche nodded. "You're sure you're fit, now?"

I nodded.

"Good." Goldsche looked at his aristocratic friend. "Hans? Would you care to enlighten the captain?"

"Certainly." Von Dohnanyi put down his cigarette holder, removed his spectacles and then a neatly folded handkerchief and started to clean the lenses.

I stubbed out my cigarette, opened my notebook, and prepared to take some notes.

Von Dohnanyi shook his head. "Please, just listen for now, if you would, Captain," he said. "When I'm finished, you'll perhaps understand my request that no notes are taken of this meeting."

I closed the notebook and waited.

"Following the Gleiwitz incident, German forces invaded Poland on September first, 1939, and sixteen days later the Red Army invaded from the east, in accordance with the Molotov-Ribbentrop Pact signed between our two countries on August twenty-third, 1939. Germany annexed western Poland and the Soviet Union incorporated the eastern half into its Ukrainian and Belorussian republics. Some four hundred thousand Polish troops were taken prisoner by the Wehrmacht, while at least another quarter of a million Poles were captured by the Red Army. It is the fate of those Polish men taken prisoner by the Russians with which we are concerned here. Ever since the Wehrmacht invaded the Soviet Union—"

"Germany's always been unlucky that way," I said. "With her friends, I mean."

Ignoring my sarcasm, von Dohnanyi put his glasses back on and continued: "Possibly even as soon as August 1941, the Abwehr has been receiving reports of a mass murder of Polish officers that took place in the spring or early summer of 1940. But where this took place was anyone's guess. Until now, perhaps.

"There's a signals regiment, the 537th, commanded by a Lieutenant Colonel Friedrich Ahrens, stationed in a place called Gnezdovo near Smolensk—I understand from Judge Goldsche that you've been to Smolensk, Captain Gunther?"

"Yes, sir. I was there in the summer of 1941."

He nodded. "That's good. Then you'll know the sort of country I'm talking about."

"It's a dump," I said. "I can't see why we thought it worth capturing at all."

"Er, yes." Von Dohnanyi smiled patiently. "Apparently Gnezdovo is an area of thick forest to the west of the city, with wolves and other wild animals, and right now, as you might expect, the whole area is under a thick blanket of snow. The 537th is stationed in a castle or villa in the forest that was formerly used by the Russian secret police—the NKVD. They employ a number of HIWIs—Russian POWs like those glaziers in the corridor—and several weeks ago some of those HIWIs reported that a wolf had dug up some human remains in the forest. Having investigated the site for himself, Ahrens reported finding not one but several human bones. The report was passed on to us in the Abwehr, and we then set about evaluating this intelligence. A number of possibilities have presented themselves.

"One: that the bones are from a mass grave of political prisoners murdered by the NKVD during the so-called Great Purge of 1937 to 1938 following the first and second Moscow trials. We estimate as many as a million Soviet citizens were killed and that they are buried in mass graves all over an area west of Moscow hundreds of square kilometers in size.

"Two: that the bones are from a mass grave of missing Polish officers. The Soviet government has assured the Polish prime minister in exile, General Sikorski, that all Polish prisoners of war were freed in 1940, after having been transported to Manchuria, and that the Soviets have simply lost track of many of these men because of the war, but it seems clear to our sources in London that the Poles do not believe them. A key factor in the Abwehr's suspicion that these bones might be those of a Polish officer is the fact that this explanation would fit with previous intelligence reports about Polish officers who were seen at the local railway station in Gnezdovo in May 1940. Remarks made by Foreign Minister Molotov to von Ribbentrop at the signing of the Non-Aggression Pact in 1939 have always led us to suppose that Stalin has a deep hatred for the Poles that dates from the Soviet defeat in the Polish-Soviet War of 1919–20. Also, his son was killed by Polish partisans in 1939.

"Three: the mass grave is the site of a battle between the Wehrmacht and the Red Army. This is perhaps the most unlikely scenario as the Battle of Smolensk took place largely to the south of Smolensk and not the west. Moreover, the Wehrmacht took over three hundred thousand Red Army soldiers prisoner and most of these men remain alive, incarcerated in a camp to the northeast of Smolensk."

"Or working in the corridor outside," I said helpfully.

"Please, Gunther," said Goldsche. "Let him finish."

"Four: this is perhaps the most politically sensitive of all the possibilities and is also why I have asked you to forbear from taking notes, Captain Gunther."

It wasn't difficult to guess why von Dohnanyi hesitated to describe the fourth possibility; it was hard to talk about this subject—hard for him and even harder for me, who had firsthand experience of some of these dreadful things that were so "politically sensitive."

"Four is the possibility that this is one of many mass graves in the region full of Jews murdered by the SS," I said.

Von Dohnanyi nodded. "The SS is very secretive about these matters," he said. "But we have information that a special battalion of SS attached to Gottlob Berger's Group B and commanded by an Obersturmführer by the name of Oskar Dirlewanger was active in the area immediately west of Smolensk during the spring of last year. There are no accurate figures available, but one estimate we have holds Dirlewanger's single battalion responsible for the murders of at least fourteen thousand people."

"The last thing we want to do is step on the toes of the SS," said Goldsche. "Which means this is a matter requiring great confidentiality. Frankly, there will be hell to pay if we go around uncovering mass graves of their making."

"That's a delicate way of putting it, Judge," I said. "Since I assume it's me you want to send down to Smolensk and investigate this, then I'm supposed to make sure that this is the correct mass grave we're uncovering, is that what you mean?"

"In a nutshell, yes," said Goldsche. "Right now the ground is frozen hard so there's no possibility of digging for more bodies. Not for several weeks. Until then, we need to find out all we can. So if you could spend a couple of days down there. Speak to some of the locals, visit the site, evaluate the situation, and then come back to Berlin and report directly to me. If it is our jurisdiction, then we can organize a full war crimes inquiry with a proper judge almost immediately." He shrugged. "But to send a judge at this stage would be too much."

"Agreed," said von Dohnanyi. "It would send the wrong signal. Best to keep things low-key at this stage."

"Let me check my mental shorthand, gentlemen," I said. "About just what you want me to do. So as I know, for sure. If this mass grave is full of Jews, then I'm to forget about it. But if it's full of Polish officers, then it's the bureau's meat. Is that what you're saying?"

"That's not a very subtle way of putting it," said von Dohnanyi, "but yes. That's exactly what's required of you, Captain Gunther."

For a moment he glanced up at the landscape above Goldsche's fireplace as if wishing he could have been there instead of a smoky office in Berlin, and I felt a sneer start to gather at the edge of my mouth. The picture was one of those Italian *campagnas* painted at the end of a summer's day, when the light is interesting to a painter, and some tiny old men with long beards and wearing togas are standing around a ruined classical landscape and asking themselves who's going to carry out the necessary building repairs because all the young men are away at the wars. They didn't have Russian POWs to fix their windows in those Arcadian days.

My sneer expanded to full contempt for his delicate sensibility.

"Oh, but it won't be subtle, gentlemen," I said. "I can promise you that much. Certainly nowhere near as subtle as in that nice picture. Smolensk is no bucolic demi-paradise. It's a ruin, all right, but it's a ruin because that's how our tanks and artillery have left it. It's a ruin that's full of ugly, frightened people who were only just managing to eke out a living when the Wehrmacht turned up demanding to be fed and watered for not much money. Zeus won't be seducing Io, it'll be a Fritz trying to rape some poor peasant girl. And in Smolensk the pretty landscape isn't covered in an amber glow of warm Italian sunlight but a hard permafrost. No, it won't be subtle. And believe me, there's nothing subtle about a body that's been in the ground. It's surprising how indelicate something like that turns out to be and how quickly it becomes something very unpleasant indeed. There's the smell, for example. Bodies have a habit of decomposing when they've been in the earth for a while."

I lit another cigarette and enjoyed their joint discomfort. There was a silence for a long moment. Von Dohnanyi looked nervous about something—more nervous than what he had just told me suggested, perhaps. Or maybe he just wanted to hit me. I get a lot of that.

"But I take your point," I added, more helpfully this time, "about the SS, I mean. We wouldn't want to upset them, now would we? And believe me, I know what I'm talking about—I've done it before so I'm equally anxious not to do it again."

"There is a fifth possibility," added Goldsche, "which is why I would prefer to have a proper detective on the scene."

"And that is?"

"I would like you to make absolutely sure that this whole thing is not some ghastly lie dreamed up by the Ministry of Propaganda. That this body has not been deliberately planted there to play first us and then the world's media like a grand piano. Because make no mistake about it, gentlemen, that's exactly what will happen if this does turn out to be the dwarf's ring."

I nodded. "Fair enough. But you're forgetting a sixth possibility, surely."

Von Dohnanyi frowned. "And what is that?"

"If this does turn out to be a mass grave, that it's full of Polish officers that the German Army murdered."

Von Dohnanyi shook his head. "Impossible," he said.

"Is it? I don't see how your second possibility can even exist without the possibility of the sixth one, too."

"That's logically true," admitted von Dohnanyi. "But the fact remains that the German Army does not murder prisoners of war."

I grinned. "Oh, well, that's all right then. Forgive me for mentioning it, sir."

Von Dohnanyi colored a little; you don't get a lot of sarcasm in the concert hall or the Imperial Court; and I doubt he'd spoken to a real policeman since 1928, when, like every other aristocrat, he'd applied for a firearm permit so he could shoot wild boar and the odd Bolshevik.

"Besides," he continued, "this part of Russia has only been in German hands since September 1941. There's that, and the fact that it's a matter of military record which Poles were prisoners of Germany and which were prisoners of the Soviet Union. This information is already known to the Polish government in London. For that reason alone it should be easy to establish if any of these men were prisoners of the Red Army. Which is why I myself think it's highly improbable that this could be something manufactured by the Ministry of Propaganda. Because it would be all too easy to disprove."

"Perhaps you're right, Hans," admitted the judge.

"I am right," insisted von Dohnanyi. "You know I'm right."

"Nevertheless," said the judge, "I want to be sure exactly what we're dealing with here. And as quickly as possible. So, will you do it, Gunther? Will you go down there and see what you can find out?"

I had little appetite to see Smolensk again or, for that matter, anywhere else in Russia. The whole country filled me with a combination of fear and shame, for there was no doubt that whatever crimes the Red Army had committed in the name of Communism, the SS had committed equally heinous ones in the name of Nazism. Probably our crimes were more heinous. Executing enemy officers in uniform was one thing—I had some experience of that myself—but murdering women and children was quite another.

"Yes, sir. I'll go. Of course I'll go."

"Good fellow," said the judge. "As I said already, if there's even a hint that this is the handiwork of those thugs in the SS, don't do anything—get the hell out of Smolensk as quickly as possible, come straight home, and pretend you know nothing at all about it."

"With pleasure."

I smiled wryly and shook my head as I wondered what magic mountaintop these two men were on. Perhaps you had to be a judge or an aristocrat to look down from the heights and see what was important here—important for Germany. Me, I had more pressing concerns; myself, for example. And from where I was sitting the whole business of investigating the mass murder of some Poles looked a lot like one donkey calling another donkey "long ears."

"Is there something wrong?" asked von Dohnanyi.

"Only that it's a little difficult for me to see how anyone might think Nazi Germany could ever occupy moral high ground on an issue like this."

"An investigation and then a white book could prove extremely useful in restoring our reputation for fair play and probity in the eyes of the world," said the judge. "When all this is over."

So that was it. A white book. An evidentiary record that influential and honorable men like Judge Goldsche and Court Official von Dohnanyi could produce from a Foreign Office archive after the war was concluded to show other influential and honorable men from England and America that not all Germans had behaved as badly as the Nazis, or that the Russians had been just as bad as we were, or something similar. I had my doubts about that working out.

"Mark my words," said Dohnanyi, "if this is what I think it is, then it's just a beginning. We have to start rebuilding our moral fabric somewhere."

"Tell that to the SS," I said.

WEDNESDAY, MARCH 10, 1943

A t six A.M. on a bitterly cold Berlin morning I arrived at Tegel airfield to board my flight to Russia. A long journey lay ahead, although only half of the other ten passengers climbing aboard the three-engined Ju52 were actually going as far as Smolensk. Most, it seemed, were getting off at the end of the first leg of the journey— Berlin to Rastenburg—which was a mere four hours. After that there was a second leg, to Minsk, which took another four hours, before the third leg—two hours—to Smolensk. With stops for refueling and a pilot change in Minsk, the whole journey to Smolensk was scheduled to take eleven and a half hours, all of which helped explain why it was me being sent down there instead of some fat-arsed judge with a bad back from the Wehrmacht legal department. So I was surprised when I discovered that one of the other dozen or so passengers arriving on the tarmac in a chauffeur-driven private Mercedes was none other than the fastidious court official from the Abwehr, Hans von Dohnanyi.

"Is this a coincidence?" I asked cheerfully. "Or did you come to see me off?"

"I'm sorry?" He frowned. "Oh, I didn't recognize you. You're flying to Smolensk, aren't you, Captain Bernhard?"

"Unless you know something different," I said. "And my name is Gunther, Captain Bernhard Gunther."

"Yes, of course. No, as it happens I'm traveling with you on the same plane. I was going to take the train and then changed my mind. But now I'm not so sure I made the right choice."

"I'm afraid you're between the wall and a fierce dog with that one," I said.

We climbed aboard and took our seats along the corrugated fuselage: it was like sitting inside a workman's hut.

"Are you getting off at the Wolf's Lair?" I asked. "Or going all the way to Smolensk?"

"No, I'm going all the way." Quickly he added, "I have some urgent and unexpected Abwehr business to attend to with Field Marshal von Kluge at his headquarters."

"Bring a packed lunch, did you?"

"Hmm?"

I nodded at the parcel he was holding under his arm.

"This? No, it's not my lunch. It's a gift for someone. Some Cointreau."

"Cointreau. Real coffee. Is there nothing beyond your great father's talents?"

Von Dohnanyi smiled his thin smile, stretched his thinner neck over his tailored tunic collar. "Would you excuse me please, Captain."

He waved at two staff officers with red stripes on their trousers and then went to sit beside them at the opposite end of the aircraft, just behind the cockpit. Even on a Ju52 people like von Dohnanyi and the staff officers managed somehow to make their own first class; it wasn't that the seats were any better up front, just that none of these flamingos really wanted to talk with junior officers like me.

I lit a cigarette and tried to make myself comfortable. The

engines started and the door closed. The copilot locked the door and put his hand on one of two beam-mounted machine guns that could be moved up and down the length of the aircraft.

"We're a crew member short, gentlemen," he said. "So does anyone know how to use one of these?"

I looked at my fellow passengers. No one spoke, and I wondered what the point was of transporting any of these men nearer the front; none of them looked as though they could have worked a door lock let alone an MG15.

"I do," I said, raising my hand.

"Good," said the copilot. "There's a one-in-a-hundred chance we'll run into an RAF mosquito as we're flying out of Berlin, so stay on the gun for the next fifteen minutes, eh?"

"By all means," I said. "But what about in Smolensk?"

The copilot shook his head. "The front line is eight hundred kilometers east of Smolensk. That's too far for Russian fighters."

"Well, that's a relief," said someone.

"Don't worry." The copilot grinned. "The cold'll probably kill you long before then."

We took off in the early morning light and when we were airborne, I stood up, slid the window open, and poked the MG outside, expectantly. The saddle drum held seventy-five rounds but my hands were soon so cold I didn't much fancy our chances of hitting anything with it and was quite relieved when the copilot shouted back that I could stand down. I was even more relieved to close the window against the freezing air that was filling the aircraft.

I sat down, tucked my numb hands under my armpits, and tried to go to sleep.

FOUR HOURS LATER as we approached Rastenburg, in Eastern Prussia, people turned around in their seats and, looking out the windows, eagerly tried to catch a glimpse of the Leader's headquarters, nicknamed the Wolf's Lair.

"You won't see it," said some know-it-all who'd been there before. "All of the buildings are camouflaged. If you could see it, then so could the fucking RAF."

"If they could get this far," said someone else.

"They weren't supposed to get as far as Berlin," said another, "but somehow, against all predictions, they did."

We landed a few kilometers west of the Wolf's Lair, and I went to look for an early lunch or a late breakfast and, finding neither, I sat in a hut that was almost as cold as the plane and ate some meager cheese sandwiches I had brought with me just in case. I didn't see von Dohnanyi again until we were back on the plane.

The air between Rastenburg and Minsk was rougher, and from time to time the Junkers would drop like a stone before hitting the bottom of the pocket like a water bucket in a well. It wasn't long before von Dohnanyi was starting to look very green.

"Perhaps you should drink some of those spirits," I said, which was a crude way of telling him that I wouldn't have minded a drop of it myself.

"What?"

"Your friend's Cointreau. You should drink some to settle your stomach."

He looked baffled for a minute and then shook his head, weakly.

One of the other passengers, an SS lieutenant who had boarded the plane at Rastenburg, produced a hip flask of peach schnapps and handed it around. I took a bite off it just as we hit another big air pocket and this one seemed to jolt all the life out of von Dohnanyi, who fell onto the fuselage floor in a dead faint. Overcoming my natural instinct, which was always to leave the people in the first class to look after themselves, I knelt down beside him, loosened the collar on his tunic, and poured some of the lieutenant's schnapps between his lips. That was when I saw the address on von Dohnanyi's parcel, which was still under his seat.

Colonel Helmuth Stieff, Wehrmacht Coordination Dept., Anger Castle, Wolf's Lair, Rastenburg, Prussia.

Von Dohnanyi opened his eyes, sighed, and then sat up.

"You just fainted, that's all," I said. "Might be best if you lay on the floor for a bit."

So he did, and actually managed to sleep for a couple of hours while, from time to time, I wondered if von Dohnanyi had simply forgotten to deliver his bottle of Cointreau to his friend Colonel Stieff at the Wolf's Lair, or if, perhaps, he had changed his mind about handing over such a generous present. If the booze was anything like the coffee, it was certain to be high-quality stuff, much too good to give away. He could hardly have forgotten about the parcel since I was certain he had taken it with him when we got off the plane in Rastenburg. So why hadn't he given it to one of the many orderlies for delivery to Colonel Stieff, or even, if he didn't trust them, to one of the other staff officers who were going straight to the Wolf's Lair? Of course, one of them might equally have told von Dohnanyi that Stieff was no longer at the Wolf's Lair; that would have explained everything. But like an itch that kept on coming back, no amount of scratching I did seemed to take away from the fact that von Dohnanyi's failure to deliver his precious bottle just seemed strange.

There's not an awful lot to do on a four-hour flight between Rastenburg and Minsk.

IT WAS STILL LIGHT BY THE TIME we reached Smolensk several hours later, but only just. For almost an hour before that we'd been flying over an endless, thick green carpet of trees. It seemed there were more trees in Russia than anywhere else on earth. There were so many trees that at times the Junkers seemed almost immobile in the air, and I felt as if we were drifting over a primordial landscape.

I suppose Russia is as near as you can get to what the earth must have been like thousands of years ago—in more ways than one; probably it was an excellent place to be a squirrel, although perhaps not such an excellent place to be a man. If you were intent on hiding the bodies of thousands of Jews or Polish officers, this looked like a good place to do it. You could have hidden all manner of crimes in a landscape like the one below our aircraft, and the sight of it filled me with dread not just for what I might find down there but also for what I might find myself faced with again. It was only a dark possibility but I knew instinctively that in the winter of 1943, this was no place to be an SD officer with a guilty conscience.

Von Dohnanyi had made a full recovery by the time a clearing in the forest finally appeared to the north of the city like a long green swimming pool, and we landed. Steps were wheeled quickly into place on the tarmac and we stepped out into a wind that quickly cut a jagged hole in my greatcoat, then my torso, leaving me feeling as cold as a frozen herring and, in the center of that enormous tract of forest, just as out of place. I pulled my crusher about my frozen ears and looked around for a sign of someone from the signals regiment who was supposed to meet me. Meanwhile, my erstwhile traveling companion paid me no attention as he came down the steps of the aircraft and was immediately met by two senior officers—one of them a general with more fur on his collar than an eskimo—and seemed quite indifferent to my own lack of transport as, laughing loudly, he and his pals shook hands while an orderly loaded his luggage into their large staff car.

A Tatra with a little black and yellow flag bearing the number 537 on the hood drew up next to the staff car and two officers climbed out. Seeing the general, the two officers saluted, were cursorily acknowledged, and then walked toward me. The Tatra had its top up but there were no windows and it seemed another cold journey lay ahead of me.

"Captain Gunther?" said the taller man.

"Yes, sir."

"I'm Lieutenant Colonel Ahrens, of the 537th Signals," he said. "This is Lieutenant Rex, my adjutant. Welcome to Smolensk. Rex was going to meet you by himself but at the last minute I thought I'd join him and put you fully in the picture on the way back to the castle."

"I'm very glad you did, sir."

A moment later the staff car drove away.

"Who were the flamingos?" I asked.

"General von Tresckow," said Ahrens. "With Colonel von Gersdorff. I can't say I recognized the third officer." Ahrens had a lugubrious sort of face—he was not unhandsome—and an even more lugubrious voice.

"Ah, that explains it."

"How do you mean?"

"The third officer—the one you didn't recognize, the one who got off the plane—he was also an aristocrat," I explained.

"It figures," said Ahrens. "Field Marshal von Kluge runs Army Group HQ like it's a branch of the German Club. I get my orders from General Oberhauser. He's a professional soldier, like me. He's not an aristocrat—and not so bad, as staff officers go. My predecessor, Colonel Bedenck, used to say that you never really know exactly how many staff officers there are until you try and get into an air raid shelter."

"I like the sound of your old colonel," I said, walking toward the Tatra. "He and I sound as if we're cut from the same cloth."

"Your cloth is a little darker than his, perhaps," said Ahrens pointedly. "Especially the cloth of your other uniform—the dress one. After what he saw in Minsk, Bedenck could hardly bear to be in the same room as an officer of the SS or SD. Since you're to be billeted with us for security reasons, I might as well confess I feel much the same way. I was a little surprised when Major General Oster from the Abwehr telephoned and told me that the bureau was sending an SD man down here. There's little love lost between the SD and the Wehrmacht in my corner."

I grinned. "I appreciate a man who comes right out and says what's on his mind. There's not a lot of that around since Stalingrad. Especially in uniform. So as one professional to another, let me tell you this. My other uniform is a cheap suit and a felt hat. I'm not the Gestapo, I'm just a policeman from Kripo who used to work homicide, and I'm not here to spy on anyone. I intend on going home to Berlin just as soon as I've finished looking at all the evidence you've gathered, but I tell you frankly, sir, mostly I'm just looking out for myself and I don't give a damn what your secrets are."

I put my hand on a long shovel that was attached to the Tatra's hood; the little cars were no good in mud or on snow and frequently you had to dig them out or shovel gravel under the wheels: there was probably a sack of it behind the backseat.

"But if I am lying to you, Colonel, you have my permission to bang me on the head with this and have your men bury me in the woods. On the other hand, you might think I've already said enough to bury me yourself."

"Fair enough, Captain." Colonel Ahrens smiled and then took out a little cigarette case. He offered one to me and to his lieutenant. "I appreciate your candor."

We puffed them into life until it was almost impossible to distinguish smoke from our hot breath in the freezing cold air.

"Now then," I said. "You mentioned something about being billeted with you? If I didn't need it to go back to Berlin, I could cheerfully hope that I never again saw a Junkers 52."

"Of course," said Ahrens. "You must be exhausted."

We climbed into the Tatra. A corporal named Rose was at the wheel, and we were soon bowling along quite a decent road.

"YOU'LL BE STAYING WITH US IN THE CASTLE," said Ahrens. "That's Dnieper Castle, which is along the main road to Vitebsk. Nearly all of Army Group Center, the Air Force Corps, the Gestapo, and my lot are located west of Smolensk, in and around a place called Krasny Bor. The general staff is headquartered in a nearby health resort, which is as good as it gets around here, but we're not badly off at the castle in Signals. Are we, Rex?"

"No, sir. We're well set, I think."

"There's a cinema and a sauna—there's even a rifle range. Grub's pretty good, you'll be glad to hear. Most of us—at least the officers, anyway—we don't actually go into Smolensk itself very much at all." Ahrens waved at some onion dome spires on the horizon to our left. "But it's not a bad place, to be honest. Rather historic, really. There are more churches hereabouts than you could polish the floor with. Rex is your man for that sort of thing, aren't you, Lieutenant?"

"Yes, sir," said Rex. "There's a nice cathedral, Captain. The Assumption. I do recommend you see that while you're here. That is, if you're not too busy. By rights it shouldn't be there at all: during the Siege of Smolensk at the beginning of the seventeenth century, the defenders of the city locked themselves in the crypt, where there was an ammunition depot, and blew it and themselves up to prevent it from falling into Polish hands. History repeats itself, of course. The local NKVD used to keep some of its own personnel and domestic case files in the crypt of the Assumption Cathedral—to protect them against the Luftwaffe—and when it became clear that the city was about to be captured by us, they tried to blow them up, like they did in Kiev, at the city's Duma building. Only the explosives didn't go off."

"I knew there was a reason it wasn't on my itinerary."

"Oh, the cathedral is quite safe," said Rex. "Most of the explosive has been removed, but our engineers still think there are lots of hidden bombs in the crypt. One of our men had his face blown off when he opened a filing cabinet down there. So it's just the crypt that remains out of bounds to visitors. Most of the material is of limited military intelligence value and probably out of date by now, so the more time that passes, the less important it seems to risk looking for it." He shrugged. "Anyway, it's really a very impressive building. Napoleon certainly thought so."

"I had no idea he got this far," I said.

"Oh yes," said Rex. "He really was the Hitler of—" Rex stopped midsentence.

"The Hitler of his day," I said, smiling at the nervous lieutenant. "Yes, I can see how that comparison works very well for us all."

"We're not used to visitors, as you can see," said Ahrens. "On the whole, we keep ourselves to ourselves. For no other reason than secrecy. Well, you'd expect tight security with a signals regiment. We have a map room that indicates the disposition of all our troops, from which our future military intentions are plain. And of course, all of the group's communications come through us. It goes without saying that this room and the actual telephone room are barred to ordinary access. But we do have lots of Ivans working at the castle—four HIWIs who are permanently on site and some female personnel who come in every day from Smolensk to cook and skivvy for us. But every German unit has Ivans working for them in Smolensk."

"How many of you are there?"

"Three officers, not including myself, and about twenty noncommissioned officers and men," said Ahrens.

"And how long have you been here?"

"Me personally? Since the end of November 1941. If I remember rightly, on thirtieth November."

"What about partisans? Get any trouble from them?"

"None to speak of. At least not close to Smolensk. But we have had air attacks."

"Really? The pilot on the plane said this was too far east for the Ivan air force."

"Well, he would, wouldn't he? The Luftwaffe is under strict orders to maintain that bullshit argument. But it's just not true. No, we've had air attacks, all right. One of the troop houses in our compound was badly damaged early last year. Since then we've had a big problem with German troops cutting down the wood around the castle for fuel. That's the Katyn Wood. The trees provide us with excellent antiaircraft cover so I've had to forbid entry to the Katyn Wood to all German soldiers. It's caused problems because this obliges our troops to forage farther afield, which they're reluctant to do, of course, since that exposes them to the risk of partisan attack."

This was the first time I'd heard the name Katyn Wood.

"So tell me about this body? The one the wolf discovered?" I laughed.

"What's funny?"

"Only that we've got a wolf and some woodcutters, and a castle. I can't help thinking there should be a couple of lost children in this story—not to mention a wicked wizard."

"Maybe you're it, Captain."

"Maybe I am. I do make a wicked fire tongs punch. At least I used to when you could get any brown rum and oranges."

"Fire tongs punch." Ahrens repeated the words dreamily and shook his head. "Yes, I'd almost forgotten that."

"Me too, until I mentioned it." I shivered.

"I could certainly use a cup now," said Lieutenant Rex.

"Just another enjoyable thing that sneaked out of Germany's back door and left no forwarding address," I said.

"You know, you're a strange fellow for an SD officer," said Ahrens.

"That's what General Heydrich told me once." I shrugged. "Words to that effect, anyway—I'm not exactly sure. He had me chained to a wall and was torturing my girlfriend at the time."

I laughed at their obvious discomfort, which in truth was probably less than mine. I was hardly as used to the cold as they were and the rush of freezing air through the windowless Tatra took my breath away.

"You were about to say, about the body," I said.

"Back in December 1941, shortly after I arrived in Smolensk, one of my men pointed out that there was a sort of mound in our little wood and that upon this mound was a birch cross. The HIWIs mentioned some shootings had taken place in the Katyn Wood the year before. Shortly after that I said something about it in passing to Colonel von Gersdorff, who's our local chief of intelligence, and he said he, too, had heard something about this but that I shouldn't be surprised because this kind of Bolshevik brutality was exactly what we were fighting against."

"Yes. That's what he would say, I suppose."

"Then in January I saw a wolf in our wood, which was unusual because they don't come so near the city."

"Like the partisans," I said.

"Exactly. Mostly they stay farther west. Von Kluge hunts them with his own Russian *Putzer*."

"So he's not particularly worried about partisans?"

"Hardly. He used to go after wild boar but in winter he prefers to hunt wolves from a plane. A Storch he keeps down here. Doesn't even bother to land and collect the fur, most of the time. I think he just likes killing things."

"Around these parts that's infectious," I said. "Anyway, you were saying about the wolf."

"It had been on the mound in the Katyn Wood, next to the cross, and had dug up some human bones, which must have taken a while as the ground is still like iron. I suppose it was hungry. I had a doctor take a look at the remains and he declared that they were human. I decided it must be a soldier's grave and informed the officer in charge of war graves around here. I also reported the discovery to Lieutenant Voss of the field police. And I put it in my report to group, who must have passed it on to the Abwehr because they telephoned and said you were coming. They also told me not to talk about it with anyone else."

"And have you?"

"Until now, no."

"Good. Let's keep it that way."

It was dark by the time we reached the castle, which wasn't really a castle at all but a two-story white stucco villa of about fourteen or fifteen rooms, one of which was assigned temporarily to me. After an excellent dinner with real meat and potatoes, I went with Ahrens on a short tour and it quickly became obvious that he was rather proud of his "castle" and even prouder of his men. The villa was warm and hospitable, with a large roaring log fire in the main entrance hall; and, as Ahrens had promised, there was even a small cinema where once a week a German film was screened; but Ahrens was especially proud of his homemade honey because, with the help of a local Russian couple, he kept an apiary in the castle grounds. Clearly his men loved him. There were worse places to see out a war than Dnieper Castle, and besides, it's difficult to dislike a man who is so enthusiastic about bees and honey. The honey was delicious, there was plenty of hot water for a bath, and my bed was warm and comfortable. Fueled up on honey and schnapps, I slept like a worker bee in a temperature-controlled hive and dreamed about a crooked house with a witch in it and being lost in the woods with a wolf prowling around; the house even had a sauna and a small cinema and venison for supper. It wasn't a nightmare because the witch turned out to like sitting in the sauna, which was how we got to know each other a lot better. You can get to know anyone well in a sauna, even a witch.

6

THURSDAY, MARCH 11, 1943

I awoke early the next morning feeling a little tired from the flight but keen to get on with my inquiry because, of course, I was even keener to return home. After breakfast, Ahrens got the key to the cold storeroom where the remains were stored and we went down to the basement to examine these. I found a large tarpaulin laid out on the stone floor. Ahrens drew back the top part to reveal what looked like a tibia, a fibula, a femur, and half a pelvis. I lit a cigarette—it was better than the stale, meaty smell coming off the bones—and dropped down on my haunches to take a closer look.

"What's this?" I asked, handling the tarpaulin.

"From an Opel Blitz," said Ahrens.

I nodded and let the smoke drift up my nostrils. There wasn't much to say about the bones except that these were human and that an animal—presumably the wolf—had been chewing them.

"What happened to the wolf?" I asked.

"We chased it off," said Ahrens.

"Seen any wolves since?"

"I haven't but some of the men might have. We can ask, if you like."

"Yes. And I'd like to see the spot where these remains were found."

"Of course."

We fetched our greatcoats and were joined outside by Lieutenant Hodt and Oberfeldwebel Krimminski from the 537th, who had been guarding against German soldiers looking to take wood for their fires. At my request, the Oberfeldwebel had brought an entrenching tool. We walked north along the snow-covered castle road, toward the Vitebsk highway. The forest was mostly birch trees, some of them recently felled, which seemed to bear out the colonel's story regarding troop foraging.

"There's a fence about a kilometer away that marks the perimeter of the castle land," said Ahrens. "But there must have been some sort of a fight around here as you can still see some trenches and foxholes."

A little farther on we turned west off the road and began the more difficult task of walking in the snow. A couple of hundred meters away we came upon a mound and a cross made from two pieces of birch.

"It's about here that we came across the wolf and the remains," explained Ahrens. "Krimminski? The captain was wondering if any of us had seen the animal since."

"No," said Krimminski. "But we've heard wolves at night."

"Any tracks?"

"If there were any, the snow covered them up. It snows most nights around here."

"So we wouldn't know if the wolf had come back for seconds?" I said.

"It's possible, sir," said Krimminski. "But I haven't seen any signs of that having happened."

"This birch cross," I said. "Who put it there?"

"Nobody seems to know," said Ahrens. "Although Lieutenant Hodt has a theory. Don't you, Hodt?"

"Yes, sir. I think this is not the first time human remains have been found around here. My theory is that when it happened before, the locals reburied them and erected the cross."

"Good theory," I said. "Did you ask them about it?"

"No one tells us very much about anything," said Hodt. "They're still afraid of the NKVD."

"I shall want to speak to some of these locals of yours," I said.

"We get on pretty well with our HIWIs," said Ahrens. "It didn't seem worth upsetting the saucer of milk by accusing anyone of lying."

"All the same," I said, "I shall still want to speak to them."

"Then you'd better speak to the Susanins," said Ahrens. "They're the couple who we have most to do with. They look after the hives and tell the Russian staff what to do in the castle."

"Who else is there?"

"Let's see, there's Tsanava and Abakumov—they look after our chickens—Moskalenko, who chops wood for us. The laundry is done by Olga and Irina. Our cooks are Tanya and Rudolfovich. Marusya, the kitchen maid. But look here, I don't want you bullying them, Captain Gunther. There's a status quo here I wouldn't want to be disturbed."

"Colonel Ahrens," I said. "If this does turn out to be a grave full of dead Polish officers, then it's probably already too late for that."

Ahrens swore under his breath.

"That is, unless you yourselves shot some Polish officers," I said. "Or perhaps the SS. I can more or less guarantee that no one back in Berlin is interested in uncovering any evidence of that."

"We haven't shot any Poles," sighed Ahrens. "Here, or anywhere else."

"What about Ivans? You must have captured a lot of Red Army after the Battle of Smolensk. Did you shoot any of them, perhaps?"

"We captured about seventy thousand men, many of whom are now held in Camp 126, about twenty-five kilometers to the west of Smolensk. And there's another camp in Vitebsk. You are welcome to go and take a look at them for yourself, Captain Gunther." He bit his lip for a moment before continuing: "I'm told that conditions there have improved, but in the beginning there were so many Russian POWs that conditions in the Ivan camps were extremely harsh."

"So what you're saying is that there was probably no need to shoot them when they could just as easily be starved to death."

"This is a signals regiment, damn it," said Ahrens. "The welfare of Russian POWs is not my department."

"No, of course not. I wasn't suggesting that it was. I'm merely trying to establish the facts here. In wartime people have a habit of forgetting where they've left them. Don't you agree, Colonel?"

"Perhaps," he said stiffly.

"Your predecessor, Colonel Bedenck. What about him? Did he shoot anyone in this wood, perhaps?"

"No," insisted Ahrens.

"How can you be sure of that? You weren't here."

"I was here, sir," said Lieutenant Hodt. "When Colonel Bedenck was in command of the 537th. And you have my word that no one has been shot in this wood by us. No Russians and no Poles."

"Good enough," I said. "All right then, what about the SS? Special Action Group B was stationed in Smolensk for a while. Is it possible the SS left a few thousand calling cards down there?"

"We've been at this castle since the beginning," said Hodt. "The SS were active elsewhere. And before you ask, I'm certain of that because this is a signals regiment. I myself set up their SS command post with telephone and teletype. And the local Gestapo. All of their communications with Group HQ would have come through us. Telephone and teletype. And all their other traffic with Berlin. If any Poles had been shot by the SS, I'm certain I would have known about it."

"Then you might also know if any Jews had been shot around here."

Hodt looked awkward for a moment. "Yes," he said. "I would."

"And were there?"

Hodt hesitated.

"Come now, Lieutenant," I said. "There's no need to be coy about this. We both know the SS have been murdering Jews in Russia since the first day of Operation Barbarossa. I've heard tell that as many as half a million people were butchered in the first six months alone." I shrugged. "Look, all I'm trying to do is establish a perimeter of safe inquiry. A pale beyond which it's not wise for me to go walking in my size forty-six policeman's boots. Because the last thing any of us wants to do is to lift the lid of their hive." I glanced at Ahrens. "That's right, isn't it? Bees? They don't like it when you open their hive, right?"

"Um, no, you're right," he said. "They don't particularly like it." He nodded. "And let me answer that question. About the SS. And what they've been up to around here."

He led me a short distance away from the others. We walked carefully as the ground was icy and uneven under the snow. To me the Katyn Wood felt like a dismal place in a country that was full of equally dismal places. Cold air hung damp around us like a fine curtain while elsewhere pockets of mist rolled into hollows in the ground like the smoke from invisible artillery. Crows growled their contempt for my inquiries in the tops of the trees, and overhead a barrage balloon was moored to prevent overflights by enemy aircraft. Ahrens lit another cigarette and yawned a steamy plume.

"It's hard to believe but we prefer it here in winter," he said. "In just a few weeks from now this whole wood will be full of mosquitoes. They drive you mad. Just one of many things that drives you mad out here." He shook his head. "Look, Captain Gunther, none of us in this regiment is very political. Most of us just want to win this war quickly and go home—if such a thing is still possible after Stalingrad. When that happened, we all listened to the radio, to hear what Goebbels would say about it. Did you hear the speech? From the Sportpalast?"

"I heard it." I shrugged. "I live in Berlin. It was so loud I could hear every word Joey said without even having to turn on the fucking radio."

"Then you recall how he asked the German people if they wanted a war more radical than anything ever imagined. Total war, he called it."

"He has quite a turn of phrase, does our Mahatma Propagandi."

"Yes. Only it seems to me—to all of us at the castle—that total war is what we've had on this front since day one, and I don't recall anyone asking any of us if this is what we wanted." Ahrens nodded at a line of new trees. "Over there is the road to Vitebsk. Vitebsk is less than a hundred kilometers west of here. Before the war there were fifty thousand Jews living there. As soon as the Wehrmacht took over the city, the Jews living there started to suffer. In July of 1941 a ghetto was established on the right bank of the Zapadnaya Dvina River and most of the Jews who hadn't run away and joined the partisans or just emigrated east were rounded up and forced to live in it: about sixteen thousand people. A wooden stockade was built around the ghetto and inside this, conditions were very hard: forced labor, star-vation rations. Probably as many as ten thousand died of hunger and disease. Meanwhile, at least two thousand of them were murdered on some pretext or another at a place called Mazurino. Then the or-ders came for the liquidation of the ghetto. I myself saw those orders on the teletype—orders from the Reichsführer SS in Berlin. The pre-text was that there was typhoid in the ghetto. Maybe there was, maybe there wasn't. I myself delivered a copy of those orders for Field Marshal von Kluge, informing him of what was happening in his area. Later on I learned that about five thousand of the Jews who remained alive in the ghetto were driven out into the remote country-side, where they were all shot. That's the trouble with being part of a signals regiment, Captain. It's very hard not to know what's going on, but God knows I really wish I didn't. So, to answer your question specifically—about that beehive you were referring to—halfway to

Vitebsk is a town called Rudnya, and if I were you I should confine my inquiries to anywhere east of there. Understand?"

"Yes, sir. Thank you. Colonel, since you mentioned the Mahatma, I have another question. Actually, it was something my boss mentioned to me back in Berlin. About the Mahatma and his men."

Ahrens nodded. "Ask it."

"Has anyone from the Propaganda Ministry ever been here?"

"Here in Smolensk?"

"No, here at the castle."

"At the castle? Why on earth would they come here?"

I shook my head. "It doesn't matter. It wouldn't surprise me if they'd been here to film all those Soviet POWs you told me about, that's all. To help prove to the folks back home that we were winning this war."

Of course, this wasn't the reason I'd asked about the Propaganda Ministry but I couldn't see how I could explain my suspicions without calling the colonel a liar.

"Do you think we're winning this war?" he asked.

"Winning or losing," I said. "Neither one looks good for Germany. Not the Germany I know and love."

Ahrens nodded. "There have been days," he said, "many days, when I find it hard to like what I am or what we're doing, Captain. I, too, love my country but not what's being done in its name, and there are times when I can't look my own reflection in the eye. Do you understand?"

"Yes. And I recognize myself when I hear you talking treason."

"Then you're in the right place," he said. "You hear as much as we do in the 537th, then you'll know that there's plenty of treason talked in Smolensk. This might be one reason why the Leader is coming here on a morale-building visit."

"Hitler's coming here to Smolensk?"

"On Saturday. For a meeting with von Kluge. That's supposed to be a secret, by the way. So don't mention it, will you? Although everyone and his dog seems to know about it."

ALONE, WITH AN ENTRENCHING TOOL IN MY HAND, I took a walk around the Katyn Wood. I went slowly down a slope into a dip in the ground that seemed to be a natural amphitheater and even slower up the other side with my army boots sounding like an old horse eating oats as they crunched down in the snow. I don't know what I was looking for. The frozen ground underneath the snow was as hard as granite and my futile attempts at excavation merely amused the crows. A hammer and chisel might have yielded better results. In spite of the birch cross, it was hard to imagine much had ever taken place in that wood; I wondered if really anything of significance had happened there since Napoleon. Already it felt like I was on a wild-goose chase. Besides, I cared little for the Poles. I'd never liked them any more than the English, who, apparently able to ignore the role that perfidious Poland had played during the Czech crisis of 1938—it wasn't just the Nazis who had marched in there, it was the Poles, too, in pursuit of their own territorial claims—had stupidly come to the aid of Poland in 1939. The few bones I had seen back in the castle were evidence of nothing very much. A Russian soldier who had died in his foxhole, perhaps, and later been found by a hungry wolf? It was probably the best thing that could have happened to the Ivan given the awful situation Ahrens had described at Camp 126. Starving to death was easy to do in a world policed and patrolled by my own tenderhearted countrymen.

For half an hour I blundered around, getting colder. Even wearing gloves my hands felt frozen and my ears ached as if someone had hit them with the entrenching tool. What on earth were we doing in this desolate permafrosted country, so very far from home? The living space Hitler craved so much was fit only for the wolves and crows. It made no sense at all, but then very little of what the Nazis did made much sense to me. But I doubt that I was the only one who was beginning to suspect that Stalingrad might have the same significance as the retreat of Napoleon's Grand Army from Moscow; surely everyone except Hitler and the generals knew we were finished in Russia.

In the distance close to the road to Vitebsk a couple of sentries pretended to look the other way but I could hear their laughter quite clearly: there was something about the Katyn Wood that had a curious effect on sound, holding it within the line of trees like water in a bowl. But their opinion just made me more determined to find something. Being bloody-minded and proving other people wrong is what being a detective is all about. It's one of the things that made me so popular with my many friends and colleagues.

Scraping at the snow and occasionally reaching to pick something up, I found an empty packet of German cigarettes, a buckle off a German carbine sling, and a piece of twisted wire. Quite a haul for half an hour's work. I was just about to call it a day when I turned too quickly on my heel, slipped and fell down the slope, twisting my knee in a way that left it feeling stiff and painful for days afterward; I swore loudly and, still sitting in the snow, picked up my crusher, hauled it back on my head. A glance at the sentries near the road revealed that they had their backs turned squarely to me, which probably meant that they didn't want to be seen laughing at the SD officer who'd fallen on his arse.

I put down my hand to push myself up, which was when I found an object that was only part frozen to the ground. I pulled hard and the object came away in my hand. It was a boot—a riding boot of the kind worn by an officer. I put the boot to one side and, still sitting, set to work scraping at the frozen ground on either side of me with the entrenching tool. A few minutes later I had a small metallic object in my hand. It was a button. I pocketed the button and, recovering the boot, stood up and limped back to the castle, where I washed my little find very carefully in warm water.

On the face of the button was an eagle.

. . .

IN THE AFTERNOON I INTERVIEWED THE SUSANINS, the Russian couple who helped to look after the 537th at Dnieper Castle. They were in their sixties and as wary and unsmiling as an old sepia photograph. Oleg Susanin wore a black peasant's blouse with a belt, dark trousers, a gray felt hat, and a longish beard; his wife looked not dissimilar. Since their German was better than my Russian but with a vocabulary that was restricted to food, fuel, laundry, and bees, Ahrens had arranged for me to have the services of a translator from Group headquarters—a Russian called Peshkov.

He was a shifty-looking fellow with round pince-nez glasses and a Hitler mustache; he wore a German Army greatcoat, a pair of German officer's boots, and a red bow tie with white polka dots; later on Ahrens told me he'd grown the mustache in order to look more pro-German.

"That's a matter of opinion," I said. Peshkov spoke excellent German.

"It's an honor to be working for you, sir," he said. "I'm entirely at your service while you're in Smolensk. Day or night. You have only to ask. You can usually leave a message for me with the adjutant, sir. At Krasny Bor. I make myself available there every morning at nine o'clock precisely."

But while Peshkov was quite fluent in German, he never smiled or laughed and was completely different from the Russian who had accompanied me to Dnieper Castle from Group HQ at Krasny Bor, a man called Dyakov, who seemed to be a sort of local hunting guide and general servant for von Kluge—his *Putzer*. Ahrens explained that German soldiers had rescued Dyakov from an NKVD murder squad.

"He's quite a fellow," said Ahrens, as he continued to introduce me to the two Russians. "Aren't you, Dyakov? A complete rogue, probably, but Field Marshal von Kluge seems to trust him implicitly, so I've no choice but to trust him, too."

"Thank you, sir," said Dyakov.

"He seems to have a soft spot for Marusya, our kitchen maid, so when he's not with von Kluge he's usually here, aren't you, Dyakov?"

Dyakov shrugged. "This is very special girl, sir. I should like to marry her but Marusya says no and, until she does, I must keep trying. If there was any work for her somewhere else, I guess I'd be there instead."

"Peshkov, on the other hand, hasn't a soft spot for anyone other than Peshkov," added Ahrens. "Isn't that right, Peshkov?"

Peshkov shrugged. "A man has to make a living, sir."

"We think he might be a secret Jew," continued Ahrens, "but no one can be bothered to find out for sure. Besides, his German is so good it would be a shame if we had to get rid of him."

Both Peshkov and Dyakov were Zeps—Zeppelin volunteers, which is what we called all the Russians who worked for us who were not POWs; those were HIWIs. Dyakov wore a heavy coat with a lamb's-wool collar, a fur hat, and a pair of black leather German pilot's gloves that he said were a gift from the field marshal, just like the Mauser Safari rifle he carried on a sheepskin strap over his shoulder. Dyakov was a tall, dark, curly-haired fellow with a thick beard, hands the size of a balalaika, and, unlike Peshkov, his face always wore a broad and engaging smile.

"You take the field marshal wolf hunting," I said to Dyakov. "Is that right?"

"Yes, sir."

"See many wolves around here?"

"Me? No. But it's been a very cold winter. Hunger brings them nearer to the city in search of scraps. A wolf can get a good meal out of an old piece of leather, you know."

We all went to sit in the castle kitchen, which was the warmest place in the house, and drank black Russian tea from a battered samovar, sweetening it with some of the honey that Ahrens made. The delicious smell of the sweetened tea wasn't quite strong enough to mask the dark smell of the Russians.

Peshkov liked the tea but he didn't much like the Susanins. He spoke roughly to them—rougher than I would have liked under the circumstances.

"Ask them if they remember any Poles in this area," I told him.

Peshkov put the question and then translated what Susanin had said. "He says that in the spring of 1940 he saw more than two hundred Poles in uniform in railway trucks at Gnezdovo station. The train waited for an hour or so and then started again, going southeast toward Voronezh."

"How did they know they were Poles?"

Peshkov repeated the question in Russian and then answered: "One of the men in the railway wagons asked Susanin where they were. The man said he was Polish then."

"What was that word they used?" I asked. "*Stolypinka*s?"

Peshkov shrugged. "I haven't heard it before."

"Yes, sir," said Dyakov. "*Stolypinka*s were the prison wagons named after the Russian prime minister who introduced them under the tsars. To deport Russians to Siberia."

"How far is the station from here?" I asked.

"About five kilometers west," said Peshkov.

"Did any of these Poles get out of the wagons?"

"Get out? Why should they get out, sir?" asked Peshkov.

"To stretch their legs, perhaps. Or be taken somewhere else?"

Peshkov translated, listened to Susanin's answer, and then shook his head. "No, none of them. He's sure of that. The doors remained chained, sir."

"What about this place? Were there ever any executions around here? Of Jews? Of Russians, perhaps? And why is there a cross in the middle of the Katyn Wood?"

The woman never spoke at all and Oleg Susanin's answers were short and to the point, but I've questioned enough men in my time to know when someone is holding something back. Or lying.

"He says that when NKVD had this house they were forbidden to come to Dnieper Castle for security reasons so they don't know what went on here," said Peshkov.

"There was a fence all the way around the land then," added Dyakov. "Since the Germans arrived, the fence has been broken down by soldiers foraging for firewood but some of it is still there."

"Don't be so rough with them," I told Peshkov. "They're not accused of anything. Tell them there's nothing to be afraid of."

Peshkov translated again and, uncertainly, the Susanins both nodded a faint smile in my direction. But Peshkov remained contemptuous.

"Take my word for it, boss," he said. "You have to speak roughly to these people or they won't answer at all. The *babulya* is a real peasant, and the *starik* is a stupid *bulbash* who's spent his whole life in fear of the party. They're still terrified the NKVD will come back—even after eighteen months of German occupation. As a matter of fact, I'm a little surprised these two are still here. It goes without saying that if those *mudak*s ever do come back here, these two will be Russian fertilizer. Know what I'm saying? Day one, they'll be shot just because they worked for you fellows. With all due respect to your colonel, about the only thing that's kept them here are their beehives."

"Like Tolstoy, yes?" Dyakov laughed loudly. "Still, it makes for a nice cup of tea, yes?"

"Aren't you afraid of what will happen if the NKVD comes back?"

Peshkov glanced at Dyakov and shrugged.

"No, sir," said Peshkov. "I don't believe they are coming back."

"That is a matter of opinion," I said.

"Me? I don't have any beehives, boss." Dyakov grinned widely. "There's nothing to keep Alok Dyakov here in Smolensk. No, sir, when the shit starts coming up through the floor, I'm going to Germany with the field marshal. If it was just being shot, I could live with that, if you know what I mean. But there's plenty worse the NKVD can do to a man than put a tap in the back of your head. Believe me, I know what I'm talking about."

"What was the NKVD doing here?" I asked. "Here. In this house."

"I don't know, sir," said Peshkov. "Frankly, it was best never to ask such questions. To mind one's own business."

"It's a nice house. With a cinema. What do you think they were doing? Watching *Battleship Potemkin*? *Alexander Nevsky*? You must have some idea, Dyakov. What's your opinion?"

"You want me to guess? I guess they were here getting drunk on vodka and watching movies, yes."

I nodded. "Thank you. Thank you for your help. I am very grateful to you both."

"I am glad to have been of assistance," said Peshkov.

It was hard to know which of them was lying—Peshkov, Dyakov, or the Susanins—but I knew someone was. I had the proof of that in my own trouser pocket. Even as I nodded and smiled at the Russians, I had my hand around the button I had found in Katyn Wood.

When I went outside on my own to think things over, Dyakov followed me.

"Peshkov speaks good German," I said. "Where did he learn?"

"At university. Peshkov's a very clever man. But me, I learned German at a place called Terezin, in Czechoslovakia. When I was a boy I was prisoner of the Austrian Army in 1915. I like Austrians. But I like Germans more. Austrians are not very friendly. After the war I was a schoolteacher. Is why NKVD arrested me."

"They arrested you because you were a schoolteacher?"

Dyakov laughed loudly. "I teach German, sir. That is fine in 1940 when Stalin and Hitler are friends. But when Germany attacks Russia, then NKVD think I am enemy and arrest me."

"Did they arrest Peshkov, too?"

Dyakov shrugged. "No, sir. But he wasn't teaching German, sir. Before the war I believe he worked at the electricity power station, sir. I believe he learned to do this job in Germany. With Siemens. Is very important job, so that could be why NKVD didn't arrest him."

"Why isn't Peshkov doing that job now?"

Dyakov grinned. "Because there's no money to be made doing that. The Germans at Krasny Bor pay him very well, sir. Good money. Better than electricity worker. Besides, there are Germans running electricity power station now. They don't trust Russians to do this."

"And the hunting? Who taught you to hunt?"

"My father was hunter, sir. He taught me to shoot." Dyakov grinned. "You see, sir? I've had very good teachers. My father and the Austrians."

7

FRIDAY, MARCH 12, 1943

I awoke thinking I must be back in the trenches because there was a strong smell of something horrible in my nostrils. The smell was like a dead rat only worse, and I spent the next ten minutes sniffing the air in various areas of my room in the castle before finally I decided that the source of the stink was underneath my own bed. And it was only when I went down on my hands and knees to look that I remembered the frozen leather boot I had tossed on the floor the previous morning; except that the boot and whatever was still in the boot was now frozen no longer.

I took a deep breath, and at the same time I looked inside the leg of the boot, I squeezed the toe. There were several hard objects inside it. They were the remains of a decayed foot to add to the colonel's collection of bones on the floor of the cold storeroom downstairs. I had a good idea that the foot and the leg bones wrapped in the tarpaulin had belonged to the same man because the boot had been chewed in several places, presumably by the wolf. But there was something else in the boot besides a dead Pole's stinking foot, and gradually I peeled out of the leg a piece of oiled paper that must have been wrapped around the dead man's calf. At first I was inclined to believe that the Pole had simply tried to insulate his leg against the cold, much as I did with my own poorer quality boots; but newspaper would have done for that—oiled paper was for preserving things, not keeping them warm.

I unfolded the paper as best I could using the leg of the bed and a chair; it was folded in half and inside the fold were several typed sheets of onionskin paper. But in spite of the oiled paper, what was written was almost illegible and it was clear it was going to require the resources of a laboratory to decipher what was written on these pages.

Until the ground thawed it was hard to see how I was going to make much more progress with this preliminary investigation, and it looked as if the button would have to be evidence enough. But I wasn't happy about that. One button, an old boot, and a few bones didn't seem like much of a haul to take back to Berlin. I badly wanted to know what was written on the pages before I mentioned them to anyone. I wasn't about to make myself or the bureau a sucker for some elaborate lie dreamed up by the Propaganda Ministry. All the same, I couldn't help but think that if the Mahatma's men had planted evidence of a massacre in the Katyn Wood, they'd have made it a little more obvious and easy for someone like me to find.

I dressed and went downstairs to find some breakfast.

Colonel Ahrens looked pleased when I told him I had probably concluded my investigation and would be returning to Berlin just as soon as possible; he looked a lot less pleased when I told him that I had made no firm conclusions.

"At this stage I really can't say if the bureau will want to take this any further. Sorry, sir, but that's just the way it is. I'll be off the back of your collar just as soon as I can get on a plane home."

"You won't get a flight out of here today. Saturday looks like a better bet. Or even Sunday. There will be plenty of planes arriving here tomorrow."

"Of course," I said. "The Leader. He's coming here, isn't he?"

"Yes. Look, I'll telephone the airfield and arrange things for you. Until then you're welcome to make use of the facilities here at the castle. There's a shooting range if you care for that kind of thing. And there's a movie in the theater this afternoon and evening. All leave is canceled from midnight tonight, so the movie has been brought forward. I'm afraid it's *Jew Süss*. All we could get at short notice."

"No, thanks," I said. "It's not one of my favorites." I shrugged. "You know, maybe I'll take a look at the local cathedral after all."

"Good idea," said the colonel. "I'll lend you a car."

"Thank you, sir. And if you could give me a map of the city, I'd be grateful. From a distance it's hard to tell one onion dome from another."

I DIDN'T GIVE A DAMN ABOUT THE CATHEDRAL. I had no intention of looking at the cathedral or anything else, for that matter, but I didn't want Colonel Ahrens knowing that. Besides, I don't believe in tourism during wartime, not anymore. Sure, when I was stationed in Paris during 1940 I'd walked about a bit with a Baedeker and seen a few of the sights—Les Invalides, the Eiffel Tower—but that was Paris; you could always read a Frenchman in a way you couldn't ever do with a Czech or an Ivan. I'd learned a bit of caution since then, and even in Prague I didn't go abroad with the Baedeker very much. Not that there ever were any Baedekers written about Russia—what would have been the point?—but the principle holds good, I think, as two examples might serve to illustrate.

Heinz Seldte was a lieutenant in a police battalion I knew from the Alex in the early thirties; I helped get him a leg up into Kripo. He was one of the first Germans into the city of Kiev in September 1941, and on a quiet summer's afternoon he decided to go and look at the city's Duma building on Khreshchatyk, which is the main street—

apparently it was a big deal with a spire and a statue of the archangel Michael, the patron saint of Kiev. What he didn't know—what nobody knew—was that the retreating Red Army had booby-trapped the whole fucking street with dynamite, which they exploded with radio-controlled fuses from over four hundred kilometers away. The historic buildings of Khreshchatyk—the Germans renamed the ruins Eichhornstrasse—were never seen again; nor was Heinz Seldte.

Victor Lungwitz was a waiter from the Hotel Adlon, he waited tables because he couldn't make a living at being an artist. He joined an SS Panzer Division in 1939 and was sent to Belarus as part of Operation Barbarossa. When he was off duty he liked drawing churches, of which Minsk has almost as many as Smolensk. One day he went to look at some old church on the edge of town; it was called the Red Church, which ought to have put him on his guard. They found Victor's drawing but no sign of him; a few days later a mutilated body was found in some marshland nearby; it took them a while to identify poor Victor; the partisans had cut almost everything off his head—his nose, his lips, his eyelids, his ears—before cutting off his genitals and letting him bleed to death.

When you fight a war with a Baedeker, you don't always know what you're going to see.

In the colonel's drafty little Tatra I drove east along the Vitebsk highway with Smolensk in front of me and the Dnieper River on my right. For most of the way the road ran between two railway lines, and as I passed Arsenalstrasse and a cemetery on my left I saw the main station; it was a huge icing cake of a place with four square corner towers and an enormous archway entrance. Like a lot of buildings in Smolensk, it was painted green, and either green meant something significant in that part of Russia or green was the only color of paint they'd had in the stores the last time anyone had thought of carrying out some building maintenance. Russia being Russia, I tended to subscribe to the second explanation.

A little farther down the road, I stopped to consult my map and then turned south down Brückenstrasse, which sounded promising given that I needed to find a bridge to cross the river.

According to the map the west and east bridges were destroyed and that left three in the middle or, if you were a Russian, a log raft passenger ferry that resembled something from my time at a boys' summer camp on Rügen Island. On the north bank of the river I slowed the car as I came in sight of the local Kremlin—a fortress enclosing the center of the ancient city of Smolensk; on a hilltop, behind the castellated redbrick walls built by Boris Godunov, stood the city's cathedral with its distinctive pepper-pot domes and tall white walls, and looking to my eyes as ugly as an outsized wood-burning stove. At least now I could say that I'd seen it.

I showed my papers to the military police guards at the checkpoint on the Peter and Paul bridge, asked for directions to the German Kommandatura, and was directed to go south on Hauptstrasse.

"You can't miss it, sir," said the bridge sentry. "It's opposite Sparkassenstrasse. If you find yourself on Magazinstrasse, you'll have gone too far."

"Are all Smolensk street names in German?"

"Of course. Makes it a lot easier to get around, don't you think?"

"It certainly does if you're German," I said.

"Isn't that what it's all about, sir?" The sentry grinned. "We're trying to make it as much like home as possible."

"That'll be the day."

I drove on and in the shadow of the Kremlin wall on my right, I went along Hauptstrasse until I saw what was obviously the Kommandatura—a gray stone building with a pillared portico and several Nazi Party flags. An extensive series of German street pointers had been erected in the square in front of this building—many of them on a broken Soviet tank—but the general effect was not one of clarity of direction but confusion; a sentry stood in the middle of the pointers to help Germans make sense of their own signs. The red of the flags on the Kommandatura added an almost welcome splash of color in a city that was as gray and green as a dead elephant. Underneath the flags a dozen or so soldiers were watching a boy riding bareback on a spavined white horse perform a few tricks with the nag; from time to time they would toss a few coins onto the cobbled street, where they were collected by an old man wearing a white cap and jacket who might have been some relation to the boy or possibly the horse. Seeing me, two of the soldiers came over as I pulled up and saluted.

"Can't leave it there, sir," said one. "Security. Best leave it around the corner on Kreuzstrasse, next to the local cinema. Always plenty of room there."

Three very ragged children—two boys and a girl, I think—watched me park the Tatra in front of some German propaganda posters that were almost as scruffy as they were. I'd seen some poor children in my time but none as poor as these three urchins. Despite the cold, all of them were barefoot and carrying foraging bags and mess tins; they looked as if they had to fend for themselves and were not having much success, although they appeared to be healthy enough. All of this looked a long way from the smiling faces and the soup bowls and the large loaves of bread depicted on the posters. Were their parents alive? Did they even have a roof over their heads? Was it any of my business? I felt a strong pang of regret as momentarily I considered the carefree life they might have been enjoying before my countrymen arrived during the summer of 1941. I wasn't the type who ever carried chocolate so I gave each of them a cigarette, assuming they were more likely to trade than smoke it. There are times when I wonder where charity would be without us smokers.

"Thank you," said the oldest child, speaking German—a boy maybe ten or eleven. His coat had more patches than the map in my pocket, and on his head was a side cap or what the more graphically minded German soldier sometimes called a cunt cover. He tucked the cigarette behind his ear for later, like a real workingman. "German cigarettes are good. Better than Russian cigarettes. You're very kind, sir."

"No, I'm not," I said. "None of us are. Just remember that and you won't ever be disappointed."

Inside the Kommandatura I asked the desk clerk where I could find an officer and was directed to the first floor, and there I spoke to a slimy fat Wehrmacht lieutenant who could have given a whole week's rations to the children outside and not even noticed. His army belt was on its last notch and looked as if it might have appreciated some time to relax a little.

"Those people in the street outside? Doesn't it bother you they look so desperate?"

"They're Slavs," he said, as if that was all the excuse needed. "Things were pretty backward in Smolensk before we got here. And believe me, the local Ivans are a lot better off now than they ever were under the Bolsheviks."

"So is the tsar and his family but I don't figure they think that's a good thing."

The lieutenant frowned. "Was there something specific I could help you with, sir? Or did you just come in here to give your conscience a little air?"

I nodded. "You're right. I'm sorry. That's exactly what I was doing. Forgive me. As a matter of fact, I'm looking for some sort of scientific laboratory."

"In Smolensk?"

I nodded. "Somewhere that might own a stereo microscope. I need to carry out some tests."

The lieutenant picked up the telephone and turned the call handle. "Give me the department store," he said to the operator. Catching my eye, he explained: "Most of the officers stationed here in Smolensk are using the local department store as a barracks."

"That must be handy if you need a new pair of underpants."

The lieutenant laughed. "Conrad? It's Herbert. I have an officer of SD who's trying to find a scientific laboratory here in Smolensk. Any ideas?"

He listened for a moment, uttered a few words of thanks, and then replaced the receiver.

"You could try the Smolensk State Medical Academy," he said. "It's under German control so you should be able to find what you're looking for there."

We went to the window and he pointed to the south.

"About half a kilometer down Rote-Kreuzer Strasse and on your right. Can hardly miss it. Big canary-yellow building. Looks like the Charlottenburg Palace in Berlin."

"It sounds impressive," I said, and walked to the door. "I guess the Ivans in Smolensk can't have been as backward as all that."

IT WAS A SHORT DRIVE TO THE Smolensk State Medical Academy and, as promised, it wasn't easy to miss; the academy was enormous but, like a lot of buildings in Smolensk, the place showed signs of the ferocity of the battle waged by the retreating Red Army, with many of the windows on the five stories boarded up, and the yellow stucco façade pitted with hundreds of bullet holes. The triple arches of the entrance were protected with sandbags, and on the roof was a Nazi flag and what looked like an antiaircraft gun. While I was there an ambulance pulled up out front and disgorged several heavily bandaged men on stretchers.

When the German medical personnel and Soviet nurses on the front desk were done admitting the new arrivals I explained my mission to one of the orderlies. The man listened patiently and then led the way up and through the enormous hospital, which was full of German soldiers who had been wounded during the Battle of Smolensk and were still awaiting repatriation to the Fatherland. We reached a corridor on the fifth floor, where there was not one but several laboratories, and he presented me courteously to a small man wearing a white coat that was a couple of sizes too big for him, as well as mittens and a Soviet tank crewman's helmet, which he snatched off when he saw me standing there. The bow was unctuous but understandable when dealing with SD officers.

"Captain Gunther, this is Dr. Batov," said the orderly. "He's in charge of the scientific laboratories here at the academy. He speaks German and I'm sure he will be able to assist you."

When the orderly left us alone, Batov looked sheepishly at the tanker's helmet. "This ridiculous hat, it keeps the head warm," he explained. "It's cold in this hospital."

"I noticed that, sir."

"The boilers are coal-fired," he said, "and there's not so much coal about for things like heating a hospital. There's not much coal around for anything."

I offered him a cigarette and he took one and tucked it behind his ear. I lit one myself and looked around. The lab was reasonably well equipped for the purposes of instructing Russian medical students; there were several workbenches with gas taps, burners, chemical hoods, balances, flasks, and several stereo microscopes.

"What can I do for you?" he asked.

"I was hoping I might be able to use one of your stereo microscopes for a while," I said.

"Yes, of course," he said, ushering me toward the instrument. "Are you a scientist, Captain?"

"No, sir, I'm a policeman. From Berlin. Before the war we'd just started using stereo microscopes in ballistics work. To identify and match bullets from the bodies of murder victims."

Batov paused by the stereo microscope and switched on a light beside it. "And do you have a bullet you wish to examine now, Captain?"

"No. It's some typewritten papers I wanted to take a look at. The paper got damp and some of the words are hard to read." I paused, wondering how much I could tell him. "Actually, it's more complicated than that. These papers have been exposed to cadaveric fluid. From a decaying body. They were inside a boot in which the human leg wearing it had disintegrated down to the bone."

Batov nodded. "May I see?"

I showed him the papers.

"Even with a stereo microscope this will be difficult," he said thoughtfully. "Best of all would be to use infrared rays, but unfortunately we're not equipped with that kind of advanced technology here at the academy. Perhaps it would be best to have them treated in Berlin after all."

"I have good reasons for preferring to see what can be achieved here right now in Smolensk."

"Then you'll probably need to wash these documents with chloroform or xylol," he said. "I could do this for you, if you like."

"Yes. I'd be grateful if you could. Thanks."

"But may I ask, exactly what are you hoping to achieve?"

"If nothing else I'd like to be able to find out what language the papers are written in."

"Well, we can treat one sheet of paper, perhaps, and see how that works."

Batov went to look for some chemicals and then started to wash one of the pages; while he worked I sat and smoked a cigarette and dreamed that I was back in Berlin, having dinner with Renata at the Hotel Adlon. Not that we ever did have dinner at the Adlon, but it wouldn't have been much of a daydream if any of it had been remotely possible.

When Batov had finished cleaning the page he dried it carefully, flattened the paper with a sheet of glass, and then arranged the page underneath the prism of the microscope.

I drew an electric light a little closer and looked through the eyepieces while I adjusted the zoom control. A blurred word moved into focus. The alphabet wasn't Cyrillic and the words weren't written in German.

"What's the Russian word for soldier?" I asked Batov.

"*Soldat.*"

"I thought so. *Żołnierz.* That's the Polish word for soldier. Here's another. *Wywiad.* No idea what that means."

"It means 'intelligence,'" said Batov.

"Does it?"

"Yes. My wife was Ukrainian-Polish, sir, from the Subcarpathian province. She studied medicine here before the war."

"Was?"

"She's dead now."

"I'm sorry to hear that, Doctor."

"Polish." Batov paused and then added, "The language on the document. That's a relief."

I looked up from the eyepieces. "Why is that?"

"If it's in Polish it means I can offer to help you," explained Batov. "If it was in Russian—well, I could hardly betray my own country to the enemy, now could I?"

I smiled. "No, I suppose not."

He pointed at the stereo microscope. "May I have a look?"

"Be my guest."

Batov looked through the eyepieces for a moment and then nodded. "Yes, this is written in Polish. Which makes me think that a better division of labor would be if I read out the words—in German, of course—and you wrote them down. That way—in time—you would know the entire contents of the document."

Batov sat up straight and looked at me. He was dark and rather earnest, with a thick mustache and gentle eyes.

"You mean one word at a time?" I pulled a face.

"It's a laborious method, I do agree, but it has the merit of also being certain, don't you think? A couple of hours and perhaps all of your questions about this document might be answered, and perhaps, if you agreed, I might earn a little bit of money for my family.

Or perhaps you might give me something I can trade on Bazarnaya Square."

He shrugged. "Alternatively, you are welcome to borrow the stereo microscope and work on your own, perhaps." He smiled uncertainly. "I don't know. To be perfectly honest, I'm not used to German officers asking me for permission to do anything in this academy."

I nodded. "All right. It's a deal." I took out my wallet and handed over some of the occupation reichsmarks the bureau office in Berlin had issued me with. Then I handed him the rest of the bills as well. "Here. Take it all. With any luck I'm flying home tomorrow."

"Then we had better get started," said Batov.

IT WAS LATE WHEN I GOT BACK to Dnieper Castle. Most of the men were having dinner. I joined the officers' table in the mess, where chicken was on the menu. I tried not to think about the three ragged children I'd seen in Smolensk that afternoon while I was eating, but it wasn't easy.

"We were beginning to worry," said Colonel Ahrens. "Can't be too careful around here."

"What did you think of our cathedral?" asked Lieutenant Rex.

"Very impressive," I said.

"Glinka, the composer, came from Smolensk," added Rex. "I'm rather fond of Glinka. He's the father of Russian classical music."

"That's nice," I said. "To know who your father is. It's not everyone who can say that these days."

After dinner the colonel and I went to his office for a smoke and a quiet word—or at least as quiet as could be achieved given that it was next to the castle's cinema theater. Through the wall I could hear Süss Oppenheimer pleading for his life in front of the implacable burghers of the Stuttgart Town Council. It made an uncomfortable sound track to what promised to be an equally uncomfortable conversation.

He sat behind his desk facing a good deal of paperwork. "You don't mind if I work while we talk? I have to compile these duty logs for tomorrow. Who's manning the telephone exchange, that kind of thing. I have to post this on the notice board before nine o'clock so everyone knows where they're supposed to be tomorrow. Von Kluge will have my guts if there's a problem with our telecommunications when Hitler's here."

"He's flying from Rastenburg?"

"No, from his forward HQ, at Vinnitsa, in the Ukraine. His staff call it the Werewolf HQ. But don't ask me why. I believe he's going on to Rastenburg tomorrow night."

"He gets around, does our leader."

"Your flight back to Berlin is fixed for early tomorrow afternoon," said Ahrens. "I don't mind saying that I wish I was coming with you. The news from the front is not good. I'd hate to be in von Kluge's boots when the Leader drops in for a chat tomorrow and demands a new offensive this spring. Frankly, our troops aren't nearly up to that task."

"Tell me, Colonel, how soon is the ground around here likely to thaw?"

"End of March, beginning of April. Why?"

I shrugged and looked generally apologetic.

"You're coming back?"

"Not me," I said. "Someone else."

"What the hell for?"

"We won't know for sure until we find a complete body, of course, but I've a pretty shrewd idea that there are Polish soldiers buried in your wood."

"I don't believe it."

"I'm afraid it's true. Just as soon as the ground thaws, my boss, Judge Goldsche, will probably send a senior army judge and a forensic pathologist down here to take charge of the investigation."

"But you heard the Susanins," said Ahrens. "The only Poles they saw around here remained on the train at Gnezdovo."

I thought it best to avoid telling him that either the Susanins or perhaps Peshkov were clearly lying. I'd caused enough trouble for Ahrens already. Instead I handed him the button.

"I found this," I said. "And the remains of a man's foot in an officer's riding boot."

"I don't see that a fucking button and a boot tells us very much."

"I won't know for sure until I consult an expert, but that looks to me like a Polish eagle on the button."

"Balls," he said angrily. "If you ask me, that button could just as easily be from the coat of a Russian White Army soldier. There were whites under General Denikin fighting the reds in this area until at least 1922. No, you must be mistaken. I don't see how something like that could have been covered up. I ask you. Does this place feel like somewhere that's built in the middle of a mass grave?"

"When I was at the Alex, Colonel, the only time we ever paid much attention to our feelings was when it was lunchtime. It's evidence that counts. Evidence like this little button, the human bones, those two hundred Polish officers in the railway siding. You see, I think they did get off that train. I think they maybe came here and were shot by NKVD in your wood. I've some experience of these murder squads, you know."

I hardly wanted to tell the colonel about the document in Polish I had discovered and that Dr. Batov had painstakingly translated for me with his stereo microscope. I figured that the fewer people who knew about that the better. But I had little doubt that the bones found in Katyn Wood had belonged to a Polish soldier; and the bureau seemed certain to have a major war crimes investigation in Smolensk just as soon as I could get home to Berlin and make my report to Judge Goldsche.

"But look here, if there are two hundred Poles buried out there, what difference will it make to those poor buggers now? Answer me that. Couldn't you pretend that there's nothing of interest here? And then we can get on with our lives and the normal business of trying to get through this war alive."

"Look, Colonel, I'm just a policeman. It's not up to me what happens here. I'll make my report to the bureau and, after that, then it's up to the bosses and to the legal department of the High Command. But if that button does turn out to be Polish—"

I left my sentence unfinished. It was hard to know exactly what the result of such a discovery might look like but I sensed that the colonel's cozy little world at Dnieper Castle was about to come to an end.

And so I think did he, because he swore loudly, a couple of times.

SATURDAY, MARCH 13, 1943

It snowed again during the night and the room was so cold I had to wear my greatcoat in bed. The window frosted on the inside and there were tiny icicles on the iron bedstead, as if a frozen fairy had tiptoed along the metalwork while I had been trying to sleep. It wasn't just the cold that kept me awake; every so often I thought of those three barefoot children and wished I'd given them something more than a few cigarettes.

After breakfast I tried to stay out of the way. I hardly wanted to remind Colonel Ahrens by my presence that I was soon to be replaced by a judge from the War Crimes Bureau. And unlike many of the men in the 537th, I had no great desire to be up at dawn to stand on the main road to Vitebsk and wave to the Leader as he drove from the airport to an early lunch with Field Marshal von Kluge at his headquarters. So I borrowed a typewriter from the signals office and spent the time before the flight back to Berlin writing up my report for Judge Goldsche.

It was dull work and a lot of the time I was looking out the window, which was how I came to see Peshkov, the translator with the toothbrush mustache, having a furious argument with Oleg Susanin, at the end of which Susanin pushed the other man onto the ground. There was nothing very interesting about this except that it's always interesting to see a man who looks a bit like Adolf Hitler being shoved around. And so seldom seen.

After lunch Lieutenant Hodt drove me to the airport, where security was predictably tight—as tight as I'd ever seen: there was a whole platoon of Waffen SS Grenadiers guarding two specially equipped Focke-Wulf Condors and a squadron of Messerschmitt fighters that were waiting to escort the real Hitler's flight to Rastenburg.

Hodt left me in the main airport building, where an advance party of Hitler's staff officers were enjoying a last cigarette before the Leader's convoy arrived—it seemed that the Leader did not permit smoking aboard his own plane.

While I was waiting, a young bespectacled Wehrmacht lieutenant came into the hall and asked the assembled company which of us was Colonel Brandt. An officer wearing a gold equestrian's badge on his army tunic stepped forward and identified himself, whereupon the lieutenant clicked his heels and announced he was Lieutenant von Schlabrendorff and that he had brought a parcel from General von Tresckow for Colonel Stieff. My interest in this little exchange was only piqued when the lieutenant handed over the very same package containing two bottles of Cointreau that Court Official von Dohnanyi—to whom von Schlabrendorff bore a strong resemblance— had brought with him on the plane from Berlin the previous Wednesday. This made me wonder—again—why von Dohnanyi had not delivered the parcel to someone when we'd touched down in Rastenburg. Perhaps if I'd been a proper security service officer I might have made some mention of this fact—which struck me as suspicious—but I had enough on my plate already without interfering with the job of the Gestapo or the Leader's uniformed RSD bodyguards. Besides, my interest in the matter faded as a burly flight sergeant entered the hall and announced that our own flight to Berlin had been delayed until lunchtime the following day.

"What?" exclaimed another officer—a major with an impressive scar on his face. "Why?"

"Technical problems, sir."

"Better we find out on the ground than when we're in the air," I told the major, and went to look for a telephone.

9

SUNDAY, MARCH 14, 1943

I spent another night at Dnieper Castle; and this time my sleep was interrupted not by cold, or by thoughts of the three ragged children I'd met—and certainly not by any spiritual feeling about what might have happened in Katyn Wood—but by Lieutenant Hodt arriving in my room.

"Captain Gunther," he said.

"Yes, what is it, Lieutenant?"

"Colonel Ahrens apologizes for disturbing you and requests that you join him as soon as possible. His car is outside in front of the castle."

"Outside? Why? What's happened?"

"It would be best if the colonel explained things to you, sir," said Hodt.

"Yes. Yes, of course. What time is it?"

"Two A.M., sir."

"Shit."

I got dressed and went outside. An army Kübelwagen was waiting in the snow with the engine running. I climbed in alongside Colonel Ahrens and behind another officer I hadn't seen before. Around the second officer's neck was a metal gorget that identified him as a member of the uniformed field police, which was the easily recognized equivalent of the Kripo beer token I carried in my coat pocket from when I'd been a plainclothes detective. It was already obvious to me that we weren't going to the local library. As soon as I was seated, the NCO driving the bucket punched it loudly into gear and we set off swiftly down the drive.

"Captain Gunther, this is Lieutenant Voss of the field police."

"If it wasn't so late I might be pleased to meet you, Lieutenant."

"Captain Gunther works for the War Crimes Bureau in Berlin," explained Ahrens. "But before that he was a Kripo police commissar at the Alex."

"What's this all about, Colonel?" I asked Ahrens.

"Two of my men have been murdered, Captain."

"I'm sorry to hear that, Colonel. Was it partisans?"

"That's what we're hoping you can help us to find out."

"I guess there's no harm in hoping," I said sourly.

We drove east along the road to Smolensk. A sign on the road said PARTISAN DANGER AHEAD. SINGLE VEHICLES STOP! HOLD WEAPONS READY.

"It looks like you've already made up your minds," I observed.

"You're the expert," said Voss. "Perhaps, when you've taken a look at the scene, you'll tell us what you think."

"Why not?" I said. "As long as everyone remembers that I'm boarding a plane back to Berlin in ten hours."

"Just take a look," said Ahrens. "Please. Then, if you wish, you can take your flight home."

The "if you wish" part I didn't like at all but I kept my mouth shut. Lately I'd got a lot better at doing that. Besides, I could see the colonel was upset and telling him I really didn't give a damn about who had killed his men wasn't exactly going to smooth my already delayed departure from Smolensk. I wanted to stay on in that city like I wanted to remain in an ice-cold bath.

A few blocks west of the railway station the road split and we took the southern route down Schlachthofstrasse before turning right onto Dnieperstrasse, where the driver skidded to a halt. We got out and walked past an Opel Blitz that was full of field policemen and down a snow-covered slope to the edge of the Dnieper River, where another bucket wagon was parked with its spotlight trained on two bodies lying side by side at the water's half-frozen edge. Two of the lieutenant's men were standing beside the bodies and stamping their feet against the cold and the damp. The river looked as black as the Styx and almost as still in the moonlit silence.

Voss handed me a flashlight and, although I was keen not to be involved, I made a nice show of casting a professional eye over the lieutenant's crime scene. It was easy enough to call: two men in uniform, their bare heads bashed in and their throats neatly cut from ear to ear like a clown's big smile, and blood all over the snow that, in the moonlight, hardly looked like blood at all.

"Lieutenant? See if you can't find their cunt covers, will you?"

"Their what?"

"Their hats, their fucking hats. Find them."

Voss looked at one of his men and passed on the order. The man scrambled back up the bank.

"And see if you can't find a murder weapon, while you're at it," I shouted after him. "Some kind of a knife or bayonet."

"Yes, sir."

"So what's the story so far?" I asked no one in particular and without much interest in an answer.

"Sergeant Ribe and Corporal Greiss," said the colonel. "Two of my best men. They were on switchboard and coding duty until about four o'clock this afternoon, after the Leader left."

"Doing what?"

"Manning the telephone exchange. The radio. Decoding teletype messages with the Enigma machine."

"So when they went off duty, they left the castle, how? In a bucket wagon?"

"No, on foot," said Ahrens. "You can walk it in half an hour."

"Only if it's worth your while, I'd have thought. What's the attraction around here? Don't tell me it's that church near the railway station or I'll start to worry I've been missing out on something important."

"The Peter and Paul? No."

"There's a swimming bath that's used by the army on Dnieperstrasse," said Voss. "It seems they went there to swim and use the steam room, after which they both went next door."

"And next door is?"

"A brothel," said Voss. "In the Hotel Glinka. Or what used to be the Hotel Glinka."

"Ah yes, Glinka, I remember him. He's the father of Russian classical music, isn't he?" I yawned loudly. "I'm looking forward to acquainting myself with some of his music. It'll make a pleasant change from a cold Russian wind. Christ, my ears feel like something bit them."

"The whores in the brothel claim the two men were there until eleven and then left," said Voss. "No trouble. No fights. Nothing suspicious."

"Whores? Why wasn't I told? I just spent the evening alone with a good book."

"It wasn't a place for German officers," said Voss. "It was a place for enlisted men. A cyria."

"What's a cyria?" I asked.

"A roundup brothel."

"Ah," I said. "So, strictly speaking, they weren't whores at all. Just innocent girls from out of town who'd been pressed into some horizontal service for the Fatherland. Now I'm glad I stayed in with my book. Who found them?"

"I beg your pardon?"

"The bodies? Who found them? A whore? Another Fritz? The Volga boatman? Who?"

"An SS sergeant came out of the Glinka for a breath of fresh air," explained Voss. "He'd had a lot to drink and was feeling ill, he says. He saw a figure bent over these two men down here and thought he was witnessing a robbery. He challenged the man, who ran off in the direction of the west bridge." Lieutenant Voss pointed along the riverbank. "That way."

"Which is ruined, right? So we can assume he wasn't looking to make it across the river tonight. Not unless he was a hell of a swimmer."

"Correct. The sergeant pursued the figure for a while but lost him in the darkness. A moment later he heard an engine start up and a vehicle driving away. He claims it sounded like a motorcycle, although I must say I don't know how he could tell that without seeing it."

"Hmm. Which way did the bike go? Did he say?"

"West," said Voss. "It never came back."

I lit a cigarette to stop me from yawning again. "Did he give you a description of the man he saw? Not that it matters if he was drunk."

"Says it was too dark."

I glanced up at the moon. There were a few clouds and, from time to time, one of these drew a dark curtain over the moon but nothing in the way of weather that looked at all likely to delay a flight back to Berlin.

"That's possible, I suppose."

Then I looked back at the two dead men. There's something particularly awful about a man who's had his throat cut; I suppose it's the way it reminds you of an animal sacrifice, not to mention the sheer quantity of blood that's involved. But there was an extra dimension of horror to the way these two men had been butchered—that was indeed the word—for such was the force used to cut their throats that each man's head had almost been severed so that the spine was clearly visible. If I'd looked closely I could probably have seen what each had had for dinner. Instead I lifted their hands to check for defensive cuts, but there were none.

"I seem to recall that the partisans are fond of removing the heads of captured German soldiers," I said.

"It has been known," allowed Voss. "And not just their heads."

"So it may be our killer meant to do the same but was disturbed by the SS sergeant," I said.

"Yes, sir."

"On the other hand, their sidearms are still holstered and the flaps are still buttoned, which means they weren't afraid of him." I started going through one of the men's pockets. "Which is another mark against this being partisans. And almost certainly a partisan would have taken these weapons. Weapons are more valuable than money. Still, there's no sign of a wallet."

"It's here, sir," said Voss, producing a wallet. "Sorry. I took both of their wallets when I was trying to identify them earlier."

"May I see one of those?"

Voss handed me a wallet. I spent a couple of minutes going through the contents and found several banknotes.

"I guess these whores aren't charging much money. This man has plenty of cash left. Which is unusual for a man leaving a brothel. So. The motive wasn't robbery but something else. But what?" I shone the flashlight up the slope toward the street and the brothel. "Perhaps just murder. It looks as if their throats were cut here, as they lay on the ground."

"How do you work that out?" asked Colonel Ahrens.

"The blood has soaked the hair on the backs of their heads," I said. "If their throats had been cut while they were standing up it would be all down the front of their tunics. Which it isn't. Most of it is on the snow here. Neat job, too. Almost surgical. Like their throats were cut by someone who knew what he was doing."

The field policeman came back with one of the dead men's caps in his hand. "Found the caps on the street, sir. Left the other where it was so you could take a look for yourself."

I took the cap and opened it up and found blood and hair on the inside.

"Come on," I said smartly. "Show me." And then to Ahrens and Voss, "You wait here, gentlemen."

I followed the man back up the bank, to a spot on the street where another field policeman was standing with his flashlight trained helpfully on the other cap. I picked it up and inspected the inside; there was blood in this one, too. Then I walked back down the bank to Ahrens and Voss, pointing the flashlight one way and then the other.

"The killer probably hit them on the head up on the street," I said. "And then dragged them down here where it was quiet, to kill them both."

"Do you think it was partisans?"

"How should I know? But I suppose unless we can prove it wasn't, the Gestapo will want to execute some locals just to show everyone they're on the job and taking things seriously, as only the Gestapo can."

"Yes," said Voss. "I hadn't thought of that."

"That's probably why you're not working for the Gestapo, Lieutenant. Wait a minute. What's this?"

Something glinted in the snow—something metallic. But it wasn't a knife or a bayonet.

"Anyone know what this is?"

We were looking at two rippled pieces of springy, flat metal that were joined together by a small oval socket at the end; the pieces of metal shifted around like a pair of playing cards in my fingers. Colonel Ahrens took the object from my hand and examined it for himself.

"I think it's the inside of a scabbard," he said. "For a German bayonet."

"Sure about that?"

"Yes," said Ahrens. "This is meant to hold the bayonet in place.

Stops it from jumping out. Here, you." Ahrens spoke to the field policeman. "Are you carrying a bayonet?"

"Yes, sir."

"Hand it over. And the scabbard."

The policeman did as he was told and with the aid of his Swiss officer's knife the colonel had soon extracted the holding screw from the man's scabbard and withdrew an identical spring interior.

"I had no idea that's how the bayonet stays sheathed," said Voss. "Interesting."

We went back up the slope toward the Hotel Glinka. "Tell me, Colonel, are there any other brothels in Smolensk?"

"I really wouldn't know," he said stiffly.

"Yes, there are, Captain Gunther," said Voss. "There's the Hotel Moskva to the southeast of the city, and the Hotel Archangel near the Kommandatura. But the Glinka is the nearest to the castle and the 537th Signals."

"You certainly know your brothels, Lieutenant," I said.

"As a field policeman, you have to."

"So if they were on foot, as you say, Colonel, it's likely the Glinka would have been their establishment of choice."

"I wouldn't know about that, either," said the colonel.

"No, of course not." I sighed and looked at my watch, wishing I was already at the airport. "Maybe I should keep my questions to myself, Colonel, but I had the head-hammered idea you actually wanted my help with this."

The Glinka was a fussy-looking white building with more architecturally effeminate flourishes than a courtier's lace handkerchief; on the roof there was a short castellated spire with a weather vane; on the street was an archway entrance with thick, pepper-pot columns that put you in mind of a cut-price Philistine temple, and I half expected to find some muscular Ivan chained between them for the amusement of a local fertility god. As it was, there was just a bearded doorman holding a rusty saber and wearing a red Cossack coat and an unlikely chest full of cheap medals. In Paris they might have made something out of a doorway like that, just as they might have made the interior of the place seem attractive or even elegant, with plenty of French mirrors, gilt furniture, and silk curtains—the French know how to run a decent brothel in the same way they know what makes a good restaurant—but Smolensk is a long way from Paris, and the Glinka was a hundred thousand kilometers from being a decent brothel. It was just a sausage counter—a cheap bang house where simply walking through the dirty glass door and catching the strong smell in the air of cheap perfume and male seed made you think you were risking a dose of drip. I felt sorry for any man who went there, although not as sorry as I felt for the girls, many of them Polish—and a few of them as young as fifteen—who'd been taken from their homes for "agricultural work" in Germany.

A few minutes of conversation with a selection of these unfortunates was enough to discover that Ribe and Greiss had been regulars at the Glinka, that they had behaved themselves impeccably—or at least as impeccably as was required in the circumstances—and that they had left alone just before eleven P.M., which was more than enough time for them to get back to the castle for the midnight roll call. And I quickly formed the impression that the ghastly fate that had befallen the two soldiers could have had little or nothing to do with what had happened in the Glinka.

When I had finished questioning the Polish whores of the Glinka, I went outside and gratefully drew a deep breath of clean, cold air. Colonel Ahrens and Lieutenant Voss followed and waited for me to say something. But when I closed my eyes for a moment and leaned against one of the entrance pillars, the colonel interrupted my thoughts impatiently.

"Well, Captain Gunther," he said. "Please tell us. What impression have you formed?"

I lit a cigarette and shook my head. "That there are times when being a man seems almost as bad as being a German," I said.

"Really, Captain, you are a most exasperating fellow. Try to forget your personal feelings and concentrate on your job as a policeman, please. You know damned well I'm talking about my boys and what might have happened to them."

I threw my cigarette onto the ground angrily and then felt angrier for wasting a good cigarette.

"That's good coming from you, Colonel. You wake me up to help out the local field police with an extra set of cop's eyes and then you put on your spurs and try to get stiff when the cop's eyes see something they don't like. If you ask me, your damned boys had it coming if they were in there. I feel bad enough just going through the door of a wurst hut like that, see? But then I'm peculiar that way. Maybe you're right. Sometimes I forget that I'm a German soldier."

"Look, I only asked about my men—they were murdered, after all."

"You got stiff with me, and if there's one thing a Berliner hates it's someone who gets stiff with him. You might be a colonel but don't ever try to push a ramrod up my ass, sir."

"Captain Gunther, you have a most violent temper."

"Maybe that's because I'm tired of people thinking that any of this shit really matters. *Your men were murdered*. That would be laughable if this whole situation in Russia wasn't so tragic. You talk about murder like it still means something. In case you hadn't noticed, Colonel, we're all of us in the worst place in the world with one boot in the fucking abyss, and we're pretending that there's law and order and something worth fighting for. But there isn't. Not now. There's just insanity and chaos and slaughter and maybe something worse that's yet to come. It's only a couple of days since you told me that sixteen thousand Jews from the Vitebsk ghetto ended up in the river or as human fertilizer. Sixteen thousand people. And I'm supposed to give a damn about a couple of off-duty Fritzes who got their throats cut outside the local sausage counter."

"I can see that you are a man under strain, sir," said the colonel.

"We all are," I allowed. "It's the strain of constantly having to look the other way. Well, I don't mind telling you, the muscles in my neck are getting tired."

Colonel Ahrens seethed quietly. "I'm still awaiting an answer to a perfectly reasonable question, Captain."

"All right, I'll tell you what I think, and you can tell me that I'm deluded and then the lieutenant here can take me to the airport. Colonel, your men were killed by a German soldier. Their sidearms were still holstered so they didn't believe they were in any danger, and in this moonlight it's highly unlikely the murderer could have surprised them. Could be they even knew their killer. It's an uncomfortable forensic fact but most people do know the person who murders them."

"I can't believe what you're saying," said Ahrens.

"I'll give you some more reasons why I believe what I do in a moment," I said. "But if I may? The initial attack probably occurred on the street. The murderer hit them on the head with a blunt instrument and most likely threw it into the river. He must have been quite powerful because that's how it looks from their head injuries. I wouldn't be at all surprised if Ribe and Greiss might eventually have died from those blows alone. Then he dragged them down to the river. His doing that is another reason to assume he was strong. He made damned sure of what he was doing, too, from the size of the bayonet cuts. I've seen cart horses with smaller mouths than those wounds. He cut their throats while they were still unconscious, so he must have wanted to make sure they were dead. And I think that's significant. Also, I had the impression that the laceration ends higher on one side of each man's neck than the other. The left side of the neck, as you look at it, which might suggest a left-handed man.

"Now then: maybe he was disturbed and maybe he wasn't. It's possible he meant to push the bodies into the water and let them float away to give him more time to escape. That's what I would have done. With or without a head, a body that's been in the water takes a while to start talking back to a pathologist—even an experienced one, and I don't imagine there are too many of those in Smolensk right now.

"When he got on his toes and made a run along the riverbank, he was running for his motorcycle—yes, I don't doubt the SS sergeant was right about that. There's nothing else sounds like an air-cooled BMW. Not even Glinka. Partisans can steal motorcycles, of course. But they'd hardly be brazen enough to ride one around right here in Smolensk, with so many checkpoints around the city. If he parked the bike to the west, his name wouldn't appear on a field policeman's checklist, either. And let's not forget that it was a German murder weapon, too. According to the witness, the bike drove west along the road to Vitebsk. And given that the west bridge is down, it's certain that he didn't cross the river. Which means your murderer must be stationed out that way. To the west of Smolensk. I expect you'll find the bayonet somewhere on that road, Lieutenant. Without the spring in the scabbard, it might even have fallen out."

"But if he drove west," said the colonel, "that would mean you think he must have been going to the 537th at the castle, the general staff at Krasny Bor, or the Gestapo at Gnezdovo."

"That's right," I said. "If I were you, Colonel, I'd check out the vehicle logs at all three. Chances are that's how you'll catch your man. German bike, German knife, and the perpetrator stationed along the road to Vitebsk."

"You're not serious," said the colonel. "About where the perpetrator is now serving, I mean."

"I can't say that I envy you the job of unsticking some of those damned alibis, Colonel. But like it or not, that's just how it is with murder. It rarely ever unravels as neatly as an unwanted woolen pullover. Now, as to why he killed them, well, that's harder to answer. But since we've eliminated robbery and a fight over a favorite whore, that suggests this was murder with a detestable motive, according to the way the law writes it. In other words, it was killing with intent. That's right, gentlemen, he set out to kill them both. The question is, why today? Why today and not yesterday, or the day before, or last weekend? Was it just opportunity, or could there have been some other reason? You'll only find that out, Colonel, when you look into these two lives much more closely. Discover who they really were and you'll find your motive, and when you find that, you'll be a damned sight nearer to finding their killer."

I lit another cigarette and smiled. I felt calmer now that I'd let off some steam.

"You could find them," said the colonel. "If you stayed on a while, here in Smolensk."

"Oh no," I said. "Not me." I looked at my watch. "In eight hours I'm going back to Berlin. And I'm not coming back again. Not ever. Not even if they put a bayonet to my throat. Now, if you don't mind, I'd like to return to the castle. It's possible I can still get a little sleep before my journey."

SIX HOURS LATER LIEUTENANT REX was outside the front door of the castle waiting to drive me to the Smolensk airport. It was a beautiful clear morning with a sky as blue as the cross on a Prussian imperial flag and—if there was such a thing—surely a perfect day for flying. After almost four days in Smolensk, I was actually looking forward to spending twelve hours aboard a freezing plane. The regimental cook from Dnieper Castle had prepared a large flask of coffee and some sandwiches for me, and I'd even managed to get a Capuchin hood from army stores to wear under my crusher to help keep my ears warm. Life felt good. I had a book and a recent newspaper and the whole day to myself.

"The colonel presents his compliments," said Rex, "and apologizes for not seeing you off himself, but he was unavoidably detained at Group headquarters."

I shrugged. "In view of the events of last night, I imagine he has a lot to talk about," I said.

"Yes, sir."

Rex was quiet, for which I was grateful, and which I attributed to the loss of his two comrades. I didn't mention them. That was someone else's problem now. All I cared about was getting on the plane back to Berlin before something else happened to keep me in Smolensk. I certainly wouldn't have put it past Colonel Ahrens to speak to Field Marshal von Kluge and have my departure delayed long enough for me to investigate the murders. And von Kluge could do it; I might have been SD but I was still attached to the War Crimes Bureau and that meant I was under army orders.

A short way past the railway station, we turned north onto Lazarettstrasse to find a small crowd gathered on a patch of waste ground on the corner of Grosse Lermontowstrasse. Suddenly I felt sick to my stomach, as if I had swallowed poison.

"Stop the car," I told Rex.

"It might be best if we don't, sir," said Rex. "We've no escort, and if that crowd turns ugly, it'll be just you and me."

"Stop the fucking car, Lieutenant."

I got out of the bucket wagon, unbuttoned my holster, and walked toward the crowd, which parted in sullen silence to admit my passage. Horror does not need the dark, and sometimes a truly evil deed shuns the shadows. A makeshift gallows had been erected like so many tent poles from which six dead bodies were now hanging, five of them young men and all of them obviously Russian from their clothes. The men were still wearing their peasant-style caps. Around the neck of the central figure—a young woman who was wearing a headscarf, and missing one shoe—was a placard written in German and then Russian: WE ARE PARTISANS AND LAST NIGHT WE MURDERED TWO GERMAN SOLDIERS. None of them had been dead for very long—a pool of urine underneath one of the corpses that was turning in the wind had yet to freeze. It was one of the saddest sights I'd ever seen and I felt a strong sense of shame—the same kind of shame I felt the first time I came to Russia and witnessed what happened to the Jews in Minsk.

"Why did they do it? Last night I made it perfectly clear to every-one that it wasn't partisans who murdered those men. I distinctly told your colonel. And I told Lieutenant Voss. I am certain they both un-derstood that Ribe and Greiss were murdered by a German soldier. All of the available evidence points that way."

"Yes, sir, I heard what happened."

"I meant all of it, too. Without exception."

Lieutenant Rex backed toward me as if he didn't want to take his eyes off the crowd, but to be fair it might just as easily have been that he didn't want to look at the six people hanging from a beech-log gibbet.

"I can assure you that this execution wasn't anything to do with the colonel or the field police," explained Rex.

"No?"

"No, sir."

"Well, at least now I understand why your colonel didn't want to accompany me to the airport himself. That was clever of him. He could hardly have avoided seeing this, could he?"

"He wasn't happy about it, sir, but what could he do? This is down to the local Gestapo. It's them who carry out executions in Smolensk, not the army. And in spite of what you said just now—that it was a German soldier who murdered Ribe and Greiss—I believe they still thought it was necessary to make a point to the people of Smolensk that the murders of Germans will not go unpunished. At least that was the colonel's information."

"Even if innocent people are punished," I said.

"Oh, these people weren't innocent," said Rex. "Not exactly, any-way. I believe they were already being held in the Kiewerstrasse prison, for one thing or another. Black marketers and thieves, probably. We get a lot of them in Smolensk." Rex had drawn his pistol and was hold-ing it stiffly at his side. "Now, if you don't mind, we really ought to get out of here before they string us up beside these others."

"You know, I should have realized something like this might

happen," I said. "I should have gone to Gestapo headquarters last night and told them myself. Made an official report. They would have listened to the little fucking skull and crossbones on my hat."

"Sir. We ought to go."

"Yes. Yes, of course." I sighed. "Take me to the airport. The sooner I get out of this hellhole the better."

Looking more than a little relieved, Rex followed me back to the car and suddenly he was full of talk that was mostly explanation and evasion of the kind I'd often heard before and would doubtless hear again.

"No one likes to see that sort of thing," he said, as we drove north up Flugplatzstrasse. "Public executions. Least of all me. I'm just a lieutenant of signals. I worked for Siemens in Berlin before the war, you know. Installing telephones in people's houses. Fortunately, I don't have to get involved with that side of it. You know—police actions. So far I've got through this war without shooting anyone, and with any luck, that's not going to change. Frankly, I could no more hang a bunch of civilians than I could play a Schubert impromptu. If you ask me, sir, the Ivans are decent salt-of-the-earth fellows just trying to feed themselves and their families, most of them. But try telling that to the Gestapo. With them everything is ideological—all Ivans are Bolsheviks and commissars and there's never any room for compromise. It's always 'Let's make an example of someone to deter the rest,' you know? If it wasn't for them and the SS—what happened over at the ghetto in Vitebsk was quite unnecessary—well, really, Smolensk is not such a bad place at all."

"And there's even a fine cathedral. Yes, you mentioned it before. I just don't think I know what a cathedral is for, Lieutenant. Not anymore."

IT'S HARD TO FEEL GOOD about your homeland when so many of your fellow countrymen behave with such callous brutality. Leaving

Smolensk far below and behind me, my heart and mind felt as severely jolted by the sight of those five hanged men and one woman as the plane soon was by pockets of warmer air that the pilot called "turbulence." This was so heart-stoppingly severe that two of the plane's other passengers—a colonel from the Abwehr named von Gersdorff, who was one of the aristocrats that had met von Dohnanyi at Smolensk airport the previous Wednesday, and an SS major—were swiftly crossing themselves and praying out loud; I wondered how much good a prayer in German could be. For a while the two officers' prayers provided a source of some small sadistic pleasure to me; they were a satisfactory hint that there might be some justice in an unjust world, and the way I was feeling I would hardly have cared if our plane had met with a catastrophic accident.

Perhaps it was the vigorous shaking of the plane we endured for over an hour that banged something loose in my head. I had been thinking about Captain Max Schottlander, who was the Polish author of the military intelligence report—for this was what it was—I had found inside his frozen boot, and which Dr. Batov had translated for me. Suddenly, as if the lurching movement of the plane had brought part of my brain to life, I wondered what effect might be achieved if ever I was to disclose the report's contents—although to whom these contents might be disclosed was hard to answer. For a moment a number of ideas as to just what could be done crowded my brain all at once; but finding no more than a fleeting thought attached to each, these ideas seemed to vanish simultaneously, as if a warmer, more hospitable mind than my own had been required to give them all a chance to thrive, like so many of Colonel Ahrens's bees.

What was more certain and enduring in my mind was the belief that what I had discovered in that boot was now a source of no small danger to me.

10

THURSDAY, MARCH 18, 1943

There were hundreds of snowdrops growing in the garden of the flower house; spring was in the air and I was back in Berlin; the Russian city of Kharkov had been retaken by von Manstein's forces, and, the previous day, a number of prominent state and Party figures had been named in the trial of a notorious Berlin butcher called August Nöthling. He'd been accused of profiteering, although it would have been more accurate to have described his real crime as that of having supplied large quantities of meat without the requisite food coupons to high government officials such as Frick, Rust, Darré, Hierl, Brauchitsch, and Raeder. Frick, the minister of the Interior, had received more than a hundred kilos of poultry—this at a time when it was rumored the Food Ministry was considering reducing the daily meat ration by fifty grams.

All of this ought to have put me in a better mood—generally speaking there was nothing I enjoyed more than a very public scandal involving the Nazis. But Judge Goldsche had asked me to come and see him a second time to discuss my report on Katyn Wood and, although he had already dispatched Judge Conrad to Smolensk to take charge of an investigation that was still unofficial and secret, I had a bad feeling my part in it was not yet over. The reason for this feeling was simple: despite having been back in the office for three days, I had yet to be assigned to another case, even though a new one was already demanding a high level of investigation.

Grischino was an area to the northwest of Stalino, in Russia. Following a counteroffensive in February, the area had been retaken by the Seventh Armored Division, which found that almost everyone in a German field hospital—wounded soldiers, female nurses, civilian workers—some six hundred people including eighty-nine Italians, had been murdered by the retreating Red Army. For good measure the reds had raped the nurses before cutting off their breasts and then slitting their throats. Several judges—Knobloch, Block, Wulle, and Goebel—were already in Ekaterinovka taking depositions from local witnesses, and this left the bureau severely overstretched; there were a few survivors from the Grischino Massacre now in Berlin's Charité Hospital who had yet to be deposed by a bureau member, and I could not understand why Goldsche hadn't asked me to do it immediately upon my return from Smolensk. I'd seen the photographs that were supplied by the Propaganda Service Battalion. In one particular house, the bodies were piled up to a height of 1.5 meters. Another picture of ten German soldiers lying in a line by the side of the road showed that the skulls of the men had been flattened to one-third of their normal size, as if someone had driven a truck or a tank over them, most likely while they were still alive. Grischino was the worst war crime committed against Germans I had seen since coming to the bureau, but the judge did not seem inclined to discuss it with me.

"These murders in Smolensk that you looked into," he said, lighting his pipe. "Is there anything in that for us, do you think?"

Brahms was playing on the radio in his office, which suggested we were going to have a very private conversation.

"I assume you mean the two soldiers from the signals regiment and not the six civilians the Gestapo hanged in the street."

"I wish they wouldn't overreact like that," said Goldsche. "Killing innocent people in retaliation. It really compromises what we're about in this department. You can dress that kind of thing up any way you like but it's still a crime."

"Will you tell them or shall I?"

"Oh, I think it's best coming from you, don't you think? After all, you used to work for Heydrich, Bernie. I'm sure Müller will listen to you."

"I'll get right on it, Judge."

Goldsche chuckled and sucked on his pipe. The chimney in his office must have been bomb-damaged—which was common enough in Berlin—because it was hard to distinguish the smoke off the coal fire from the smoke off his pipe.

"I'm certain it was a German who killed them both," I said. My eyes were starting to water, although that could just as easily have been the syrupy Brahms. "It was probably an argument about a whore. That's one case we can leave to the local field police."

"What's he like, this Lieutenant Ludwig Voss?"

"He's a good man, I think. Anyway, I told Judge Conrad he could rely on him. Not so sure about Colonel Ahrens. The man is a little too protective of his men to be really helpful to us. His men and his bees."

"Bees?"

"He keeps an apiary at the castle where the 537th are quartered, which is right in the middle of Katyn Wood. For the honey."

"I don't suppose he gave you any?"

"Honey? No. In fact, by the time I left I got the distinct impression he didn't like me at all."

"Well, there are going to be plenty of bees buzzing around his ears before this particular investigation's over," observed Goldsche. "And I expect that's why, don't you?"

"I'll bet August Nöthling could have sold you some honey."

"He's a butcher."

"Maybe so. But he still managed to supply twenty kilos of chocolate to the minister of the Interior and the field marshal."

"That's exactly what one would expect of a man like Frick. But I certainly didn't expect it of Field Marshal von Brauchitsch."

"When you've been retired by the Leader, what else can an old soldier do but eat if he's not to fade away?"

The judge smiled.

"So what now?" I asked. "For me, I mean. Why don't you let me depose those wounded soldiers in the Charité? The ones from Grischino."

"Actually, I'm going to depose them myself. Just to keep my hand in. Anyway, I was hoping to catch two birds with one trap. I suffer from fearful indigestion and it occurred to me I might persuade one of the doctors or the nurses to let me have a bottle of liver salts. There's none to be had in any of the shops."

"As you wish. I'm certainly not going to stand between you and your liver. Look, I'm not anxious to head back to Russia but it strikes me there's a lot of work to do in Stalino, right now. That's near Kharkov, isn't it?"

"That depends on what you mean by near. It's three hundred kilometers south of Kharkov. That's much too far to send you, Bernie. I need you here in Berlin. Especially now and this weekend."

"Would you mind telling me why?"

"I've been warned by the Ministry of Propaganda that we can expect a summons to the Prince Carl Palace at any time. So that we might brief the minister himself on what you discovered in Katyn Wood."

I let out a groan.

"No, listen, Bernie, I want you to make sure that there is nothing in your report with which he can find fault. I don't think the bureau can afford to disappoint him again so soon after the disappointment he felt after we lost our witness to the sinking of the SS *Hrotsvitha von Gandersheim*."

"I should have thought that overcoming disappointment is what propaganda is all about."

"Besides, it's Heroes' Memorial Day this Sunday. Hitler's inspecting an exhibition of captured Soviet military material and making a speech, and I need someone with a uniform to accompany me to the Armory Building and help represent this department. All of the general staff will be there, as usual."

"Find someone else, Judge. Please. I'm no Nazi. You know that."

"That's what everyone in this department says. And there is no one else. It seems that this weekend there is only you and me."

"It will be just another rant by the great necromancer about Bolshevik poison. But now I begin to understand. That's why there are so many judges from the bureau out of town, isn't it? They're avoiding this duty."

"That's very true. None of them want to be anywhere near Berlin this weekend." He puffed his pipe for a moment and then added, "Perhaps they're afraid of failing to show the proper amount of respect and enthusiasm for the Leader's ability to lead our nation in such a solemn moment of national commemoration." He shrugged. "On the other hand, they might just be afraid."

I lit a cigarette—if you can't beat them, join them—and took a long drag before speaking again.

"Wait a minute. Is something going to happen, Judge? At the Armory? To the general staff?"

"I think something is going to happen, yes," said the judge. "But not to the general staff. At least not right away. Afterward it's quite possible there may be some kind of overreaction on the part of the Gestapo and the SS. Of the kind we were discussing earlier. So I wouldn't forget your firearm, if I were you. In fact, I'd be very grateful if you made sure you brought it with you. I've never been much of a shot with a pistol."

Even as the judge was speaking I remembered a remark made by Colonel Ahrens during one of our more frank conversations—something about the amount of treason talked in Smolensk—and suddenly a lot of what I'd seen seemed to make sense: the package addressed to Colonel Stieff in Rastenburg that von Dohnanyi had carried all the way from Berlin and which—strangely—Lieutenant von Schlabrendorff had asked Colonel Brandt to carry on Hitler's plane back to Rastenburg must surely have been a bomb, albeit a bomb that hadn't exploded.

And what better motive could there have been for someone to have killed a couple of telephonists than the possibility that they had overheard the details of a plan to kill Hitler? But when that plan had failed, another plan must have been put into action. That made sense, too; Hitler was increasingly a recluse and the opportunities to kill him were few and far between. All the same, if this was indeed why the two telephonists had been murdered, I found the act repugnant; Hitler certainly deserved to die and secrecy was undoubtedly important if his assassination was ever to be carried out, but not if that meant the cold-blooded murder of two innocent men. Or was I just being naïve?

"Sure," I said. "The mist clears. I begin to see the elf-king, father. He's near."

The judge frowned, trying to recognize my allusion. "Goethe?"

I nodded. "Tell me something, Judge," I said. "I suppose von Dohnanyi's involved."

"Christ, is it that obvious?"

"Not to everyone," I said. "But I'm a detective, remember? It's my job to smell when the fuse is burning. However, if I've guessed, it's possible others might guess, too." I shrugged. "Maybe that's why the bomb didn't go off on Hitler's plane. Because someone else figured it out."

"Christ," muttered the judge. "How did you know about that?"

"You know, for an intelligence officer with the Abwehr, your friend isn't very clever," I said. "Brave, but not very smart. He and I were on the same plane down to Smolensk. If you're going to carry a parcel that's addressed to someone in Rastenburg, it looks a lot less suspicious if you deliver it the first time you're there."

"That parcel you saw was only ever the backup plan to Plan A."

"And what was that? Fix the brakes on Hitler's car? Nobble the vegetarian option in the officers' mess? Push him over in the snow? The trouble with these damned aristocrats is that they know everything about good manners and being a gentleman and absolutely nothing about cold-blooded murder. If you're going to do this kind of thing, you need a professional. Like the person who murdered those two telephonists. Now, he knew what he was doing."

"I don't know for sure what the plan was then."

"So what *do* you know? I mean, how are they going to try it this time?"

"Another bomb, I believe."

I smiled. "You know, your salesmanship stinks, Judge. You invite me along to a party and then tell me that a bomb is going to explode while we're there. My enthusiasm for Sunday morning is diminishing all the time."

"A very brave officer from Army Group Center in Smolensk, who has the duty of taking Hitler round an exhibition of captured Soviet weaponry, has agreed to carry a bomb in his jacket pocket. I believe it's his plan to be as close to the Leader as possible when it goes off."

I wondered if this officer was the Abwehr colonel I'd seen on the plane back from Smolensk. I would have asked the judge but I thought I'd probably unnerved him quite enough with my remarks about von Dohnanyi. I certainly didn't want Goldsche calling this officer and telling him to call off the assassination just because of what I'd guessed.

"Then we'd better just hope for the best," I said. "Usually that's the only option available in Nazi Germany."

11

SUNDAY, MARCH 21, 1943

The Zeughaus or Arsenal was a baroque building of pinkish stone on Unter den Linden that housed a military museum. In the center of the façade was a classical open pediment, and surrounding the roof was a spindle balustrade along which were arranged a series of twelve or fourteen suits of classical armor, made of stone, and empty, as if ready to be claimed by a busload of Greek heroes. But I was inclined to think of these empty suits of armor as belonging to men who were already dead and therefore more typical of Nazi Germany and the disastrous war we were now waging in Russia. This seemed especially true on the first Heroes' Memorial Day that Berlin had witnessed since the surrender at Stalingrad; and there would have been many of the several hundred officers who paraded in front of the huge staircase on the north side of the inner courtyard to hear the Leader's ten-minute speech who had the same unpalatable thought as me: our true heroes were lying under several feet of Russian snow, and all the memorials in the world wouldn't alter the fact that Hitler's retreat from Moscow would not be long in following Napoleon's, and with equally terminal effect upon his leadership.

It was, however, a more imminent termination to Hitler's leadership that many of us were praying for on that particular Sunday morning. We stood there to attention, under the barrels of the ten-centimeter field guns Army Group Center had taken from the reds, and I for one could cheerfully have wished that someone would have fired a fragmentation shell at our beloved leader; the ten-centimeter K353 delivered a seventeen-kilogram shell containing about six hundred bullets and was devastating to fifty percent of targets in a twenty- to forty-meter area. Which sounded just fine to me. I would probably have been killed, as well, but that was all right just as long as the Leader didn't walk away from an explosion.

We listened to a somber piece of Bruckner that did little to make anyone feel optimistic about anything; then, bare-headed and wearing a gray leather greatcoat, the Leader walked to the lectern and, like a malevolent fisherman casting a long line into an infernal black lake, he sought to hook our lowered spirits with an announcement of a lifting of the ban on vacations for serving men because the front had been "stabilized." Then he got to more standard fare about the Jews, and the Bolsheviks, the warmonger Churchill, and how the enemies of the Reich meant to abduct and then to sterilize our male youth before eventually slaughtering us in our beds.

In that place of war and destruction, Hitler's cold, hard voice seemed darker and more subdued than normal, which did nothing to encourage any feeling at all, let alone soldierly sentiment for fallen comrades. It was like listening to the sepulchral tones of Mephistopheles as, in some cavernous mountain hall, he threatened us all with hell. Only the threats were no good; hell was waiting just down the road and we all knew it. You could smell it in the air like hops from a local brewery.

In spite of all Judge Goldsche had told me, I didn't really believe anything was going to happen to Hitler; but it certainly didn't stop me hoping that Colonel von Gersdorff—for that was the Abwehr assassin's name and, as I'd suspected, he was indeed the officer who had been on the plane back from Smolensk—would prove me wrong.

As the Leader finished speaking, everyone—myself included—applauded enthusiastically; I glanced at my watch and told myself that I was applauding because Hitler's speech had lasted a comparatively short ten minutes; but this was a lie and I knew it: applauding a speech by the Leader was a simple condition of self-preservation—the hall was full of Gestapo. Acknowledging the applause with a perfunctory Hitler salute, the Leader walked to the entrance of the exhibition, where he was greeted by the colonel and, at a distance—a safe one, I hoped—the rest of us followed.

According to the judge, von Gersdorff's tour of the exhibition was due to last thirty minutes; in the event, it lasted less than five. As I entered the exhibition hall where a number of Napoleonic standards were on display, I saw the Leader turn on his heel and then move quickly through a side door and out of the Arsenal onto the riverbank, leaving his would-be assassin bewildered by a thus unexpected turn of events; short of chasing after Hitler and throwing himself into the back of his Mercedes, von Gersdorff's attempt to kill the Leader looked very much as if it was over before it had even begun.

"That wasn't supposed to happen," muttered the judge. "Something's gone wrong. Hitler must have been tipped off."

I glanced around the exhibition hall. Those members of Hitler's SS bodyguard who still remained behind seemed quite relaxed. Others—officers with red stripes on their trouser legs, who were presumably in on the plot—rather less so.

"I don't think that's the case," I said. "There doesn't seem to be any sign of alarm on the part of the SS."

"Yes, you're right." The judge shook his head. "Christ, the man's luck is uncanny. Damn him, he seems to have an instinct for self-preservation."

Von Gersdorff continued standing where he was, seemingly at a loss about what to do next, his mouth wide open like the Engelberg Tunnel. Around him were several officers who clearly had no idea the colonel was carrying explosives that might go off at any moment.

"I'm not so sure about your friend's instinct for self-preservation," I said.

"What?"

"Colonel von Gersdorff. He's still carrying a bomb, isn't he?"

"Oh God, yes. What's he going to do?"

For another minute or so we watched, and gradually it became quite clear to us that von Gersdorff wasn't going to do anything. He kept looking around as if wondering why he was still there and had not yet been blown to smithereens. Suddenly it seemed I had to get him out of there: brave men of conscience were rather thin on the ground in Germany in 1943. I had the evidence of my own shaving mirror to remind me of that.

"Wait here," I told the judge.

I walked quickly through the exhibition, pushing my way past the other officers toward the colonel; I stopped in front of him and bowed politely. He was about forty, dark and balding, and if I had doubted his courage, there was always the Iron Cross, First Class, around his neck—not to mention what he had hidden in his greatcoat pocket—to remind me. I figured I had a less than even chance of being blown up; my heart was in my mouth and my knees were shaking so much only my boots were holding me up; it might have been Heroes' Memorial Day but I wasn't feeling in the least bit heroic.

"You must come with me, Colonel," I said quietly. "Now, sir, if you don't mind."

Seeing me and, more importantly, the little silver death's head on my cap and the witchcraft badge on my sleeve, von Gersdorff smiled a sad smile, as though he were being arrested, which was my intention—or at least to leave him with the impression that he was being arrested. His hands were shaking and he was as pale as a Prussian winter's day but still he remained rooted to the spot.

"It would be best for everyone if you didn't wait any longer, sir," I said firmly.

"Yes," he said, with a quiet air of resignation. "Yes, of course."

"This way, please."

I turned on my heel and walked out of the exhibition hall. I didn't look around. I didn't need to. I could hear von Gersdorff's boots on the wooden floor immediately behind me. But on our way out of the exhibition hall, an SD captain called Wetzel, whom I knew from the Gestapo, took my arm.

"Is everything all right?" he asked. "Why did the Leader leave so abruptly?"

"I don't know why," I said, pulling my arm away from his grip. "But it seems something he said has left the colonel feeling a little upset, that's all. So if you'll excuse us."

I looked around. By now I could see the fear in von Gersdorff's eyes; but was he afraid of me or—more likely—the bomb in his pocket?

"This way, sir," I said, and led him to a lavatory, where the colonel hesitated, so I was obliged to take him by the elbow and thrust him urgently inside. I checked the six cubicles to see that there was no one else in there. We were in luck; we were alone.

"I'll keep watch," I said, "while you defuse the device. Quickly, please."

"You mean you're not arresting me?"

"No," I said, positioning myself immediately behind the door. "Now disarm that fucking bomb before we both find out the true meaning of Heroes' Memorial Day."

Von Gersdorff nodded and walked over to a row of sinks. "Actually, there are two bombs," he said, and from the pockets of his greatcoat he carefully withdrew two flat objects that were each about the size of a rifle magazine. "The explosives are British. Clam mines used for sabotage. Odd that the Tommy ordnance for this kind of work should be better than ours. But the fuses are German. Ten-minute mercury sticks."

"Well, it's good that we can make something right," I said. "Makes me feel really proud."

"I'm not so sure about that," he said. "I can't understand why they haven't gone off yet."

Someone pushed at the lavatory door and I opened it just a crack. It was Wetzel again, his long hooked nose and thin mustache looking very rat-like through the gap in the door.

"Is everything all right, Captain Gunther?" he asked.

"Better find another one," I told him. "The colonel's being sick, I'm afraid."

"Do you want me to have someone fetch a mop and a bucket?"

"No," I said. "There's no need for that. Look, it's kind of you to offer your help but the colonel is a bit of a mess, so it might be best if you left us alone for a minute, all right?"

Wetzel glanced over my shoulder as if he didn't quite believe my story.

"Sure?"

"Sure."

He nodded and went away, and I looked anxiously around to see von Gersdorff carefully withdrawing the fuses from one of the mines.

"It'll be me throwing up if you don't hurry up and defuse those things," I said. "That fucking Gestapo captain is going to come back any minute. I just know he is."

"I still don't understand why the Leader left so quickly," said von Gersdorff. "I was about to show him Napoleon's hat. Left behind in his coach after Waterloo and recovered by Prussian soldiers."

"Napoleon was defeated. Perhaps he doesn't like to be reminded of that. Especially now we're doing so well in Russia."

"Yes, perhaps. Nor do I really understand why you're helping me."

"Let's just say I hate to see a brave man blow himself up just because he's dumb enough to forget he's got a bomb in his pocket. How's it coming along?"

"Are you nervous?"

"Whatever gave you that idea? I always get a kick out of being

125

near explosives that are about to go off. But next time I'll be sure to wear some armor plating underneath my coat and some earplugs."

"I'm not that brave, you know," he said. "But since my wife died last year—"

Von Gersdorff removed the second fuse and dropped the two mercury sticks into the lavatory.

"Are they safe?" I asked.

"Yes," he said, pocketing the two mines again. "And thank you. I don't know what came over me. I suppose I must have just frozen— like a rabbit caught in a car's headlights."

"Yes," I said, "that's certainly what it looked like."

He came to attention immediately in front of me, clicked his heels and bowed his head.

"Rudolf Christoph Freiherr von Gersdorff," he said. "At your service, Captain. Whom do I have the honor of thanking?"

"No." I smiled and shook my head. "No, I don't think so."

"I don't understand. I should like to know your name, Captain. And then I should like to take you to my club and buy us both a drink. To calm our nerves. It's just around the corner."

"That's kind of you, Colonel von Gersdorff. But perhaps it's best you don't know who I am. Just in case the Gestapo should ask you for a list of all the people who helped you organize this little disaster. Besides, it's hardly the kind of name that someone like you would ever remember."

Von Gersdorff straightened perceptibly, as if I had suggested he was a Bolshevik. "Are you suggesting that I would ever betray the names of brother officers? Of German patriots?"

"Believe me, everyone has his limit where the Gestapo is concerned."

"That would not be the conduct of an officer and a gentleman."

"Of course it wouldn't. And that's why the Gestapo don't employ officers and gentlemen. They employ sadistic thugs who can break a man as easily as one of those mercury sticks of yours."

"Very well," he said. "If that's the way you want it."

Von Gersdorff walked stiffly toward the lavatory door like a man—or more accurately an aristocrat—who had been grossly insulted by a common little captain.

"Wait a minute, Colonel," I said. "There's a particularly nosy Gestapo officer outside that door who believes you came in here to throw up. At least I hope he does. I'm afraid it was the only story I could think of in the circumstances." I ran the tap to fill one of the basins. "Like I say, he's a suspicious bastard and he already smells a rat so we'd better make my story look a little more convincing, don't you think? Come here."

"What are you going to do?"

"Save your life, I hope." I scooped some water into my hands and threw it onto the front of his tunic. "And mine, perhaps. Here, hold still."

"Hang on. This is my dress uniform."

"I don't for a minute doubt your courage, Colonel. But I happen to know this is your second failure within as many weeks so I am not confident that you or any of the people working with you really know what the hell you're doing. You and your posh friends seem to lack all of the lethal qualities that are necessary to be assassins. Let's just leave it there, shall we? No names, no thank-yous, no explanations, just goodbye."

I threw some more water onto the front of von Gersdorff and, hearing the door open, I just had time to haul the towel off the roller and to start mopping down his front. I turned to see Wetzel standing in the room. The smile on his rodent's face looked anything but friendly.

"Is everything all right?" he said.

"I told you it was, didn't I?" I said irritably. "Jesus Christ."

"Yes, you did, but—"

"I didn't flush the lavatory," murmured von Gersdorff. "Those sticks are still in there."

"Shut up and let me do the talking," I said.

Von Gersdorff nodded.

"What's got into you, Wetzel?" I said. "Damn it all, can't you take a fucking hint? I said I was handling it."

"I have the distinct impression that there's something not quite right in here," said Wetzel.

"I didn't know you were a plumber. But go ahead. Be my guest. Now you're here, see if you can unblock the toilet." I threw the towel aside, gave the colonel a quick up and down and then nodded. "There you go, sir. A little damp, perhaps, but you'll do."

"I'm sorry," said von Gersdorff.

"That's all right. Could happen to anyone."

Wetzel wasn't the type to back away from an insult; he picked up a clothes brush and tossed it to me. I caught it, too.

"Why don't you brush him down while you're at it?" said Wetzel. "A new career as a gentleman's valet or a lavatory attendant would seem appropriate in the circumstances."

"Thanks." I fussed at the colonel's shoulders for a few seconds and then put down the brush. It was probably a safer although rather less pleasurable option than trying to shove it up Wetzel's rectum.

Wetzel sniffed the air, loudly. "It certainly doesn't smell like someone has been ill in here," he said. "Why is that, I wonder?"

I laughed.

"Did I say something funny, Captain Gunther?"

"The things the Gestapo will try and pinch you for these days." I nodded at the six cubicles next to us. "Why don't you check that the colonel here flushed the toilet while you're at it, Wetzel?"

There was a bottle of lime water on the shelf behind the basins. I picked it up, pulled out the cork, and splashed some onto the colonel's hands. He rubbed them on his cheeks.

"I'm all right now, Captain Gunther," he said. "Thank you for your assistance. It was most kind of you. I shan't forget this. I really thought I was about to faint back there."

Wetzel glanced behind the door of the first cubicle.

I laughed again. "Find anything, Wetzel? A Jew on the wing, perhaps?"

"We have an old saying in the Gestapo, Captain," said Wetzel. "A simple search is always better than suspicion."

He stepped into the second cubicle.

"It's the last one," murmured von Gersdorff.

I nodded.

"The way you say that, Wetzel, it sounds homespun, almost friendly," I said.

"The Gestapo is not unfriendly," said Wetzel. "So long as someone's not an enemy of the state."

He came out of the second cubicle and went into the third.

"Well, there are none of those in here," I said brightly. "In case you didn't notice, the colonel was about to guide the Leader around the exhibition. They don't let just anyone do that, I expect."

"And how is it that you two are friends, Captain?"

"Not that it's any of your damned business, but I've just got back from Army Group Center in Smolensk," I said. "That's where the colonel is stationed. We were on the same plane back to Berlin. Isn't that right, Colonel?"

"Yes," said von Gersdorff. "All of the exhibits for today's display were collected by Army Group Center. The enormous honor of being the Leader's guide this morning fell to me, I'm happy to say. However, I think I must have picked up some sort of bacillus while I was down there. I just hope that the Leader doesn't get it."

"Please God he doesn't," I said.

Wetzel stepped into the fourth cubicle. I saw him glance into the toilet bowl. If he did the same in the sixth and last cubicle he would surely see the two mercury sticks and we would be arrested, and that would be the end of us. It was whispered around the Alex that Georg Elser—the Munich bomber of November 1939—had been tortured by Heinrich Himmler, in person, following his unsuccessful attempt to assassinate the Leader; the rumor was that Himmler had almost kicked the man to death. It was anyone's guess what had happened to him since then, but the same rumor said he had been starved to death in Sachsenhausen. About assassins the Nazis were never anything less than vengeful and vindictive.

"Is that why he left so abruptly, do you think?" I asked. "Because he could see that you were ill and didn't want to catch it himself?"

"Perhaps." Von Gersdorff closed his eyes and nodded, catching on at last. "I think it might have been, yes."

"I can't say I blame him," I said. "There was typhoid around Smolensk when we left. In Vitebsk, wasn't it? Where all those Jews died?"

"That's what I told the Leader," said von Gersdorff. "When he visited our headquarters in Smolensk last weekend."

"Typhoid?" Wetzel frowned.

"I don't think I have typhoid," said von Gersdorff. "At least I hope not." He clutched his stomach. "However, I do feel rather ill again. If you'll excuse me, gentlemen, I'm afraid I am going to throw up once more."

The colonel moved away from me and presented himself immediately in front of the Gestapo captain, who recoiled noticeably as, for a brief moment, von Gersdorff placed a hand on his shoulder before launching himself into the last cubicle; he closed and then locked the door hurriedly behind him. There was a short pause and then we heard the sound of him retching loudly. I had to hand it to the colonel. He was a hell of an actor. By now I was almost convinced myself that he was ill.

Wetzel and I faced each other with obvious dislike.

"There's nothing personal in this. The fact I don't like you, Captain Gunther, has nothing to do with what I'm doing here."

"Make sure you flush that machine pistol, Colonel," I said loudly, through the door. "And while you're at it, those two bombs in your pockets."

"I'm just doing my job, Captain," said Wetzel. "That's all. I'm just trying to make sure that everything is in order."

"Sure you are," I said pleasantly. "But in case you didn't notice, the cat's already been swept downriver. I don't doubt the Leader would be most impressed with your efforts to ensure his safety, Captain Wetzel, but he's gone—back to the Reich chancellery and a nice lunch, I'll be bound."

Von Gersdorff retched again.

I went over to the basin and started to wash my hands furiously.

"I forget," I said. "Is typhoid caught in the air or do you have to eat something that's been contaminated?"

For a moment Captain Wetzel hesitated. Then he quickly washed his hands. I handed him the towel. Wetzel started to dry his hands, remembered that I'd used the towel to purportedly wipe the vomit off the colonel's tunic, and dropped it abruptly on the floor; then he turned and left.

I let out a breath, leaned against the wall, and lit a cigarette.

"He's gone," I announced. "You can come out now." I took a deep drag of smoke and shook my head. "I'm impressed with the way you kept up with all that puking. It sounded very convincing. I think you'd have made quite an actor, Colonel."

The cubicle door opened slowly to reveal a very pale-looking von Gersdorff.

"I'm afraid it wasn't an act," he said. "What with the bombs and that fucking Gestapo captain, my nerves are shot to pieces."

"Perfectly understandable," I said. "It's not every day that you try to blow yourself up. That sort of thing takes guts."

"It's not every day you fail, either," he said bitterly. "Another ten minutes and Adolf Hitler would have been dead."

I gave him a cigarette and lit it with the butt of my own.

"Got any family?"

"A daughter."

"Then don't be so hard on yourself. Think of her. We might still have Hitler, but she still has you, and that's what's important right now."

"Thank you." For a moment von Gersdorff's eyes filled up; then he nodded and wiped them quickly with the back of his hand. "I wonder why he did leave so abruptly."

"You ask me? The man isn't human at all. Either that or he got a sniff of that cologne you were wearing before I splashed that lime water on your hands. It was horrible."

Von Gersdorff smiled.

"You know what?" I said. "I think we need that drink after all. You mentioned a club? Around the corner?"

"I thought you wanted to keep fools like me at arm's length."

"That was before that stupid captain opened his mouth and told you my name," I said. "And what better company for one fool than another?"

"Is that what we are? Fools?"

"Certainly. But at least we know we're fools. And in today's Germany, that counts as a kind of wisdom."

WE WENT TO THE GERMAN CLUB—formerly the Herrenclub—at number two Jäger Strasse, which was a red sandstone neo-Baroque hatchery for anyone with a *von* in his name and the kind of place where you felt improperly dressed without a red stripe on your trouser leg and a Knight's Cross around your neck. I'd been there once before but only because I'd mistaken the place for Nero's golden palace and they'd mistaken me for the mailman. Naturally, women were not allowed. It was bad enough for the members to see the witchcraft badge on my tunic in there; if they had seen a female in that place someone would probably have fetched a red-hot stool.

Von Gersdorff ordered a bottle of Prince Bismarck; they shouldn't have had any but of course they did because it was the German Club and the seventy-seven princes and thirty-eight German counts who were among the members might have wondered what things were coming to when you couldn't get a decent bottle of schnapps. I daresay that August Nöthling wasn't the only shopkeeper in Berlin who knew how to get around the country's strict rationing. We drank it neat, cold, and quickly with quiet patriotic toasts that someone eavesdropping on our conversation might have considered treasonable and it was fortunate that we were in the bowling alley, which was empty.

After a while we were both a little drunk and bowled a few, which was when I informed von Gersdorff of one aspect of the plot to kill Hitler I found repellent.

"Something's been nagging me ever since I got back from Smolensk," I said.

"Oh? And what's that?"

"I don't mind you trying to blow Hitler up," I said. "But I do mind about the two telephonists in Smolensk who had their throats cut because they overheard something they shouldn't have."

Von Gersdorff stopped bowling and shook his head. "I'm afraid I don't know what you're talking about," he said. "When did this happen?"

"In the early hours of Sunday, March thirteenth," I said. "The same day the Leader visited Smolensk. Two telephonists from the 537th were found murdered on the banks of the Dnieper River near a brothel called the Hotel Glinka. I was the investigating officer. Unofficially, anyway."

"Really, I know nothing about this," he insisted. "And I can assure you, Captain Gunther, that there is no one at Army Group HQ who would commit such a crime. Or, indeed, order such a crime to be carried out."

"You're sure about that?"

"Of course I'm sure. These are officers and gentlemen we're

talking about." He lit a cigarette and shook his head. "But, look, this sounds much more like partisans? What makes you so sure it wasn't some damned Popov who murdered them?"

I gave him the reasons. "Their throats had been cut with a German bayonet. And the murderer escaped riding a BMW motorcycle west, in the direction of Group headquarters. Also, I suspect the two victims knew their murderer."

"God, how awful. But if it happened near a brothel, as you say, then perhaps it was just a soldier's argument about a prostitute."

I shrugged. "The local Gestapo hanged some innocent people for the crime, of course. In retaliation. So a proper sense of order has been restored. Anyway, I just thought I'd ask your opinion." I shook my head. "Perhaps it was an argument about a whore after all."

I didn't really believe that. Not that it mattered very much what I believed about the murders now I was back in Berlin. Trying to figure out who murdered the two army telephonists was down to Lieutenant Voss in Smolensk and, I told myself—and I told von Gersdorff—that if I never saw the place until the year 2043 it would be a hundred years too soon.

12

MONDAY, MARCH 22, 1943

It was his right leg. The minister limped into his office in the Leopold Palace at speed, and if the carpet hadn't been so thick and the distance between the huge door and his desk hadn't been quite so vast we might not have noticed the shiny special shoe and the even shinier metal brace. Well, almost. We were looking out for it, of course: there were so many jokes told about Joey's cloven hoof that it was even more notorious than he was—almost a Berlin tourist attraction—and the judge and I kept a close eye on his clot foot just so we could say that we'd seen it, in just the same way you wanted to be able to say you'd seen Lotte the bear in the pit at Köllnischer Park, or Anita Berber at the Heaven and Hell Club.

As Goebbels limped into the room, the judge and I stood up and saluted in the customary way and he flapped a delicate little hand back over his shoulder in imitation of the way the Leader did it—as if swatting an irritating mosquito, or dismissing some sycophant, of which there seemed to be a plentiful supply in the Ministry of Public Enlightenment and Propaganda. I suppose it was just that kind of place: before the ministry took over the building in 1933 the palace had been the residence of the Hohenzollerns—the royal family of Prussia, which had employed more than a few sycophants itself.

Goebbels was all smiles and apologies for keeping us waiting. It made a nice change from the kind of hate that was usually heard spilling out of his narrow mouth.

"Gentlemen, gentlemen, please forgive me," he said in a deeply resonant voice that belied his dwarfish stature. "I've been on the telephone complaining to the High Command about the situation we found at Kharkov. Field Marshal von Bock had reported that all German supplies would be destroyed rather than left behind for the enemy, but when Field Marshal von Manstein took the city again he discovered large quantities of our supplies still undestroyed. Can you believe it? Of course von Bock blames Paulus, and now that Paulus is conveniently a prisoner of the Bolsheviks, who is there to contradict him? I know some of these people are your friends, Judge, but really, it beggars belief. It's hard enough to win a war without being lied to by people on your own side. The Wehrmacht really needs to be combed out. Did you know that the generals are demanding rations for thirteen million soldiers when there are only nine million Germans under arms? I tell you, the Leader ought to take the severest action against someone."

Goebbels sat down behind his desk and almost vanished until he leaned forward on his chair. I was tempted to go and fetch him a cushion but, in spite of his continuing smile, there was good reason to doubt he had a sense of humor. For one, he was short and I've never yet met a short man who could laugh at himself as easily as a taller one; and that's as true a picture of the world as anything you'll find in Kant or Hegel. For another, he was a doctor of philosophy and nobody in Germany ever calls himself doctor unless he wants to impress upon other people how impeccably serious he really is.

"How are you, Judge?"

"Fine, sir, thank you."

"And your family?"

"We're all fine, sir, thank you for asking."

The doctor clasped his hands and bounced them excitedly on the blotter, as if chopping herbs with a mezzaluna. He wasn't wearing a wedding band, although he was famously married; maybe he figured that none of the starlets at the UFA studios in Babelsberg he was reputedly fond of banging would recall having seen the pictures that had been in every German magazine of the minister marrying Magda Quandt.

"It's a great pity your investigation into the sinking of that hospital ship didn't come off," Goebbels said to me. "The British are experts at occupying the moral high ground. That would have removed them from it, permanently, make no mistake. But this is even better, I think. Yes, I read your report with great interest, Captain Gunther, great interest."

"Thank you, Herr Doctor."

"Have we met before? Your name seems familiar to me. I mean, before you were with the War Crimes Bureau."

"No, I'd certainly have remembered meeting you, sir."

"There was a Gunther who used to be a detective with Kripo. Rather a good one, by all accounts. He was the man who arrested Gormann, the strangler."

"Yes, sir, that was me."

"Well, that must be it."

I was already nervous about meeting Dr. Goebbels. About ten years ago I'd been asked to drop a case as a favor to Joey, but I hadn't and I wondered if this was what he remembered. And our little exchange did nothing to make me feel any less like a man sitting on hot coals. The judge was equally nervous—at least he kept tugging at the stud of his wing collar and flexing his neck before he answered the minister's questions, as if his throat required a little more space to swallow whatever it was that he was going to have to agree to.

"So, do you really think it's a possibility?" Goebbels asked him. "That there is some sort of a mass grave hidden down there?"

"There are lots of secret graves in that part of the world," he said carefully. "The problem is making absolutely sure that this is the right one: that this is indeed the site of a war crime committed by the NKVD."

He nodded at a manila file that lay on top of a copy of that day's *Völkischer Beobachter*.

"It's all there in Gunther's report, sir."

"Nevertheless, I should like to hear the captain talk about it himself," Goebbels said smoothly. "My own experience of written reports is that you can usually get more out of the man who wrote it than the report itself. That's what the Leader says. 'Men are my books,' he says. I tend to agree with that sentiment."

I stirred a little under the minister's sharp eye.

"Yes," I said, "I do think it's a possibility. A strong possibility. The local inhabitants are quite unequivocal that there isn't a grave in Katyn Wood. However, I believe that's probably a good sign that there is. They're lying, of course."

"Why would they lie?" Goebbels frowned almost as if he regarded lying as something quite inexplicable and beyond all countenancing.

"The NKVD might be gone from Smolensk but the people are still afraid of them. More than they're afraid of us, I think. And they've got good reason. For twenty years the NKVD—and before them the OGPU and the Cheka—have been murdering Russians wholesale." I shrugged. "We've only been doing it for eighteen months."

Goebbels thought that was very funny.

"I'll say one thing for Stalin," he said, "he knows the best way to treat the Russian people. Mass murder is as primitive a language as there is, but it's the best language in which to talk to them."

"So, there's that," I said. "And there's the fact that what they actually told me flies in the face of what I found lying on the ground."

"The bones and the button—yes, of course." Goebbels pinched his lower lip thoughtfully.

"It's not much to go on, I'll admit, but I've had it verified as belonging to the greatcoat of a Polish officer."

"Is it possible that the coat could have been stolen from a Polish officer by a Red Army soldier, who was subsequently killed in the Battle of Smolensk?" asked Goebbels.

"That's a good question. What you say is certainly a possibility. But against that are the numerous intelligence reports the Abwehr had received of Polish officers seen on a train parked in a local railway siding. These would seem to confirm at least that at some stage in 1940 there were certainly Poles in the vicinity of Smolensk."

"Many or all of whom may have been murdered by the NKVD," said Goebbels.

"But we won't really know for sure that there's more than one body until the ground thaws and we're able to carry out a proper exhumation."

"When is that thaw likely to happen?"

"A couple of weeks at least," I said.

Goebbels grimaced with impatience. "There's no way of speeding this up? Building fires on the ground, for example? Surely there must be something we can do."

"Not without the risk of destroying important evidence," said Goldsche.

"I'm afraid that for the moment we're at the mercy of the Russian winter," I said.

Goebbels took his long chin in his hands and frowned. "Yes, yes of course."

He was wearing a gray three-piece suit with wide lapels, a white shirt, and a striped tie. The tie was without any sort of knot, just a party badge for a tiepin—like a nurse's collar—which added a fussy and curiously feminine touch to his appearance.

"Gentlemen, I hear what you say. However, at the risk of stating the obvious, let me make quite clear to you both the enormous propaganda value to us that this investigation presents. After the disaster of Stalingrad and the likelihood of another disaster in Tunisia, we need a coup like this. Jews all over the world are doing their best to make Bolshevism look innocent and to represent it as a lesser danger to world peace than National Socialism. They maintain the lie that the dastardly deeds typical of the Russian beast simply never happened. Indeed, in Jewish circles in London and Washington the present slogan is that the Soviet Union is destined to lead Europe. We cannot allow this to pass unchallenged. It is our job to stop this. It's only Germany that stands between these monsters and the rest of Europe, and it's time that Roosevelt and Churchill woke up to this fact."

He must have suddenly realized he wasn't giving a speech in the Sports Palace because he came to an abrupt stop.

A few seconds passed before Judge Goldsche spoke. "Yes, sir. Of course you're right."

"The very second the ground down there thaws, I want a dig to commence," said Goebbels. "We can't afford any delay in this matter."

"Yes, sir," agreed the judge.

"But since we have a little time before then," continued Goebbels, "two weeks, you say, Captain Gunther?"

I nodded.

"Might I ask a question, Herr Reich Minister?" said the judge. "You say 'we.' Are you referring to Germany as a whole or to this particular ministry?"

"Why do you ask, Judge Goldsche?"

"Because the standard protocol is that the Bureau of War Crimes prepares investigative reports and the Foreign Office publishes them as white books. Reich Minister von Ribbentrop doesn't like it when the normal protocol is ignored."

"Von Ribbentrop." Goebbels snorted with disgust. "In case you hadn't noticed, Judge Goldsche, the current foreign policy of this country is to wage total war on its enemies. There is no other foreign policy. We use von Ribbentrop to speak to the Italians and the Japanese and not much else." Goebbels grinned at his own joke. "No, you can leave the Foreign Office to me, gentlemen. Let them publish their silly white book, if that makes them happy. But this investigation is a propaganda matter now. Your first port of call in this matter is me. Is that clear?"

"Yes, Herr Reich Minister," said the judge, who looked sorry he'd ever mentioned a white book.

"More importantly, perhaps we can turn this delay to advantage. Let us suppose for a moment that it is indeed a mass grave containing some unfortunate Polish officers. I should like to hear your thoughts on the proper way to go about handling things when eventually we're able."

The judge looked puzzled. "In the usual way, Herr Doctor. We should act carefully and with patience. We must allow the evidence to lead us, as it always does. The business of judicial forensic inquiry is never something that can be rushed, sir. It requires painstaking attention to detail."

Goebbels did not look satisfied with this answer. "No, with respect, that won't do at all. We're talking about the crime of the century here, not a tomb in the Valley of the Kings."

He flicked open a cigarette box on the desk and invited us to help ourselves. Goldsche declined in order to continue his line of argument but I took one: the box was made of white enamel with a handsome gold eagle on the lid and the cigarettes were Trummers, which I hadn't seen—or, more importantly, smoked—since before the war. I was tempted to take two and put one behind my ear for later.

"If the evidence is to sustain the investigation, we must proceed with caution, sir," said the judge. "I've never seen an investigation that was improved by haste. It contributes to error of interpretation. When we rush things we leave ourselves vulnerable to criticism by enemy propaganda: that we faked something, perhaps."

But Goebbels was hardly listening. "This goes beyond all normal protocols," he said, trying to stifle a yawn. "I thought I made that clear already. Look, the Leader himself has taken an interest in this case. Our intelligence sources in London inform us that relations between the Soviets and the Polish government in exile are already under considerable strain. It's my estimation that this would certainly break those relations altogether. No, my dear judge, we cannot allow the evidence to lead us, as you say. That is much too passive a response to an opportunity like this. If you'll forgive me for saying so, your approach, while being very proper as you say, lacks imagination."

For once I couldn't help but agree with the minister but I kept my own counsel; Goldsche was my boss, after all, and I had no wish to embarrass the man by disagreeing with him in front of Dr. Goebbels. But perhaps Goebbels sensed something like this and when our meeting was apparently over and the judge and I were being ushered to the door, the minister asked me to wait behind.

"There's something else I wish to discuss with you, Captain," he said. "If you'll forgive us, Johannes, it's a private matter."

"Yes, of course, Herr Reich Minister," said Goldsche, who, looking a little nonplussed, was led out of the building by one of the minister's younger lackeys.

Goebbels closed the door and politely ushered me over to a sitting area—a yellow sofa and some armchairs—under a window as tall as a hop-picker's wooden legs in what passed for a cozy corner of his office. Outside was the Wilhelmplatz and the underground railway station, which is where I could have wished to be—anywhere but the place in which I was now sitting down for a quiet tête-à-tête with a man I thought I despised. But the greater discomfort I was feeling came from the realization that—in person at least—Goebbels was courteous and intelligent, even charming; it was hard to connect the man I was talking to with the malignant demagogue I'd heard on the radio ranting at the Sports Palace for "total war."

"Is there really a private matter you want to discuss with me?" I asked. "Or was that just a way of getting rid of the judge?"

But the minister of Enlightenment and Propaganda was not a man to be hurried by a nobody like me.

"When my ministry first moved into this beautiful house, back in 1933, I had some builders from the SA come in during the night to knock off all the stucco and wainscoting. Well, what else were those thugs good for except to smash things? Believe me, this place was like something in aspic jelly and badly in need of some modernization. After the Great War, the building had been occupied by some of those old Prussian farts from the Foreign Office, and when they turned up the next day to take away their papers—you can't imagine how much dust there was on those—they were absolutely horror-struck at what had been done to their precious building. It was actually quite amusing. They walked around with their mouths open, gasping like fish in a trawlerman's net, and protesting loudly to me in their posh, High German accents about what had happened in here. One of them even said, 'Herr Reich Minister, do you know that you might be put in prison for this?' Can you imagine it? Some of these old Prussians belong in a damned museum.

"And these judges in the War Crimes Bureau, they're not much more than relics themselves, Captain. Their attitudes, their working methods, their accents are positively antediluvian. Even the way they dress. You would think it was 1903 and not 1943. How can a man feel comfortable in a stiff collar? It's criminal to ask a man to dress like that just because he happens to be a lawyer. I'm afraid every time I look at Judge Goldsche I see the previous British prime minister—that old fool Neville Chamberlain with his ridiculous umbrella."

"An umbrella is only ridiculous if it's not raining, Herr Reich Minister. But really, the judge is not the fool he looks. If he sounds ridiculous and slow, that's just how law is. However, I think I get the picture."

"Of course you do. You used to be a top detective. That means you know about law in real life, not what's in a lot of dusty legal textbooks. I could have spent the next hour talking to Judge Gold-sche and he'd have given me the same old nonsense about 'standard practice' and 'proper procedure.'" Goebbels shrugged. "That's why I sent him away. I want a different approach. What I don't want is all his Prussian stucco and dusty wainscoting and piss-elegant protocol. You understand?"

"Yes. I understand."

"So, you can speak freely now that he's gone. I could sense that you didn't agree with what he was saying but that you were too loyal to say so. That's commendable. However, unlike the judge, you've actually been on the scene. You know Smolensk. And you've been a cop at the Alex and that means something. It means that whatever your politics used to be, your methods were the most modern in Europe. The Alex always had that reputation, did it not?"

"Yes. It did, for a while."

"Look, Captain Gunther, whatever you say here and now will be in confidence. But I want your own opinions about how best to han-dle this investigation, not his."

"You mean if we do find some more bodies in Katyn Wood when it thaws?"

Goebbels nodded. "Exactly."

"There's no guarantee we will. And there's another thing. The SS were busy in that area. There are Ivans digging for food down there who worry that they're going to pull a lot more than a potato out of the ground. Frankly, it's probably a lot easier to find a field that doesn't contain a mass grave than one that does."

"Yes, I know and I agree—we'll have to be careful. But the but-ton. There is the button you found."

"Yes, there's the button."

I didn't mention the Polish captain's intelligence report—the one

I'd found in his boot; it had left me in no doubt that there were Polish officers buried in Katyn Wood but I had some very good reasons for not mentioning this to the minister—my own safety being the most important.

"Take your time," said Goebbels. "I've got plenty of time this morning. Would you like some coffee? Let's have some coffee." He picked up the telephone on the coffee table. "Bring us coffee," he said curtly. He replaced the receiver and settled back on the sofa.

I stood up and helped myself to another Trummer—not because I wanted another smoke but because I needed time to arrive at an answer.

"Gunther, I know you've handled large-scale, high-profile murder inquiries under the eyes of the press before," he said.

"Not always satisfactorily, sir."

"That's true. Back in 1932, I seem to remember you screwing up a press conference in the police museum at the Alex to talk about the lust murder of a young girl. As I recall, you had a small disagreement with a reporter by the name of Fritz Allgeier. From *Der Angriff.*"

Der Angriff was the newspaper set up by Joseph Goebbels during the last days of the Weimar Republic. And I had good reason to remember the incident now. During the course of the investigation—which proved fruitless, as the killer was never apprehended—I'd been asked by a man named Rudolf Diels, who subsequently took charge of the Gestapo, to drive the case into a sand dune. Anita Schwarz had been a cripple, and Diels had hoped to move the case out of the public eye in order to spare the feelings of the similarly disabled Goebbels. I refused, which did little to help my career in Kripo, although at the time it was already more or less over. Soon after that I left Kripo altogether and stayed out of the force until, some five years later, Heydrich obliged me to return.

"You have an excellent memory, sir." I felt my chest tighten but it was nothing to do with the cigarette I was smoking. "I don't remember what your newspaper said about that press conference, but the *Beobachter* described me as a liberal left-wing stooge. Are you sure you want my opinions about this investigation?"

"I remember that, too." Goebbels grinned. "You were a stooge, through no fault of your own, however. But look, all that's behind us."

"I'm relieved you think so."

"We're fighting for our survival now."

"I can't disagree with that."

"So please. Give me your best thoughts about what we should do."

"Very well." I took a deep breath and told him what I thought. "Look, sir, there's a cop's way to run an investigation, there's a lawyer's way to run one, and then there's a Prussian lawyer's way of doing it. It seems to me that what you want is the first because it's the quickest. The minute you put lawyers in charge of something, everything runs slow. It's like oiling a watch with treacle. And if I tell you that this needs a cop running things down there, it's not because I want the job. Frankly, I never want to see the place again. No. It's because there's an extra factor here."

"What's that?"

"The way I look at it is this, and I hope you'll forgive my foolhardy honesty here, but it seems to me that you need this inquiry to be completed urgently, within the next three months—before the Soviets overrun our positions."

"Don't you believe in our final victory, Captain?"

"Everyone on the Russian front knows that the whole thing is going to come down to Stalin's math. When we recaptured Kharkov it cost the reds seventy thousand men and us almost five thousand. The difference is that while the Ivans can afford to lose seventy thousand men, we can ill afford to lose five thousand. After Stalingrad, there's a good chance of a Russian counterattack this summer—on Kharkov and on Smolensk." I shrugged. "So, this inquiry has to be handled quickly. Before the end of the summer. Perhaps earlier."

Goebbels nodded. "Let's suppose for a moment that I agree with you," he said. "And I don't say that I do. The Leader certainly doesn't. He believes that once the colossus that is the Soviet Union starts to totter, it will suffer an historic collapse, after which we'll have nothing to fear from an Anglo-American invasion."

I nodded. "I'm sure the Leader knows the situation better than me, Herr Reich Minister."

"But go ahead anyway. What else would you recommend?"

The coffee arrived. It gave me time to fetch another cigarette from the elegant box on the table and to wonder if I should mention another idea. Good coffee has that effect on me.

"As I see it, we've got two weeks before we can do anything— and I think it's going to take two weeks to make this happen. I mean, it won't be easy."

"Go on."

"This is going to sound crazy," I said.

Goebbels shrugged. "Speak freely, please."

I pulled a face, and then drank some coffee while I mulled it over for another second.

"You know, I talk to my mother a lot," confessed Goebbels. "Mostly in the evening when I return from work. I always think she knows the voice of the people much better than me. Better than a lot of the so-called experts who judge things from the ivory tower of scientific inquiry. What I always learn from her is this: the man who succeeds is the man who is able to reduce problems to their simplest terms and who has the courage of his convictions—despite the objections of intellectuals. The courage to speak, perhaps, even when he believes that what he is suggesting sounds like madness. So, please, Captain, let me be the judge of what's crazy and what isn't."

I shrugged. It seemed ridiculous for me to be worrying about the image of Germany abroad. Would one less crime laid at our door really make any difference? But I had to believe there was a possibility it might.

"Coffee's good," I said. "And so are the cigarettes. You know, a lot of doctors say smoking is not good for you. Mostly I ignore doctors. After the trenches I tend to believe in things like fate and a bullet with my name on it. But right now a lot of doctors is what I think we need. Yes, sir, as many corpse handlers as we can muster. In other words, a lot of forensic pathologists and from all over Europe, too. Enough to make this look like an independent inquiry, if such a thing is possible in the middle of a war. An international commission, perhaps."

"You mean assembled in Smolensk?"

"Yes. We dig the bodies up under the eyes of the whole world so that no one can say that Germany was responsible."

"You know, that's quite an audacious idea."

"And we should try to make sure that anyone from the government or the National Socialist party, but especially the SS and the SD, has as little to do with the investigation as possible."

"This is interesting. How do you mean?"

"We could put the whole investigation under the control of the International Red Cross. Better still, under the control of the Polish Red Cross, if they'll wear it. We could even arrange for a few journalists to accompany the commission to Smolensk. From the neutral countries—Sweden and Switzerland. And perhaps some senior Allied prisoners of war—a few British and American generals, if we have any. To use as witnesses. We could put them under parole and let them have free access to the site." I shrugged. "When I was a cop handling a murder inquiry, you had to let the press in on things. When you didn't, they'd think you were trying to hide something. And that's especially true here."

Goebbels was nodding. "I like this idea," he said. "I like it very much. We can take pictures and shoot newsreel like it's a proper news story. And we could also let the neutral-country journalists go where they want, speak to whoever they want. Everything in the open. Yes, that's excellent."

"The Gestapo will hate that, of course. But that's good, too. The press and the experts will see that and draw their own conclusions: that there are no secrets in Smolensk. At least there are no German secrets."

"You leave the Gestapo to me," said Goebbels. "I can handle those bastards."

"There is one argument against it, however," I said. "And it's a pretty damned important one."

"And what is that?"

"I should think that anyone in Germany who is related to one of our men taken prisoner at Stalingrad would find it profoundly worrying to be reminded of what the reds are capable of. I mean, there's no telling that our boys haven't met or will meet the same fate as those Polish officers."

"That's true," he said. "And it's a terrible thought. But if they're dead, they're dead and there's nothing we can do about that. On the other hand, if they're still alive, I tend to think that shining a light on this particular crime might actually help to keep them that way. After all, the Russians are certain to deny responsibility for these poor Poles and it would hardly support their argument if they were unable to show the world that their German POWs are alive."

I nodded. Joey could be pretty persuasive. But he hadn't finished with me yet. In fact, he'd hardly even started.

"You know, it's right what you said—about lawyers. I've never liked them very much. Most people think I'm a lawyer myself, because of my Ph.D. But my doctoral thesis at Heidelberg University was about a romantic playwright called Wilhelm von Schütz. He was the first to translate Casanova's memoirs into German."

For a moment I wondered if this might be why Joey was such a womanizer.

"I even wrote a novel, you know. I was a very open, Renaissance sort of fellow. After that I was a journalist and I gained a real respect for policemen."

I let that one go; during the Weimar Republic, my old boss at

Kripo, Bernhard Weiss, had been a frequent target of the Nazi newspapers because he was a Jew, and at one time Weiss had even sued Goebbels for libel and won. But when the Nazis took power, Weiss had been obliged to flee for his life to Czechoslovakia, and then England.

"And of course two of my favorite movies are about the Berlin police: *M* and *The Testament of Dr. Mabuse.* Subversive and hardly conducive to the public good but really quite brilliant, too."

I had the vague memory that the Nazis had banned *Mabuse* but I couldn't remember for sure. When the minister of Propaganda is interested in your opinion, it tends to affect your concentration.

"So, I agree with you one hundred percent," he said. "A policeman is what this investigation needs most. Someone who's in charge but not obviously in charge, if you know what I mean. It could even be someone authorized by this ministry to do everything, from securing the area—after all, there might be some Russian saboteurs down there who'd like to conceal the truth from the world—to ensuring the full cooperation of those damned flamingos at Army Group Center. They won't like this any more than the Gestapo. Von Kluge and von Tresckow. Believe me, I've had to put up with that kind of snobbery all my life."

This sounded worryingly like my own opinion.

Goebbels took out a cigarette case and quickly lit a cigarette, warming to his own train of thought. I had a horrible feeling that he was measuring me up for the job he was starting to describe.

"And of course it will have to be someone who can make sure that there is no wasted time. Perhaps you're right about that, too. About Stalin's math. And think about it, Captain Gunther. Think about the sheer diplomatic and logistical nightmare of making sure that all those foreigners and journalists are allowed to do their jobs without interference. Think about the overwhelming need for there to be one man behind the scenes, making sure that everything runs smoothly. Yes, I do ask you to think about that, please. You've been there. You know what's what. In short, what this investigation needs is a man to manage the site and the situation. Yes, it's obvious to me that this investigation needs *you*, Captain Gunther."

I started to disagree but Goebbels was already waving away my objections with the back of his hand.

"Yes, yes, I know you said you didn't want to return to Smolensk and I can't blame you for that. Frankly, I can't think of anything worse than being away from Berlin. Especially when it's a dump like Smolensk. But I'm appealing to you, Captain. Your country needs you. Germany is asking you to help clear her name of this bestial deed. If, like me, you want the truth about this awful crime to be laid at the door of the Bolshevik barbarians who carried it out, then you'll accept this task."

"I don't know what to say, sir. I mean, it's flattering, of course. But I'm not at all diplomatic."

"Yes, I'd noticed that already." He shrugged apologetically. "If you do this service for me, you will not find me ungrateful. You'll soon find that I'm a good person to have on your side, Captain. And I've a long memory, as you already know." He started to wag his finger at me in the same way I'd seen him do on the newsreels. "Maybe not today, maybe not tomorrow, but I never forget my friends."

There was, of course, an opposite side to this coin but Goebbels was too clever to draw it to my attention right away, not while he was still trying to seduce me. On the whole, I prefer to do the seducing myself, but it was increasingly clear to me that there wasn't going to be room for me to refuse a man who only had to pick up the telephone again and instead of ordering coffee instruct one of his lackeys to have the Gestapo turn up at the door on Wilhelmplatz to give me a lift to Prinz Albrechtsrasse. So I listened, and after a while I started to nod my compliance, and when he asked me straight out, yes or no, if I would take the job, I said I would.

He smiled and nodded his appreciation. "Good, good. I appreciate it. Look, I've not made that journey myself but I know it's a brutal one so I'll have my own plane fly you down there. Shall we say tomorrow? You can have whatever you need."

"Yes, Herr Reich Minister."

"I'll speak to von Kluge himself and make sure you have his full cooperation as well as the best accommodation that's available. And of course I'll draw up some letters patent explaining your powers as my plenipotentiary."

I didn't much like the idea of representing Goebbels in Smolensk; it was one thing taking charge of the Katyn Wood investigation and an international commission; but I hardly wanted soldiers looking at me and seeing the cutout of a man with a clot foot and a sharp line in suits and phrase-making.

"These things have a habit of not remaining secret for very long," I said carefully. "Especially in the field. For form's sake it would be best if the powers granted to me in your letter made it quite clear that I am acting as a member of the War Crimes Bureau and not the Ministry of Propaganda. It wouldn't look good if one of those journalists or perhaps someone from the International Red Cross gained the impression that we were trying to stage-manage the situation. That would discredit everything."

"Yes, yes, you're right, of course. For the same reason, you had better go down there wearing a different uniform. An army uniform, perhaps. It's best we keep the SS and the SD as far away from the scene as possible."

"That most of all, sir."

He stood up and ushered me to the door of his office.

"While you're down there I shall expect regular reports on the teletype. And don't worry about Judge Goldsche, I shall telephone him immediately and explain the situation. I shall simply say that all of this was my idea, not yours. Which of course he'll believe." He grinned. "I flatter myself that I can be very persuasive."

He opened the door and walked me down the magnificent staircase so quickly I hardly noticed the limp, which was, I suppose, the general idea.

"For a while after your time in Kripo you were a private detective, weren't you?"

"Yes, I was."

"When you get back we'll talk again. About another service you might be able to do for me this summer. And which you'll certainly find is considerably to your advantage."

"Yes, sir. Thank you."

The sun was shining and as I walked out of the ministry onto Wilhelmplatz it seemed to me that my own shadow had more substance and character than I did, as if the body occluding the light behind it had been cursed into spineless insignificance by some evil troll, and for no good reason I stopped and spat onto the black contour as if I had been spitting onto my own body. It didn't make me feel any better; in lieu of bending my own ear with accusations of cowardice and craven cooperation with a man and a government I loathed, it was nothing more—or less—than an expression of the dislike I now felt for my own person. Sure, I told myself, I had said yes to Goebbels because I wanted to do something to help restore Germany's reputation abroad, but I knew this was only partly true. Mostly I agreed with the diabolic doctor because I was afraid of him. Fear. It's a problem I often have with the Nazis. It's a problem every German has with the Nazis. At least those Germans who are still alive.

PART TWO

1

FRIDAY, MARCH 26, 1943

The spring thaw in Smolensk still looked to be a long way off. A fresh layer of snow covered the broken cobbles and twisted tramlines of Gefängnisstrasse, a fairly typical-looking street in the south of the city—typical only by the standards of the Spanish Peninsular War, that is; in Smolensk, there were times when I found myself looking around for Goya and his sketchbook. In the turret of a burned-out tank on the corner of Friedhofstrasse was the blackened corpse of a dead Ivan made more macabre by the sign in German he was holding in a skeletal hand directing traffic north, to Commandant's Square. A horse was dragging a sled laden with an impossible quantity of logs while its one-armed owner, swaddled in quilted rags and with a length of string for a belt, walked slowly alongside smoking a pungent pipe. A babushka wearing several headscarves had set up a stall by the prison door and was selling kittens and puppies, but not as pets; on her feet were waterproof shoes made from old car tires. Beside her, a bearded man was carrying a yoke with a pail of milk on each end and holding a tin mug in his hand; I bought a mugful and drank the best milk I'd tasted in a long time—cold and delicious. The man himself looked just like Tolstoy—even the dogs in Smolensk looked like Tolstoy.

"Jews are your eternal enemies!" proclaimed the poster on the bulletin board by the front door of the prison. "Stalin and Jews belong to the same gang of criminals."

As if to make sure you understood the message, there was a large drawing of a Jew's head against the background of a Star of David; the Jew was winking in a sly, dishonest way and, as if to remind everyone that this race was not to be trusted, the poster listed the names of thirty or forty Jews who had been convicted of various offenses. Their fates were not mentioned but you didn't need to be Hanussen the clairvoyant to divine what this would have been: in Smolensk, there was only one punishment for anything if you were a Russian.

The prison was an assemblage of five ancient buildings from the time of the tsars, all grouped around a central courtyard, although two were little better than ruins. The high brick wall of the courtyard had a large shell hole in it that had been covered with a screen of barbed wire, and the whole area was observed by a guard in a watchtower with a machine gun and a searchlight. As I crossed the courtyard and headed into the main prison building, I heard the sound of a woman weeping. And if all of that wasn't depressing enough, there was the simple window-frame gallows they were erecting in the prison yard; it wasn't tall enough to guarantee the mercy of a broken neck, and whoever the gallows was meant for faced death by strangulation; which is about as depressing as it gets.

In spite of the hole in the prison yard wall, security was tight: once you were through the hellish main door, there was a floor-to-ceiling turnstile to negotiate and then a couple of steel doors that, when they closed behind you, made you think you were Doctor Faustus. I shivered a little just to be in the place, especially when a tall, skinny guard walked me down a circular flight of iron stairs into the depths of the prison and along a beige-tiled corridor that smelled strongly of misery, which, as anyone will tell you, is a subtle mixture of hope, despair, rancid cooking fat, and men's piss.

I was visiting the local prison to take the witness statements of two German NCOs accused of rape and murder. They were both from a division of Panzergrenadiers—the third. I met the two NCOs one after the other in a cage with a table and two chairs and a bare lightbulb. The floor was covered in a grit or sand that cracked under my shoes like spilled sugar.

The first NCO they brought to me had a jaw the size of the Crimea and bags under his eyes, as if he hadn't slept in a while; that was understandable, given his situation, which was serious. There were red marks on his neck and chest, as if someone had stubbed out several cigarettes on his body.

"Corporal Hermichen?"

"Who are you?" he asked. "And why am I still in here?"

"My name is Captain Gunther and I'm from the Wehrmacht War Crimes Bureau, which ought to give you a clue why I am here."

"Is that some kind of a cop?"

"I used to be a cop. A detective. At the Alex."

"I haven't committed any war crime," he protested.

"I'm afraid the priest says different, which is why you were arrested."

"Priest." The corporal's tone was scathing.

"The one you left for dead."

"Rasputin, more like. Have you seen him? That so-called priest? Black devil."

I offered him a cigarette and, after he took it, I lit it and explained that his commanding officer, Field Marshal von Kluge, had asked me to come to the prison and determine if there were indeed grounds for a court-martial.

The corporal grunted his thanks for the cigarette and studied the hot end for a moment as if comparing it with his own situation.

"Incidentally, those marks on your chest and neck," I said. "They look like cigarette burns. How did you come by them?"

"They're not cigarette burns," he said. "They're bites. From the bedbugs. A whole fucking army of bedbugs." He took a nervous puff and started to scratch eloquently.

"So why don't you tell me what happened? In your own words."

He shook his head. "I certainly haven't committed any war crimes."

"All right. Let's talk about the other fellow, your comrade, Sergeant Kuhr. He's quite a fellow, isn't he? Iron Cross, First Class, old fighter—that means he was a member of the Nazi Party before the Reichstag election of 1930, doesn't it?"

"I've got nothing to say about Wilhelm Kuhr," said Hermichen.

"That's a pity because this is your one chance to put out your side of the story. I'll be speaking to him after you, and I expect he'll tell me his side of the story. So if he blames it all on you, it will be your misfortune. From where I'm sitting, you both look guilty as hell, but generally speaking military courts like to balance justice with clemency, albeit in a completely arbitrary way. And my guess is they'll only convict one of you. The question is, which one? You or Sergeant Kuhr?"

"I really don't understand what this shit is all about. Even if I did kill those two Ivans—and I'm not saying I did—what the fuck?"

"They weren't Ivans," I said. "They were just a couple of laundry maids."

"Well, whatever I'm supposed to have done, the SS has done a lot fucking worse—Sloboda, Polotsk, Bychitsa, Biskatovo. I went through those places. They must have shot three hundred Jews in those four villages alone. But I don't see anyone charging those bastards with murder."

"*Rape* and murder," I said, reminding him of the whole charge that had been laid against him. I shrugged. "Look, I tend to agree with you. For the reasons you mentioned, the whole idea of charging idiots like you with war crimes in this theater strikes me as absurd. However, the field marshal feels rather differently about these things. He's not like you or me. He's the old-fashioned type. An aristocrat. The kind who believes there's a proper way to conduct yourself if you're a soldier in the Wehrmacht, and an example must be made of someone who deviates from that standard. Especially since you were both part of the platoon guarding his headquarters at Krasny Bor. Which is hard luck for you, Corporal. He's determined to make an example of you and Sergeant Kuhr unless I can persuade him that there's been a mistake."

"What sort of example?"

"They'll try you tomorrow and, after they find you guilty, they'll hang you on Sunday. Right here in the yard outside. They were erecting the gallows as I came through the door of the prison. That kind of an example."

"They wouldn't," he said.

"I'm afraid they would. And they do. I've seen it. The commanders are coming down hard on that kind of thing." I shrugged. "I'm here to help, if I can."

"But what about Hitler's decree?" said the corporal.

"What about it?"

"I heard about this barbarian decree the Leader had made that said it wasn't the same standard required out here, see? On account of how the Slavs are fucking barbarians." He shrugged. "I mean, anyone can see that, can't they? I mean, look at them. Life means less down here than it does back home. Anyone can see that."

"The Ivans are not so bad. Just people, trying to survive, make a living."

"No, they're hardly human. Barbarians is right."

"By the way, it's not called the barbarian decree, you blockhead," I sneered. "It's the Barbarossa Decree, after the German Holy Roman emperor of the same name. He led the Third Crusade, which is probably why we chose to name the military operation we've mounted against the Soviet Union after him in the first place. Out of some misplaced sense of fucking history. Not that you'd know much about history. What you do know is that this decree was not passed on to the local field commanders by von Kluge. Like a lot of those old-style general staff officers, the field marshal chose to sit on Hitler's decree—you might say, even to ignore it altogether. And it certainly didn't apply to those men guarding Army Group Center headquarters. What the SS and the SD do is their affair. And I must tell you this: if you and your old fighter friend were gambling on an appeal to Berlin over the field marshal's head, I'm here to say you can forget it. That's just not going to happen. So you'd better start talking."

Corporal Hermichen hung his head and sighed. "That bad, eh?"

"Damned right, that bad. My advice to you is to make a statement as quickly as possible in the hope of saving your neck. I'm not really interested in whether you hang or not. No, what I'm more interested in was the way you—or your sergeant—killed those two women."

"I didn't have anything to do with that. That was Sergeant Kuhr. He killed them both. Rape—yes, I went along with that. He raped the mother and I raped the daughter. But I was for letting them go. It was the sarge who insisted on killing them. I tried to talk him out of it, but he said killing them was best."

"This was in a quiet spot west of the Kremlin, right?"

The corporal nodded. "Narwastrasse. There's a little cemetery just north of there. That's where it—where it happened. We'd followed them from our barracks on Kleine Kasernestrasse, where they did the laundry, to a little chapel. The church of the Archangel Michael—Svirskaya, I think the Ivans call it. Anyway, we waited for them to come out of the church and then followed them south down Regimenstrasse. When they went in the cemetery, the sarge said they were leading us on so we could fuck them in there. That they wanted us to fuck them. Well, it wasn't like that. It wasn't like that at all."

"You followed them how?"

"Motorcycle and sidecar. The sarge was driving."

"So that means you were carrying the jerry can full of gasoline, in the sidecar."

"Yes."

"Why?"

"How do you mean?"

"The witness—the Russian Orthodox priest from the Svirskaya Church who saw you, who took the number on the bike's license plate, who you shot and left for dead—he says you burned the bodies with the gasoline, and that you had the gasoline beside you when you were raping the laundry maids. By the way, why didn't you burn his body, too?"

"We were going to. But we ran out of gasoline and he was too big to haul on top of them."

"Which one of you shot the priest?"

"The sarge. Didn't hesitate. Soon as he saw him. Pulled his Luger and let him have it. That was half an hour before we finished with the two girls, during which time we didn't hear a peep out of him, which persuaded us he was dead. But of course it was just a flesh wound and he was just knocked out. Fell down and banged the back of his head. I mean, how were we to know?"

"Tell me something, Corporal, would you have shot him again if you'd known he was still alive?"

"You mean me, sir? Yes, I was so scared I would have."

"Now tell me about when you murdered the two women."

"Not me, sir. I told you. It was the sarge."

"All right. He cut their throats, didn't he?"

"Yes, sir. With his bayonet."

"Why did he do that, do you think? Instead of shooting them the way you say he'd shot the priest."

The corporal thought for a moment and then tossed his cigarette end onto the floor, where he ground it underneath the heel of his boot.

"Sergeant Kuhr is a good soldier, sir. And brave. I never knew a braver one. But he's a cruel man, so he is, and he likes to use a knife. It's not the first time I saw him use a blade on a man—on someone. We took an Ivan prisoner near Minsk and the sarge murdered him in cold blood with his knife, although I don't remember if he used his bayonet or not. He slit the Ivan's throat before cutting his whole fucking head off. Never seen anything like it."

"When you saw that, did you have the impression that he'd done that before? I mean, cut a man's throat."

"Yes, sir. He seemed to know exactly what he was doing. Well, that was bad but this time—with the two girls, I mean—that was worse. And it wasn't the sight that lives with me, sir. It was the sound. You can't explain that, the way they kept on breathing through their throats. It was horrible. I couldn't believe it that he killed them that way. The two girls, I mean. I really couldn't believe it. I threw up. That's how bad it was. They were still breathing through their throats like a couple of slaughtered pigs when the sarge poured the gasoline on them."

"Did he set them alight? Or did you?" I paused. "It was your lighter that the field police found near the scene of the crime. With your name on it—Erich?"

"My nerves were gone. I'd lit a cigarette to get something inside myself. The sarge snatched the nail out of my hand and tossed it onto the bodies. But he used so much gasoline that it almost took my fucking eyebrows off when they went up. I fell over backwards to get away from the flames. Must have dropped the lighter then. In some long grass. Looked for it but by then the sarge was back on the bike and starting it up. I thought he'd drive away without me so I just left it."

I nodded, lit a cigarette, and sucked hard on the loosely packed end. The smoke helped to cure the degraded feeling I had from listening to this sordid story. I'd come across many evil bastards and heard some loathsome stories in my time with Kripo—the Alex wasn't known as Gray Misery for nothing—but there was something about this particular crime I found more ghastly than I could ever have imagined. Perhaps it was just the idea of the two Russian women—Akulina and Klavdiya Eltsina—surviving the Battle for Smolensk that had killed Akulina's husband, Artem, and keeping themselves alive by doing the laundry of their gentlemanly German conquerors, two of whom would rape and murder them both in the most squalid, inhuman way. I'd come across the sensation if not the facts that were peculiar to this case many times before, of course: I suppose it's just the curse of hindsight, the way you see the fate that was always hanging over people like the Eltsinas—the way it seemed they were meant to meet two bastards like Hermichen and Kuhr and then be raped and murdered in a snow-covered cemetery in Smolensk. Suddenly I wanted to leave, to go outside and throw up and then breathe some fresh air; but I forced myself to sit there with Corporal Hermichen, not because I thought I could help him but because I had more questions—questions about another pair of murders that had been nagging at me ever since I'd been back from Berlin.

"I believe your story. It's just dirty enough to smell right. Naturally, Sergeant Kuhr will pay you the same compliment you paid him: that it was all your idea. But that's the thing about three stripes and a first-class hero badge. It's generally assumed you're not so easily led."

"I'm telling you the truth."

"Let me ask you something, Corporal. Almost two weeks ago—on March thirteenth—two army telephonists from the 537th Signals Regiment were murdered near the Hotel Glinka."

"I heard."

"Their bodies were found on the riverbank. Their throats had been cut from ear to ear. With a German bayonet. A witness reported a possible suspect leaving the scene on a BMW motorcycle and heading west along the road to Vitebsk. Which might easily have taken him to Krasny Bor."

Corporal Hermichen was nodding.

"You can see why I'm asking," I said. "The obvious similarity between those murders and the murders of the Eltsinas."

The corporal frowned. "The who?"

"The two women who were raped and murdered. Did you forget why I'm here? Don't tell me you don't know their names?"

He shook his head and then, seeing the look on my face, said, "Does it make it worse if I don't?" The sarcasm in the corporal's voice was obvious and perhaps understandable: he was right; it shouldn't have made it worse and yet somehow it did.

"Ever go to that brothel at the Hotel Glinka?"

"Every enlisted man in Smolensk has been to the Hotel Glinka," he said.

"What about on Saturday, March thirteenth? Did you go there then?"

"Nope."

"You seem very sure of that."

"March thirteenth was the weekend of Hitler's visit," said Hermichen. "How could I forget? All leave was canceled."

"But after he'd flown back home?"

He shook his head. "Needed special permission of the CO, didn't you? Those two fellows from the 537th must have been the classroom favorites. Most fellows stayed in the barracks casino that weekend." He shrugged. "Easy enough to check my story, I'd have thought. I played cards until late."

"And Sergeant Kuhr?"

Hermichen shrugged. "Him, too."

"Being a sergeant, could he have slipped out without permission?"

"Maybe. But look, even if he did, the sarge just isn't the type to murder two of our own. Not over a whore. Not over anything. Look, he hated Jews—well, everyone hates the Jews—and he hated Ivans, but that was it. He'd have done anything for another German. He certainly wouldn't have cut some Fritz's throat. Kuhr may be a bastard but he's a German bastard." Hermichen smiled and shook his head. "Oh, I can see how tempting it would be to bolt a couple of unsolved murders on the end of these ones—kind of like making a new tapeworm German word. Well, it won't work. Take it from me, Captain Gunther, you're carving the wrong piece of wood."

"Maybe," I said.

"As a matter of fact, I'm certain of it."

"How so?"

"Look, sir, I'm in a tight spot, I can see that now. I appreciate you trying to help me. Who knows, maybe I can help you in return. For example, maybe I can give you some information that might help you catch your murderer—the one that really killed those two army telephonists."

"What sort of information?"

"Oh no. I couldn't tell you while I'm in this place. I'd have nothing to trade if I told you what I know, now." He shrugged. "You know, the way I heard it, they weren't killed by partisans."

"What did you hear?"

"The field police like to keep a tight lid on the pickle jar in case some of the vinegar spills. The Gestapo hanged some locals just to make the Ivans think we thought they did it. Doesn't do to let the Ivans know how easy it is to kill us. Something like that. But it wasn't the partisans, was it?"

"So I get you out of here and you tell me some important truth you claim you know, is that it?"

"That's right."

I smiled. "Suppose I don't care for the truth? Suppose all I care about is police housekeeping. After all, it suits everyone at headquarters if we can hang you both for those murders at the same time as we hang you for these new ones. It looks a lot tidier that way. Generally, I don't approve of that sort of thing but I might make an exception in your case, Corporal. Alibi or not, I bet I can make another charge of murder stick against you and your sergeant. In fact, I'm sure of it."

"Can you? My alibi is solid silver, sir. Lots of other men saw me that night because I played skat until about two A.M. Everyone knows I'm good at skat. I won three grand hands in a row. Almost sixty marks. The losers won't forget that evening in a hurry. So, good luck trying to prove I was somewhere else."

"It's not me who needs the good luck. Maybe I didn't mention the gallows they're building in the yard for after your fair trial and the rope with your name on it."

"I've been thinking about nothing else since you got here."

"What if I get you out of here and I'm disappointed? Generally speaking, I don't much like disappointment. I might find it hard to get over that. No, the best I can do for you is to plead your case to the field marshal. You have my word on it."

"Your word? Didn't I already say? That isn't good enough."

I stood up to leave.

"Forget it, Hermichen. I'm not selling any life insurance today. My book is full. You're all risk, sonny. And I can't see the profit in it."

"The profit ought to be obvious. You solve the case, your career advances, you draw down a bigger paycheck, and your wife gets to buy a nicer coat. That's how it works with you people, isn't it?"

"I'm not the ambitious type. My career—such as it is—went down the toilet a long time ago. My wife is dead, soldier. And I really don't care very much who killed those two telephonists. Not anymore. What's two more dead Germans after Stalingrad?"

"Sure you care. I can see it in your blue eyes and on your clever cop's face. Not knowing something eats away at guys like you— sometimes it gets to be an illness. It's like the crossword puzzle in the paper. Solving crimes, arresting murderers—it's the only way that bulls like you can live with yourself. Almost as if you have to show you're better than anyone else on account of how you figured out whodunit."

I called for the guard and he came back to unlock the door.

"This isn't over between you and me, copper," Hermichen said. "You know it and I know it." He stayed where he was and sneered some more. "So go ahead and walk. We both know you'll be back."

"I might come back at that. Just to see you on tiptoes."

"Well, don't count on any last words. Because there won't be any. Until then my deal is on the table. Got that? The day I'm out of here, I talk."

I shook my head and walked out and tried to laugh off Corporal Hermichen like a bad joke. Him, thinking he could make me feel dizzy. Only, he was right, of course, and I hated him for it. I didn't like it that someone—a German—had murdered those two men and thought he was probably in the clear by now. That was understandable in a place like Russia, where everyone else was getting away with murder every day. And I wouldn't have minded an Ivan doing it. After all, we were at war. Killing Germans—that was what they were supposed to do. But a German killing Germans was something else. That was uncomradely.

Outside in the prison yard they were adding some timber to strengthen the uprights of the gallows so they could hang the two NCOs side by side, like partners in crime. It was only Ivans they hanged in public; these two men were going to be hanged in private. Everyone—soldiers and citizens alike—would get to hear about it, of course. Just to ensure that everyone in Smolensk—German and Russian—behaved themselves. The Wehrmacht was thoughtful that way.

The question was, did I hate Corporal Hermichen enough to say nothing on his behalf and let him hang?

KRASNY BOR HAD BEEN A SOVIET HEALTH RESORT eight kilometers west of Smolensk. There were some lakes and mineral springs and plenty of trees, which ensured a steady supply of fresh oxygen to the resort every morning, but otherwise it was difficult to perceive the health benefits that might have resulted from a sojourn there. In winter the place was frozen solid; in summer it was reported to be plagued with mosquitoes; the mineral springs tasted like a fisherman's bathwater; certainly Krasny Bor did not compare favorably with more famous German health resorts like Baden-Baden, where expensive hotels and uninterrupted luxury were the order of the day, and which was doubtless why the likes of Richard Wagner—not to mention quite a few Russians like Dostoevsky—used to go there, year after year. It was easy to see why Dostoevsky hadn't bothered with Krasny Bor; the resort wasn't much more than a collection of log cabins. But it was as near to luxury as there existed anywhere in Smolensk, and this—as well as its privacy and seclusion, which made the resort easy to guard—was why Field Marshal von Kluge had chosen it to be the headquarters of Army Group Center.

For an old Prussian Junker, the field marshal was not without a sense of humor; he especially enjoyed making jokes about the negligible health benefits of living at Krasny Bor. Von Kluge's jokes were usually at the expense of the Russians and, although very cruel, these were often loudly appreciated by Alok Dyakov, who was von Kluge's *Putzer*. Von Kluge might have had a sense of humor but he was ruthless, too; he also fancied himself a military lawyer, as I soon discovered after sitting down on one of the rattan-backed chairs in his cozy log-cabin office.

"Thank you for doing this, Captain Gunther," he said, glancing over my typed report. "I appreciate it's not why you're here in Smolensk, but until we can have a party of Russian POWs start digging in Katyn Wood, it's best that you keep yourself useful."

He glanced out the window for a moment, shifted the curtain with his hand, and shook his head grimly.

"It'll be a while yet, I think. Dyakov thinks at least another week before it starts to thaw, don't you, Alok?"

The Russian, sitting at a plain wooden table to our right, nodded. "At least a week," he said. "Maybe longer."

"How are your quarters?"

"Very comfortable, sir, thank you."

Von Kluge stood up and, leaning against a section of plain brick wall, he carried on reading my report with the aid of a pair of half-moon glasses. Most of his office was made of wood but the wall contained a regular series of square apertures that heated the room because behind the wall was a large and powerful stove that also heated the officers' mess.

"So," he said finally. "You seem to think they're guilty as charged."

The field marshal was tall with a receding chin and a receding hairline; his manner was rather more robust as was his intelligence; his men called him Clever Hans.

"The evidence points that way, sir," I said. "However, Sergeant Kuhr looks to be the more culpable of the two. My own impression of Kuhr is that he would be a very hard man to resist. I think Corporal Hermichen was only complying with the wishes of his senior NCO."

"And this is why you're recommending clemency for him?"

"Yes, sir."

"But not for Kuhr?"

"I don't think I made any recommendations at all with regard to Sergeant Kuhr."

"Kuhr is by far the better soldier," said von Kluge. "And you're right, he is a most forceful fellow."

"You know him?"

"It was I who gave Sergeant Kuhr his Iron Cross, First Class. I have the greatest respect for him, as a fighting man." Von Kluge put my report down on the corner of a fancy Biedermeier desk that looked a little out of place in his otherwise sparely furnished office, and lit a cigarette. "Corporal Hermichen, I don't know at all. But I hardly see how you can rape anyone in compliance with a senior officer's wishes. No matter how hard that officer is to resist, as you say. After all, when one takes into account the resistance of the poor victim, and the necessity of the corporal being sufficiently aroused to carry out the rape—he doesn't deny that, I see—then I fail to understand how a defense of coercion can possibly apply here." The field marshal shook his head. "I've never understood rape. To me, resistance is not and could never be a corollary of sexual arousal. Compliance is the only aphrodisiac I can appreciate."

"Then I would argue for clemency for the corporal on the basis of the fact that it was the sergeant who cut the victims' throats. He doesn't deny that. Hermichen says he was against it."

"And yet the corporal also mentions the presence of the jerry can before the rape actually commenced. That looks bad for him. I ask you, Captain, what purpose did he think the gasoline was there to serve? A prophylactic, perhaps? I have actually heard of such a thing—soldiers are very stupid, there's no end to what they will do to themselves to avoid a dose of jelly, or what they'll do to women to avoid a pregnancy. No, he must have known that Sergeant Kuhr intended something more lethal as part of the whole disgusting enterprise. He must have suspected that Sergeant Kuhr was intent on the disposal of the bodies. Which means he still managed to carry out the rape in the full knowledge of that fact. Which takes some doing."

Von Kluge turned to his Russian jester. "Have you ever raped a woman, Alok?"

Dyakov stopped lighting his pipe and grinned. "Sometimes, possibly," he said, "perhaps I have gained the wrong impression from a girl and went too far, too soon. Maybe this is rape, maybe this isn't, I don't know. What I can say is that for me, this would be a cause of some regret."

"We'll take that as a yes," said von Kluge. "Rape and consent, I think it's all the same with Ivans like Dyakov, but that's no reason our men should behave in this fashion. Rape is terribly bad for discipline, you know."

"But you understand I never did such a thing with other men," protested Dyakov. "As part of an enterprise, as your lordship says. And as for killing a girl afterward, this is without any excuse." Dyakov shook his head. "Such a man is not a man at all, and deserves to be severely punished."

Von Kluge turned to me. "You see? Even my pet pig can't excuse such appalling behavior. Even Dyakov thinks they should both hang."

Dyakov stood up. "Excuse me, but I didn't say that, your lordship. Not exactly, no. Personally, I would spare the sergeant, and if you spare him, you must also spare the other, too."

"But why?" asked von Kluge.

"I know this sergeant, too, like you, sir. He is a very good fighter. Very brave. The best. He has killed many Bolsheviks, and if you spare his life he will kill many more of the bastards. Can Germany afford to lose such an experienced fighting man as this? A respected combat sergeant with an Iron Cross, First Class? I don't think so." He shrugged. "To my mind, it is unrealistic to expect a soldier to kill your enemies one day and then to behave like a gentleman toward them the next. It makes no sense."

"Nevertheless, that is what I do expect," said von Kluge. "But perhaps you're right, Alok. We shall see."

"I don't know about Sergeant Kuhr," I said, "but there's still another argument in favor of sparing Corporal Hermichen from the rope."

As von Kluge raised an eyebrow at me the telephone rang. He picked up the receiver, listened for a moment, said "Yes," and then replaced the receiver.

"Well, what is it?" he asked me. "Your other argument, Captain?"

"It's this, sir. I think he has some information that might be valuable, sir."

I hesitated for a moment as I heard the small voice of the operator still on the line. Von Kluge heard it, too, and picked it up angrily. "For two weeks now I've been telling your people that this telephone isn't working properly," he said to the operator. "I want it fixed today or I shall want to know why." He banged the receiver down. "I'm surrounded by idiots." He looked at me as if I might have been another idiot.

"You were saying?"

"If you remember, sir, a couple of weeks ago there were two murders in Smolensk. A couple of off-duty soldiers had their throats cut."

"I thought that was partisans," said von Kluge. "I distinctly remember it was partisans. And the Gestapo hanging five people for it, the day after Hitler visited Smolensk. As an example to the city."

"It was six people," I said. "And the ones they hanged didn't kill our men."

"I do appreciate that, Captain," said von Kluge. "I'm not a complete fool. Naturally, they meant the executions to serve as a message to the partisans—an eloquent message of the kind that Voltaire mentions in his play *Candide*."

"I don't know the play. But I think I know the message."

"And I thought you were an educated man, Gunther. Pity."

"And I do know a possible lead when I hear one, sir. It's my belief that another German soldier murdered those two men and that Corporal Hermichen might be able to provide some information that could lead to the killer's apprehension. That is, if the corporal's life was spared."

"Are you suggesting that we do a deal with Corporal Hermichen—that he tells you what you want to know in return for a more lenient sentence?"

"That's exactly what I'm suggesting."

"And what about Sergeant Kuhr? Does he have any information pertinent to this other inquiry?"

"No, sir."

"But if he did have any useful information, would you be recommending that the court spares his life, too?"

"I suppose I would. Information—good information—is rather difficult to come by in any police inquiry. A lot of the time we rely on informers, but they're thin on the ground in wartime. Over the years I've developed a nose for when a man has a story to tell. I think Corporal Hermichen is just such a man. I'm not saying that he doesn't deserve to be punished—what happened was bestial, truly bestial. I just happen to believe that perhaps sparing one man might result in the apprehension of another equally bestial criminal. Amid so much death and so much killing, a murder is very easy to get away with in this part of the world. That bothers me. It bothers me a lot. I think that if we take our time here and act judiciously, we can throw a stone and hit two birds instead of one."

"That sort of thing may pass for proper procedure at Berlin Alexanderplatz," said von Kluge. "But the Wehrmacht High Command does not enter into negotiations with rapists and murderers. According to you, we should spare the corporal because he has some important information, but we should also convict the sergeant who isn't fortunate enough to have any such useful information—information that it ought to have been the corporal's duty as a German soldier to share with his superiors long before now. I like Corporal Hermichen even less now that you've told me this, Gunther. He strikes me as a very untrustworthy sort of fellow. You surely can't expect my court to make a deal with a man like that."

"I would like to solve that crime, sir," I said.

"I appreciate your professional zeal, Captain. But surely the field police are dealing with that crime? Or the Gestapo? It's what they're for."

"Lieutenant Voss of the field police is a good man, sir. But it's my information that there are still no suspects."

"Isn't it possible that the corporal and the sergeant also murdered these two other fellows? Have you thought of that?"

Patiently I explained all of the facts and why I thought Kuhr and Hermichen were innocent of those earlier crimes—not least the fact that both men had cast-iron alibis for the night in question—but the field marshal wasn't having any of this.

"The trouble with you detective fellows," he said, "is that you place too much emphasis on fancy notions like alibis. When you've handled as many military courts as I have, you soon get to know all of the common soldier's tricks and to understand just what they're capable of. They're all liars, Gunther. All of them. Alibis mean nothing in the German Army. The ordinary Fritz in uniform will lie for his comrade just as soon as you or I would fart. Playing skat in the mess here until two o' clock? No, I'm afraid it just won't do. From what you've told me about the bayonet and the motorcycle, it seems perfectly obvious that you've already got the two most likely perpetrators for that crime, too."

I glanced at Dyakov but Dyakov pursed his lips and shook his head discreetly and it was then plain to me that there was little point in arguing with von Kluge. All the same, I tried.

"But, sir—"

"No buts, Gunther. We'll try 'em both in the morning. And hang the bastards after lunch."

I nodded curtly and then got up to leave.

"Oh, and Gunther. I'd like you to prosecute, if you wouldn't mind."

"I'm not a lawyer, sir. I'm not sure I know how."

"I'm aware of that."

"Couldn't Judge Conrad do it?"

Johannes Conrad was the bureau judge that Goldsche had already dispatched to Smolensk. Since his arrival, he and Gerhard Buhtz—a professor of forensic medicine from Berlin—had been kicking their heels waiting for more evidence of a massacre.

"Judge Conrad is going to judge the case, with me and General von Tresckow. Look, I'm not asking you to cross-examine them or anything like that. You can leave that to me. Just lay the facts and the evidence before the court—for appearance's sake—and we'll do the rest. You must have done that before, when you were a police commissar."

"Might I ask who's going to defend the men?"

"This isn't meant to be an adversarial process," said von Kluge. "It's a court of inquiry. Their guilt or innocence isn't to be determined by advocacy but by the facts. Still, perhaps you're right—under the circumstances someone ought to speak for them. I'll appoint an officer from my own staff to give them a fair shake. Von Tresckow's adjutant, Lieutenant von Schlabrendorff. He trained as a lawyer, I think. Interesting fellow, von Schlabrendorff—his mother's the great-great-granddaughter of Wilhelm the First, the Elector of Hesse, which means that he's related to the present king of Great Britain."

"I could do it more effectively, sir. Defend the men. Instead of prosecuting them. I'd feel more comfortable doing that. After all, it will give me another chance of arguing for clemency on behalf of Corporal Hermichen."

"No, no, no," he said testily. "I've given you a job to do. Now, damned well do it. That's an order."

2

SATURDAY, MARCH 27, 1943

The trial of Sergeant Kuhr and Corporal Hermichen took place the following morning at the Army Kommandatura, in Smolensk, which was less than a kilometer north of the prison. Outside, the air had turned to the color of lead and it was obvious that snow was on the way, which most people agreed was a good thing as it meant the temperature was starting to climb.

Judge Conrad took the role of presiding judge with Field Marshal von Kluge and General von Tresckow assisting; Lieutenant von Schlabrendorff spoke for the accused; and I presented the facts that were ranged against them. But before proceedings commenced I spoke to Hermichen briefly and urged him to tell me anything he knew about the murders of the two telephonists.

"In return I'll inform the court that you have given the field police some important information that might lead to the arrest of another criminal," I said. "Which might weigh well with them—enough to show you some leniency."

"I told you, sir. When I know I'm off the hook, I'll tell you everything."

"That isn't going to happen."

"Then I'll have to take my chances."

The hearing—it was hardly a trial—took less than an hour. I knew it was within my remit to press for a verdict and a sentence, but in the event I did neither as I had little appetite for urging upon the court the execution of a man I suspected could solve a crime. About Sergeant Kuhr I felt more ambivalent. But there was another factor, too. Before the Nazis, I had strongly believed in capital punishment. Every cop in Berlin had believed in that. In my time at the Alex I had even attended a few executions, and while I took no satisfaction in the sight of a murderer being led kicking and screaming to the guillotine, I felt justice had been served and the victims had been properly avenged. Since Operation Barbarossa and the invasion of the Soviet Union, I had come to think that every German had played some part in a crime greater than had ever been seen in any courtroom and, to that extent, I felt less than comfortable with the whole hypocrisy of prosecuting two soldiers for doing what an SS man from any police battalion would have considered to be all in a day's work.

To his credit, von Schlabrendorff spoke well for the accused men and the three judges actually seemed inclined to give his words some weight before they retired to consider their verdict. But it didn't take the trio long before they were back in the courtroom and Judge Conrad was pronouncing a sentence of death, to be carried out immediately.

As the men were led away, Hermichen turned and called to me:

"Looks like you were right, sir."

"I'm sorry about that. Really, I am."

"Are you coming to see the show?"

"No," I said.

"Perhaps I'll tell you what you want to know just before they put the noose around my neck," said Hermichen. "Perhaps."

"Forget it," I said. "I won't be there."

But I knew I would be, of course.

IT WAS COLD IN THE PRISON YARD. Snow was falling gently from the breathless sky as if thousands of tiny Alpine paratroopers were taking part in some huge airborne invasion of the Soviet Union. It silently covered the crossbar of the gallows, turning its simple dark geometry into something almost benign, like a length of cotton wool on the Christmas crib in a quiet country church, or a layer of cream on a Black Forest cake. The two ropes that were curled underneath the icing-sugared beam might have been decorative; while below these tenantless holes in the air, the little flight of precarious wooden steps that led the way to pendulous death looked like something that had been provided by a more thoughtful soul, as if some child might have had need of them to reach a sink to wash its hands.

In spite of what was about to happen, it was hard not to think of children. The prison was surrounded by Russian schools—one on Feldstrasse, one on Kiewerstrasse, and one on Krassnyistrasse—and as I'd parked my car outside the prison a snowball fight had been in progress and the sound of their playing and laughter now filled the freezing air like a flight of emigrating birds. For the two men who were awaiting their fate that carefree sound must have provoked a painful memory of happier times; even I found it depressing, reminding me as it did of someone I'd once been and wouldn't be again.

Those of us who had assembled to see the sentence carried out— myself, Colonel Ahrens, Judge Conrad, Lieutenant von Schlabrendorff, Lieutenant Voss, several noncommissioned members of the field police, and some army prison guards—put out our cigarettes respectfully as two men approached the gallows; we relaxed a little as we realized they were only prison guards and watched as they began to push and pull at the beams as if testing the frame's strength until, satisfied that the wooden edifice would perform its function, one of them lifted a thumb in the direction of the prison door. There was a short interval and then the two condemned men emerged with their hands tied in front of them and walked slowly toward the gallows, looking to one side and then the other in a sort of helpless, cornered way, as if searching for a means of escape or some sign that they had been reprieved. They were wearing boots and breeches but no tunics, and their white collarless shirts were almost too bright to contemplate.

Seeing me, Corporal Hermichen smiled and mouthed a greeting and, thinking he now meant to tell me what I wanted to know, I moved closer to the gallows, where the guards were already urging the two men up the wooden steps. Reluctantly they complied and the steps wobbled ominously.

Sergeant Kuhr looked up at the noose as if wondering if it was equal to the business of hanging him, and now that I was nearer, I could see it was a fair question as the rope was little more than a length of striped cord, like something that might have been used to hang a Christmas decoration—it hardly looked strong enough to hang a fully grown man.

"Picked a nice fucking day for it," he said. And then: "All this fuss over a bit of Ivan cunt. Incredible." He bowed his head for a moment as the executioner lassoed it and tightened the rope under his left ear. "Hurry up, I'm getting cold."

"Be a lot warmer where you're going," said the executioner, and the sergeant laughed.

"Won't be sorry to leave this godforsaken place," he said.

"So you came after all," Hermichen said to me.

"Yes."

"I knew you would." He grinned. "You can't afford to risk it, can you? The possibility that I might say who really killed those two telephonists. Our German friend on the motorcycle. With the razor-sharp bayonet. We saw him, you know. That night." Hermichen opened his hands and then clasped them tightly again. "I've been thinking of him a lot. They'd hang him, too, if he was caught."

"That's always a possibility," I said.

"Aye, but the thing is, I'm not in favor of hanging anyone, for obvious reasons."

"There's not much time," I said.

"Talk about stating the fucking obvious," snarled Sergeant Kuhr.

Overcoming a powerful sense of shame, I remained where I was as the executioner pulled the noose over Hermichen's head; just by being there it seemed as if I was actively assisting in a degrading act of human wickedness no less cruel or violent than that meted out to the two Russian women the pair had raped and murdered. Two more deaths in this terrible place seemed hardly to matter; and yet—I asked myself—when would the killing stop? There seemed to be no end to it.

"Please, Corporal," I said. "I urge you to tell me. For the sake of those two dead comrades."

"More to them than met the eye, too. Least that's what people say."

I swallowed hard, almost as if it had been me with the noose around my neck, drew a deep breath, and pushed my chin toward my shoulder. I felt the bones and gristle of my own vertebrae crunch like a mouthful of Brazil nuts. It was good to be alive—to draw breath; sometimes you had to be reminded of that.

"Surely you wouldn't want their murderer to go unpunished— or worse, to go to your own death suspected of having killed them yourself."

"Can't see it matters much either way," said Sergeant Kuhr. "Not to us, eh, Erich?" He laughed.

Hermichen lifted his hands and wiped some snowflakes from his hair and face with scrupulous care. "He's got a point," he said.

The executioner dismounted the steps, checked the knots of the ropes tied to the uprights, and contemplated the terrible sight in front of him. He looked at me and then back at the two condemned men, whereupon he placed his shiny black boot on the steps their lives were resting on. "Say what you want to say," the executioner told them roughly. "And hurry up about it. Haven't got all day."

"I changed my mind," said Hermichen. "I've got nothing to say, after all." And with that he closed his eyes and began to pray.

"That's the spirit," said Sergeant Kuhr. "Fuck 'em. Fuck 'em all."

The executioner glanced over at Judge Conrad, who was nominally in charge of the execution. He was a stern-looking man who wore horn-rimmed glasses, but all the same, he'd seen enough for one day and he took them off and tucked them into the pocket of his greatcoat; then he nodded curtly. For his sake I hoped he was now seeing a blur of what was happening. He was a thoroughly decent man and I didn't blame him for the sentence, not in the least bit; he had done his duty and given his verdict on the basis of the evidence.

The executioner himself wasn't much more than a boy but he went about his job with ruthless efficiency and little more sign of emotion than if he had been about to kick at the sidewalls of a set of tires. Instead he placed the instep of his boot on the wooden steps and—almost carelessly—pushed them over.

The two condemned men dropped several centimeters and then swung like coat hangers, their legs cycling furiously on bicycles that weren't there; and all the time their necks seemed to grow longer, like soccer players straining to head the ball at a goal. Both men groaned loudly and steam enveloped their torsos as they lost control of their bladders. I turned away with a feeling of profound disgust and anger that I had been tricked by Corporal Hermichen into witnessing his squalid death.

It makes for a hell of a weekend when you're obliged to attend a hanging.

. . .

I WENT TO THE ZADNEPROVSKY MARKET on Bazarnaya Square, where you could buy all manner of things; even in winter the square was full of enterprising Russians with something to sell now that the constraints of Communism had been removed: an icon, an old vase, a homemade broom, jars of pickled beets and onions, some radishes, quilted clothing, pencils, snow shovels, hand-carved chess sets and pipes, portraits of Stalin, portraits of Hitler, unexploded propaganda grenades, cigarette papers, safety matches, lend-lease fuel packs for preparing food, lend-lease meat rations, lend-lease anti-gas goggles, lend-lease first aid kits, bundled copies of a satirical magazine called *Crocodile*, back issues of *Pravda* that were useful for starting a fire, packets of Mahorka—this was Red Army tobacco (so strong it was like inhaling your very first cigarette)—and of course numerous Red Army souvenirs—these were popular with German soldiers, especially RKKA helmets, medals, tobacco tins, butter cans, spoons, razors, liquid polish, TT pistol holsters, wrist compasses, trench shovels, map cases, cavalry sabers, and—most popular of all—SVT bayonets.

I wasn't in search of any of this stuff. A souvenir was something you bought to remind you of somewhere, and although it wasn't yet over, I knew I didn't ever want to be reminded of my time in Smolensk; after the day I'd just had I wanted to forget about it as quickly as possible. So I went to Bazarnaya Square with something else in mind: a source of cheap oblivion.

I bought two large bottles of home-brewed beer—brewski—and was about to buy a bottle of *samogon*—the cheap but powerful homemade spirit we Germans were always being warned not to drink—when I saw a familiar face. It was Dr. Batov, from the Smolensk State Medical Academy.

"You don't want this stuff," he said, removing the *samogon* from my hand. "Not if you want to see yourself in the mirror tomorrow."

"That was rather the point," I said. "I'm not sure I do. I heard the thing to do was pour the *samogon* into the brewski and drink the mixture. *Yorsh*, it's called, isn't it?"

"For an intelligent man you have some very stupid ideas. If you drink two and a half liters of *yorsh* you may never see again. I suppose I should be glad if an enemy soldier kills or blinds himself, but I can easily make an exception in your case. What happened? I thought you weren't coming back. Or is your return to Smolensk a punishment for discovering their dirty little secret?"

He was talking about the Polish intelligence report we had translated in his laboratory with the aid of the stereo microscope.

"Actually, I decided to keep my mouth shut about that," I said. "At least for now. My life seems precarious enough without rocking the steps it's standing on. No, I'm back here in Smolensk on other duties. Although I certainly wish I wasn't. I just want to get drunk and to forget more than I care to remember. It's been that sort of a day, I'm afraid."

And I told him where I'd been and what I'd seen.

Batov shook his head. "It's a curious example your generals try to make," he said. "Hanging one kind of German soldier for behaving like another kind of German soldier. Do they suppose it will make us dislike the Germans a little less if you execute one of your own for killing Russians—after all, that's what you're here for, isn't it? To get rid of us so that you can live in the space made by our absence? There's a kind of schizophrenia working here."

"That's just a medical name for hypocrisy," I said. "Which is the homage the Wehrmacht pays to virtue. Honor and justice in Germany are just a delusion. But it's a delusion that someone in my line of work has to deal with every day. Sometimes I think that the greater insanity is not to be found in our leaders but in the judges I work for."

"I'm a doctor. So I prefer medical names. But if your government is schizophrenic, then mine is certainly dangerously paranoid. You've no idea."

"No. But it might be amusing to compare notes."

Batov smiled. "Come with me," he said. "I'll show you where you can buy the better stuff. It's not great, but it won't put you in hospital. At the SSMA we're rather short of beds as it is."

We went to another corner of the square—a quieter corner, on Kaufstrasse—where a man with a face like a box of iron filings and with whom Batov had clearly dealt before sold me a *chekuschka*, which was a quarter liter of vodka from Estonia. The bottle was asymmetrical in a way that made you think you were already drunk, and the stuff looked no less suspicious than the *samogon* but Batov assured me it was good stuff, which was probably why I decided to buy two and suggested he keep me company.

"Drinking alone is never a good idea," I said. "Especially when you're by yourself."

"I was on my way to the bakery on Brückenstrasse." He shrugged. "But the chances are they won't have any bread anyway. And even when they do, it's like eating earth. So yes, I would like that. I live south of the river. On Gudonow Strasse. We can go there and drink these bottles, if you like."

"Why do you use the German names for the streets and not your own Russian names?"

"Because then you wouldn't know where I was talking about. Of course, this might just be a cunning trap. Me being an Ivan, I could have decided to lure you back to my place where some partisans are waiting to cut off your ears and nose and your balls."

"You'd be doing me a favor. It's my ears and nose and my balls that seem to get me in trouble." I nodded firmly. "Let's go, Doctor. It would be nice to spend time with a Russian who's not an Ivan, or a Popov, or a Slav, or a subhuman. It would be good to be with a Russian who's just a man."

"Oh my God, you're an idealist," said Batov. "And clearly a dangerous one at that. It's obvious to me that you've been sent here to

Russia to put that idealism severely to the test. Which is perfectly understandable. And rather perceptive of your superiors. Russia is the best place for a cruel experiment like that. This is the country for cruel experiments—it's where idealists are sent to die, my friend. Killing people who believe in things is our national sport."

With the bottles in Batov's empty shopping bag, we went and found my car and drove over the rickety temporary wooden bridge that connected the southern part of the city with the northern part: German engineers had been busy. But Russian women were, it seemed, no less industrious; on the banks of the Dnieper they were already hard at work building the wooden rafts that would transport things into the city when the river was properly navigable.

"Is it the women who do all the work here?" I asked.

"Someone has to, don't you think? It will be the same for you Germans one day, you mark my words. It's always the women who rebuild the civilizations that the men have done their best to destroy."

Batov lived alone in a surprisingly spacious apartment in a largely undamaged building that was painted the same shade of green as many of the churches and public buildings.

"Is there some reason why every other building has been painted green?" I asked. "Camouflage, perhaps?"

"I think green was the only color available," said Batov. "This is Russia. Explanations are usually commonplace. We probably exceeded some sort of five-year plan for paint production only no one thought to produce more than one color. Very likely blue paint was made the previous year. Blue is the right color for a lot of these buildings, by the way. Historically speaking."

Inside, the apartment was a series of rooms connected by a long corridor that ran along the wall facing onto the street; built into this long wall was a series of bookshelves that were full of books. The apartment smelled of furniture polish and fried food and tobacco.

"That's quite a collection you have there," I said.

Batov shrugged. "They serve a double purpose. As well as keeping me busy—I love to read—they help to insulate the corridor against the cold. It's doubly fortunate that Russians write such thick books. Perhaps that's why."

We went into a cozy little drawing room that was heated with a tall brown ceramic stove that stood in the corner like a petrified tree. While I glanced around the room, Batov pushed some wood in the brass door on the grate and closed it again. I knew his wife was dead but there were no pictures of her to be seen and this puzzled me as there were many marks on the wallpaper where framed pictures had been hanging as well as many photographs of Batov himself and a girl I presumed was his daughter.

"Your wife," I said. "Was she killed in the war?"

"No, she died before the war," he said, fetching some small glasses, some black bread, and some pickles.

"Do you have a picture of her?"

"Somewhere," he said, waving a hand at the apartment and its contents. "In a box in the bedroom, I think. You're wondering why I keep her hidden, perhaps? Like an old pair of gloves."

"I was rather."

He sat down and I poured two glasses.

"Here's to her, anyway," I said. "What was her name?"

"Jelena. Yes, here's to her. And to the memory of your own wife."

We threw the glasses back and then banged them down on the table. I nodded. "Not bad," I said. "Not bad at all. So that's *chekuschka*."

"*Chekuschka* is really what we call the size of the bottle, not the stuff that's in it," he said. "The vodka is cheap stuff but nowadays that's all there is."

I nodded. "Your wife," I said. "I didn't mean to pry. Really, it's none of my business."

"It's not because I didn't love her that I keep her photographs hidden," explained Batov, "but because in 1937 she was arrested by the NKVD after she had been accused of anti-Soviet agitation and wrecking. It was a difficult time for the country. Many were arrested or simply disappeared. I don't display her photographs because I'm afraid to do so would be to risk the same thing happening to me. I could hang them up again, of course. After all, it's not as if the NKVD are likely to come calling while you Germans are here in Smolensk. But somehow I haven't had the courage. Courage is another thing that's in short supply in Smolensk these days."

"What did happen?" I said. "To Jelena, I mean? After she was arrested?"

"She was shot. At that particular time in Soviet history arrest and a bullet in the back of the head were more or less synonymous. Anyway, that's what they told me. A letter came in the post, which was thoughtful of them—so many people never learn these things for sure. No, I was lucky that way. She was Ukrainian-Polish, you see. I think I told you before—when you came to the hospital—she was from the Subcarpathian province. As a Pole she was a member of a so-called fifth column community, and this made the authorities suspicious of her. The charge was nonsense, of course. Jelena was an excellent doctor and devoted to all of her patients. But that certainly didn't stop the authorities from alleging she had secretly poisoned many of her Russian patients. I imagine they tortured her to get her to implicate me, but as you can see, I'm still here, so I don't think she could have told them what they wanted. Now I blame myself for not leaving Russia and going to live with her in Poland. Perhaps she would be alive if we had left. But that's true of millions, I shouldn't wonder. Jews, especially, but Poles, too. Since the war of 1920 it's been almost as difficult to be Polish under the Bolsheviks as it is to be Jewish under the Germans. It's an old historical scar but, as always, these scars run deep. The Russians lost, you see. Soviet forces under

Marshal Tukhachevsky were defeated by General Pilsudski outside Warsaw—the so-called Miracle on the Vistula. Stalin always blamed Tukhachevsky, and for his part he blamed Stalin. There was no love lost between them, so really it's amazing that Tukhachevsky lasted as long as he did. But he was arrested in 1937 and he and his wife and two brothers were shot. I believe his three sisters and a daughter were sent to penal camps. So I suppose I and my daughter can count ourselves lucky in that we're still here to tell the tale. I told you the name of this street is Gudonow Street. It is. But before the war it used to be called Tukhachevsky Street. And just living on a street with this name was a cause for suspicion. Really, you look like you think I'm exaggerating but I'm not. People were arrested for much less than that."

"And I thought Hitler was bad."

Batov smiled. "Hitler is just a minor demon in hell, but Stalin is the devil himself."

We tossed another couple of glasses back and ate the bread and pickles—Batov called these little snacks *zakuski*—and it wasn't long before we had finished the first bottle, which he then placed beside the leg of the table.

"In Russia an empty on the table is a bad omen," he said. "And we can't afford any of those on Tukhachevsky Street. It's bad enough that I have a *fashisty* in my apartment. The floor lady will cross herself three times if she sees a Hans in the building and think her building has been cursed. Many at the hospital feel the same way about you *germantse*. It's odd, but for some Russians there's really not much difference between you Germans and the Poles. I suppose that might be because there are parts of Poland that used to be German, which became Polish, and now they're German again."

"Yes," I said. "East Prussia."

"To a Russian, that's much too complicated. Better to hate you all. Safer, too. For us."

"You might say that it's the Poles who have brought me back here to Smolensk," I said. I told Batov about Katyn Wood and how we were waiting for a thaw to begin so we could start digging.

Batov brushed up his thick, Stalin-sized mustache with the inside of his hand; he didn't say anything for a moment but his dark, shadowy eyes were full of questions that were mostly for himself, I think. The face was lean and the nose keen-looking, even fastidious, and the bushy black mustache almost designed to protect his nostrils from some of the less pleasant smells that afflicted any resident of Smolensk; and probably not just the smells: the words and ideas of any governmental tyranny can stink as bad as any backed-up sewer. For a moment he hung his head almost as if he was feeling shame.

"You must understand that in spite of all this, I love my country, Herr Gunther," he said. "Very much. I am in love with Mother Russia. Her music, her literature, her art, the ballet—yes, I love the ballet. My daughter, too. It is still her life. There's nothing she wishes more than to be a great ballerina like Anna Pavlova and dance *The Dying Swan* in Paris. But I love the truth more. Yes, even in Russia. And I hate all cruelty."

I sensed he was about to tell me something, so I lit two cigarettes, handed him one silently, opened the second bottle, and then refilled our glasses.

"When I joined my profession I took an oath to help my fellow man," he said. "But lately this has become increasingly difficult. The situation here in Smolensk is terrible. Of course, you know that. You have eyes and you're not a fool. But it was no less terrible before you Germans arrived here with your new street names and your Aryan superiority. Wagner is a great composer, yes, but is he any greater than Tchaikovsky, or Mussorgsky? I think not. Things have been done here in Russia that no civilized country should ever have countenanced doing against another civilized country. Not just by you, but by us, the Russians, too. And one of those things was what was done to the Poles."

"If I didn't know you were here, Dr. Batov, I'd say I was talking to myself."

"Perhaps that's why I feel able to tell you about this," he said. "When first we met I sensed you are someone who is trying to be a good man. In spite of the uniform you are wearing. Although it's odd—I could have sworn it was a different one the last time you were here."

"It is different," I said. "But that's a long story. For another time."

"I don't say that you are a good man, Captain Gunther—you are still a captain, yes?"

I nodded.

"No, you are not a good man. There are none of us can claim to be that, today. I think we must all make compromises to stay alive. When my wife was arrested, the authorities made me sign another piece of paper saying that I recognized the justice of the sentence given to her. I didn't want to do that, but I did it all the same. I told myself Jelena would have wanted me to sign it, only the truth is that I signed it because if I hadn't, they would have arrested me. Was there any sense in us both being dead? I don't think so. And yet—"

He had a smile that was full of brilliantly white teeth and it returned briefly to his thoughtful, almost preoccupied face but only as a way of preventing the tears in his eyes from increasing in quantity; he blinked them away and tossed back the drink I had poured for him.

I looked away out of something like decency and glanced over the books that were piled next to his chair. They all looked like they'd been read but I wondered if just one of them contained a single truth like the one I guessed he knew as well as I did; that being dead is probably the worst thing that can happen to you—after this nothing matters very much, especially not what other people say about you; as long as you can draw breath you've got a chance of turning around whatever nastiness you've been involved in; at least that was what I was praying when I prayed at all.

Batov wiped his mustache with the back of his hand. "I haven't drunk vodka like this in a long time," he said. "Frankly, I haven't been able to afford it. Even before you Germans turned up, things were very hard. And they're not about to get easier. For me, at any rate."

"That's why we're drinking, isn't it? To forget about shit like that. Because life is shit but the alternative is always worse. At least that's the way it looks to me. I'm in a dark place but the other side of the curtain looks even darker to me. And it frightens me."

"You sound like a Russian now. It must be the vodka, Captain Gunther. What you say is quite correct, and that's why any Russian drinks. We pretend to live because dying is much more reality than we can cope with. Which reminds me of a story—about drinking *yorsh*, as a matter of fact. That stuff is lethal. Even to those who are themselves lethal. Perhaps them most of all because they have so much more to forget. Let's see now, yes, it would have been May of 1940 when two senior NKVD officers arrived at the state hospital in a Zis driven by a blue-hat NCO. Because of who they were and the power they wield—the power of life and death—I was asked to supervise their medical treatment myself. I say 'asked' but it would be more accurate to say that the blue-hat NCO put a gun to my head and told me that if they died, he would come back to the hospital and personally blow my brains out. He actually took out a gun and put it to my head, just to make the point. He even made me help carry the two officers out of the back of the truck, which I will never forget as long as I live. As I dropped the tailgate I thought the two men had been seriously injured because the floor of the truck was covered in blood. Only the blood was not theirs. And in fact the two NKVD men were not injured at all but blind drunk. The NCO was pretty drunk himself. They'd all been drinking *yorsh* for several days and the two officers were suffering from acute alcoholic poisoning. Also on the floor of the truck I saw several leather aprons and a briefcase that fell on the ground as we carried the men out and burst open: it was full of automatic pistols."

"Do you remember the names of these men?"

"Yes. One was a Major Vasili Mikhailovich Blokhin, and the other was a Lieutenant Rudakov—Arkady Rudakov. But I don't remember the NCO. And really, who they were is not important because almost immediately I knew what they were. These people are the worst we have, you know. State-sanctioned psychopaths. Well, everyone in Russia knows this type: unlike most people, this kind of NKVD man doesn't give a damn what he says about anything or anyone. And always he is threatening to shoot you, as if it means nothing to him because he does it so often. I mean, this kind of a fellow handles guns like I handle a stethoscope. When he wakes up in the morning he probably reaches for his gun before he scratches his own balls. He shoots someone with less thought than you or I would stamp on an ant.

"If you were to magnify a flea several thousand times, you'd have an idea of what these men are like. Ugly and bloated with blood, with thin legs and hairy, fat bodies. If you squashed one of them there would be such a great quantity of blood that came bursting out of their bodies that you would see nothing but red. Then there were their uniforms: the blue hats, the double TT shoulder holsters, and the Orders of the Badge of Honor on their *gymnasterka* tunics— they would have received those orders from Stalin himself for their service in 1937 and 1938. In other words, one of these men might easily have been the very man who shot my own dear wife.

"For a glorious moment it seemed that fate had placed these men in my hands, and I felt my Hippocratic oath was no longer of importance beside the exciting possibility of meting out some kind of rough justice to one of them—perhaps to both. I mean, I actually considered murdering these men. It would have been easy enough for a doctor like me—an injection of potassium to the heart, and no one would have been at all surprised. Indeed, the lieutenant regained consciousness long enough to get up off the trolley he was on and fall down again, and when he fell he hit the back of his head on the floor and fractured his skull. I told myself I would be doing the world a favor if I killed them both. It would have been like putting down a couple of dangerous dogs. Instead I ordered fluid replacement, dextrose solutions, thiamine and oxygen and set about trying to restore them to full health." He paused and then frowned. "Why did I do that? Was it because I am a decent man? Or is morality just a form of cowardice, as Hamlet says? I don't know the answer to that. I treated them. And I continued treating them as I would have treated any other man. Even now it seems quite perplexing to me.

"Gradually I discovered more about what they had been doing. Not least because, in his delirium, one of them—the major—told me what their duties had been and why they were drunk. They'd been celebrating after carrying out a successful special operation near the station at Gnezdovo. I'm sure I don't have to tell a German what a 'special operation' amounts to. You Germans use this euphemism, too, don't you? When you want to kill thousands of people and pretend that it's something sanitary. And this merely confirmed a local rumor that had been running for a while: the road to Vitebsk had been closed for several days, and a trainload of men had been seen in a railway siding. At the time I had no idea that these men were Poles and it was only later I discovered that a whole trainload of Poles had been systematically liquidated."

"Did he tell you that, too?" I asked.

"Yes, the major told me. The other one—the one who fractured his skull—didn't recover from his injury. But periodically the major was talkative. Fortunately, he never remembered anything he had told me, and naturally I denied that he had said anything while he'd been unconscious. It's odd, but I've never told anyone what he told me until now. It's even odder that I should be telling all this to a German. After all, there's many a mass grave in this part of the world that's full of Jews murdered by the SS. I assume your government now wishes to try to make anti-Soviet propaganda out of this incident."

"You assume correctly, Dr. Batov. They wish to look on in a little pantomime of horror as they find the bodies of hundreds of Polish officers while carefully sidestepping the burial pits of their own making."

"Then your Dr. Goebbels has a greater opportunity to shame us than perhaps even he suspects. You can forget there being hundreds of men. There are at least four thousand Polish officers buried in Katyn Wood. And if half of what Major Blokhin told me in his delirium is accurate, then Katyn is just the tip of the iceberg. God knows how many tens of thousands of Poles are buried in locations farther afield: Kharkov. Mednoe. Kalinin."

"For God's sake, why?" I asked. "All because of the defeat in 1920?"

Batov shrugged. "No, not just that, I think. It was probably also because Stalin feared that Poles would behave like the Finns and join the German side. Like I said, for Russians, Poles and Germans are virtually coterminous. It's the same reason why as many as sixty thousand Estonians, Latvians, and Lithuanians were also murdered by the NKVD. Killing them was probably just seen as a simple way of making sure that eventually they didn't kill us."

"Stalin's math," I said. "I never did like math all that much. I'd forgotten how much until I came to Russia." I shook my head. "Even so, it's hard to imagine. Even for a German. The things that men are capable of. It beggars belief."

"Perhaps it's hard to imagine in Germany. But not in Russia. I'm afraid we Russians are rather more inclined to believe the worst of our government than you Germans are. But then, we've had a lot more practice. We've had the Bolsheviks and the Cheka since 1917. And before that we had the tsar and the Cheka. It's often forgotten what a bloody tyrant Nicholas the Second was. Perhaps a million

Russians were murdered by him, too. So, you see, we're used to being murdered by our own government. You've only had Hitler and your Gestapo since 1933. Besides, it's all easy enough to prove, isn't it? What happened to these Poles. All you have to do is dig up Katyn Wood."

I shrugged. "But even if we do that, I still think it will suit plenty of people to say that it was Germany who killed those men. Frankly, I think Goebbels is wasting his time, although I wouldn't dream of telling him that. The Americans and the British have invested too much in Uncle Joe to turn away from him now. It might be embarrassing for it to be proved in front of the world what they already know in their heart of hearts—that the Bolsheviks are every bit as loathsome as the Nazis. Embarrassing, yes, but I don't think it will really change very much, do you?"

Batov was quiet for a moment. His eyes flicked to one side and for a moment I thought he was listening to something I couldn't hear—a neighbor, perhaps, or even someone else in the apartment. But when he took a deep breath and clasped his hands tightly for a moment— so tightly his knuckles whitened—I realized he was steeling himself to tell me something even more important.

"What if I could prove definitively that the NKVD murdered those Poles? What if I told you I had evidence of what Major Blokhin and his men had done here—here in Smolensk and in Katyn Wood? What would you say to that, my German friend?"

"Well, things might be different, I suppose." I paused, lit another cigarette, and pushed the packet across the table toward Batov. "But different for who?"

"I mean, could they be any different for me and my daughter?"

"Do you mean money? I can give you money. I can get more money if what I can give you is not enough."

"No. Your money is no good. Nor is our money, if it comes to that. There's nothing to buy with money. Not in Smolensk. You

certainly cannot buy the one thing I need most of all—a future for me and my daughter. There's no future for us here. You see, when the Red Army recaptures Smolensk—as, with respect, inevitably it will—there will be a dreadful reckoning in this city. The NKVD will conduct a new witch hunt to find all of those traitors who did business with the Germans. And as someone who has been questioned before, whose wife was a spy and a wrecker, then I'm automatically suspect. But if that weren't enough, then as someone whose hospital is full of wounded German soldiers—which is aiding and abetting the enemy, plain and simple—the fact of the matter is that I will be one of the very first to be shot. My daughter, too, probably. I have less chance of surviving this war than an ant on the floor."

"How old is she? Your daughter?"

"Fifteen. No, our only chance of being alive this time next year is if I can persuade you Germans to take me back to Germany with you as a—what do you call it?"

"A Zeppelin volunteer."

Batov nodded.

"*Can* you prove it?"

He nodded again. "I have the proof. Enough proof for it to seem almost suspicious. But it is proof nonetheless. It is proof that cannot be questioned. *Enyoperovezhempe geraenka.*" He glanced out the window. "It's stopped snowing," he said. "We could walk, I suppose. It's not far to the hospital. Me, I walk there every day. But you Germans don't much like walking. I've noticed that when you invade someone else's country, you do it at great speed, and in as many vehicles as you can. You Germans, with your cars and your autobahns. Yes, I should like to see those. Germany must be a beautiful country if people want to get from one place to another at such enormous speed. Here, no one is ever in a hurry to go anywhere else in Russia. What would be the point? They know it's just as shitty somewhere else as the place you are now." He grinned. "Are you too drunk to drive that car of yours?"

"I'm too drunk to take proper care of a pretty girl, but I'm never too drunk to drive a car. And certainly not in Russia. If I hit someone or something, I'm not likely to care very much. I'm a German, right? So fuck it. Besides, a bit of fresh air will sober me up in no time."

"Again spoken like a true Russian. We have plenty of fresh air in Russia. Much more than we need."

"That's why we came," I said. "At least according to Hitler. We needed the space to breathe. That's why we hanged those two German soldiers this morning. It's all part of the master race's master plan to extend our living space." I laughed. "I'm drunk. That's the only reason why it seems funny, I suppose."

"In Russia, that's the only reason anything ever seems funny, my friend."

We left the apartment and I drove us down to the hospital. Despite the fresh snow, with all the cracks and potholes the car had little trouble in gripping the road; I felt like I was bouncing around on the floor of the plane from Berlin.

"Do you remember I told you about Lieutenant Rudakov and how he fell and cracked his head on the floor, while he was drunk?" asked Batov.

"Yes." I swerved to avoid a cart and a horse in the middle of the road. "I'm beginning to understand how he must have been feeling."

"The lieutenant suffered a depressed skull fracture. I was able to repair his skull, but not his brain. The pressure on his brain caused a hemorrhage, damaging delicate tissue—speech centers, mainly. That and the acute insult to his system that was the amount of alcohol consumed was enough to render him an invalid. Most of the time he's little better than a marrow. Quite a decent-looking marrow, actually, as he still has a few moments of lucidity."

"Christ, Batov, you don't mean to say he's alive—that he's still here? In your hospital?"

"Of course he's still here. This is his hometown. Where better to care for him than the Smolensk State Medical Academy?"

. . .

THE MAN IN THE WHEELCHAIR did not look like a man who had helped murder five thousand people but then, as I'd learned from firsthand experience, few men do. There were men in SS police battalions with faces like Handel's favorite choirboys, who could charm the birds from the trees. Sometimes, for murder to take place, murderers must be full of smiles.

Arkady Rudakov's ears were of normal size, his forehead was as upright as a parlor piano, his eyes and nose were quite symmetrical, and his arms were of the usual length and without any tattoos; he didn't even drool in a way that might have been described as savage or atavistic, and after Batov's description of an enlarged flea, bloated with blood, it was almost a disappointment to meet a handsome, open-faced little man of about thirty, with a full head of luxuriant dark hair, a smiling, feminine mouth, small hands, and warm brown eyes. He looked like a tailor or a baker—someone who was good with people instead of someone who was merely good at killing them.

Rudakov's voice was no less improbable. Every few seconds he would say the same thing: "*U me-nya vsyo v po-ryadke, spasiba. U me-nya vsyo v po-ryadke, spasiba.*" He had a cartoonish sort of voice, as if his chest was never quite filled with enough breath to make a man's full voice, or as if someone had tried to strangle him.

"What does he keep saying?" I asked Batov.

"He says, 'Everything is all right, thank you,'" said Batov. "Of course, he's not all right. Never will be again. But he thinks he is. Which is a small mercy, I suppose. At first when officers from the NKVD came to visit him they would ask if he was all right and he would make this answer. But it was soon evident that he didn't tend to say much else." Batov shrugged. "It was a very Soviet answer, of course. Always when someone in Russia asks you how things are, you make this answer, because you never know who's listening. Any other answer would be unpatriotic, of course. But even the blockheads of the NKVD realized that there was something seriously wrong with this fellow. That's probably the only reason they left him here and alive, because they didn't think he was likely to pose any kind of threat to them. I suspect if he'd been the gabby type, they'd have taken him away and shot him."

"*U me-nya vsyo v po-ryadke, spasiba.*"

I pulled a face. "I can see why they weren't worried. With all due respect, Dr. Batov, I can't see this fellow making much of a witness. Not one that would satisfy the Ministry of Propaganda, anyway."

"As I said, there are times when he's quite lucid," said Batov. "It's like a window in his mind opens and a whole load of fresh air and light flood in. During this time he is capable of conducting a conversation. Which is when he told me all about the murders in Katyn Wood: curiously, it's the numbers he seems to remember. For example, he told me that among the dead were a Polish admiral, two generals, twenty-four colonels, seventy-nine lieutenant colonels, two hundred and fifty-eight majors, six hundred and fifty-four captains, seventeen naval captains, three thousand five hundred sergeants, and seven army chaplains—in all, some four thousand one hundred and eighty-three men. Did I say five thousand? No, it's just over four. These lucid periods never last long, however, but because of what he says I thought it best to keep him here, in a locked room. For his protection. Not to mention my own. And most of the other people in this hospital. There are one or two nurses who share this secret. But only the ones I trust."

We were in a private room on the uppermost floor of the hospital. There was a bed and an armchair and a radio—everything a man who was no longer in possession of his senses might have needed. On the wall was a picture of Stalin, which was enough to persuade me that I was probably the first German who'd been in there since the Battle for Smolensk. Any self-respecting German would probably have smashed the glass, which might be why I chose to ignore it.

"*U me-nya vsyo v po-ryadke, spasiba.*"

Batov regarded his patient kindly and, leaning over him for a moment, stroked his cheek with the back of his hand.

"*Kak skazhesh,*" Batov said gently to Rudakov. "*Kak skazhesh. Ti khoroshi drug.*"

"So much for wanting to kill him," I said.

"You mean me?" Batov shrugged. "What good would that do? Look at him. It would be like killing a child."

"If you'd been to school in Berlin, Doctor, you'd know why that's not always a bad idea." I lit a cigarette. "Some of the damned children I knew." The match caught the loon's eyes like a hypnotist's gold watch. Experimentally, I moved it one way, the other way, and then flicked it onto his forehead, just to see if he was putting on a dumb show. If it was an act, his middle name must have been Stanislavski.

"*Blagodaryu,*" muttered the loon.

"*Nyezachto.*" I put the cigarette in his mouth and he smoked it automatically. "These lucid periods. Can they be predicted?"

"Unfortunately not. It's possible I might be able to bring him out of it temporarily with therapeutic chemical shock—perhaps methylamphetamine, or thiopental, if I could get some. But there's no telling what permanent effect that might have on what's left of his mind."

"Let's not tell that to the ministry," I said. "I doubt they'd be much interested in an NKVD lieutenant's future welfare."

"No, indeed."

"I suppose we could film him being questioned, when he is being lucid," I said thoughtfully. "But it's hardly ideal for what's required here." I shook my head. "And besides, the people I work for—they're judges. Generally speaking, they like a witness to look like he knows what day it is. I doubt this fellow knows his arse from his earhole."

Batov did not look perturbed by my skepticism.

"I'm not saying that we can't use this fellow," I added. "It's just that it might be said by our critics that, being feeble-minded, he just repeats what we want him to say. Like a puppet."

"I said I had proof," said Batov. "I didn't say he was it. Rudakov's only the cherry on the cake. The real proof is something else."

"I'm listening."

"Ya-veh paryatkeh, spasiba."

"When Rudakov turned up here he had some bags," said Batov. "In the bags were some ledgers and an FED—a camera—and in the camera was a roll of exposed film. The ledgers contained a list of names: yes, it was about four thousand names." He let that revelation hang in the air for a moment.

"I see."

"After Rudakov had been here for a while I had the film developed. The NKVD—they took pictures. Like they were on some sort of hunting trip or safari. Trophy pictures of them actually shooting Poles. Like they were actually proud of what they'd done. Men with their wrists bound together with wire and kneeling on the edge of a trench while Rudakov and his friends shot them in the back of the head." Batov looked apologetic. "It's hard to believe that anyone would want to commemorate such acts, but they did."

"The SS does this sort of thing, too," I said. "It's hardly peculiar to the NKVD."

"I still have the ledgers and I still have the enlargements I made. Together they are all the evidence anyone could need of exactly what happened in Katyn Wood. Even for the exactingly high standards of your German judges."

"Sounds like the blue hats had themselves quite a holiday. Could I see these pictures? And the ledgers?"

Batov looked evasive. "I can only show you one picture just now," he said. "I keep it here, with Arkady, and from time to time I show it to him in order to try to stimulate what's left of his memory about who he was."

Dr. Batov lifted the picture of Stalin and unpeeled a 210 × 297mm–sized black-and-white photograph.

"I keep this hidden for obvious reasons," he added, handing me the picture.

In the photograph were three NKVD officers who appeared to be relaxing for the camera. They were wearing their traditional *gymnasterka* tunics with crossbelts and riding breeches with high boots; one man was seated in a wicker-basket chair, with another on the arm; Rudakov was standing beside them; each man was holding a Nagant revolver in his right hand and making the same curious hand sign—I suppose you'd call it the cuckold's horns—with his left. Behind them was a building that I recognized immediately as Dnieper Castle, where the 537th Signals was now based.

"The man in the center is Blokhin," said Batov. "The major I was telling you about—the one who was dead drunk. The man sitting on the arm of the chair is the blue-hat NCO who drove them both here."

"The hand sign," I remarked. "What does it mean?"

"I think it's a Freemason sign," said Batov. "I'm not sure. I've heard that a lot of NKVD are Freemasons—lots of people are in Russia, even today. But I'm not sure."

"And this was on the same roll of film as what? I mean, what's in these other pictures?"

"Polish officers being shot by Blokhin and Rudakov. Piles of bodies. These three drinking. More buddy shots. The rest of the material—the pictures and the ledgers—are somewhere safe. When my daughter and I have travel documents to get us to Berlin, I will give you everything. You have my word on it. You understand it's Germans I don't trust, Captain Gunther, not you."

"Kind of you to say so."

"I expect you will have to speak to your superiors about all of this," said Batov. He sat down on the bed and wiped his forehead with a loud sigh. "I'm really drunk."

"I doubt that." I grinned at him. "You were right what you said back in the marketplace when I was just a kraut buying brewski. For a clever man, I'm also a stupid one. I rather imagine you planned this touching little scene, Dr. Batov. I might not have had my balls cut off by partisans, nonetheless you did a swell job of bringing me here to your parlor so you could put a tattoo on my chest like a drunken Cossack in one of your oversized novels. I don't blame you. Really, I don't. Blame is for people with clearer consciences than mine. But don't overplay your part, Doctor. The audience doesn't like it. That's lesson one in the Stanislavski book of acting like someone who's on the level."

Batov grinned back at me. "You're right, of course. I might not have been selling vodka or brewski but I've got something to sell just like anyone else who goes to the market. When you showed up here at the hospital the first time with that Polish intelligence report, it was obvious to me where you must have got it from. I wanted to tell you about the lieutenant then, but I didn't quite have the guts. Then you left and I figured my chance was gone. That is, until I spotted you in the market this afternoon. When I saw you, it seemed too good to be true that you should be back here in Smolensk."

"I get a lot of that."

"So. Do we have a deal?"

"I think so. Only it might take a little while. You'll have to be patient."

"I'm Russian. Patience is something we're born with."

"Sure, sure. That's out of the same book as not putting any empties on the table. You don't believe that shit any more than I do. But here's something that you can believe. And this comes straight from the shoulder holster. When you made that crack about not trusting Germans, you implied you know what you're doing, but I still wonder if you do. You tell me you've got evidence of what happened in Katyn Wood and I tell you I'm prepared to buy your story. But I'm not the one who owns the store. You'll be making a deal with the devil here, not me. You appreciate that, don't you? Once you're out in the open with this, I can't protect you. Unlike me, you see, the Nazis are not the kind of people who can handle much disappointment. If they think for a minute you're holding out on them in any way, they're liable to reach for their pistols. The Gestapo is just as likely to put a bullet in your head as your own secret police. At that point, I'll be looking out for myself, see? Generally speaking, it's what I do best. I won't have time or even the inclination to do any special pleading for you and your daughter's ballet lessons."

"I know what I'm doing," he insisted. "I've thought about the risks. Really, I have. And I don't think I have anything to lose."

"When people say that kind of thing, mostly I don't believe them, or I think they haven't thought things through. But I imagine you really do know what you're doing. You're right, I don't think you have anything to lose. Just your life. And what's that worth in the current market? In my case, it's not much, and in yours, it's nothing at all. And in between there's probably just a lot of misplaced optimism. Mine, mostly."

3

MONDAY, MARCH 29, 1943

How did Saturday's execution go?" asked Field Marshal von Kluge. "Did those two sergeants die well?"

"Only one of them was a sergeant, sir. The other man was a corporal."

"Yes, yes, of course. But the question still stands, Gunther."

"I'm not sure it's even possible to die well when you're struggling for breath on the end of a length of cord, sir."

"Do you take me for an idiot? What I mean is, did they die bravely? As bravely as any German soldier ought to die? After all, there's always the chance that a condemned man will do or say something that reflects badly on the German Army. Cowardice in the ranks is even more intolerable than wanton criminality. How did they acquit themselves?"

"They died bravely, sir. I'm not sure I could have met the hangman with such apparent equanimity."

"Nonsense, Captain. I don't doubt your own courage for a moment. Any man with an Iron Cross like you knows what real bravery is. A German soldier should know how to die well. It's expected."

We were in the field marshal's office at Krasny Bor. Von Kluge had made a start on a large cigar and, in spite of the subject matter, was about as relaxed as a man can look when he's got a red stripe on his leg and a Knight's Cross around his neck. Of his pet Russian, Dyakov, there was no sign, although there was a large dog occupying a space next to the heat vents in the brick wall that could easily have been mistaken for him. The dog was licking his balls and, as I envied his ability to do something like that, I reflected that he was almost certainly the happiest creature in all of Smolensk.

"And did they say anything? Any last words of contrition?"

"No, and they didn't say anything about the murders of those two NCOs, either," I said. "Which was a pity."

"Leave this matter to the field police, Captain Gunther. That's my advice. I'm sure they will apprehend the true culprit before very long. Do you want to know why I'm so confident about that? Because I have forty-two years' experience in the military to draw upon. During that time I've learned that such incidents as these have a habit of repeating themselves. A man who has cut the throats of two men will before long cut the throats of some others. Almost certainly."

"That's exactly what I was hoping to prevent. I'm a little sentimental that way."

"Yes, you must be. Not to mention symbiotic and coadjuvant. Military law is not collaborative, Captain. We do not make deals with those who are beneath us. Our existence is based on unquestioning obedience and power, and we must always be merciless so that we triumph even when it seems that we might be crushed. The command of power is justified only by itself. I'd rather two more men were sacrificed on the altar of expediency than our military authority should ever be compromised in the distasteful way you proposed. A deal you called it. Ghastly idea. We shall win this war if our men recognize that there is only one way to win it and that is to fight according to their duty, ruthlessly and without expectation of favor or mercy."

It was a nice little speech, and while it might have been original, I thought it much more likely that Hitler had said something like that when he and the field marshal had been alone together in this very same office a few weeks ago. The bit about fighting ruthlessly and without expectation of favor or mercy had the Leader's rhetorical fingerprints all over it.

"Oh, by the way, Captain," said von Kluge, changing the subject, "when I took the dog for a walk this morning, he could smell a change in the air. I know that because almost immediately we were outside he started to paw at a piece of ground. As if he was digging for rabbits. He hasn't done that since the autumn of last year. I can't say I noticed anything different myself. But then I'm not a dog. You can't fool a dog about such things."

He paused for a moment and sucked on the cigar.

"What I'm saying is that the ground in Smolensk is melting, Gunther. Spring is here and so is the thaw. If the dog can dig, then so can you."

"I'll get right on it."

"Please do. I don't mind telling you I dislike this whole affair. And I especially dislike the Ministry of Propaganda. It is my sincerest wish that we begin and conclude this investigation as quickly as possible—that we remove our morbid gaze from the unfortunate past of this benighted region and concentrate only upon the future and on how we are going to fight a war against a resurgent Red Army now, in 1943. I tell you frankly, Captain, I am going to need all of my resources to win this war, and I cannot afford to spare any of my men and especially not my officers in an effort that can kill none of the enemy. Consequently, when your excavations commence, I should prefer it if the War Crimes Bureau uses only Russian prisoner of war labor. That seems only fitting. I think it would be demeaning for German soldiers to occupy themselves with digging up dead bodies left behind by the Bolsheviks. Von Schlabrendorff will help you there.

And my man Dyakov, of course. He's an expert on handling HIWI Russian labor. We used a contingent of Ivan workers to rebuild a bridge across the Dnieper last spring and Dyakov knows who the good workers are. Hopefully some of them are still alive. Perhaps you might mention this to Judge Conrad when next you see him."

"I'll do that, sir."

"I doubt that the world really gives a damn about any of this. It's my personal opinion that the minister is deluded if he thinks the Allies are going to fall out of love with each other just because the Russians might have murdered a few Poles."

"It's probably more than a few, sir. My sources indicate to me that it could be at least four thousand."

"And what about all of the ethnic Germans who were killed by Poles in 1939? In Posen, my own part of the world, the Poles—especially Polish soldiers—behaved like barbarians. Entire families of Germans were murdered. The women were raped and the men were frequently tortured before they were murdered. As many as two thousand Germans were murdered by the Poles in Posen alone. Two thousand. Some of my own family were obliged to flee for their lives. My house was ransacked. Read the white book that your own department prepared for the Foreign Office if you don't believe me. No one in East Prussia is going to care what happened to some Poles. I certainly don't. I tell you, they could find the whole Polish Army buried in Katyn Wood and I wouldn't give a damn."

"I didn't know you were from Posen."

"Well, now you do." Von Kluge puffed at his cigar and waved at me. "Was there another matter you wanted to see me about?"

"Yes, sir, there was."

I told von Kluge about Dr. Batov and his offer to furnish us with the hard evidence that would prove that the Soviets had murdered thousands of Poles in Katyn Wood.

"I believe he has a ledger with the names of all the dead, as well as some photographs of the crime in actual progress. The only trouble is, he's scared that he and his daughter will be murdered if the NKVD retakes Smolensk."

"He's not wrong about that. There will be a bloodbath in this city if ever the reds are in charge again. It will make your Katyn Wood massacre look like the teddy bears' picnic. I should think any right-minded Russian would be very anxious to prevent that from happening."

"Exactly. Dr. Batov would feel a lot safer if they could come and live in Berlin, sir."

"In Berlin?" Von Kluge chuckled. "I don't doubt it. I should like to be back in Berlin myself. Yes, indeed. A stroll in the Tiergarten before champagne at the Adlon, then the opera followed by dinner at Horcher's. Berlin is lovely at this time of year. The Adlon is lovely. Yes, I shouldn't mind a bit of that myself."

"He'd simply like some assurances to that effect. Before he cooperates with Judge Conrad's investigation. What he has could be really useful to us, sir. To Germany."

"And this doctor of yours can furnish you with evidence? To the bureau's satisfaction?"

"I do believe he can, sir."

Von Kluge sighed a cloud of cigar smoke and shook his head, as if in pity of me and my tiresome conversation.

"I wonder about you, Gunther, I really do. Prior to becoming a policeman, what were you? A car salesman? You keep bringing me deals you tell me I have to make. First it was those two NCOs, and now it's this damned Russian doctor. Don't you know anyone in this city who's prepared to do something for nothing—because he thinks he has a simple patriotic duty to bring forward the truth?"

"He's not a German, sir. He's a Russian. Duty doesn't come into it, nor patriotism, for that matter. He's simply a man trying to save his own life and that of his daughter. Right now he's attending injured German soldiers in the Smolensk State Medical Academy. If he was a patriot, he'd have cleared off like the rest of them and left us to heal our own sick and wounded. If ever he's captured, that alone will earn him a death sentence. Surely we should be prepared to assist him simply for that service?"

"If we were to offer every damned Ivan German citizenship because he has collaborated with us, we'd never hear the end of it. And where would the purity of the German race be then, eh? Eh? Not that I believe in that nonsense myself. But the Leader does."

"Sir, he's offering us a lot more than just collaboration. He's willing to furnish us with the means of proving to the world what manner of opponent we're fighting. Isn't that worth some sort of reward? And surely that's what we're already offering any man who joins General Vlasov's Russian Liberation Army. It's written in this Smolensk Proclamation that our planes have been dropping on Soviet positions that if they come over to us, we'll put them in German uniforms and give them a better life."

"I tell you straight, Captain Gunther, the Leader doesn't like these Zeppelin volunteers. He doesn't trust them. Doesn't trust any damned Slavs. Take this General Vlasov—the Leader doesn't care for him at all. I tell you now, his damned Russian Liberation Army is an idea that will never get off the ground. They can drop all the leaflets they like on Soviet positions but his Smolensk Proclamation is a dead fucking goose. I happen to know that the Leader believes he will need someone as strong and ruthless as Stalin to keep control of Greater Germany in the Urals. The last thing he wants is this Vlasov trying to overthrow him." Von Kluge shook his head. "They're a shifty lot these Ivans, Gunther. You watch out for this doctor, that's my advice."

"And what about you, sir?"

"How do you mean?"

"Your man, Alok Dyakov. He's a Slav. Do you trust him?"

"Of course I trust him. And why not? I saved his life. The man is completely loyal to me. He's proved that again and again."

"And what are you planning to do with him when all of this is over? Will you leave him here? Or take him with you?"

"My affairs are none of your business, Gunther. Don't be so damned impertinent."

"You're absolutely right. I apologize. Your affairs are none of my business. But, sir, if you'll only think about this for a moment. From what he's already told me, Dr. Batov has good reason to hate the Bolsheviks and, more especially, the NKVD. They murdered his wife. Consequently, I'm convinced that he's every bit as keen to serve Germany as your man Dyakov. Or Peshkov."

"Who the hell is Peshkov?"

"The Group translator, sir. But Dr. Batov is every bit as keen on serving Germany as him or Alok Dyakov."

"It certainly doesn't sound like it. By your own account, this doctor seems keener on saving his own skin than serving Germany. But I will take the matter under consideration, Captain, and give you my answer later, after I've returned from hunting."

"Thank you, sir." As I got up to leave, the dog left off licking his balls and looked up at me expectantly, as if hoping I might suggest another more interesting activity. Not that I could ever have suggested anything that made more sense; not in Smolensk. "Are you hunting wolves?" I asked. "Or something else?"

For a moment I was tempted to ask if he was hunting Poles, but it was plain I'd aggravated the field marshal quite enough already.

"Yes, wolves. Wonderful creatures. Dyakov seems to have an instinctive understanding of how they think. Do you hunt yourself, Captain Gunther?"

"No."

"Waste of a life. A man should hunt. Especially in this part of the world. We used to hunt wolves in East Prussia when I was a boy. So did the Kaiser, you know. He's a tricky customer to hunt—the wolf. Even trickier than wild boar, let me tell you. Very elusive and cunning. We hunted a lot of wild boar when first we were in this neck of the woods. But they're all gone, I think."

I went outside the field marshal's bungalow and quickly pulled on my coat. The air wasn't as dry as it had been the day before, and the moisture in it seemed to confirm what von Kluge had told me; and not just moisture—the sound of a woodpecker's beak against the trunk of a tree carried through the surrounding forest like distant machine-gun fire; it felt like the thaw was finally on the way.

A car was waiting in front of the veranda steps and beside it stood Dyakov with two hunting rifles slung over his shoulders, smoking a pipe. He nodded to me and bared his big white teeth in what passed for a smile. There was indeed something wolf-like about him, but he wasn't the only one who was equipped with blue eyes and an instinctive understanding of how wolves think; I had a few cunning ideas myself, and I certainly wasn't about to place Dr. Batov's future exclusively in the delicate hands of Günther von Kluge. Too much was now at stake to trust that the field marshal would grant the Russian's wish; it was plain to me that I was going to have to send a teletype to the Ministry of Propaganda in Berlin as soon as possible—that if, because of some prejudice about Slavs, the field marshal wasn't prepared to give Batov what he wanted in return for what we wanted, then I would have to go over von Kluge's head and persuade Dr. Goebbels to do it instead.

I set off for the castle in the Tatra. Out of the gate, I turned left; I hadn't driven very far when I saw Peshkov walking in the same direction. I considered just driving on but it was hard to ignore a man who had gone out of his way to look like Adolf Hitler—perhaps that was the thinking behind the mustache and the longish, forward-combed hair; and besides, it was obvious he was also headed for the castle.

"Want a lift?" I asked, drawing up beside him on the empty road.

"You're very kind, sir." He loosened the length of rope around his waist that held his coat together and climbed into the passenger seat. "It's not everyone who would stop to pick up a Russian. Especially on a road as quiet as this one."

"Maybe it's because you don't look particularly Russian." I slammed the car in gear and drove on.

"You mean my mustache, don't you? And my hair."

"I most certainly do."

"I've had this mustache for many years," he explained. "Well before the Germans invaded Russia. It's not such an unusual style in Russia. Genrikh Yagoda, who was chief of the secret police until 1936, had the very same mustache."

"What happened to him?"

"He was demoted from the directorship of the NKVD in 1936, arrested in 1937, and became one of the defendants at the last great show trial—the so-called Trial of the Twenty-One. He was found guilty, of course, and shot in 1938. For being a German spy."

"Maybe it was the mustache."

"Perhaps, sir." Peshkov shrugged. "Yes, that's certainly possible."

"That was a joke," I said.

"Yes, sir. I know it was."

"Well, I expect his successor will meet a similar fate one day."

"He already has, sir. Nikolai Yezhov was also a German spy. He disappeared in 1940. It's assumed he, too, was shot. Lavrentiy Beria is the new head of the NKVD. It's Beria who masterminded the deaths of all these poor Polish officers. With Stalin's approval, of course."

"You seem to know a lot about this subject, Peshkov."

"I have given a statement concerning what I know about these deaths to your Judge Conrad, sir. I should certainly be willing to talk to you further about this matter. But it's true, while my own subject is electrical engineering, sir, I have always been rather more interested in politics and current affairs."

"Not a very healthy interest to have in Russia."

"No, sir. Not every country is as lucky with its system of government as Germany."

I left that one unanswered as we arrived at the castle. Peshkov thanked me profusely for the ride and then went to the adjutant's hut, leaving me wondering how it was that an electrical engineer knew so much about the history of Russia's most secret organization.

WITH THE LONG-HANDLE SPADE from the hood of the Tatra I scraped at a spot near the birch cross where the first human bones had been found; the ground shifted under the point of the metal and black Russian earth darkened the furrow I'd made in the melting snow. I threw down the spade and burrowed my fingertips into the soil like a farmer eager to sow some seed.

"I thought it was you," said a voice behind me.

I stood up and looked around. It was Colonel von Gersdorff.

"I was surprised to hear that you were back in Smolensk," said von Gersdorff. "I seem to remember you telling me in Berlin that you never wanted to come back here."

"I never did. But Joey the Crip thought I was in need of a vacation, so he sent me down here to get away from it all."

"Yes. That's what I heard. It certainly beats a holiday on Rügen Island."

"And you?" I asked him. "What brings you out here to the castle? If I seem a little nervous about talking to you, I'm just worried you might have another bomb in your coat pocket."

Von Gersdorff grinned. "Oh, I'm here a lot. The Abwehr likes a report on what happens in Smolensk sent to the Tirpitzufer every day. Only, I don't like to do it up at Krasny Bor. Not any longer. You never know who's listening. Place is crawling with Ivans."

"Yes, I know, I was just talking to Peshkov. And before that, to Dyakov."

"Shifty characters both, in my opinion. I keep raising the matter of the sheer number of Ivans who are working for us inside the perimeter of the safe zone we've established at Krasny Bor, but von Kluge won't hear of any changes to these arrangements. He's a man who's always had lots of servants, and since most of those who were German servants are now in the army, that means having Russians on the staff. When we first came out here, he brought his butler from Poland, but the poor bastard was killed by a partisan sniper not long after he got here. So now he makes do with his *Putzer*, Dyakov. But as it happens, it's not the Russians von Kluge is suspicious of, it's other Germans. In particular the Gestapo. And although I hate to say it, that does make things extra difficult when it comes to maintaining tight security at Krasny Bor. Even the Gestapo has its uses.

"We've tried to have the Gestapo run checks on the backgrounds of some of these Russians but it's more or less impossible. Most of the time we have to go on the local mayor's word that such and such a person is trustworthy, which is hopeless, of course. So I prefer to do my encoding and decoding down here at the castle. Colonel Ahrens is a decent fellow. He gives me the exclusive use of a room here so I can send my stuff in private. I'd just come out of the castle when I saw you trailing up here with the spade in your hand."

"The ground is softening."

"So, we can start digging. Tomorrow, perhaps."

"I never was much for waiting on tomorrow," I said. "Not when I can make a start today."

I took off my coat and my jacket and handed them to him. "D'you mind?"

"My dear fellow, not at all." Von Gersdorff folded them over his arm and lit a cigarette. "I love to watch another man work."

I rolled up my sleeves, collected the shovel off the ground, and started to dig.

"So why is von Kluge suspicious of Germans?" I asked him.

"He's scared, I suppose."

"Of what?"

"Do you remember a military court official called von Dohnanyi?"

"Yes, I met him in Berlin. He's Abwehr, too, isn't he?"

Von Gersdorff nodded. "He's the deputy head of the Abwehr's central section under Major General Oster. A few weeks ago—just before the Leader visited von Kluge at Group headquarters—von Dohnanyi came down here to meet with von Kluge and General von Tresckow."

"I was on the same plane as him," I said, stabbing at the ground with the spade.

"I didn't know that. Von Dohnanyi is back in Berlin now, but he was here in Smolensk to add his voice to my own and the general's and to those of some other officers who would like to see Hitler dead."

"Let me guess: von Schlabrendorff and von Boeselager."

"Yes, how did you know?"

I shook my head and carried on digging. "A lucky guess, that's all. Go on with your story."

"We asked the field marshal to join us in a plan to assassinate Hitler and Himmler when they came down here on the thirteenth. The idea was that we would all of us draw our pistols and shoot them both dead in the officers' mess at Krasny Bor. Something like that is a lot easier here than it would be at Rastenburg. At the Wolf's Lair, he's more or less untouchable. Officers have to give up their pistols before they can be in a room with Hitler. Which is why he remains there so much, of course. Hitler's not stupid. He knows there are plenty of people in Germany who would like to see him dead. Anyway, von Kluge agreed to join the conspiracy, but when Himmler didn't show up with Hitler, he changed his mind."

"I really can't fault the field marshal's logic," I said. "You know, if someone does kill the Leader, they'd better make sure to shoot Himmler and the rest of the gang. When you decapitate a snake, the body keeps on writhing and the head remains deadly for quite a while afterward."

"Yes, you're right."

"I have to hand it to you people. Three attempts to kill Hitler in as many weeks and all of them botched. You would think that a group of senior army officers would know how to kill one man. It's what you're supposed to be good at, damn it. None of you seemed to have any trouble slaughtering millions during the Great War. But it seems beyond any of you to kill Hitler. Next thing you'll be telling me you were planning to use silver bullets to shoot the bastard."

For a moment von Gersdorff looked embarrassed.

"And let me guess—now von Kluge is scared that someone will talk," I said. "Is that it?"

"Yes. There's a rumor going around Berlin that Hans von Dohnanyi is going to be arrested. If he is, then of course the Gestapo may find out a lot more than even they were expecting."

"What kind of a rumor?"

"How do you mean?"

"Generally speaking, the Gestapo likes to keep who they're planning to arrest under their black hats—at least until the small hours of the morning when they call. You know—it stops people from escaping and that kind of thing. If there is a rumor, it could mean they started it because they want him to run and maybe flush out another rabbit they're interested in pursuing. That kind of rumor—a rumor with foundation. Yes, they're not above doing that from time to time. Or it could just be the kind of rumor that's spread by a man's enemies to make him feel insecure and undermine him at work. It's what the English call 'a Roman holiday,' when a gladiator was butchered for the pleasure of others. You'd be surprised at the damage a rumor like that can do to a man. It takes nerves of steel to withstand the Berlin gossipmongers."

"As a matter of fact, Captain Gunther, it was you who started this rumor."

"Me?" I stopped digging for a moment. "What the hell are you talking about, Colonel? I never started any rumor."

"Apparently, when you met von Dohnanyi in Judge Goldsche's office in Berlin three weeks ago, you mentioned that the Gestapo had been to see you—I believe it was while you were in the hospital—to ask you questions about some Jew you knew called Meyer—who his friends were, that kind of thing."

I frowned, remembering the air raid by the RAF on the night of the first of March that had almost killed me.

"That's right. Franz Meyer was going to be a witness in a war crimes investigation. Until the RAF dropped a bomb on his apartment and took half of his head off. The Gestapo seemed to think Meyer might have been mixed up in some sort of currency smuggling racket in order to help persuade the Swiss to offer asylum to a group of Jews. But I don't see—"

"Did the Gestapo mention someone called Pastor Dietrich Bonhoeffer?"

"Yes."

"It was Pastor Bonhoeffer and Hans von Dohnanyi who were smuggling foreign currency to bribe the Swiss to take refugee Jews from Germany."

"I see."

"And it was that meeting between von Dohnanyi and Judge Goldsche at the War Crimes Bureau that prompted him to help lend his weight to persuading von Kluge that a group of like-minded army officers—"

"By which you mean Prussian aristocrats, of course."

Von Gersdorff was silent for a moment. "Yes, I suppose you're right. Is that why you think we bungled it? Because we're aristocrats?"

I shrugged. "It crossed my mind."

I spat on my hands and started digging again. It was hard work but the ground came away on the flat of my spade in heavy, half-frozen lumps that I hoped would turn out to be layers of peaty history. Von Gersdorff kicked carelessly at one near the toe of his boot and watched it roll slowly down the slope like a very muddy football. For all either of us knew, it might have been a mud-encrusted skull.

"If you think it was snobbery that kept the plot within a small circle of aristocrats, you're wrong," he said. "It was simply the over-riding need for total secrecy."

"Yes, I can see how that was an advantage. And you felt more comfortable placing your trust in a man with a *von* in his name, is that it?"

"Something like that."

"That doesn't sound a little like snobbery?"

"Perhaps it does at that," admitted von Gersdorff. "Look, trust is something that's very hard to find these days. You find it where you can."

"Talking of snobbery," I said, "I spent the morning trying to per-suade the field marshal to sign some papers that would allow a local Russian doctor to go and live in Berlin. He works at the Smolensk State Medical Academy and he claims to have documentary evidence of who's buried here. Ledgers, photographs—he's even got an Ivan hidden in a private room who was part of the NKVD murder squad that carried out this atrocity. Bit of a soft pear, alas, after some sig-nificant roof damage—but the doctor is straight out of the prayer book: every wish comes true if he gives us what we want. But he won't do it if he has to stay on in Smolensk. I can't think of a more deserving case for a homeland pass, but Clever Hans seems to have his blue eyes dead set against it. I just don't understand. I thought if anyone would be on his side about this it would be a man with a Rus-sian servant. But the field marshal seems to think Dyakov is an ex-ception and that Slavs are not much better than farmyard animals."

"It's the Poles he really hates."

"Yes. He told me. But Poles aren't Russians. That's rather the point of who and what's buried here, I imagine."

"In von Kluge's eyes—Polacks, Ivans, Popovs, they're all the same."

"Which seems to be the exact opposite of the way the Russians think—about the Polacks, I mean. As far as they're concerned, Polacks and Germans are virtually the same thing."

"I know. But that's just how this story is. It doesn't make your job any easier, but I doubt von Kluge is going to grant a homeland pass to anyone, with the possible exception of Dyakov."

"So what's the story with Dyakov?"

Von Gersdorff shrugged. "The field marshal has only the one hunting dog. I suppose he felt there was no reason why he couldn't have another."

"I never did like dogs much, myself. Never even owned one. Still, from what I gather, it's relatively easy to know all about a dog. You just buy them when they're puppies and throw them a bone now and then. But with a man—even a Russian—I imagine it's maybe a little more complicated than that."

"Lieutenant Voss of the field police is the man to speak to about Dyakov. If you're interested in him. Are you interested in him?"

"It's only that the field marshal recommended I speak to von Schlabrendorff and Dyakov about drafting in some HIWI labor to dig up this whole damned wood. I like to know who I'm working with."

"Von Schlabrendorff is a good man. Did you know that he's—?"

"Yes, I know. His mother's the great-great-granddaughter of Wilhelm the First, the Elector of Hesse, which means that he's related to the present king of Great Britain. That kind of pedigree should come in very useful when it comes to exhuming several thousand bodies."

"Actually, I was about to tell you that he's my cousin." Von Gersdorff smiled with good grace. "But I certainly think you can trust Dyakov to find a few Ivans to do the digging."

I stopped digging for a moment and leaned forward to take a closer look before scraping at what looked to be a human skull and the back of a man's coat.

"Is that what I think it is?" asked von Gersdorff. He turned and waved one of the sentries over.

The man arrived at the double, came to attention, and saluted.

"Fetch some water," von Gersdorff ordered. "And a brush."

"What sort of brush, sir?"

"A hand brush," I said. "From a dustpan, if you can find one."

"Yes, sir." The soldier went away at the double in the direction of the castle.

Meanwhile, I kept on scraping at the half-covered cadaver with the point of my spade, finally revealing two twisted hands bound tight together with a length of wire. I'd never seen anyone who'd been run over and flattened by a tank, but if I had I supposed that this is what it would have looked like. In the Great War I'd stumbled across the bodies of men buried in the mud of Flanders but somehow this felt very different. Perhaps it was the certainty that there were so many other bodies buried there; or perhaps it was the wire wound around the almost skeletal wrists of the corpse that left me lost for words. There are no good deaths, but perhaps some are better than others. There are even deaths—execution by firing squad, for example—that seem to give the victim a little bit of dignity; the man lying facedown in the dirt of Katyn Wood had certainly died a death that was a long way from that. A more wretched sight would have been hard to imagine.

Von Gersdorff was already crossing himself solemnly.

The soldier arrived back with a brush and a canteen of water. He handed them to me, and I started brushing the mud away from the skull before washing it with the water to reveal a small hole in the back of the skull, and then probing it with my forefinger. Von Gersdorff squatted down beside me and touched the perfect bullet hole experimentally.

"A standard NKVD *vyshka*," he remarked. "A nine-gram airmail from Stalin."

"You speak Russian?"

"I'm an intelligence officer. It's sort of expected." He stood up and nodded. "I also have French, English, and some Polish."

"How does that come about?" I asked. "You speaking Polish?"

"I was born in Silesia. In Lubin. You know, if it hadn't been for Frederick the Great bringing Lubin back into Prussia in 1742, I might well have been one of the Polish officers lying in this mass grave."

"There's an amusing thought."

"Well, it looks like you've found what everyone has been looking for, Gunther."

"Not me," I said.

"How's that?"

"Maybe I didn't make myself clear," I said. "I'm not really here. Those are my orders. The SD and the Ministry of Propaganda are supposed to be a hundred kilometers from this site. Which is why I'm wearing an army uniform instead of an SD one."

"Yes, I was wondering about that."

"Even so, that might not stand close inspection. So I haven't found anything. I think the report had better state that you found this body. All right?"

"All right. If that's what you want."

"Who knows?" I said. "You might need to make yourself popular with all the people you let down when you didn't blow yourself up at the Arsenal."

"When you put it like that, it's a wonder I can look myself in the eye every morning."

"I wouldn't know about that. It's a long time since I so much as glanced at a mirror."

WITH ITS CHINTZ-CURTAINED WINDOW, oak farmhouse chairs, open fireplace, and framed watercolors of Berlin's historic sites, the signals office was as neat as an old maid's parlor. Underneath a shelf full of books and steel helmets there was a large table where plaintext messages could be written out on sheets of lined yellow paper. On this was a clean white tablecloth, a vase of dried flowers, a samovar full of hot Russian tea, and a polished onyx ashtray. Ranged along the wall were a twenty-four-line switchboard, a five-watt Hagenuk transceiver, a big Magnetophon reel-to-reel tape recorder, a Siemens sheet-writer teletype machine, and an Enigma rotor cipher machine with a Schreibmax printer attachment that could print all the letters of the alphabet onto a narrow paper ribbon, which meant the signal officer operating the Enigma didn't have to see the decrypted plaintext information.

The under-officer in charge of the signals room was an open-faced young man with reddish hair and amber-framed spectacles; his hands were delicate and his touch on the massive Torn's transmitting key was—according to Colonel Ahrens—as sure as a concert pianist's. His name was Martin Quidde, and he was assisted by an even younger-looking radio master recently arrived from the signals kindergarten in Lubeck, who had a nervously twitching thigh that looked as if it was permanently receiving a telegraph transmission from home. The pair of them regarded me with watchful respect, as though I were a chunk of raw pitchblende.

"Relax, boys," I said. "I'm not in an SD uniform now."

Quidde shrugged, as if such a thing hardly mattered to him, and he was right, of course, it didn't, not in Nazi Germany, where a uniform was a guarantee only that a man was afflicted with duties and superiors, and everyone—from some squirt in a pair of leather shorts to an old lady in a housecoat—could prove to be the Gestapo informer who revealed some careless word or patriotic shortcoming that put you in a concentration camp.

"I'm not Gestapo and I'm not Abwehr. I'm just a prick from Berlin who's here to do some amateur archaeology."

"Are there really four thousand Poles buried in our front garden, sir?" Quidde was quoting the figure I had included in my telemessage to Goebbels.

"That's what it said on my message to the ministry, didn't it?"

"Do you reckon they murdered them out there?"

"That's certainly what it looks like," I said. "Brought them to the side of an open grave in twos and threes and shot them in the back of the head."

The younger signaler, whose name was Lutz and who was manning the switchboard, answered a call only he heard and began to shift the cables in the switchboard around like so many chess pieces.

"General von Tresckow," he said into his headset. "I have General Goerdeler for you, sir."

"Makes you think what we're fighting, eh, sir?" said Quidde.

"Yes, it certainly does," I said. "We certainly can't teach Ivan anything about cruelty, murder, and deceit."

"You know, I've often had a peculiar feeling that something was not quite right about this place," said Quidde.

"I get that feeling back in Berlin, sometimes," I said, being deliberately ambiguous again; it was up to Quidde what he chose to hear. "When I'm visiting friends who live near the old Reichstag. I don't believe in ghosts myself, but it's easy to understand why so many others do."

Lutz started to deal with another call on the switchboard.

I offered Quidde a cigarette to try to fool him into thinking I was an all-around decent guy. He didn't expect a white rabbit, of course, but for a couple of free cigarettes he seemed prepared to pretend that my black hat might just be empty; it's why people like me smoke, I guess. In return he served me some hot Russian tea in a little glass with a lump of real sugar, and while I waited to receive confirmation that the ministry had received my message in full, Quidde asked me if any progress had been made in identifying the murderer of his two fellow signalers, Sergeant Ribe and Corporal Greiss.

I shook my head. "I appreciate that those men were comrades of yours, Corporal," I told Quidde. "But really, I'm the wrong man to ask about it. I'm not the investigating officer. It's Lieutenant Voss of the field police who's working that case. You should ask him, or the colonel, of course."

"Maybe so, sir," said Quidde. "But with all due respect to Lieutenant Voss, sir, he's not a detective, is he? He's just the local kennel hound. And as for the colonel, well, all he really cares about are his bloody bees. Look, sir, everyone here at the castle knows that before you were in the SD you used to be a top bull at the Alex."

"Not even a top donkey, Corporal." I grinned. "Thanks, but they gelded all the best cops back in thirty-three."

"And everyone knows it was Voss and the colonel who asked you to go down to the Hotel Glinka to take a look at the crime scene. The word is that it was you who figured it wasn't an Ivan that killed them—who chalked out another Fritz for it. And now everyone figures you're still interested in finding out who killed them on account of how it was you that was trying to get that rapist bastard they hanged last Saturday to give up what he knew about the murders."

"Colonel Ahrens," said Lutz, "I have Lieutenant Hodt for you, sir."

I shrugged and sipped my sweet tea before lighting one up for myself—one of the several handfuls of Trummers and a bottle of cognac I had stolen from Joey's private plane on the flight down from Berlin; the cognac was long gone but the cigarettes were lasting nicely. I breathed the biscuity-smelling smoke deep into the walls of my chest, and as I paused to wait for my head to clear, I pondered how to answer the corporal's perfectly reasonable arguments. He was right, of course: in spite of von Kluge's fairly explicit order to forget all about the case of the two dead signalers, I was still very much interested in finding out who killed them. It takes a lot to shoo me away from a real crime; others—one or two of them even more powerful than Field Marshal von Kluge—had tried to warn me off something before and it didn't take then, either. We Germans have a great capacity for ignoring other people and what they tell us; it's what makes us so damned German. It's always been like that, I guess. Rome tells Martin Luther to lay off and does he lay off?—does he hell. Beethoven goes deaf and, in spite of what his doctors advise, he carries on writing music; well, who needs ears to listen to a whole symphony? And if a mere field marshal stands in the way of your investigation's progress, then you simply go over his head, to the minister of Propaganda. Von Kluge was going to love me when he discovered what I'd done. And my continuing interest in the murders of Ribe and Greiss would be of small consequence beside the greater irritation that would be afforded to him when Joey the Crip pulled rank over Clever Hans and told him that Dr. Batov was to be allowed to come to Berlin after all—because I had no doubt the minister *would* agree to it. One thing you could say in defense of Joseph Goebbels was that he always knew a good thing when he saw it.

"Some people don't mind loose ends," I said. "But me, I always like to make the ends meet and sometimes tie a nice bow with them. I was in the trenches during the last war, Corporal Quidde. It bothered me then when men got killed for no good reason, and it bothers me now. Look, I tried my best. But it was no damned good. The fellow wouldn't talk. Always assuming, that is, he really did know something about what happened. I wouldn't have put it past Hermichen to have strung me along, just for the sheer joy of it. Maybe he was playing for time. Murderers are like that, sometimes. If we believed everything they told us, the prisons would be empty and the guillotines would rust over."

Quidde was spared from having to answer; he pressed a hand to his headphones as the Torn woke from its sleep like the robot in *Metropolis.*

"I think this must be your acknowledgment from Berlin, sir," he said, and picking up a pencil, he began to write.

When he had finished he handed the message to me and waited patiently while I read it.

YOUR MESSAGE ACKNOWLEDGED. MINISTRY OF PUBLIC EN-
LIGHTENMENT AND PROPAGANDA. AWAIT FURTHER ORDERS.

Underneath that message was another:

BE CAREFUL WHAT YOU SAY. LUTZ IS GESTAPO. THEY RE-
CRUITED HIM WHILE HE WAS STILL AT SIGNALS SCHOOL IN LU-
BECK. DON'T WANT TO SAY ANYTHING IN FRONT OF HIM. I
HAVE INFORMATION ABOUT RIBE AND GREISS THAT MIGHT
HAVE A BEARING ON THEIR DEATHS BUT I AM WORRIED THIS
COULD GET ME KILLED. MEET ME IN THE GLINKA GARDEN ON
WEDNESDAY AFTERNOON AT FOUR P.M. AND COME ALONE.
NOD IF YOU AGREE.

I nodded. "Yes, that's fine," I said, and put the folded-up message in my pocket.

4

WEDNESDAY, MARCH 31, 1943

Goldsche had appointed Judge Conrad to be in overall charge of the Katyn Wood investigation for the bureau. Conrad was a senior judge from Lomitz, near Wittenberg, and while he could be a little gruff, I liked him. In his early fifties, Conrad had served with distinction in the Great War; after a stint as a public prosecutor in Hildesheim, he had joined the Army Justice Service in 1931 and had been a lawyer in the army ever since. Like most of the judges in the War Crimes Bureau, Johannes Conrad was no Nazi, and so neither of us felt comfortable at the idea of working closely with Army Group Center's own advisory coroner, Dr. Gerhard Buhtz, whom von Kluge had succeeded in imposing on the bureau's bosses as the man in charge of the forensic part of the investigation.

On the face of it, Buhtz, a former professor of forensic medicine and criminal law from Breslau University and an expert on ballistics, was extremely well qualified, but he certainly wouldn't have been my choice or Conrad's for such a politically sensitive role since, prior to his appointment in August 1941 as the coroner of Army Group Center, Gerhard Buhtz had been a colonel in the SS and an early member of the Nazi Party. Buhtz had also been the head of the SD in Jena, and Conrad argued that his being part of our investigation was a not-so-subtle attempt by von Kluge to undermine it from the very outset.

"Buhtz is a fanatical Nazi," Conrad told me on our way to a clearing in Katyn Wood where a meeting had been arranged with Buhtz, Ludwig Voss, and Alok Dyakov. "If any of that bastard's history gets out when the international commission is here, it will fuck everything up."

"What sort of history?" I asked.

"While he was in Jena, Buhtz was in charge of carrying out autopsies on prisoners who were shot while trying to escape from Buchenwald KZ. You can imagine what that meant, and what Buhtz's death certificates were worth in terms of honesty. And then there was some scandal involving the Buchenwald camp doctor. Fellow named Werner Kircher, who's now the chief physician with the RSHA in Berlin."

"Isn't he the deputy director of the forensic pathology unit?"

"That's right. He is."

"I thought I knew the name. So what was the scandal?"

"Apparently Buhtz persuaded Kircher to let him remove the head of a young SS corporal who had been murdered by some prisoners."

"He actually cut the head off?"

"Yes, so that he could study it in the lab. Turns out he had quite a collection. God only knows what they did to the prisoners. Anyway, Himmler found out about it and went crazy that an SS man should be treated with such disrespect. Buhtz got kicked out of the SS, which is why he went first to Breslau and then to Army Group Center. The man is a barbarian. If the commission or any of these reporters picks up on the fact that Buhtz was at Buchenwald, it will make us all look bad. I mean, what price the German search for truth and justice in Katyn when our leading pathologist is little better than a mad scientist?"

"It would be just like von Kluge to hope that something like that would put a stick in our spokes."

For a moment I thought of the two dead signalers near the Hotel

Glinka and how their heads had been almost completely severed by someone—a German—who clearly knew what he was doing. And I wondered about Buhtz again as he arrived on a BMW motorcycle.

I went down to greet him and watched him climb off the machine and remove his leather helmet and goggles. Then I introduced myself; I even held his leather coat while he found his glasses and his Wehrmacht officer's cap.

"My compliments, it's a brave man who rides a motorcycle on these roads," I said.

"Not really," said Buhtz. "Not if you know what you're doing. And I like my independence. There is so much time wasted in this theater just waiting for a driver from the car pool."

"You have a point."

"Besides, at this time of year the air is so fresh that one feels alive on a motorcycle in a way one never could in the back of a car."

"There's plenty of fresh air in my car," I said. "Of course, not having any windows helps with that." I looked at the motorcycle more closely: it was an R75, also known as the "Type Russia," and could cope with a wide variety of terrain. "But can you really carry all your stuff on this?"

"Of course," said Buhtz, and, throwing open one of the leather panniers, he took out a full anatomist's dissection set and spread it out on the BMW's saddle. "I never travel without my magician's box of tricks. It would be like a plumber arriving without any tools."

One particular knife caught my eye. It was glitteringly sharp and as long as my forearm. It wasn't a bayonet but it looked just the thing to cut a man's throat back to the bone. "That's one hell of a blade," I said.

"That's my amputation knife," he said. "Pathology in the field is largely just tourism. You turn up, you see the sights, you take a few photographs, and then you go home. But I like to have a decent catlin about my person just in case I want a little souvenir." He chuckled grimly. "Some of these surgical knives, including that one, were my father's."

He rewrapped his tools and I handed him back his coat and led the way up to the birch cross, where the others were waiting for us. The snow was almost all melted and the ground felt softer. I swatted a fly away and reflected that winter really was behind us now, but with the Russians certain to mount a new offensive before very long, there were few Germans in Smolensk who could have looked upon the spring and summer of 1943 with any great optimism.

"I understand you think there may be as many as four thousand men buried in this wood," Buhtz said as we climbed the slope toward the waiting men.

"At least."

"And are we planning to exhume all of them?"

"I think we should exhume as many as we can in the time that's available to us before the Russians begin a new campaign," I said. "Who knows when that will start and what the outcome will be?"

"Then I shall have my work cut out for me," he said. "I shall need some assistants, of course. Doctors Lang, Miller, and Schmidt from Berlin, and Dr. Walter Specht, who's a chemist. Also, there's a former student of mine from Breslau I should like to send for: Dr. Kramsta."

"I BELIEVE THE REICH HEALTH LEADER in Berlin, Dr. Conti, has already put these matters in hand," I said.

"I sincerely hope so. But look, Leonard Conti is not always reliable. In fact, I should say that as the RSHA physician he's been nothing short of incompetent. A disaster. My advice to you, Captain Gunther, would be that you should keep the ministry on his tail to make sure everything that is supposed to happen does happen."

"Certainly, Professor. I'll do that. Now, let's meet the others and get started."

I walked him over to where Judge Conrad, Colonel Ahrens, Lieutenant Voss, Peshkov, and Alok Dyakov were waiting for us.

Buhtz was in his mid-forties, stout and powerful-looking, with a bowlegged way of walking—although that might have been the fact that he had just climbed off a large motorcycle. He already knew the other men, who returned his brisk "Heil Hitler" with a notable lack of enthusiasm; he shook his head in exasperation and then dropped down on his haunches to inspect the most recently discovered cadaver.

As Voss lit a cigarette, Buhtz looked at him irritably. "Please put that cigarette out, Lieutenant." And then to Judge Conrad: "That's really got to stop," he said. "Immediately."

"Oh, surely," said Conrad.

"Do you hear?" Buhtz said to Voss. "There's to be no smoking anywhere on this site from now on. I don't want this damned crime scene spoiled by so much as a soldier's spit or a boot print. Colonel Ahrens, any man caught smoking in this wood is to be put on charge, is that clear?"

"Yes, Professor," said Friedrich Ahrens. "I'll pass that on right away."

"Please do so."

Buhtz stood up and looked down the slope toward the road. "We're going to need some sort of hut or house here for the postmortem work," he said. "With trestle tables, the stronger the better. At least six, so work on several bodies can be carried out at once. Results will seem more significant if they are made simultaneously. Oh yes, and buckets, stretchers, aprons, rubber gloves, some sort of water supply so medical personnel can wash human material and themselves, and electric lighting, of course. Some police photographers, too. They'll need a good source of light, of course. Microscopes, petri dishes, slides, scalpels, and about fifty liters of formaldehyde."

Voss was making copious notes.

"Then I think we shall need a second hut for a field laboratory.

Also, I shall be providing you with details of procedures for identifying and marking the bodies, as well as for preserving the personal effects we find on them. From what I've seen so far, the bodies appear to have been covered in sand, the weight of which will have pressed them into one large sandwich. Not a very nice one, either. The chances are there's quite a foul soup down there. This whole site is going to smell worse than a dead dog's arse when we start the actual exhumations."

Colonel Ahrens groaned. "This used to be such a great place to have a billet. And now it's little better than a charnel house." He glanced angrily at me, almost as if he held me personally responsible for what had happened in Katyn Wood.

"Sorry about that, Colonel," said Conrad. "But it's now the most important crime scene in Europe. Isn't that right, Gunther?"

"Yes, sir."

"Which reminds me," said Buhtz. "Lieutenant Voss?"

"Sir."

"Your field police will need to organize a team of men to comb this whole area for more graves. I want to know where there are Polish graves, where there are Russian graves, and where there are . . . something else. If there's a fucking cat buried within a thousand meters of this spot, I want to know about it. This task requires accuracy and intelligence and, of course, scrupulous honesty, so it should be carried out by Germans, not Russians. As for the digging on the site itself, I understand Russian HIWIs are to be used. Which is fine as long as they can understand orders and work to direction."

"Alok Dyakov is organizing a special team of men," I said.

"Yes, sir." Dyakov snatched off his fur hat and bowed obsequiously to Professor Buhtz. "Every day Herr Peshkov and myself will be here in Katyn Wood to act as your foremen, sir. I have a team of forty men I've used before. You tell me what you want them to do, and we will make sure they do it. Isn't that right, Peshkov?"

Peshkov nodded. "Certainly," he said quietly.

"No problem," continued Dyakov. "I choose only good men. Good workers. Honest, too. I don't think you want men who help themselves to what they find in the dirt."

"Good point," agreed Buhtz. "Voss? You'd better organize a round-the-clock team of night watchmen. To protect this site from looters. It should be clear that anyone looting this site will suffer the severest penalty. And that includes German soldiers. Them most of all. A higher standard is expected of a German, I think."

"I'll organize some signage to that effect, sir," said Voss.

"Please do that. But more importantly, please organize the team of night watchmen."

"Sir," said Dyakov. "If I might make a small request? Perhaps the men digging here could receive some rewards. A small incentive, yes? Some extra rations. More food. Some vodka and cigarettes. On account of the fact that this will be very smelly, very unpleasant work. Not to mention all the mosquitoes there are in this wood in summer. Better that workers are happy than resentful, yes? In Soviet Union no workers are rewarded properly. They pretend to pay us and we pretend to work. But Germans are not like this. Workers are paid well in Germany, yes?"

I glanced at Conrad, who nodded. "I don't see why not," he said. "After all, we are not communists. Yes, I agree."

Buhtz nodded. "I shall also require the services of a local undertaker. Catafalques for the bodies that we exhume and dissect and eventually rebury. Good ones. Airtight, if possible. I feel obliged to remind you once again that the smell here in the wood is going to become very bad. And you make a good point about mosquitoes, Herr Dyakov. The insects are already quite irritating enough in this part of the world, but as the weather improves, these will become a severe hazard. Not to mention all the flies and maggots we will find on the cadavers. You will need to make provision for some sort of pesticide. DDT is the most recently synthesized and the best. But you can use Zyklon B if that's not readily available. I happen to know for

236

a fact that Zyklon B is in plentiful supply in parts of Poland and the Ukraine."

"Zyklon B," said Voss, continuing to write.

"In most cases, gentlemen, we shall attempt to remove bodies intact," said Buhtz. "However, in the meantime . . ."

He approached the corpse I had uncovered with a spade just forty-eight hours earlier and drew back the piece of sacking I had used to cover it up again.

"I propose to make an immediate start with this fellow."

He probed the bullet hole in the back of the skull with his forefinger for a moment.

"Judge Conrad," he said. "I wonder if you would be kind enough to make a contemporaneous note for me, while I make a preliminary examination of this cadaver's skull."

"Certainly, Professor," said Conrad, and, taking out pencil and paper, he prepared to write.

Buhtz dug around the skull with his fingers to make enough room to lift it clear of the earth it was lying in. He peered closely at the top and the front of the skull and then said, "Victim A appears to have suffered a bullet wound to the occipital bone, close to the opening of the lower part of the skull, consistent with his being shot, execution style, in the back of the head and at close range. There appears to be a point of exit in the forehead, which leads me to suppose that the bullet no longer remains within the skull cavity."

He unwrapped his bundle of surgical instruments on the ground and, selecting the large amputation knife I had seen earlier, he began to cut into the bones of the neck.

"However, by measuring the size of these holes we may be able to arrive at an early determination of the caliber of the weapon that was used to execute this man."

There was no hesitation in the way he used the knife, and I wondered if he could have removed the head of a living man with such skill and alacrity. When the head was completely severed, he lifted the skull and wrapped it carefully in the piece of sacking and laid it on the ground by the feet of Lieutenant Voss.

Meanwhile, I glanced at Judge Conrad, who caught my eye and nodded silently, as if the professor's actions here in Katyn Wood confirmed the curious story he had told me about the removal of the SS corporal's head in Buchenwald.

It was Dyakov's keen eyes that spotted the shell casing. It was lying on the ground in the spot that had been recently occupied by the dead Polish officer's skull. He dropped down on his haunches and rubbed in the dirt for a moment before coming up with the small object in his thick fingers.

"What's that you've found?" asked Buhtz.

"Sir, it looks like a shell casing," said Dyakov. "Perhaps the same shell that contained the very bullet that killed this poor Polish man."

Buhtz took the shell casing from Dyakov and held it up to the light. "Excellent," he said. "Well done, Dyakov. We're off to a flying start, I think. Thank you, gentlemen. If anyone needs me, I will be in my laboratory at Krasny Bor. With any luck, this time tomorrow we'll already be able to say what kind of weapon killed this fellow."

I had to admit that Buhtz was more impressive than I had been expecting. We watched him walk back down the slope to his motorcycle. He was carrying the skull under his arm and looked like a referee walking away from a game of soccer with the ball.

Conrad sneered after him. "What did I tell you?" he murmured.

"Oh, I don't know," I said, "he seemed to know what he was about."

"Maybe," Conrad said grudgingly. "Maybe he does. But he'll boil that head tonight and make a soup out of it. Just you see if I'm wrong."

Lieutenant Voss sniffed the air. "It smells bad already," he said.

"Plenty bad," agreed Dyakov. "And if we smell it, then so will the wolves. It might not just be the looters we have to worry about.

Maybe they'll come back for a free meal. It might even be dangerous. Believe me, you don't want to meet a pack of hungry wolves at night."

"Would a wolf really eat something that's been dead for this long?" asked Lieutenant Voss.

Dyakov grinned. "Sure. Why not? A wolf is not so particular if his meat is kosher or not. Filling his stomach with something—anything—is more important. Even if he throws most of it up, for sure something will stay down, you can guarantee it. Hey, Colonel, maybe you should increase the guard on the wood from tonight."

"Please don't tell me my duty, Dyakov," said Ahrens. "You might enjoy the field marshal's confidence, but you don't yet enjoy mine." With a face like a thundercloud, he walked down the slope just as we heard the sound of Buhtz's motorcycle start up and then roar away.

"What's up with Ahrens?" asked Judge Conrad. "The silly ass."

"He's all right," insisted Dyakov. "He just doesn't like it that this nice place is already starting to look and smell like a shit heap." He laughed a big vulgar laugh. "That's the trouble with you Germans. You have such sensitive noses. We Russians don't even notice it when things smell bad. Eh, Peshkov?" He elbowed the other man, who winced uncomfortably and then moved away.

"That's why we've got the same rotten government we've had since 1917," added Dyakov. "Because we have no sense of smell."

BACK IN THE SIGNALS ROOM AT DNIEPER CASTLE there was a message for me from Berlin. Martin Quidde had already gone off duty and it was his junior signaler, Lutz—the man who Quidde believed was working secretly in the 537th for the Gestapo—who handed me the yellow envelope. He knew what the message said, of course, because it was he who had decoded it, but I could see he was keen to ask me a question and because when I can I like to keep the Gestapo as close as possible, I offered him a Trummer from my little cigarette case and acted as if I was happy to talk for a while. But what I really wanted was to have someone in the Gestapo looking out for me, and sometimes, when you're looking for a man to cover your back, it's best to recruit the very person whose job it might be to put a knife in it.

"Thanks very much, sir," he said, puffing with obvious enthusiasm. "These are the best cigarettes I've tasted in a while."

"Don't mention it."

"Quidde says you're not in the army at all but in the SD."

"That should tell you something."

"It should?"

"It should tell you that you can trust me. That you can be frank with me."

Lutz nodded but it was plain I was going to have to let him have the run of the line for a while before I could land him at my feet.

"This is not something that would be true of everyone in the 537th," I said carefully. "Not everyone is committed to the Party the way you and I are, Lutz. In spite of all evidence to the contrary, loyalty—real loyalty—is a comparatively rare thing these days. People say 'Heil Hitler' with alacrity but for most of them it doesn't mean a damned thing."

"That's very true."

"It's just a figure of speech, a trope. Do you know what a trope is, Lutz?"

"I'm not sure I do, sir."

"It's a word or phrase that has almost become a cliché. It implies that for some people the words no longer mean anything very much, that the words have been turned away from their normal meaning. A lot of people say 'Heil Hitler' and make the salute merely as a way of ensuring that they don't get into trouble with the Gestapo. But Hitler doesn't mean much for these men, and certainly not what he means for you and me, Lutz. By which I mean SD men and Gestapo men. I'm right, aren't I? That you're with the Gestapo? No, you don't need to answer that. I know what I know. But what I don't yet know is if I can rely on you, Lutz. That I can count on you in a way I can count on no one else in this regiment. That I can talk to you in confidence, perhaps, and that you can speak to me in the same way. Do I make myself plain?"

"Yes, sir. You can count on me, sir."

"Good. Now tell me something, Lutz, did you know those two dead signalers well?"

"Yes, well enough."

"Were they good Nazis?"

"They were—" He hesitated. "They were good signalers, sir."

"That's not what I asked you."

Lutz hesitated again, but this time it was only for a moment. "No, sir. Neither of them could ever have been described as that, I think. In fact, I had already reported them to the Gestapo because I suspected them of being involved in some local black market."

I shrugged. "That's not uncommon with people who work in signals and in stores."

"I also reported them for certain remarks I considered to be disloyal. This was a couple of months ago. In February. Immediately after Stalingrad. What they said seemed especially disloyal after Stalingrad."

"You reported them to the Gestapo station at Gnezdovo, here in Smolensk?"

"Yes. To a Captain Hammerschmidt."

"And what did he do?"

"Nothing. Nothing at all." Lutz colored a little. "Ribe and Greiss weren't even questioned, and I asked myself why I had bothered. I mean, it's no small thing to denounce someone for treason, especially when it's a comrade."

"Is that what it was, do you think? Treason?"

"Oh yes. They were always making jokes about the leadership. I asked them to stop but they took no notice. If anything, it got worse.

When the Leader was here a few weeks ago, I suggested we go down to the road and watch out for his car as it drove past on the way to headquarters at Krasny Bor. They just laughed and proceeded to make more jokes about the Leader. Which made me really angry, sir. These were capital crimes, after all. I mean, here we are, in the midst of a war for our very survival, and these two bastards were undermining the nation's will to self-defense. Frankly, I'm not at all sorry they are dead, sir, if it means I no longer have to listen to that kind of crap."

"Do you remember any of these jokes?"

"Yes, sir. One. Only I'd rather not repeat it."

"Come now, Lutz. No one is going to assume that it was your joke."

"Very well, sir. It goes like this. A bishop is visiting a local church, and in the vestibule he notices three pictures hanging on the wall. There's one of Hitler and one of Göring and there's a picture of Jesus in the middle. The bishop questions the pastor of the church about this arrangement and the pastor tells the bishop that these three pictures help to remind him of what it says in the Bible—that Christ was nailed up between two criminals."

I smiled to myself. I'd heard many permutations of this joke before, but not for a while. Most people who made jokes about the Nazis were just letting off steam; but for me, it always felt like an act of political resistance.

"Yes, I can see why that would make anyone very angry," I told him. "Well, you did the right thing all the same. I imagine the Gestapo had more pressing matters to deal with ahead of the Leader's visit to Smolensk. I shall certainly make a point of seeking out this Captain Hammerschmidt and asking him why he didn't think to question these men."

Lutz nodded, but he hardly looked convinced by my explanation.

"However, the next time you hear something you think affects our morale or security here in Smolensk, it might be best if you spoke to me first."

"Yes, sir."

"Good."

"There is one thing I wanted to ask you, sir."

"Go ahead, Lutz."

"This Dr. Batov who the Ministry of Enlightenment have told you can come to live in Germany. Can that be right, sir? He's a Slav, isn't he? And Slavs are racially contaminated. I thought that the whole point of our drive toward the east is to expel these inferior races, not to assimilate them into German society."

"You're right, of course, but sometimes exceptions must be made, for the greater good. Dr. Batov is going to perform a very important propaganda service for Germany. A very important service that might help to change the course of this war. I don't exaggerate. As a matter of fact, I'm going to see him now, to tell him the good news. And for him to perform this service I was speaking of."

Once again Lutz hardly looked convinced by my arguments; I wasn't surprised; that's the trouble with dyed-in-the-wool Nazis—stupidity, ignorance, and prejudice always get in the way of them seeing the bigger picture. But for that, they might be impossible to deal with.

GLINKA PARK WAS A LANDSCAPED GARDEN with trees and stupid little paths just inside the southern wall of the Kremlin with the Luther Church and the town hall a stone's throw to the east. You could smell the circus and hear the complaints of some of the animals from its menagerie farther to the west; then again, that might just have been the effect of some town drunks who were making a horizontal party of it with some booze and a little campfire and some pet dogs on the Rathausstrasse side. In the center of the park was a large statue of

Glinka; around his size-fifty-six bronze shoes was a wrought iron fence that had been made to look like music paper with notes in positions that you just knew without being able to read music were probably from his most popular symphony. With the Nazis in charge of a large part of the country, it was hard to imagine a Soviet composer finding very much to write a symphony about; unless some modern maestro felt inspired to write a new overture to victory complete with real cannons and bells and a triumphant Russian army; and now that I'd thought about it, that wasn't hard to imagine at all: 1812 and the Grand Army's disastrous retreat from Moscow was beginning to seem much more contemporary than felt comfortable. I just hoped I wasn't going to be another frozen body lying in the snow on the long road back to Berlin.

I saw Martin Quidde before he caught sight of me; he was wandering around with a leather dispatch case in one hand and a cigarette in the other, looking like he didn't have a care in the world when in fact it wasn't like that at all; as soon as he saw me he looked one way and then the other like a cornered dog, as if wondering where to run.

"Was he a great composer, do you think?" I asked him. "Did he really deserve this? Or were they just short of a nice statue to put in this park whenever it was that some boyar locked the lid on his piano for good?" I checked Glinka's dates on the pedestal. "Eighteen fifty-seven. Seems like only yesterday. Back then Germany was just a twinkle in Bismarck's blue eye. If old Blood and Iron had known then what we know now, would he have done it, d'you think? Unified all the German states into one big happy family? I wonder."

Quidde hurried me away into the trees as though we were more likely to fall under suspicion if we remained near the statue. Several times he glanced anxiously back, almost as if he expected Glinka to climb down off the pedestal and come after us with a baton and a couple of bars of serious music in his hand.

"You know, I don't think Herr Glinka minds very much what I

say about him," I said. "Not as much as a lot of other people I can think of. But then, that's true of nearly everyone these days."

"You'll feel a lot less sanguine about things when I've told you what I know," he said.

I lit a cigarette and flicked the match onto the slush-covered ground. I was smoking too much again but then Russia does that to you. It was hard to pay much attention to your health after Stalingrad, knowing that so many Russians were hoping soon to kill you.

"Then maybe I just don't want to know," I said. "Maybe I should be more like Beethoven. It seems to me like he managed to do well enough when he didn't hear a damned thing. Going deaf is probably very good for your health in Germany. These days I get the impression that listening to what other people say can be lethal. Especially listening to our leaders."

"Don't I know it?" Quidde said bitterly. He removed his helmet and rubbed his head furiously.

"Now I begin to see and hear, and I think I might be looking at a man who maybe heard a lot more than just Midge Gillars on Radio Berlin."

"If Midge knew what I know, she'd play some very different tunes. Only this time they won't be the devil's."

"Still, those tunes are the good ones, right? I should know. I'm the apostle of cheap music. Just don't tell the fellow on the pedestal."

"Did you come alone?" he asked anxiously.

I shrugged. "I was thinking of bringing a couple of showgirls. But then again, you did ask me to come alone. Now, what's this all about?"

Quidde lit another cigarette unsteadily with the stub of the old one; this did nothing for his nerves; the smoke plumed from his twitching mouth and flaring nostrils like the puff from a runaway train.

"You'd better let some hydrogen out, Corporal, or you'll float away. Take it easy. Anyone would think you're nervous."

Quidde handed me the dispatch case.

"What's this?" I asked.

"A reel of recording tape," he said.

"What do I want with this? I don't even own a tape recorder. I wouldn't even know how to work one."

"That tape was made by Friedrich Ribe," said Quidde. "And it might just be what got him killed. Only two people knew what was on that tape. And one of them is dead."

"Ribe."

Quidde nodded.

"So how did your throat escape getting cut?"

"I've asked myself the same question. I think Ribe and Greiss were killed because they were on the same duty roster. Whoever killed them must have figured they both heard what in fact only Friedrich Ribe had heard. And me, of course. Ribe wouldn't ever have let Werner Greiss listen to what's on this tape. At the time we all thought it was Greiss who was the Gestapo's canary when in fact it was Jupp Lutz all along. I only found out myself a couple of weeks ago when a friend from Lubeck wrote and told me about it."

"But Ribe played it for you," I said.

Quidde nodded. "We were friends. Good friends. Looking out for each other since way back."

I glanced inside the dispatch case, which contained a box with the letters of the German Electricity Company—AEG—printed on it.

"All right. It's not the MDR Symphony Orchestra and it's not the lost chord. So what's on this tape?"

"You remember when the Leader came to Smolensk a few weeks ago?"

"I still treasure the memory."

"Hitler had a meeting with Clever Hans in his office at Krasny Bor. In private. It was real cozy, apparently—no aides, no adjutants, just the two of them. Only, the telephone in the office hasn't been working properly. It doesn't always hang up when you drop the receiver back in the cradle, with the result that the operator continues to hear everything that's said. Well, more or less everything."

"And so Ribe decided to tape-record it?"

"Yes."

"Jesus." I sighed. "What was he thinking?"

"He wanted a souvenir. Of Hitler's voice. You get used to hearing him making a speech, but no one ever hears what he's like when he's relaxed."

"A signed photograph would have been less dangerous."

"Yes. About halfway through the tape von Kluge guesses that he and Hitler could have been overheard because he lifts the receiver and then bangs it down hard several times before the line is terminated."

"And so, what—Hitler and von Kluge were worried that the army's plans for a summer campaign in 1943 were compromised? Yes, I can see why that might bother them a bit."

"Oh, it's worse than that," said Quidde.

I shook my head. I couldn't think of anything that was worse than giving away military secrets; then again, those were the days in which my ideas of what was worse and what was worst were limited by a naïve faith in the inherent decency of my fellow Germans. After almost twenty years in the Berlin police, I thought I knew all about corruption, but if you are not corrupt yourself, then I think you cannot ever know just how corrupt others can be in their pursuit of wealth and favor. I think then I must still have believed in things like honor and integrity and duty. Life had yet to teach me the hardest lesson of all, which is that in a corrupt world about the only thing you can rely on is corruption and then death and yet more corruption, and that honor and duty have little place in a world that has had a Hitler and a Stalin in it. And perhaps the most naïve thing about my reaction was that I was actually surprised at what Quidde told me next.

"On the tape you can clearly hear Adolf Hitler and Günther von Kluge talking for almost fifteen minutes. They talk about the new summer campaign but only in passing, before Hitler starts asking von Kluge about his family estates in Prussia, and it very soon becomes more apparent that Hitler is visiting headquarters in Smolensk largely because, in spite of his declared previous generosity to the field marshal, he has heard a few rumors back in Berlin that von Kluge is somewhat dissatisfied with his leadership. Von Kluge then proceeds to make a few weak denials and insists he is committed to the future of Germany and to defeating the Red Army, before Hitler comes to the real point of his being there. First of all, Hitler mentions a check for one million marks that the German Treasury had given von Kluge in October 1942 to help improve his estates. He mentions that he'd given a similar sum to Paul von Hindenburg in 1933. He also reminds von Kluge that he'd promised to help with any future costs of running these estates and to this end he has brought his own personal checkbook with him. What you then hear is Hitler writing out another check, and while the amount isn't actually mentioned on the recording, you can hear from what the field marshal says when the Leader hands it over that this time it's at least as much as a million marks again, perhaps even more. Either way, at the end of the recorded conversation von Kluge assures the Leader of his unswerving loyalty and insists that the rumors of his own dissatisfaction were much exaggerated by those in the High Command who were jealous of his relationship with Hitler."

For a moment I closed my eyes. Almost everything was now explained—why a German had murdered the two signalers; it seemed obvious to me that the reason they had been killed was to silence them both about the discovery of this huge bribe. Someone acting for Hitler, or for von Kluge or perhaps for both of them, had murdered the two signalers. It was also clear exactly why von Kluge had decided to withdraw from an Army Group Center plot to murder Hitler while he was in Smolensk; this would have had nothing to do with the absence of Heinrich Himmler in Smolensk and everything to do with a check for approximately one million marks.

No less clear than any of this, however, was the gut-liquefying certainty that Martin Quidde had now put me in the same grave danger as himself.

I rolled my eyes and lit a cigarette. For a second the wind caught the smoke and blew it in my eyes and made them water. I wiped them with the back of my hand and then contemplated using it to try to slap some sense into Corporal Quidde. Maybe it was too late for that; but I hoped not.

"Well, that's a hell of a story," I said.

"It's true. It's all on the tape."

"Oh, I don't doubt it. Nor do I doubt the fact that I may never sleep again. I like a scary story now and then. I even liked *Nosferatu* when it was in the cinema. But your little tale is too scary even for me. What the hell do you expect me to do with this, Corporal? I'm a cop, not fucking Lohengrin. And if I want to commit suicide, I'll take a nice little holiday in Solingen before I jump off the Müngsten Bridge."

"I thought, maybe, you might get a starting handle on the case," said Quidde. "Those men were murdered, after all. What's the point in having a war crimes bureau and a field police if you don't investigate real crimes?"

I handed back the dispatch case.

"Do you need me to draw you a Euler diagram? The Nazis are in charge of Germany. They kill people who get in their way. The bureau is just window dressing, Corporal. And the field police are there to handle the rank and file when they've been on the beer—even sometimes when they've raped and murdered a couple of Russian girls—but not this. Never this. What you've just told me is the best reason I've heard so far for me to drop the case altogether. And so, there is no case. Not anymore. Not as far as I'm concerned. In fact, I may never ask another awkward question in this freezing cold, fucked-up Ivan city again."

"Then I'll speak to someone else."

"There is no one else."

"Listen, two friends and comrades of mine were murdered in cold blood. Their throats were cut like farmyard animals. Whatever they did, there was no excuse for that. Friedrich Ribe made a mistake. He should have been subject to military discipline. Even a court-martial. But not cold-blooded murder. So, maybe I'll take this somewhere else."

"There is nowhere else, you idiot."

"To the High Command, in Berlin. To Reichsführer Himmler, perhaps. Think about it. This tape is the evidence that could finish Hitler. When people hear what kind of man is leading them, they won't want to be led by him. Yes, Himmler might be just the man."

"Himmler?" I laughed. "Don't you get it, birdbrain? No one is going to touch this thing with a barge pole. They'll sweep this shit into the nearest mouse hole and you with it. Not only will you be condemning yourself to a concentration camp, but very likely you'll also be exposing all sorts of other people to danger. Better men than you, perhaps. Suppose Himmler questions von Kluge. What then? Maybe von Kluge will think to save his skin by dropping someone else in the crap. Have you thought about that?"

I was thinking of von Gersdorff's aristocratic little group of conspirators.

"Then perhaps the underground movement will be interested in publishing this," said Quidde. "I heard about this group of people in Munich who've been publishing leaflets against the Nazis. Some students. Maybe they could do a leaflet with a transcript of this tape."

"For a man who was wise enough to be scared stiff about all this ten minutes ago you're showing a remarkably stupid lack of concern for your welfare now. The group of people you are talking about are already dead. They were arrested and executed in February."

"Who said I was scared stiff? And who said I care anything about my own welfare? Look, sir, I believe in the future of Germany. And Germany won't have any kind of future unless someone does something with this tape."

"I want a future for Germany just like you do, Corporal, but I promise you, this isn't the way to bring that about."

"We'll see about that," said Quidde. He replaced his helmet on his head and, tucking the dispatch case under his arm, started to walk away.

I took his arm. "No, that's not good enough," I said. "I want your word you'll keep your mouth shut about this. That you'll destroy that tape."

"Are you kidding?"

"No, I'm not. I'm perfectly serious, Corporal. This has gone way beyond a joke, I'm afraid. You're behaving like a fool. Look, if you'll only listen to me. Maybe there is someone who would listen to the tape. A colonel in the Abwehr I know, but honestly, I don't think it's going to make much difference in the short term."

Quidde sneered his contempt and snatched his arm away and then kept on walking, with me walking after him like a supplicant lover. "Then you're in the way, aren't you?" he said.

For a moment I thought about von Gersdorff and von Boeselager, Judge Goldsche and von Dohnanyi, General von Tresckow and Lieutenant von Schlabrendorff; they may have been effete, even incompetent, but they were about the only opposition there was to Hitler and his gang. As long as these aristocrats were free, there was every chance that they might make a successful attempt on the Leader's life. And if Himmler was presented with an excuse to interrogate Field Marshal von Kluge, there was always the equal possibility that he might give up von Gersdorff and the others just to get Himmler off his back.

And if von Gersdorff was arrested, who might he eventually give up? Me, perhaps?

"I mean it," I said. "I want your word that you'll keep silent, otherwise—otherwise I'll kill you myself. There's too much at stake here. You can't be allowed to risk the lives of some good men who have already tried to kill Hitler and who—God willing—may try to kill him again. That is, if they're allowed an opportunity."

"What men? I don't believe you, Gunther."

"Men better placed than you and me to stand a chance of doing it, too. Men who are in and out of the Wolf's Lair at Rastenburg, and the Wehrwolf HQ at Vinnitsa. Men from the High Command of the German Army."

"Fuck you," Quidde said, and turned his back on me. "And fuck them, too. If they were any good they'd have done it by now."

I shook my head in exasperation. There was an important decision to be made now and absolutely no time to think it through. That's how it is with a lot of crime. It's not that you mean to commit one, it's just that you've run out of viable options. One minute you've got some stupid young fool snarling his contempt and telling you to go and fuck yourself and threatening to compromise the only extant source of viable conspiracy against Adolf Hitler, and the next you've pressed a Walther automatic against the back of his thick head and pulled the trigger and the young fool has collapsed on the wet ground with blood spraying out of his helmet like a new oil well and you're already thinking how you can make his necessary but regrettable murder look like a suicide—so that maybe the Gestapo wouldn't hang another six innocent Russians in retaliation for the death of one German.

I glanced around the little park. The drunks were too soaked to notice or to care—it was hard to tell which. From his lofty stone pedestal Glinka had seen the whole damned thing, of course; and it was odd, but for the first time I realized that the way the sculptor had caught the composer, he appeared to be listening to something; it was clever: it almost looked as if Glinka had heard the shot. Quickly I made my own pistol safe and pocketed it; then I took Corporal

Quidde's own identical Walther. I worked the slide to put one in the breech and fired another shot into the ground close by before placing the automatically cocked pistol carefully in his hand. I felt very little for the dead man—it's difficult to feel sorry for a fool—but I did feel half a pang of regret that I'd been forced to kill one damned fool for the sake of several others.

Then I picked up the second empty bullet casing and the dispatch case with the incriminating tape—leaving it there was not an option—and walked quickly away, hoping that no one would hear the sound of my loudly beating heart.

Later on it occurred to me that I had shot—or to be more exact, executed—Martin Quidde in the same way as the NKVD had murdered all those Polish officers. It's fair to say that this gave me some cause for reflection. I also learned that the music on the fence around Glinka's feet was from his opera *A Life for the Tsar*. That's not a great title for an opera. But then *A Life for a Group of Posh Traitors* doesn't have much of a ring to it, either. And on the whole, I much prefer solving a murder to committing one.

AFTER WHAT HAD HAPPENED in Glinka Park I didn't feel much like going to see Dr. Batov. I'm peculiar like that. When I kill a man in cold blood it unsettles me a little and the good news I had to tell the doctor—that the ministry had approved his resettlement to Berlin—might have sounded rather less like good news than it ought to have done. Besides, I was half expecting Lieutenant Voss of the field police to come around to Krasny Bor and take me on in the role of a consulting detective just like before; that's certainly what I wanted to happen; the fact of the matter is, I was hoping to steer his simple mind away from any wild theories he might have had about murder. I wasn't back in my tiny little wooden bungalow for very long when, true to form, he came calling.

There was something mutt-like about Voss. That might just have been the brightly polished metallic gorget he wore on a chain around his thick neck to show that he was on duty—this was the reason why most Fritzes referred to the field police as kennel hounds or attack dogs—but Voss had such a lugubriously handsome face it would have been easy to have confused him with the real thing. His earlobes were as long as his leather coat and his big brown eyes contained so much yellow that they resembled the distinctive field police badge he wore on his left arm. I've seen purebred bloodhounds that looked more human than Ludwig Voss. But he was no amateur soldier: the Eastern Front ribbon and infantry assault badge told a more heroic story than simple law enforcement. He'd seen a lot more action than manning the barrier on a turnpike.

"A fire, a kettle, a comfy chair, it's a nice place you have here, Captain Gunther," he said, glancing around my cozy room. He was so tall he'd had to stoop to come through the door.

"It's a bit Uncle Tom's cabin," I said. "But it's home. What can I do for you, Lieutenant? I'd open a bottle of champagne in your honor but I think we drank the last fifty bottles last night."

"We've found another dead signaler," he said, brushing aside the wisecrack.

"Oh, I see. This is becoming an epidemic," I said. "Was his throat cut, too?"

"I don't know yet. I just picked up the report on the radio. A couple of my men found the body in Glinka Park. I was hoping you might come and take a look at the scene with me. Just in case there's some sort of pattern to all this."

"Pattern? That's a word we cops only use back in civilization. You need sidewalks to see a pattern, Ludwig. There's no pattern to anything out here. Haven't you figured that out yet? In Smolensk everything is fucked up."

How fucked up, I was only just beginning to understand, thanks to Martin Quidde and Friedrich Ribe.

"It's Corporal Quidde."

"Quidde? I was speaking to the poor man just the other day. All right. Let's go and take a look at him."

It felt curious to be standing over the dead body of a man I had murdered myself not two hours before; investigating the death of my own victim wasn't something I'd ever done—and would prefer never to do again—but there's a first time for everything and the novelty of it helped sustain my interest long enough to inform Voss that to my rheumy but experienced eye, the deceased gave every appearance of having committed suicide.

"The gun in his mitt looks ready to fire," I said. "Actually, I'm surprised he's still holding it at all. You'd think some Ivan would have pinched it. Anyway, after careful consideration of all the available facts that can be observed here, suicide would seem to be the most obvious explanation."

"I don't know," said Voss. "Would you keep your tin helmet on if you were planning to shoot yourself?"

That ought to have given me pause, but it didn't.

"And would he have shot himself in the back of the head like that?" continued Voss. "I had the impression that most people who shoot themselves in the head put one through the side of the head."

"Which is exactly why a lot of people who do that *survive*," I said authoritatively. "Temple shots are like a sure thing at the races. Sometimes it just doesn't finish. For future reference, if you want to do it, then shoot yourself in the back of the head. The same way those Ivans killed those Poles. Nobody ever survives a shot that goes through the occipital bone like this one has. It's why they do it that way. Because they know what they're doing."

"I can see how that works, yes. But is it even possible to do it in this way—to yourself, I mean?"

I took out my own Walther—the very gun that had killed Quidde—checked the safety, lifted my elbow, and placed the muzzle of the automatic against the nape of my own neck. The demonstration was eloquent enough. It was easily possible.

"There was no need even to remove his helmet," I said.

"All right," said Voss. "Suicide. But I don't have your Alexanderplatz experience and training."

"I never mind the obvious explanation. Sometimes it's just too damned hard to be clever—clever enough to ignore what's obvious. Well, I'm not sufficiently clever to offer an alternative in this case. It's one thing shooting yourself in the head. It's something else altogether to cut your own throat. Besides, this time we even have the weapon."

Voss tugged off Quidde's helmet to reveal a hole in the man's forehead. "And it looks like we have the bullet, too," he said, inspecting the inside of the signaler's tin hat. "You can see it embedded in the metal."

"So you can," I said. "For all the good it will do us out here in Smolensk."

"Perhaps we should search his billet for a suicide note," he said.

"Yes," I agreed. "Perhaps there was a woman. Or perhaps there wasn't a woman. Either one of those can seem like a good enough reason for some Fritzes. But even if there's not a note, it won't make a difference. Who'd read it anyway, apart from you and me and maybe Colonel Ahrens?"

"Still, it's curious, don't you think? Three fellows from the one signals regiment meeting an untimely end in as many weeks."

"We're at war," I said. "Meeting an untimely end is what being in this crummy country is all about. But I take your point, Ludwig. Maybe there's something dodgy in those radio waves after all. That's what some people think, isn't it? That they're hazardous? All that energy heating up your brain? It would certainly explain what's been happening at the Ministry of Enlightenment."

"Radio waves—yes, I never thought of that," said Voss.

I smiled; I was taking to obfuscation like a duck to water, and I wondered how much muddier my wings and webbed feet could make that water before flying away from the scene of my crime.

"Those signals boys are living right next to a powerful transmitter, day in, day out. The mast at the back of the castle looks just like the lanky lad. It's a wonder they haven't sprouted aerials on their damned heads."

Voss frowned and then shook his head. "The lanky lad?"

"Sorry," I said. "That's what we Berliners call the radio tower in Charlottenburg." I shook my head. "So maybe radio waves gave poor Quidde's brain an itch that he decided he had to scratch with a bullet from a Walther automatic. Probably while he was standing up, too, from the way the blood's splattered across the grass."

"It's an interesting theory," admitted Voss. "About the radio waves. But you're not serious."

"No, it'd be hard proving it." I shook my head. "More likely he was just depressed at being out here in this shit hole and staring down the barrel of a Red Army counteroffensive this summer. I can see where he was coming from there. Smolensk would drive anyone to suicide. Frankly, I've thought about nothing else but blowing my brains out since I got here."

"That's one way of getting back home," said Voss.

"Yes, there's a curious atmosphere at Dnieper Castle and Katyn Wood. Colonel Ahrens seemed very disturbed by it himself today. Don't you think so?"

"He's certain to take this badly. I never met an officer who was more concerned with the welfare of his men."

"That does make a pleasant change, it's true." I narrowed my eyes and looked up at the trees. "But why this park? You don't suppose this fellow was a music lover, do you?"

"I dunno. It is sort of peaceful."

Hearing a loud whoop and a raucous cackle of laughter, I glanced around. The drunks were still there with the dogs and the campfire; it wasn't just novels that were absurdly long in Russia, it was drinking sessions, too; this one was starting to look a lot like *War and Peace*.

"Almost peaceful," added Voss.

"Do you speak any Russian, Voss?"

"A bit," said Voss. "Do this and do that, mostly. You know—the language of the occupier."

"It's probably a waste of time," I said, "but let's go and ask the Red Army if they saw anything."

"I'm afraid the orders come a lot more easily than the questions. And I'm not sure I'll understand the answers."

"We'll make a detective out of you yet, Ludwig."

I was pushing my luck and I knew it, but I don't play skat and I never liked dice much, so in Smolensk I was going to have to get my thrills where I could; the Hotel Glinka was off limits to suckers like me who prefer it if a girl does that sort of thing because she wants to and not because she has to; that left the impossibly thick Russian novel back in my room and the flutter from a conversation with a bunch of hard-drinking Ivans who might just have seen a civilian answering my own description shoot a German soldier in cold blood. Of course, speaking to all the possible witnesses is what a real detective would have done anyway, and I was gambling they could not or didn't care to remember anything at all. And when, after a five-minute chat with these piss-artists, Voss and I ended up with nothing but a lot of uncomprehending fearful shrugs and some very bad breath in our nostrils, I felt like a winner all the same. It wasn't like breaking the bank at Monte Carlo, but it was enough.

5

THURSDAY, APRIL 1, 1943

The following morning I went to see Dr. Batov at the Smolensk State Medical Academy. By now I had come to recognize the canary-colored building as typically Soviet—the kind of outsized hospital that was very likely the subject of some aspirin commissar's ambitious five-year plan for treating Russia's sick and injured; the bulletin boards in the enormous admissions hall still displayed yellowing Cyrillic notices boasting about the efficiency of Smolensk's medical personnel and how the number of patients treated had increased, year on year, as if the sick had been so many tractors. Given what I now knew about Stalin, I wondered what might have happened if the number of patients treated had fallen; would the communists have concluded that Russians were just becoming healthier? Or would the director of the academy have been shot for failing to meet his target? It was an interesting dilemma and pointed up a real point of difference between Nazism and Communism as forms of government: there was no room for the individual in Soviet Russia; conversely, not everything was state-managed in Germany. The Nazis never shot anyone for being stupid, inefficient, or just plain unlucky. Generally speaking, the Nazis looked for a reason to shoot you; the commies were quite happy to shoot you without any reason at all; but when you're going to be shot, what's the difference?

Batov was absent from his fifth-floor office, and when I failed to see him in his laboratory I asked a weary-looking German medical orderly if he knew where the Russian doctor was to be found. He told me that the Russian doctor hadn't been seen at the hospital for a couple of days.

"Is he ill? Is he at home? Is he just taking some time off? What?"

The orderly shrugged. "Don't know, sir. But really, it's not like him at all. He may be an Ivan but I've never known a man who was more dedicated to the patients. Not just his patients, but ours, too. He was supposed to carry out an operation on one of our men yesterday afternoon and he never showed up for it. And now the man is dead. So you can draw your own conclusions."

"What do the Russian nurses tell you?"

"Hard to say, sir. There's none of us Germans that *slyuni* much Popov and they don't *slyuni* any German. We're understaffed as it is. Half my medical orderlies have just been ordered southeast, to a place called Prokhorovka. Batov was about the only one who could talk with us, at a surgical level."

"What's at Prokhorovka?"

"No idea, sir. All I know is that it's near a city called Kursk. But it's all very secret and I shouldn't have mentioned it. Our own men weren't told where they were going. The only reason I found out was because several large boxes of wound dressings were taken from the stores here and someone had written the destination on the side."

"There's no chance that Batov wasn't swept into the same draft as them, I suppose?"

"Not a chance, sir. There's no way they'd have pressed an Ivan into service."

"Well, I'd better look for him at home, I suppose."

"If you see him, tell him to hurry back, sir. We need him more than ever now that we're so short-staffed."

It was then I thought to go and look for Batov in the private room where Rudakov was being cared for, but it was empty and the wheelchair in which I had seen him sitting was now gone; the bed didn't look as if it had been slept in and even the ashtray looked as if it hadn't been used in a while. I laid my hand on the radio, which had been on when last I'd been in that room, and it was cold. I glanced up at the picture of Stalin but he wasn't telling. He stared suspiciously at me with his dull dark eyes, and when I put my hand behind him to look for the photograph of the three NKVD men and found it missing, I started to get a bad feeling about things.

I left the hospital and drove quickly to Batov's apartment building. I rang the bell and knocked on the door but Batov didn't answer. The floor lady downstairs had an ear trumpet that looked like it had belonged to the Beethoven Museum in Bonn and she didn't speak any German, but she didn't have to; my identification was enough for her to assume I was Gestapo, I suppose—the woman certainly crossed herself enough, as Batov had said she would—and she soon found some keys and let me into Batov's apartment.

As soon as the floor lady opened the door I knew something was wrong: all of the doctor's precious books that had been so carefully arranged were now lying on the floor and, sensing I was about to discover something awful—there was a faint smell of sweet-and-sour decay in the apartment—I took the key and sent the babushka away, then closed the door behind me.

I went into Batov's drawing room. The tall ceramic stove in the corner was still warm, but Batov's motionless body was not. He lay facedown on the uncarpeted floor underneath a patchwork quilt of tossed books and newspapers and cushions; in the side of his neck was a wound like a large slice of watermelon. His bruised and battered mouth had been stuffed with a sock, and from the numbers of fingers that were missing from his right hand it was clear that someone had been preparing him to play Ravel's piano concerto for the left hand on the upright by the window or—more likely, perhaps—torturing him methodically: four severed fingers and a thumb were arranged in a vertical series along the mantelpiece like so many cigarette butts. I wondered why he'd lain still and taken it until I saw the hypodermic in his thigh and figured he'd been injected with some sort of muscle relaxant they use in surgery and by someone who knew what they were doing, too; it must have been just enough to stop him moving but not enough to stop the pain.

Had he given up the information that had prompted this treatment? From the way the apartment had been turned over and the number of fingers on display, it seemed unlikely. If someone can stand the loss of more than one finger, it can be assumed they could stand the loss of all five.

"I'm sorry," I said aloud, because I had the strong idea that Batov's suffering and death had been occasioned by the same information he had promised me—the photographic and documentary evidence of exactly what had happened in Katyn Wood. "I really am. If only—if only I'd come yesterday, the way I'd planned, then perhaps you'd still be alive."

Of course, it had already crossed my mind that Lieutenant Rudakov's absence from his room at the SSMA was an indication that he had met a similarly grisly end; but it was now that I started to wonder just how disabled the NKVD man had really been. Could Rudakov have fooled Batov into thinking his condition was perhaps worse than it was? What better way of hiding out from your NKVD colleagues than affecting a mental disability? In which case, wasn't it perfectly possible that Dr. Batov had been murdered by the very man he'd been trying to protect? And wasn't life just like that sometimes?

I went into the bedroom. I hadn't met Batov's only daughter before; I didn't even know her name; all I really knew about the girl was her age and the fact that she wouldn't ever be celebrating her sixteenth birthday or dancing *The Dying Swan* in Paris. As a homicide detective I'd seen plenty of dead bodies, many of them female; and of course it's fair to say that the war had rendered me even less sensitive than before to the sight of violent death; but nothing prepared me for the appalling sight that greeted me in that bedroom.

Batov's daughter had been tied to the four corners of the bed and tortured with a knife, like her poor father. Her killer had slit her nose horizontally and cut off both her ears before opening the veins in one of her arms; she was still wearing a pair of rubber overshoes. Very likely she must have arrived back in the apartment after the killer had failed to extract the information he wanted from her father, and he had set to work with his knife on the daughter, whose mouth was similarly stuffed with a sock to stifle her loudest screams. But where, I wondered, were her ears?

Eventually I found both of them in the breast pocket of the dead man's jacket, as if the killer had brought them into the room, one after the other, before Batov had told him what exactly he wanted to know.

A quick glance in the other bedroom confirmed that Batov had indeed talked. A picture of Lenin had been taken down from the wall and was now leaning against it; the space it had covered was just raw brickwork with several of the bricks torn out like the center of a jig-saw puzzle. There was just enough room in this rectangular hiding place—which was about the height and width of a letter box—to have hidden the ledgers and pictures Dr. Batov had promised to give to me.

In the bathroom I dropped my trousers and sat down on the toilet to do some thinking with a couple of cigarettes. Without the bloody distractions of the two bodies it was easier to reflect upon what I knew and what I thought I knew.

I knew that they had both been dead for not much more than a day: Batov's own body had been covered with books and newspapers, which meant that access for female houseflies had been more difficult, but already masses of tiny eggs yet to hatch into maggots were covering the girl's eyelids; depending on the temperature, fly eggs usually hatched into larvae within twenty-four hours—especially when a body was found indoors, where things are warmer, even in Russia. All of which meant they had probably died the previous afternoon.

I knew it was a waste of time asking the floor lady if she'd seen or heard anything; for one thing my Russian wasn't equal to the task of an interrogation, and for another her ear trumpet hardly encouraged the prospect of success. As a detective, I'd seen more promising witnesses in a mortuary. Not that I was feeling a lot like a homicide detective since murdering Martin Quidde.

I kept asking myself if there had been a way I could have avoided that; but the same answer kept on coming back at me: Quidde opening his mouth about what he knew to someone in the Gestapo, the field police, Kripo, the SS, or even the Wehrmacht would have been as good a way as any of destroying any future chance that von Gersdorff—or one of his colleagues—might get to kill Hitler. No one's life—not Quidde's and certainly not my own—was more important than that. For the same reason, I knew I was going to have to tell von Gersdorff about Quidde and the tape to prove to him that von Kluge could no longer be trusted.

I knew that Batov's killer enjoyed using a knife—a knife is such a close-quarters weapon that you have to take pleasure in the damage you can inflict on another human being. It's not a weapon for someone who's squeamish. I might have said that the man who murdered Batov and his daughter was the same man who murdered the two signalers, Ribe and Greiss—the throat cutting was similar, of course—except that the motives for these crimes looked so entirely different.

I knew I needed to find Rudakov even if he was dead in order to eliminate him as a suspect. Rudakov had heard everything Batov had told me about the documentary and photographic proof of the Katyn massacre, and he'd heard the deal Batov had demanded. If that wasn't a motive for a former NKVD officer to kill a man and his daughter, I didn't know what was. If he had killed the Batovs, then I guessed he was long gone and the field police were hardly likely to catch someone who had been resourceful enough to have faked a mental disability for the best part of three years.

I knew I had to go to the Kommandatura now and report the murders so that the field police and the local Russian cops could be summoned to the crime scene. Death had undone so many in and around Smolensk that Lieutenant Voss was going to wonder if murder was becoming infectious in the oblast that was his zone of responsibility. With four thousand men lying dead in Katyn Wood, I was beginning to wonder that myself.

But most of all I knew I was about to have a big problem with the minister for Enlightenment and Propaganda when I told him that the extra evidence I had promised him of exactly what had happened at Katyn had disappeared, along with our one potential witness, and that we were now back to having to rely on the forensics and nothing else.

In that respect, it was fortunate for Goebbels and Germany and the Katyn investigation that Gerhard Buhtz was a highly competent forensic scientist—much more competent than I or Judge Conrad had anticipated.

I was about to discover just how competent he really was.

THE OFFICERS' CANTEEN AT KRASNY BOR was a chintzy sort of place, a bit like a dining room in a provincial Swiss hotel except for the Russian waiters wearing white mess jackets and the gleaming regimental silver on the sideboard; and no provincial Swiss hotel—even one at high altitude—ever had clouds inside the dining room: near the wooden ceiling of the canteen there was always a thick layer of tobacco smoke like a blanket of persistent fog over an airfield. Sometimes I would lean back in my chair and stare up at this gray fug and try to imagine myself back at Horcher's in Berlin or even La Coupole in Paris. The food at Krasny Bor was as plentiful as it was at the

Bendlerblock and with an extensive wine list and a selection of beers that would have been the envy of any restaurant in Berlin; it was easily the best thing about being in Smolensk. The chef was a talented fellow from Brandenburg, and for Berliners like myself there was always an air of excitement when his two best dishes—Königsberger Klopse and lamprey pie—were on the menu. So I was less than pleased when, having just given my lunch order to the waiter, an orderly came and told me that Professor Buhtz was urgently requesting my presence in his laboratory hut. I might have asked the orderly to tell Buhtz to wait until after lunch but for the fact that von Kluge was seated at the next table and had certainly heard the details of the message, which, after all, came from someone who carried a major's rank in the Wehrmacht. Von Kluge was always very Prussian about such things and took a dim view of junior officers shirking their duties in favor of their stomachs; he was an abstemious man and, unlike the rest of us, wasn't much interested in the pleasures of the table. I expect he was thinking more about the pleasures of his bank account. So I stood up and went outside to find the forensic pathologist.

His makeshift laboratory was easily identifiable from the BMW motorcycle parked immediately outside. It was one of the larger huts on the outer perimeter of army headquarters at Krasny Bor. I knew Buhtz had an even larger and far better equipped laboratory in the town hospital on Hospitalstrasse near the city's main railway station, but he felt safer working at Krasny Bor on account of the fact that the previous autumn some German doctors working in the hospital at Vitebsk had been kidnapped, genitally mutilated, and then murdered by partisans.

To my surprise, I found the professor in the company of Martin Quidde, whose dead body was now lying in an open coffin on the wooden floor; a crude, Y-shaped stitch ran the length of his torso like the track for a small boy's electric train set, and the top of his skull displayed the telltale purple line of having been removed and then replaced, as if it had been the lid on a tea caddy. But it wasn't Quidde that Buhtz had summoned me to discuss in confidence; at least not right away.

"Sorry to interrupt your lunch, Gunther," he said. "I didn't want to discuss this in front of everyone in the mess."

"You're probably right, sir. It's never a good idea to discuss forensics when other men are trying to eat lunch."

"Well, this is rather urgent. And not to say sensitive. And I'm not talking about the stomachs of our fellow officers."

"What is it?" I asked coolly.

He took off his leather apron and then led me to a microscope by a frosted window. "You remember the skull I took away from Katyn Wood? Your dead Polack?"

"How could I forget? Outside of a play by William Shakespeare, it's not often you see a man with a decomposing head under his arm."

"That Polish officer wasn't—as you might have expected he would have been—shot with a Russian pistol like a Tokarev or a Nagant."

"I'd have thought the hole was too small to be from a rifle," I muttered.

Buhtz switched on a light near the microscope and invited me to take a look at the shell casing.

"No, indeed, you're quite right," he said, as I peered through the eyepiece. "Quite right. On the bottom of the shell casing that your Russian friend Dyakov found in the mass grave you'll see that the trademark and caliber are clearly visible on the brass."

He was pulling on his army tunic while he spoke. I daresay that slicing open Corporal Quidde meant he'd worked up an appetite.

"Yes," I said. "Geco 7.65. Bloody hell, that's the Gustav Genschow factory in Durlach, isn't it?"

"You really are a detective, aren't you?" said Buhtz. "Yes, it's a German shell. A 7.65 won't fit a Tokarev or a Nagant. Those pistols only take 7.62 caliber ammo. But 7.65 does fit a Walther like the one I bet you're wearing under your arm."

I shrugged. "So, what are you saying? That they were shot by Germans after all?"

"No, no. I'm saying they were shot by German weapons. You see, I happen to know that before the war, the factory exported weapons and ammunition to the Ivans in the Baltic states. The Tokarev and the Nagant are all right as far as they go. The Nagant you can actually use with a sound suppressor, unlike any other pistol, and a lot of NKVD murder squads like to use it where silence is required. It really is very quiet. But if you want to get the job done as efficiently and quickly as possible, and you don't mind about the noise—and I can't see that they would have minded, particularly, in the middle of Katyn Wood—then the Walther is your weapon of choice. I'm not being patriotic. Not in the least. The Walther doesn't jam, and it doesn't misfire. If you're shooting four thousand Polacks in one weekend then you need German pistols to get the job done. And my guess is that you'll find that all four thousand of these fellows were topped in the same way."

Now I remembered Batov describing a briefcase full of automatic pistols and I guessed that these must have been Walthers.

"Makes it a hell of a lot harder to argue that these fellows were all shot by the Ivans," I said. "There's a delegation of prominent Polacks arriving here from Warsaw, Krakow, and Lublin next week, including two fucking generals, and we're going to have to tell them that their comrades were shot with German pistols."

"You know, I wouldn't be at all surprised if the NKVD used Walthers for another reason, too. Other than their reliability. I think they might have used them to help cover their tracks. To make it look like we did it. Just in case anyone ever discovered this grave."

I groaned loudly. "The minister is going to love this," I said. "On top of everything else."

I told him about Batov and the documentary evidence that no longer was.

"Sorry," said Buhtz. "All the same, I'm going to ask the ministry to telephone the Genschow factory and see what their export records say. It's possible they can locate a batch of similar ammunition."

"But you said this is standard German issue, didn't you?"

"Yes and no. I've been working in the field of ballistics since 1932 and, even though I say so myself, I'm something of an expert in this field. I can tell you, Gunther, that while the caliber remains standard, over the years the trace metallurgy of ammunition can change quite a bit. Some years there's a bit more copper, other years there might be a bit more nickel. And depending on how old this ammunition is, we might be able to get an idea about when it was made, which would help to substantiate the export record. If we can do that, we might be able to say for sure that this bullet was part of a batch of ammo exported to the Baltic Ivans in, say, 1940, when we had the non-aggression pact with Comrade Stalin. Or even before the Nazis were in power, when we had those red-loving bastards in the SPD running the show. That would be documentary proof that they did do it and almost as good as finding a Russian-made bullet."

I saw little point in mentioning my own former allegiance to the SPD so I nodded silently and stood away from the microscope.

"So then," said Buhtz, "perhaps we'll just tell the Polish delegation what we know about the bodies that we've found so far. And leave it at that for now. No point in speculating unnecessarily. Under the circumstances, I think we should let them take over as much of the actual work at the site as possible."

"Suits me."

"By the way, do you speak any Polish?" asked Buhtz. "Because I don't."

"I thought you were at the University of Breslau?"

"For only three years," said Buhtz. "Besides, that's very much a German-speaking university. My Polish is fine for ordering a shitty meal in a restaurant, but when it comes to forensics and pathology, it's a different story. What about Johannes Conrad?"

"No Polish. Just Russian. He and some field police are busy

interrogating people in Gnezdovo to see what more the locals can tell us about what happened. I've an idea that Peshkov speaks French as well as German and Russian, so he might be of assistance. But the ministry are also sending us a reserve officer from Vienna who speaks good Polack. Lieutenant Gregor Sloventzik."

"Sounds about right," said Buhtz.

"He used to be a journalist. Which is how the ministry knows him, I think. I believe he speaks several other languages, too."

"Including diplomacy, I hope," said Buhtz. "I've never been very fluent in that."

"You and me both, Professor. And certainly not since Munich. Anyway, Sloventzik is going to handle all the translations for you, Professor."

"I'm very glad to hear it. I don't need more confusion right now. I'm afraid it's been that kind of a morning. This signaler that the field police found. Martin Quidde." He pointed at the corpse lying in a coffin on the floor near the back door. "I understand from Lieutenant Voss that you and he both thought his death was a suicide."

"Well, yes. We did." I shrugged. "There was an automatic with the hammer down still in his hand. Short of a poem clutched to his breast, it looked pretty clear-cut, I thought."

"You would think so, wouldn't you?" Buhtz grinned proudly. "But I'm afraid not. I've fired a whole clip from that weapon and there's not one of the bullets that's the same as the one I gouged out of the victim's helmet. It's as I was telling you earlier. About the metallurgy? The slug that went through his skull was standard 7.65 mil, yes. But it was a significantly heavier load with a bit more nickel in it. The corporal was shot with a seventy-three-grain load as opposed to the normal sixty-grain load that's in his pistol's magazine and which is standard issue to the 537th Signals. The seventy-three-grain load is normally issued only to the police units and the Gestapo."

He was right, of course; and—a long time ago—I'd known this, but not lately. You see enough lead flying through the air and it soon ceases to matter where it comes from and how much it weighs on a set of scales.

"So someone just tried to make it look like a suicide, is that what you're saying?" I asked, as if I really didn't know.

"That's right." Buhtz's grin widened. "And I doubt that there's another man in this whole damned country could have told you that."

"Well, that is fortunate. Although I don't imagine Lieutenant Voss is going to be all that pleased. He still hasn't solved the murders of those two other signalers."

"Nevertheless, it does establish a sort of pattern. I mean, someone really does have it in for those poor bastards in the 537th, don't you think?"

"Have you tried making a telephone call out here? It's impossible. There's your motive, I shouldn't wonder. Still, I don't suppose an Ivan would have bothered to make it look like a suicide, would he?"

"I hadn't considered that." He nodded. "Yes, that is reassuring for the Germans in this city, I suppose."

"All the same, sir, if a German was responsible for the murder, it might be a good idea not to mention any of this to the Gestapo. Just in case they go and string up more of the locals in retaliation. I mean, you know what they're like, sir. The last thing we want is an international commission arriving in Smolensk to find a makeshift gallows with some Russian pears growing on it."

"A man—a German—has been murdered, Captain Gunther. That really can't be ignored."

"No, of course not, sir. But perhaps, until this whole thing with the international commission is over, it might be to Germany's political advantage to hide this under some hay in the barn, so to speak. For appearance's sake."

"Yes, I can see that, of course. I tell you what, Captain. You used to be a police commissar at the Alex, didn't you?"

I nodded.

"Very well then. I promise to keep the murder of Corporal

Quidde quiet, Gunther, if you promise to find his murderer. Does that sound fair?"

I nodded. "Fair enough, sir. Although I'm not sure how. He's done a pretty good job so far of concealing his tracks."

"Well, do your best. And if all else fails, we can have each man with a police load in his pistol fire a round into a sandbag. That should help to narrow it down for you quite a lot."

"Thank you, sir. I might take you up on that offer."

"Please do. You've got until the end of the month. And then I really will have to tell the Gestapo. Is that agreed?"

"All right. It's a deal."

"Good. Then let's go and get some lunch. I hear it's Königsberger Klopse on the menu today."

I shook my head. "I've already eaten," I said.

But in truth, what with the smell of formaldehyde and the dead body and the prospect of investigating a murder that I'd committed myself, I had lost my appetite.

WEDNESDAY, APRIL 7, 1943

In Smolensk's Glinka Concert Hall—where else?—I attended a piano and organ recital at the invitation of Colonel von Gersdorff. On the program was Bach, Wagner, Beethoven, and Bruckner, and it was supposed to make everyone feel good about the Fatherland but it only made us all sick that we weren't at home and, in my own case, back in Berlin listening to some more cheerful music on the wireless: I could even have withstood a couple of numbers from Bruno and his Swinging Tigers. Of course, being an aristocrat, von Gersdorff had an Iron Cross in classical music. He even brought along an antiquarian, leather-bound score that he followed during Bach's *Well-Tempered Clavier,* which struck me as not only redundant but a bit flashy, too—a bit like taking the *Laws of the Game* to a soccer match.

After the recital we went for a drink at the officers' bar in Offizierstrasse, where in a quiet corner that felt as if it were a million kilometers from the bowling alley at the German Club in Berlin, the colonel told me he'd received a telemessage that Hans von Dohnanyi and Pastor Dietrich Bonhoeffer had finally been arrested by the Gestapo and were now being held at Prinz Albrechtstrasse.

"If they torture Hans, he could tell them about the Cointreau bomb and me and General von Tresckow and everything," he said uncomfortably.

"Yes, he could," I said. "In fact, it's highly likely. It's not many men who can withstand a Gestapo interrogation."

"Do you suppose they're being tortured?" he asked.

"Knowing the Gestapo?" I shrugged. "It all depends."

"On what?"

"On how powerful their friends are. You have to understand, the Gestapo are cowards. They won't put a man through a performance like that if he's especially well connected. Not until they've read the score as thoroughly as you did back in the concert hall." I shook my head. "I don't know much about the pastor—"

"His sister Christel is married to Hans. His mother is Countess Klara von Hase. Who was the granddaughter of Karl von Hase, who was pastor to Kaiser Wilhelm the Second."

"That's not the kind of connections I was referring to," I said politely. "How close is your friend Hans von Dohnanyi to Admiral Canaris?"

"Close enough for it to hurt them both. Canaris has been on an SD list of enemies for some time now—so has Hans's boss, Major General Oster."

"That figures. The RSHA never did like sharing responsibility for intelligence gathering and security. Well then, what about the Ministry of Justice? Von Dohnanyi used to work there, didn't he?"

"Yes, he did. He was Reich Minister Gürtner's special adviser, from 1934 to 1938, and got to know Hitler, Goebbels, Göring, and Himmler—the whole infernal crew."

"Then that will certainly help. You don't torture someone who was on nodding terms with the Leader until you're really very sure of what you're doing. Maybe this Gürtner fellow can help him, too."

"I'm afraid not. He died a couple of years ago. But Hans knows Erwin Bumke very well. He's a senior Nazi judge, but I'm sure he'll try to help Hans, if he can."

I shrugged. "Then he's not completely without friends. So that will deter the Gestapo, for sure. Besides, von Dohnanyi is an aristocrat and he's army and the army looks after its own. Chances are the army will insist on a military court."

"Yes, that's right," said von Gersdorff, with a palpable look of relief on his handsome face. "There are senior figures in the Wehrmacht who will try to speak for him, albeit quietly. General von Tresckow's uncle, Field Marshal von Bock, for example. And Field Marshal von Kluge, of course."

"No," I said. "I wouldn't count on Clever Hans at all."

"Nonsense," said von Gersdorff. "Von Kluge can be a bit Prussian in his sense of duty and honor but I firmly believe Günther is a good man. Henning von Tresckow has been his chief operations officer for over a year now and—"

I shook my head. "Let's get some air."

We stepped outside and walked up Grosse Kronstädter Strasse as far as the Smolensk Kremlin wall. Against a purple sky full of stars, the fortress looked as if it was made of gingerbread, like the sort of edible house I'd eaten every Christmas as a boy. There, in the cold silence, I struck a match against the brick, we lit some cigarettes, and I told him what Martin Quidde had told me.

"I can't believe it," protested von Gersdorff. "Not of a man like Günther von Kluge. He comes from a very distinguished family."

I laughed. "You really think that makes a difference, don't you? The old aristocratic code?"

"Of course. It has to. Yes, I can see you think that's very funny but this is what I've lived my whole life by. And I firmly believe it's the one thing that's going to save Germany from absolute disaster."

I shrugged. "Maybe. But I'm still right about von Kluge. You can't trust him."

"No, you're wrong. He knows my father. They're from the same part of West Prussia. Lubin and Posen aren't so very far away from each other. This corporal of yours must be mistaken."

"He's not mistaken," I said. "Not in the least."

"Are you sure?"

"Quite sure. I haven't heard it myself, but he says there's a tape recording of Hitler's conversation here in Smolensk with von Kluge. At Krasny Bor."

"My God, where?"

"It's quite safe." I took the tape out of my coat pocket and handed it to him.

Von Gersdorff looked at it blankly for a moment and shook his head. Finally, he said, "Well, if it's true, that would explain a lot. Why Günther changed his mind about us all shooting Hitler, at the very last minute. All of his prevarications are now explained. All his nit-picking objections. It's true, Henning still hasn't forgiven him for that. But this—this is something else. Something quite despicable."

"I couldn't agree more."

"The fucking bastard. And to think that Henning vetoed a bomb at Krasny Bor so as to spare Günther's life. We could have nailed Hitler there, without a shadow of a doubt. You see the problem is always the same: getting Hitler away from his headquarters, where he's well protected. I can't imagine we'll ever get him on his own like that again. Damn it all."

"Yes, that is a pity."

"This corporal," said von Gersdorff. "Can he be trusted?"

"He can now," I said.

"How can you be sure?"

"Because he's dead. I shot him. The idiot was threatening to expose this tape to all sorts of people. Well, you can imagine how that might have ended. At least I assume you can. If you can't, then maybe you're not as conspiracy-minded as I think you need to be. Nor as ruthless."

"You murdered him?"

"If you prefer that word. Yes, I murdered him. I had no choice but to kill him."

"In cold blood."

"And this from the man who was going to blow Hitler up on a Sunday."

"Yes, but Hitler is a monster. This fellow you killed was just a corporal."

"As I recall, Hitler used to be a corporal, too. And what about your Cointreau bomb? It's not just Hitler that would have been killed but his pilot and his photographer and maybe his fucking dog, for all I know."

I grinned, almost enjoying his squeamish discomfort, and then I laid out a possible chain of causation that included a compromised Field Marshal von Kluge being interviewed by the Gestapo and out of sheer panic informing them of everything he knew about all of the army plots to kill the Leader that had been hatched in Smolensk; as a teleological account it might not have satisfied Plato or Kant but it was enough to forestall any further caviling on the part of my very particular friend.

"Yes, I can see how that might have played out," said von Gersdorff. "But look, suppose someone looks into this man's death? What then?"

"Suppose you let me worry about that."

We walked back to his car and then returned to Krasny Bor. The road took us past Katyn Wood, now floodlit and heavily guarded to prevent looting, although the guards didn't seem to have deterred local citizens and off-duty German soldiers: during the day, the wood was visited by a host of sightseers who came to watch the exhumations from behind a protective cordon as von Kluge had refused to forbid them access to the site.

"How's the dig going?" he asked.

"Not so good," I said. "Many of the men we've dug up so far turn out to be German-speaking Poles. *Volksdeutsche* officers from the western side of the river Oder, which is your neck of the woods, isn't it?"

"Silesian Poles, you say?"

"That's right. Same as you might have been if your family had been rich a little farther east. I'm a little concerned that this might not play well with the Polish delegation when they arrive here the day after tomorrow. It might look as though we only give a damn about them because they're *Volksdeutsche*. As if we might not give a damn at all if they were a hundred percent Polack."

"Yes, I can see how that might be awkward."

"And it certainly hasn't helped things that someone in Berlin let out that these men were the same men who had been kept by the Soviets in two camps: Starobelsk and Kozelsk. Twelve thousand of them. Now, I'm pretty certain that, give or take a few hundred, there are only four thousand men buried in Katyn Wood. There's not a single man we've found who was at Starobelsk."

Von Gersdorff shook his head. "Yes, I heard about that from Professor Buhtz."

"That man's full of good news. He's yet to find a single Polish officer who was shot with a Russian weapon."

"There's more bad news, I'm afraid. I got a teletype from the Tirpitzufer, in Berlin. The Abwehr has warned me that we can expect a visitor at Katyn Wood tomorrow, although I must say he's hardly a distinguished one. Anything but."

"Oh? Who's that?"

"You won't like this one bit."

"You know something, Colonel? I'm getting used to that."

THURSDAY, APRIL 8, 1943

During the late summer of 1941 I'd heard a strong rumor around the Alex about an atrocity that a police battalion was supposed to have committed at a place called Babi Yar near Kiev. But it was only a rumor and—at the time—easily discounted because even then being a policeman was supposed to mean that you weren't a criminal. It's odd how quickly these things change. By the spring of 1943 I had enough experience of the Nazis to know that with them the worse a rumor sounded, the more likely it was to be true. Besides, I'd already seen something of what had happened in Minsk and that was bad enough—I was still haunted by the memory of what I'd witnessed there—but no one in Berlin ever employed the same hushed tones of horror to talk about Minsk as they used when they mentioned Babi Yar. All I knew for sure was that as many as thirty-five thousand Jewish men, women, and children had been shot in a ravine during the course of one September weekend; and that the officer commanding that operation—Colonel Paul Blobel—was now standing beside me in Katyn Wood.

I guessed Blobel was about fifty, although he looked much older. The shadows under his eyes were full of a darkness that was much more than skin deep. He was bald with a narrow, thin mouth and a long nose; it was probably my imagination but there was something of the night about Blobel, and I wouldn't have been at all surprised if the fingers and nails of the hands he held tightly behind his back had been as long as the legs of his black boots. He wore his black SD coat buttoned up to the neck like a bus conductor in winter, but he looked to all the world as if he'd been a visitor from the very pit next to which we were standing.

"You must be Captain Gunther," he said to me, in an accent that might have been from Berlin and which reminded me that among the many things a man can have for breakfast, a few of them come out of a tall bottle.

I nodded.

"Here is a letter of introduction," he said with a lisping, rodent-like earnestness, showing me a neatly typed letter. "I would ask you to pay particular attention to the signature at the bottom of the page."

I glanced over the contents, which were headed "Operation 1005" and requested that "every cooperation should be afforded the bearer in the execution of his top secret orders"; I also noted the signature; it was hard not to look at it several times, just to make sure, and then to fold it very carefully indeed before handing it back, gingerly, almost as if the paper was impregnated with sulphur and might burst into flame at any moment; the letter had been signed by the Gestapo chief himself, Heinrich Müller.

"Like I was sitting at the front of the class," I said.

"Gruppenführer Müller has entrusted me with a most delicate task," he said.

"Well, that makes a change."

"Yes." He smiled thinly. "It does, doesn't it?"

I certainly had no inclination to spend any time in the company of such a man as this. The easy thing would have been to have told him to get lost; and after all, Blobel's being there—and, moreover, wearing his SD colonel's uniform—was contrary to everything I had agreed to with Reich Minister Goebbels. But because I wanted this man gone from Katyn Wood as soon as possible, I was resolved to answer his questions and cooperate with his mission—insofar as I was able. The last thing I wanted was Blobel causing trouble at Gestapo headquarters and Blobel bringing the full authority of Müller down on our heads because I, or someone else, had obstructed him, and, worst of all, Blobel still there the next day when the Polish delegation arrived in Smolensk.

He seemed to relax a little after my poor joke and out of his pocket came a corrugated steel hip flask that was almost as big as a soldier's gas-mask can. He unscrewed the cap and offered the flask to me; as a homicide detective, I'd made it a rule never to drink with my clients but it had been a long time since I'd been able to keep up that standard. Besides, it was good schnapps and a large bite helped to dull the effect on my spirits of the company I was keeping, not to mention the business of exhuming four thousand murder victims. The stink of human decay was ever present, and I was never near the main grave for very long before I lit a cigarette or covered my nose and mouth with a cologne-soaked handkerchief.

"How can I be of assistance to you, Colonel?"

"May I speak frankly?"

I glanced back at the scene in front of us: dozens of Russian POWs were busy digging in what was now known as "Grave Number One"—an L-shaped trench that was twenty-eight meters long and sixteen meters wide. About two hundred and fifty bodies lay on the top row, but we'd estimated that as many as a thousand more corpses lay immediately underneath these. Now that the ground had thawed, the digging was easy enough; the hard part was to remove the bodies in one piece, and great care had to be taken when transferring a corpse from the grave to a stretcher, with as many as four men at once having to do the lifting.

"I don't think they'll mind," I said.

"No, perhaps not. Well then, as you probably know, about eighteen months ago—as part of Operation Barbarossa—certain police actions occurred throughout the Ukraine and Western Russia. Thousands of indigenous Jews were—shall we say, permanently resettled?"

"Why not say 'murdered'?" I shrugged. "That's what you mean, isn't it?"

"Very well. Let's say they were murdered. It really makes no difference to me how we describe it, Captain. In spite of what you may have heard, this kind of thing has nothing to do with me. And of greater importance now is what we do about it."

"I would think it's a little late for regrets, don't you?"

"You mistake me." Blobel took another swig from his flask of schnapps. "I'm not here to justify what happened. Personally, I was unable to participate in these dreadful actions for all the obvious humanitarian reasons and was obliged to return home from the front. For which I was roundly abused by General Heydrich and accused of being a sissy and fit only for manufacturing porcelain. Those were his very words."

"Heydrich always did have a certain turn of phrase," I said.

"He was most unsympathetic to me. And after all I had achieved for the security squadron."

I hesitated to take another verbal crack at him; was it possible I had misjudged Paul Blobel? That he wasn't quite the murdering war criminal that the rumors held him to be? That he and I had something in common, perhaps? Hearing Blobel's account of his treatment the previous year at the hands of Heydrich, it wasn't hard to feel that in comparison with him, I'd enjoyed something of a charmed life. Or was he just a shameless liar? It was always difficult to tell with my colleagues in the RSHA.

"My operational role here is simply one of public health," he said. "I'm not talking about the kind of metaphorical public health you hear talked about in those stupid propaganda films—you know, the ones that equate Jews with vermin? No, I'm talking about real environmental health issues. You see, many of the mass graves that were left behind after those special police actions are threatening to cause serious health problems in land that it's hoped will eventually be farmed by German emigrants. Some of the graves have become a very palpable environmental hazard and now threaten ecological disaster for their surrounding areas. What I mean to say is that leakage from some of the bodies has entered the water table and now endangers local wells and drinking water. Consequently, I have been tasked by General Müller to exhume some of those bodies and dispose of them more efficiently. And my reason for being here, in Katyn Wood, is to see if we can learn anything from the Soviets about the disposal of large numbers of dead people."

I lit a cigarette; it wasn't just the smell of the exhumation that the tobacco smoke helped to deal with but the flies, too; these were already becoming unbearable and it was still only April; Dyakov had told me that he believed the worst month for flies in Smolensk was May. Buhtz had given up trying to prevent smoking at the site. No one had reckoned on the persistence of the flies, and smoking was about the only thing that kept them off. Almost all of the Russian POWs worked in grave number one with a cigarette permanently in their mouths, which for some was payment enough for the unpleasant task that was required of them.

"It's as you can see," I said. "All of the victims so far have been shot in exactly the same way. And I do mean exactly—to within a few centimeters, from very close range, and at the same protrusion at the base of the skull. Nearly all of the exit wounds are between the nose and the hairline. Undoubtedly, the NKVD men who carried out this particular special action had done this many times before. Indeed, they'd done it so many times that they had even perfected where and how the bodies would fall into the grave. In fact, you can say with absolute certitude that no one was allowed just to fall in like a dead dog. There are maybe twelve layers of bodies in this grave. The heads of those in each row seem to be resting on the feet of the men below, and there was nothing about this that was not subject to thought and planning. When all of the men were dead, or at least shot, tons of sand were bulldozed on top, which helped to compress the bodies into one large mummified cake. Even the decomposition process appears to have been perfected by the NKVD. The fluids leaking from the bodies seem to have formed a kind of airtight seal around the cake. Finally, birch trees were replanted on top of the grave. It's really very methodical, and our biggest problem as far as exhumation is concerned has been the surface water—from melted snow—that has flooded the graves and which is why things now smell so bad. A few weeks ago you could have stood here and noticed a girl's perfume from thirty meters away. Now, as you can no doubt judge for yourself, it smells like the deepest pit in hell."

Blobel nodded but the smell didn't seem to bother him in the least.

"Yes, it does look extremely well organized down there," he admitted. "I used to be an architect and I've seen foundation works that weren't made as well as this grave. Surprising, really. One wonders how something so neat was ever discovered." He paused. "As a matter of fact, how was it discovered?"

"It would seem that a hungry wolf dug up a thigh bone," I said.

"D'you really believe that?"

I shrugged. "It hadn't occurred to me to believe anything else. Besides, there are plenty of wolves in these woods."

"Seen one?"

"No, but I've heard a few. Why? Have you an alternative theory, sir?"

"Yes. Looters. Local Ivans hunting for something of value. A watch or a wedding band—even a gold tooth. In my experience Slavs will steal anything, even if that means digging up a few dead bodies to do it. I've seen it before, in Kiev. But there's nothing new about that, of course. People have been robbing graves since the time of the Pharaohs."

"Well, they'd have been wasting their time here. We've not found much in the way of burial treasure for the afterlife on these poor fellows. I'd say the NKVD relieved them of anything valuable."

"That's standard practice with the communists, isn't it? Redistribution of wealth."

Blobel smiled at his own little joke. It was better than mine had been but I wasn't much in the mood for smiling—not with my stomach feeling the way it did.

"Tell me, Captain Gunther, are you going to burn the corpses?"

"No," I said. "The politics of the situation are very delicate and would seem to rule that out. That's what I've been told by the ministry. So we've decided to leave that particular decision to the Poles themselves. They're due here tomorrow. More than likely it seems that they're going to have to be reburied. For now, anyway."

"All of them?"

I shrugged. "Not my decision, thank God. I'm just a policeman."

"I've heard that before." Blobel smiled. "Still," he added, "burning them isn't so easy, either. Especially when the corpses are damp. Believe me, I know. And of course it's such a waste of precious gasoline and firewood. But even when you've burned them down to almost nothing, there's still the ash to dispose of—that has to be covered up, too. And, what's more, there's so little time to do things properly."

"Oh? Why's that?"

"The Russians are coming, of course. In less than six months this whole area will be overrun. And you can bet your last mark that if you don't burn these fucking bodies down to a layer of cinders, the Russians will do their damnedest to prove that we murdered them all."

"You've got a point there." I spat; it was that or retch. The smell was really getting to me now; that and the conversation. "Seen enough?" I asked him.

"Yes, I think so. You've been most helpful."

"That is a comfort."

Blobel smiled again. "Well, I can't stay here chatting, I have to catch a plane."

"Leaving so soon?"

He nodded. "I'm afraid so."

"Need a lift to the airport?" I was anxious to make sure I was rid of him before the arrival of the Polish delegation.

"That's very kind of you."

"It's not a problem. Where are you going to now?"

"Kiev. Then Riga. And then back to Kulmhof. Or Chelmno, as the locals call it."

"What's in Kulmhof?"

"Nothing good," said Blobel, "like a Titian painting gone very wrong," and I believed him; much later on I came to the conclusion it was the only true thing he said all morning.

8

The Polish Red Cross had arrived in Katyn Wood the previous day—the whole soccer team of eleven representatives, including Dr. Marian Wodziński, a stone-faced forensic specialist from Krakow, and three lab assistants. In Germany Marian tends to be a man's name, and when Lieutenant Sloventzik learned that Dr. Marian Kramsta was flying in the next day from Breslau to assist Professor Buhtz, naturally he assumed that Dr. Kramsta would be as hard on the eyes as Dr. Wodziński and asked if I wouldn't mind fetching him from the airport. I minded less when I took a closer look at the passenger list and discovered Dr. Kramsta was a Marianne; I minded not at all when I saw her patent leather pumps with pussycat grosgrain bows coming down the steps of the plane from Berlin. Her legs were no less elegant than her shoes, and the general effect, which I found to be particularly graceful, was only marred by the clumsy fool greeting her on the tarmac who managed to allow momentarily his admiration to master his manners.

"They're legs," she said. "A matching pair, last time I looked."

"You say that like I was paying them too much attention."

"Weren't you?"

"Not in the least. If I see a nice pair of legs, then naturally I just have to take a look at them. Darwin called it natural selection. You might have heard of that."

She smiled.

"I should have listened to the pilot and put them safely away in a rifle case where they can't do any harm."

"I certainly don't mind getting shot in a good cause," I said.

"That can be arranged. But for now, I'll take that as a compliment."

"I wish you would. It's been a while since I handed one out with such alacrity."

I collected her bags from the top of the steps and carried them to the car, but only just; they were heavy.

"If this is more shoes in here," I said, "I should warn you. The field marshal isn't planning any regimental balls."

"It's mostly scientific equipment," she said. "And I'm sorry it's so hard to carry."

"Really, I don't mind at all. I could fetch and carry for you all day long."

"I'll remember that."

"You know, Professor Buhtz didn't tell me he was expecting a lady in Smolensk."

"I spit a little too much tobacco juice for him to think of me as that," she said. "But I imagine he did tell you he was expecting a doctor. Oddly enough, it's possible to be both of those things, even in Germany."

"You remind me I should go back there sometime."

"Been down here long?"

"I dunno. Is Hindenburg still the president?"

"No. He died. Nine years ago."

"I guess that answers your question."

I finished putting her bags in the back of the Tatra, and she offered me a cigarette from a little tin of Caruso.

"Haven't seen any of these in a while," I said, and let her light me.

"A friend in Breslau keeps me in good cigarettes. Although for how much longer I don't know."

"That's some friend you have there." I nodded at the bags. "Is that all of them?"

"Yes. And thanks. Now all you have to do is help me with them at wherever it is we're going now. I'm just praying there's a bath."

"Oh, there is. There's even hot water to pour into it. I could scrub your back if you like."

"I see the car comes with its own spade," she said. "Is that to crack the driver over the head with if he gets any amorous ideas?"

"Sure. You could use it to bury me, too. One way or another there's a lot of that going on in this part of the world."

"So I've heard."

"I don't know if it counts as an amorous idea, but if I'd known it was you that was coming I'd have grabbed us a better ride."

"You mean with windows? And a seat instead of a saddle?"

"Let me know if you want the top down."

"Would it make any difference?"

"Probably not."

Dr. Kramsta collected a black fur stole around her neck with one hand and gathered the lapels of her matching coat with the other. Underneath a little black-beaded cloche her hair was red but not as red as her mouth, which was as full as a bowl of ripe cherries. Her chest was no less full, and for some reason I was reminded of the two churches on either side of Gendarmenmarkt—the French Church and the New Church, with their perfect matching domes. I narrowed my eyes and gave her a sideways, blurry look, but no matter how many times I did this and actively tried my best to make her look ugly, she still came out looking beautiful. She knew it, of course, and while in most women this would be a demerit, she knew that I knew that she knew it and somehow that seemed to make it just fine.

When she was as comfortable as she was ever going to be, I started the car and set off.

"You know my name," she said, "but I don't seem to know yours."

"My name is Bernhard Gunther, and I haven't talked to anyone I wanted to talk to for almost three weeks. That is, until you got off that plane. It now seems to me I've been waiting for you to show up or the world to end. For a while back there I really didn't mind which, but now that you're here, I have this sudden inexplicable urge to keep going awhile longer. Maybe even long enough to make you laugh—if that doesn't sound presumptuous."

"Make me laugh? In my line of work, that's not so easy to do, Herr Gunther. Most men give up when they get a nose of my usual brand of perfume."

"And what might that be, Doctor? Just in case I'm passing a branch of Wertheim's."

"Formaldehyde number one."

"My favorite." I shrugged. "No, really. I used to be a homicide cop at the Police Praesidium on Berlin Alexanderplatz."

"That explains your strange taste in perfume. So what are you doing in Katyn Wood? From what I hear, this isn't exactly a who-dunit. Everyone in Europe knows who the killer is."

"Right now I'm walking a tightrope between the Bureau of War Crimes and the Ministry of Enlightenment. What's more, I'm working without a net."

"Sounds like quite an act."

"It is. I'm supposed to make sure that everything here goes smoothly. Like a real police investigation. Of course, it doesn't. But then, that's Russia for you. A man who is afraid of failure should never come to Russia. It's just as well that they tried to make Bolshevism work here or we'd really be in trouble."

"That's an interesting way of looking at it."

"I've got a lot of interesting ways of looking at all sorts of things. You got anything special to do tonight?"

"I was hoping for some dinner. I'm starving."

"Dinner's at seven-thirty. And there's a good chef. From Berlin."

"After that I was hoping you might show me the cathedral."

"It'd be my pleasure."

"Cathedrals always look their best at night. Especially in Russia."

"You sound like you've been in Russia before, Dr. Kramsta."

"My father was a diplomat. As a child I lived in many interesting places: Madrid, Warsaw, and Moscow."

"And which of them did you like the best?"

"Madrid. But for the civil war, I'd probably be living there now."

"I'd have thought there were plenty of opportunities for a good doctor after a civil war."

"It will take more than a box of Traumaplast to fix that country, Herr Gunther. Besides, who ever said I was a good doctor? My bedside manner was always lacking, to say the least. I was never any good with patients. I haven't got the patience for all their aches and pains and imaginary ills. I much prefer working with the dead. The dead never complain about your lack of compassion or that you're not giving them the right medicine."

"Then you should fit right in here in Smolensk. We estimate there are at least four thousand bodies buried in Katyn Wood."

"Yes, I heard the announcement on Radio Berlin, on Tuesday night. Only they seemed to suggest it was more like twelve thousand."

I smiled. "Well, you know how Radio Berlin is with facts and figures."

At Group HQ in Krasny Bor I took Dr. Kramsta to her quarters, carried the luggage through the door, and handed her a crude little map of the compound.

"That's my hut over there, in case you need me for anything," I told her. "Right now I'm going over to the site. That's where Professor Buhtz is nearly always to be found these days. But if you like I can wait fifteen minutes and then you can come with me. Otherwise, I'll see you at dinner."

"No, I'll come with you," she said. "I'm anxious to get started."

When I returned she had changed into white trousers, a white turban, a white coat, and black boots; she looked like the Sarotti chocolate Moor, but on her that was still becoming as hell; I always did have a soft spot for women in white coats. I drove back to the wood and parked the Tatra. Straightaway she took out her handkerchief, sprinkled some Carat perfume onto it, and held it to her nose and mouth.

"You really have been down here for a while, haven't you?" she said.

"I was sorry to hear about Hindenburg."

"Gnezdovo," she said, as we walked up the slope to the edge of grave number one. "That means Goat's Hill, doesn't it?"

"Yes, but you won't see any goats around here. There are wolves in these woods. And before you say it, I don't mean me. Real ones."

"You're just saying that to scare me."

"Believe me, Doctor, there are many scarier things around here than a few wolves."

Near the top of the slope we came in sight of the recently constructed wooden shed. Several dozen corpses were laid out and, with the help of Lieutenant Sloventzik's translating, Buhtz was talking to a group of lean, grim-faced civilians who were the members of the Polish Red Cross.

Voss came over as soon as he saw me. I introduced him to Dr. Kramsta, who quickly excused herself and went to join Professor Buhtz.

"Is she the new pathologist Buhtz has been expecting?"

"Mm-hmm."

"Then I think I just decided to leave my body to science."

"Well, don't die yet. I need you here in Smolensk."

"Maybe you do, at that," he said. "I think I have a lead in the death of those signalmen."

Containing my own alarm for a moment, I nodded. "Let's hear it."

"It's rather awkward, sir."

Behind my back I clenched a fist; it wasn't that I was getting ready to hit Voss. I was trying to steel myself for what was coming.

But Voss had a very different explanation for what might have happened to Ribe and Greiss.

"Last night my men busted an army driver on his way into Krasny Bor who had a Russian girl hidden in the back of the truck. Her name is Tanya. Initially the driver said he'd just stopped to give the girl a lift, but the girl was quite a looker and dressed up to the peel—nice dress, shoes, silk stockings, and she spoke a bit of German, too. Which is unusual for a Popov peach. Also, when we searched her we found a bottle of Mystikum in her handbag. That's a pretty expensive perfume, sir, even back home."

"Yes, I begin to see. You're saying she was a silk."

"A half silk, anyway. She had a day job. Anyway, we questioned Tanya, and at first we got the Kremlin wall, but after we threatened to hand her over to the Gestapo, she started to talk, and when the driver found out what Tanya had told us, he gave us the rest of the setup. His name is Reuth, Viktor Reuth. It seems as if some of the boys on the switchboard have been running a ring of call girls. For officers. Normally all you had to do was speak to Ribe or Quidde and they would call the Hotel Glinka, where the doorman—the fellow in the Cossack coat—would go around the corner to an apartment on Olgastrasse and arrange for one of the girls to go to the department store on Kaufstrasse, where they were smuggled in the back door. But on this occasion, Tanya was told to wait outside the apartment for a driver from the Third Motorized Infantry to pick her up and bring her straight here."

I nodded. The GUM department store on Kaufstrasse was where most of the German officers were billeted in Smolensk. Krasny Bor was only for the general staff.

"The girls from Olgastrasse were a cut above the whores at the Glinka. They were chosen because they were amateurs and because they were always Aryan-looking, with nice clothes and good manners. The clothes seem to have been supplied by the members of the ring, or by German officers. Tanya—the one we picked up last night—has a day job as a nurse at the Smolensk State Medical Academy. And here's the thing that's really interesting, sir. The doorman at the Glinka—it turns out his name is Rudakov. Just like the fellow you reported as missing from the hospital, the fellow who might be a suspect in the death of Dr. Batov and his daughter. I did some checking, and it seems that Oleg Rudakov has a brother who was in the NKVD. At least according to some of the other girls we found living at the apartment in Olgastrasse."

"I see. And where is he now?"

"That's the thing, sir. He's disappeared, too. When we went to his apartment on Glasbergstrasse, the closet was empty and all his clothes were gone."

"I think that now would probably be a good time for you to tell me who the officer was that Tanya was meant for."

"It was Captain Hammerschmidt, from the Gestapo. Every Wednesday night he was the duty officer in the Gestapo office at Krasny Bor."

"The Gestapo? Well, that explains something."

I was thinking of what Lutz had told me, about how Hammerschmidt had refused to investigate the signaler's allegations of Ribe's disloyalty; but this wasn't what I told Voss.

"It explains why he didn't have Tanya brought to the Gestapo's local headquarters at Gnezdovo," I said. "I mean, it's one thing doing something illicit under the eyes of the Wehrmacht. It's something else to be doing it under the eyes of your own Gestapo colleagues."

"There's really no way of asking a question like that, is there?" said Voss. "Not of the local Gestapo chief."

"It would seem you're learning how to be a cop in modern Germany. It's best never to ask a question unless you think you already know the answer. Who else have you told about this? Among our own people, I mean."

"So far there's just me, an assistant secretary in the field police, and you. And Viktor Reuth knows, of course."

"And the signalmen who called the Glinka to arrange for a girl last night. By the way, who was that?"

"Both the girl and the driver claimed this was a long-standing arrangement between Hammerschmidt and Tanya. Every Wednesday night. There was no call from the 537th switchboard to the Glinka last night because there was no need for one."

I told myself I could always try to check this with Lutz—my new Gestapo source in the signals office.

Voss shook his head. "Look, sir. I don't want to go up against the Gestapo with this. The fact is, I don't want them checking too closely into my own background. There are one or two things—small things—I wouldn't like anyone to know about. I mean, it's nothing serious. It's not like I have a Jewish parent or anything like that, it's just that—"

"Don't worry about it. I have the same problem. I think everyone does. That's what they rely upon. That kind of fear. Normal human frailty makes cowards of us all."

Voss nodded. "Thanks," he said. "So, what do we do now?"

"I don't know. I really don't. The fact is, I think I know too much already. And I wish I didn't. I thought I had a pretty good reason why Ribe and Greiss were murdered."

"Oh? You didn't tell me. What is it, if you don't mind me asking?"

I shook my head. "Take my word for it, Lieutenant, this is another thing you don't want anyone to know about. Especially the

Gestapo. Anyway, now I find there's another equally good but very different reason that could have got them killed. They were in a vice racket. With any racket it's easy for things to go wrong—someone thinks they've been short-changed on a deal. Money's the best reason in the world to hold a grudge and commit murder. When Ribe and Greiss were found with their throats cut near the Hotel Glinka, perhaps they'd been collecting the money from the doorman who'd had it off the girls. And that's another motive for murdering them, of course. If someone saw the doorman handing them large handfuls of cash, well, that might have got their throats cut for them, too.

"And then there's the Rudakov connection. Dr. Batov was going to give me documentary evidence of what happened here at Katyn Wood. Only, someone tortured and murdered him to prevent that from happening. His patient, Lieutenant Rudakov, was one of the NKVD men who carried out this massacre. But now he's missing and so is a man who might have been his brother who was a doorman and pimp at the Glinka."

"I just thought of something, sir," said Voss. "Those two NCOs from the Panzergrenadiers we hanged for the rape and murder of two Russian women."

"What about them?"

"They were from the Third Division," explained Voss. "The Third absorbed the 386th Motorized Division, which more or less ceased to exist after Stalingrad."

"So they might have been driving for the signals racket, too," I said. "Like Viktor Reuth. Earning a little extra cash on the side. And they'd have had a better reason to be on the road more than the signals boys."

"Perhaps that was what your Corporal Hermichen wanted to trade for his life," said Voss. "That they were part of the same racket as the two dead men."

"Yes, it might," I said. "It just might."

I lit a cigarette and let the sweet tobacco smoke exorcise my nostrils of the loathsome stink of death that hung in the air. Unlike Dr. Kramsta, I didn't have any Carat to sprinkle on my handkerchief; I didn't even have a handkerchief.

"I'll want to speak to this Tanya," I said. "I'd like to find out how many more girls from the house on Olgastrasse were nurses who had day jobs at the Smolensk State Medical Academy. Where is she now?"

"Cooling her heels at the prison on Gefängnisstrasse. And probably trying to charm the guards into letting her go. Very beautiful is our Tanya. And very seductive."

"A blonde, you say?"

"Blond and blue-eyed with skin like honey. Like a girl on the front page of *New People*."

"I like her already. All the same, sometimes I think attractive women in this part of the world are just like trams, Lieutenant."

"How do you mean, sir?"

"I don't see one in weeks and then I meet two in one day."

THERE WAS NO WOMEN'S WING at Gefängnisstrasse but some of the holding cells—in which several prisoners were held at once—were for women only, which counted for something, I suppose. All of the guards were men from the army or the field police, and while they treated their female charges with respect, that was only in comparison to their male prisoners. Thanks to the many female soldiers who fought for the Red Army, it was generally held among Germans that Russian women were as potentially deadly as Russian men. Perhaps more so. The weekly Wehrmacht newspaper often had a story of a honey-trap *shluhya* going off with some unsuspecting Fritz who ended up losing more than just his virginity.

They brought Tanya to the same depressing room where I had interviewed the unfortunate Corporal Hermichen, and as soon as I saw her I realized I had seen her before, but Russian nurses' uniforms being as severe as they were, she'd looked very different from how she looked now. Voss had not exaggerated; her hair was the color of my father's pocket watch and her eyes were as blue as a midsummer moon. Tanya was the kind of blonde who could have stopped a whole division of cavalry with one flash of her underwear.

"Why am I still being kept here, please?" she asked Voss anxiously.

"This man wants to ask you a few questions, that's all," said Voss.

I nodded. "If you answer honestly, we'll probably let you go, Tanya," I told her gently. "Today, I shouldn't wonder. I don't think you've done very much wrong in the great scheme of things. Now that I've met you, I'm not sure that anyone has."

She nodded. "Thank you."

"It's not really you we're interested in but the Germans you worked with. And Oleg Rudakov, the doorman from the Glinka."

"He's run away," she said. "That's what I heard from some of the other girls."

"The girls in the apartment at Olgastrasse?"

"Yes," she said.

"Are any of them nurses, too?" I asked her. "At the Smolensk State Medical Academy?"

"Yes," she said. "Several. At least the better-looking ones who speak a bit of German."

"The ones who need the money, eh?"

"Everyone needs the money."

"Why did Oleg Rudakov run away? Because of what happened to you?"

"No. I think he ran away after what happened to Dr. Batov."

Her spoken German improved as the interview progressed. Which is more than could be said of my Russian; I had some language books, and I kept trying it out, but without much success.

"Was Dr. Batov involved with your call-girl ring?"

"Not directly. But he certainly knew about it. He helped keep us healthy. You know?"

"Yes. Have you any idea who might have killed him?"

Tanya shook her head. "No. Nobody knows. It's another reason why people are scared. It's why Oleg ran away, I think."

"Did you know that Oleg Rudakov had a brother who was a patient at the Smolensk State Medical?"

"Everyone in Smolensk knew this. The Rudakov brothers were both from Smolensk. Oleg used to give money to the hospital—to Dr. Batov—for looking after his brother, Arkady."

"Tell me about Arkady. Was he really injured as badly as Batov said he was? Or perhaps thought he was?"

"Do you mean was Arkady faking?" She shrugged. "I don't know. It's possible, I suppose. Arkady was always very clever. That's what people said. I did not know him before his injury—when he was NKVD—but to be lieutenant in NKVD you have to be clever. Clever enough never again to want to do what he and others had to do in Katyn Wood. Clever enough to find a way out, perhaps, that did not mean he, too, would be shot."

"So, you know about that, too? About what happened in Katyn Wood?"

"Everyone in Smolensk knows about this terrible thing. Everyone. Anyone who says they don't is lying. Lying because they are afraid. Or lying because they hate Germans more than they hate NKVD. I cannot say which it is because I don't know, but they are lying. Lying is best way to stay alive in this town. Three years ago, when this thing happened—yes, it was spring of 1940—the militia closed the road to Vitebsk, but they did not stop the train. I heard that people who were on the trains near Gnezdovo heard the sound of shots from Katyn Wood—at least until the NKVD came onto the trains and made sure all of the windows were closed."

"You're sure about this?" I said.

"That everyone knows what happened? Yes, I'm sure." Tanya's eyes flashed defiantly. "Just as everyone knows there were two thousand Jews from the ghetto at Vitebsk murdered by the German Army at Mazurino. Not to mention all of the Jews who were found floating in the Zapadnaya Dvina River. They say that the lampreys caught from the Zap are the biggest ever this year because of all the bodies they had to feed on."

Voss groaned, and I guessed it was because he'd eaten lamprey pie for dinner in the mess at Krasny Bor the previous evening.

I smiled. "Thank you, Tanya. You've been most helpful."

"I can go?"

"We'll take you home, if you like."

"Thank you, but no, I'll walk. Is all right at night when no one sees. But not in the day. After you Germans have gone from Smolensk, it will be pretty bad here, I think. It is best the NKVD don't know I go with Germans."

THE LOCAL GESTAPO WAS STATIONED in a two-story house next to the railway station at Gnezdovo so that officers could board the train and surprise anyone traveling on to the next stop, at Smolensk's main station. The Gestapo always loved surprises; and so did I, which was why I was there, of course—although out of consideration for Lieutenant Voss, I decided to spare him the ordeal of accompanying me to see Captain Hammerschmidt; he was in for a big surprise— perhaps the biggest surprise of his career. I pulled up in a cobbled yard next to a pair of camouflaged 260s, stepped out, and took a longer look at the building in front of me. The bullet-marked walls were painted two contrasting shades of green, the darker matching the color of the roof tiles, and there were bull's-eye windows on the upper floor; the windows on the ground floor were all heavily barred. The clock above the arched entrance had stopped at six o'clock, which might have been meant as a metaphor since that was often the time in the morning when the Gestapo preferred to call. In the grove of silver birch trees a short way from the house was a pile of sandbags fronted with an ominous-looking wooden post. Everything looked just as it ought to have done, although the building was, for my plainer taste, the wrong flavor; a sprinkling of chocolate chips on the mint ice-cream roof would hardly have looked out of place. Everything was quiet but that wasn't unusual; the Gestapo never have a problem with noisy neighbors. Even the squirrels in the trees were behaving themselves. Gradually a steam locomotive approached wheezily from the east; very sensibly it didn't stop at the deserted station. It was never a good idea to stop in the vicinity of the Gestapo. I knew that only too well, but I was never very good at listening to advice, especially my own.

I went inside, where several uniformed men behind several typewriters were doing their best to type with two fingers and to pretend that I didn't exist. So I lit a cigarette and calmly glanced over some of the paper on the bulletin board; among this was a wanted notice for Lieutenant Arkady Rudakov, which struck me as ironic since from the emblem on the bulletin board and on some of the drawers on the filing cabinets—a yellow-handle sword against a red shield—I took the house to have belonged to the NKVD before it had belonged to the Gestapo.

"Can I help you?" one of the men said in a tone that was distinctly unhelpful. From the mild outrage I could hear in his querulous voice and see on his equally peevish face, he might have been addressing an impertinent schoolboy.

"I'm looking for Captain Hammerschmidt."

I went over to the window and pretended to look outside but most of my attention was fixed on the fly running along the pane; the flies were everywhere now, following up the business of the Gestapo and the NKVD.

"Not here," he said.

"When are you expecting him back?"

"Who wants to know?" said the man.

"I do." Now I was trying to match him for arrogance and contempt, well aware that I was about to win the game, and easily, too.

"And who are you?"

I showed him my identity card, which was better than any ace, and my letter from the ministry.

The man folded.

"Sorry, sir. He was called back to Berlin, this morning. Unexpectedly."

"Did he say why?"

"Compassionate leave, sir. A death in the family."

"That's a surprise. Which is to say it isn't a surprise at all. At least not to me, anyway."

"How's that, sir?"

"What I mean is—I didn't know there was any compassion in the Gestapo."

I laid my business card on the corner of the man's desk.

"Tell him to come and find me at Group HQ," I said. "That is, when he's finished grieving in Berlin. Tell him—tell him that I'm a friend of Tanya."

DR. MARIANNE KRAMSTA HAD A noticeably galvanizing effect on the officers' mess at Krasny Bor; it was as if someone had opened a grimy window and let the sunshine into that stuffy wooden room; almost every officer in Group HQ seemed to find her attractive, which was no surprise to me and probably not to her, either, since she hadn't dressed for dinner so much as armed herself for the conquest of all the Germans in Smolensk. Perhaps this is not entirely fair: Marianne Kramsta was wearing a very fetching gray crepe dress with a matching belt and long sleeves, and while she looked good, the plain fact of the matter is that she would have looked good wearing a truck tarpaulin. I watched with some amusement as one man drew out her chair, another fetched her a glass of Mosel, a third lit her cigarette, and a fourth found her an ashtray. All in all, there was a great deal of bowing and heel-clicking and kissing of her hand, which by the end of the evening must have looked like a petri dish. Even von Kluge was struck with her and, having insisted that Dr. Kramsta and Professor Buhtz join him and General von Tresckow at the field marshal's own table, it wasn't long before he was ordering champagne—I daresay that after cashing Hitler's check he could afford it—and conducting himself like a smitten young subaltern in a romantic novel. Generally, everyone behaved as if there had been an officers' ball after all—with only one girl; and I'd almost made up my mind that the beautiful doctor had completely forgotten our date when, just after nine o'clock and underneath everyone's widening eyes, she presented herself at my own insignificant corner table holding a fur coat and asked me if I was ready to drive her into Smolensk to see the Assumption Cathedral.

I jumped up like a young subaltern myself, stubbed out a cigarette, helped the lady on with the coat, and ushered her outside to a 260 I'd borrowed for the evening from von Gersdorff. I opened the car door and ushered her inside.

"Oooh, has it got a heater?" she said when I was seated beside her.

"A heater, seats, windows, windshield wipers, it's got everything except a spade," I said, as we drove away.

"You're not kidding," she said.

I glanced to my right and saw she was holding the stock of a broom-handle Mauser on her lap. The stock was like a holster/carry-case: you clicked open the back of the stock and out came the gun that attached to it. Very neat.

"It was in the door pocket," she said. "Like a road map."

"The fellow who owns this car is with the Abwehr," I said. "He likes to get where he's going. A broom-handle Mauser will do that for you."

"A spy. How exciting."

"Be careful with that," I said instinctively. "It's probably loaded."

"Actually, it's not," she said, checking the breech for a moment. "But there's a couple of stripper clips in the door pocket. And really, you mustn't worry. I know what I'm doing. I've handled guns before."

"So I see."

"I always liked the old box cannon," she said. "That's what my brother used to call this gun. He had two."

"Two guns are always better than one. That's my philosophy."

"Sadly, it didn't work for him. He was killed in the Spanish Civil War."

"On which side?"

"Does it matter now?"

"Not to him."

She returned the Mauser to the inside of the stock and then to the leather door pocket. Then she flipped open the glove box.

"Your spy friend," said Marianne. "He doesn't believe in taking any chances, does he?"

"Hmm?" I glanced at her again and this time she was drawing a bayonet from its scabbard and scraping the edge with the flat of her thumb.

I slowed the car at the gate, waved at the sentries on duty, and drove onto the main road, where I slipped the spindle shift into neutral, lifted the clutch, pulled on the hand brake, and took a closer look at the bayonet.

"Careful, it's as sharp as a surgeon's catlin," she said.

It was a standard-issue K98 of the kind you'd have found on any German soldier's bolt-action short rifle; and she was right: the edge was paper thin.

"What's the matter?" she said. "It's just a bayonet."

"Yes. It's just a bayonet, isn't it?"

I nodded and handed it back to her to return to the glove box; after all, von Gersdorff's bayonet wasn't missing a scabbard. And I saw little point in telling her that a bayonet had been the probable weapon in the murders of four people in Smolensk, one of them a young woman who had been tortured.

"I suppose I thought that the man who owns this car wasn't exactly the type to use a knife."

I told myself he was hardly the type to blow himself up, either. I put the car back in gear and drove on.

"Then again, you can't be too careful in an enemy country at night."

"You make that sound like I should stay very close to you, Gunther."

"Like a pill I swallowed. But you're the doctor. I guess you'll know what's healthy for both of us."

"Call me Ines, would you? Most people do."

"Ines? I thought your name was Marianne."

"It is. But I never liked that name very much. When I was a girl living in Spain, I decided I much preferred to be called Ines. It's what my mother wanted to call me. Don't you think it's better?"

"Actually, it's getting better every time I think about it. I think it suits you. Like that fur and the Carat you're wearing."

All the way into Smolensk I kept Ines amused with my conversation, and her bright smiles and easy laughter were like a kind of prize in my eyes; when I spoke to her, it was as if there was no one else in the world.

We reached the outskirts of the city, and at the roadblock on the Peter and Paul bridge we showed our papers to the field police; by now my association with Lieutenant Voss meant that they were beginning to recognize me; but seeing Ines Kramsta with her legs crossed in the front seat of the Mercedes gave them a thrill.

"Watch it, boys, she's a doctor and it's castor oil for both of you if you don't let us through."

"I'd drink anything right now," confessed one of the bloodhounds.

"Mind me asking where you're going, sir?" asked the other.

"The doc wants to see the cathedral. Saint Luke is the patron saint of doctors."

"Yes, well, see if he can't be persuaded to look out for a couple of sentries in the field police while he's at it."

"We'll certainly do our best," said Ines.

There wasn't much to do in Smolensk at night if you didn't want to try the pleasures of the brothels or the local cinema, and the Cathedral Church of the Assumption was full of devout Russians and quite a few almost as devout German soldiers; you could tell they were devout by the fact that some of the Germans were praying to Our Lady and Saint Luke, but that might just have been the fact that our position in southern Russia was becoming critical; Soviet forces were now pushing west and threatening to isolate Army Group A in the Caucasus in the same way as the Sixth Army had been encircled at Stalingrad. One way or another, there was quite a lot to pray about, if you were a German. I guess the Russians were praying their cathedral might still be standing when the Germans pulled out of Smolensk. They had quite a bit to pray about, too. Either way, God was going to have to choose sides and choose soon: the godless communists or the blaspheming Germans. Who would be God with a choice like that?

Inside, standing in front of the iconostasis, we were both silent for a long while, and gradually silence gave way to reflection. With so much gold around there was plenty of that to be found. I had to admit, the cathedral was beautiful, and it wasn't just the gold that made me appreciate it; it reminded me a little of the Berlin Cathedral Church on Unter den Linden and going there at Easter with my mother. Every cathedral does that to me, which is why I tend to keep away from them. I guess Freud would have called it an Oedipus complex, but me, I think I just miss my mother.

"They say Napoleon liked the cathedral so much he threatened to kill any French soldier who stole anything off the iconostasis," I said quietly in her ear.

"That's dictators for you. Always threatening to kill someone."

"Why do people want to be dictators anyway?"

"Not people. Men. And have you noticed how they always claim to love art and architecture?"

"Maybe so, but I happen to know that Hitler didn't bother to look at this cathedral when he was here a few weeks ago. At least not from the ground. He might have had a good look at it from the air."

"Then he missed a wonderful experience."

"Amen to that. You know, I never had a date with a girl in a cathedral. I think maybe I should have tried it before now. Being here with you almost makes me believe in God."

"I think the incense is going to your head."

"Maybe you're right. I just had the megalomaniacal idea of trying to annex you for the Greater German Reich."

"I think it's time you drove me back to Krasny Bor."

"What, and miss the Kremlin in the moonlight?"

"There's always tomorrow night. If you want to. Besides, Professor Buhtz likes to start his forensic work first thing."

"The early bird catches the worm, huh?"

"In my line of work, there's always that possibility. But it's more likely the other way around. There's not much escapes worms. Believe me, you can tell a lot from them. That's one of my forensic specialties: tissue degeneration. How long a body has been dead. That kind of thing."

"You're right. I'd better drive you home."

"Hey, I thought you liked my perfume, Gunther."

"Formaldehyde number one? Oh, I do like it. But I have to get some rest, too. I'm taking a girl to see the Kremlin in the moonlight tomorrow night."

We hardly knew each other and yet, without ever having acknowledged it with so much as a word or a brushed finger, we both seemed to recognize something in the other's eyes that—against all expectation and beyond all understanding—felt as if it was determined to make us lovers. We had connected on some invisible level behind our clever conversation and common courtesies, and it would have spoiled the game if either one of us had mentioned aloud what we sincerely hoped would happen. There was no admission of what we really felt—an atavistic attraction that was more than lust and yet not love, either; words—even German words—would have been inadequate and certainly too clumsy for what we felt. No more was there any kind of objection raised to the idea of what hovered unspoken in the air between us. Never; not once. It just seemed as if we both knew it was going to happen because it was simply meant to be. Of course, that kind of thing happened a lot during the war, but still, this felt like something out of the ordinary. Perhaps it was the place we were in and what we were doing, as if there was so much death around that it would have seemed a kind of blasphemy not to have gone along with what the capricious generosity of life seemed willing to thrust upon us.

And when standing in front of her wooden door, we turned expectantly toward each other, the trees at Krasny Bor held their silvery breath, and the darkness discreetly closed its black eyes so that nothing might prevent this final coming together. But like a conductor trying to settle his orchestra for a long, silent moment, I just held her and looked at the perfect oval of her face in anticipation of the moment when I might inhale the sweet breath in her mouth and taste the subtler heaven in her lips. Then I kissed her. At the brush of my mouth on hers, I heard bees in my ears and felt a leap in my chest as strong as if the damper mechanism had been lifted on a grand piano and every string sounded at once, and my apotheosis was complete.

"Are you coming in, Bernhard Gunther?" she asked.

"I think I am," I said.

"You know something, Bernie? You ought to be a gambler, luck like yours."

9

WEDNESDAY, APRIL 28, 1943

I had to hand it to Goebbels; the minister had chosen his Katyn public relations officer carefully. Lieutenant Gregor Sloventzik wasn't even a member of the Party. Moreover, he seemed to be extremely good at what he did—a real Edward Bernays, a man who understood the science of ballyhoo extremely well; I thought I'd never met a man who was better at handling people—everyone from the field marshal to Boris Bazilevsky, the deputy mayor of Smolensk.

Sloventzik was a reserve army officer who'd worked as a journalist on the *Wiener Zeitung* before the war, which was how he knew the people at the ministry. The first state secretary in the ministry, Otto Dietrich, and Arthur Seyss-Inquart, the Austrian-born Reichskommissar for the Occupied Netherlands, were both reputed to be his close personal friends. Smooth and personable, Sloventzik was in his early forties with an easy smile and impeccable manners. He was tall, with longish hair and a hawk-face, and with his dark complexion he was no one's idea of a Nazi. He wore a tailored lieutenant's army uniform as if it had been that of a colonel and, under his right arm, he was forever carrying a large ring file that contained a wide variety of important facts and figures about what had been discovered concerning bodies in the mass grave at Katyn Wood. His efficiency and diplomatic skills were only exceeded by his great facility with languages; but his powers of diplomacy came crashing down to earth when, a matter of hours before the arrival of the international commission representatives, the Polish Red Cross decided that Sloventzik had grievously insulted the whole Polish nation and hence it was now considering returning immediately to Poland.

Count Casimir Skarzynski, the secretary general of the Polish Red Cross, with whom I had formed a closer acquaintance—I wouldn't have called it a friendship, exactly—and Archdeacon Jasinski came to my hut at Krasny Bor, where, much to the irritation of Field Marshal von Kluge, they were staying, and explained the problem.

"I don't really know who and what you are, Herr Gunther," the count said carefully. "And I don't really care. But—"

"I told you before, sir. I'm from the German War Crimes Bureau in Berlin. Before the war I was a humble policeman. A homicide detective. There used to be a law against that sort of thing, you know. When people killed other people, we put them in prison. Of course, that was before the war. Anyway, until you arrived, Judge Conrad and I were, at the invitation of the Wehrmacht, the investigating officers here in Katyn."

He nodded. "Yes. So you say."

I shrugged. "Why don't you tell me how Lieutenant Sloventzik has insulted your nation and I'll see what I can do to put that right?"

The count removed a brown homburg hat from his head and wiped his high forehead. He was a very tall, distinguished, gray-haired man of about sixty and wore a three-piece tweed suit that already looked too warm for comfort. It seemed like only yesterday that Smolensk had been too cold for comfort.

The archdeacon, more than a head shorter, wore a plain black suit and a biretta; he took off his glasses and shook his skull-like head. "I'm not sure this can be fixed," he said. "Sloventzik is being unusually obdurate. On two separate matters."

"That doesn't sound like him at all," I said. "He always seems so unfeasibly reasonable."

The count sighed. "Not this time," he said.

"Sloventzik has repeatedly informed us that our report should list twelve thousand bodies in Katyn Wood," said the archdeacon. "That is the figure provided by the German Ministry of Propaganda in its radio broadcasts. Our own information, however—from the Polish government in London—suggests a figure of less than half as many. But Sloventzik is quite adamant about this and has suggested that were he to disagree with your own government's figures, it might cost him his head. I'm afraid this has caused several members of our party to ask questions about our own safety."

"You see," added the count, "one or two members of the Polish Red Cross have friends or relations who have suffered at the hands of the Gestapo or who were even beheaded in German prisons in Warsaw and Krakow."

"I can see your point," I said. "Look, I'm sure I can sort this out, gentlemen. I'll speak to Berlin and have this matter clarified today. In the meantime, I can assure you that regarding the security of all the members of the Polish Red Cross, there is absolutely no cause for concern. And you have my apologies for whatever alarm you've encountered here today. I might add that Lieutenant Sloventzik has been working extremely hard ahead of the arrival of the international commission to make sure that everything runs smoothly. You'll appreciate that his only concern has been to make sure that this bestial crime is properly investigated. Frankly, gentlemen, I think he's been working too hard. I know I have."

"Yes, that is possible," admitted the count. "He is most diligent in many respects. There is, however, another matter, and that is the issue of the *Volksdeutsche*. Poles born in Poland for whom German, and not Polish, is their first language. Poles who before the Great War were East Prussians. *Ethnic Germans.*"

"Yes, I know what they are," I said patiently. "But what have ethnic Germans to do with any of this?"

"Many of the bodies that have been found so far were Polish officers of German origin," explained the count.

"Look, I'm sorry, gentlemen," I said, "but these officers are dead and I don't see that it matters very much now where they came from if they were butchered by the Russians."

"It matters," explained the archdeacon stiffly, "because Sloventzik has ordered a separation between those Polish officers who are discovered to be *Volksdeutsche* in origin and those who are not. The lieutenant proposes that the Silesian ethnic Germans receive separate burial. It's almost as if the rest of the Poles are to be treated as second-class citizens because they are ethnic Slavs."

"The Slavs who have been exhumed are not to be given coffins," said the count.

"Well, he's only a lieutenant. As his superior officer, it's a very simple matter for me to countermand that order. I tell him to do something, and he salutes and says, 'Yes, sir.'"

"You might reasonably think so," said the count. "Especially in a German army that prides itself on obeying orders. However, it's our belief that Sloventzik's been put up to this by Field Marshal von Kluge, who, as I'm sure you know, is a Silesian German himself. From Posen. And has no love for ethnic Poles like us."

This was more complicated; it wasn't just von Kluge who, like the late Paul von Hindenburg, was a Silesian German, it was Colonel von Gersdorff and, to my knowledge, several other senior officers at Army Group Center, many of them proud Prussian aristocrats who had narrowly escaped becoming Poles because of the Treaty of Versailles.

"I see what you mean." I offered them each a cigarette, which,

Polish cigarettes being what they were, the two Poles accepted gratefully. "And you're absolutely right. This does sound as if the field marshal is behind it. I don't think his sense of honor and pride has ever recovered from the Seven Years' War. However, I can promise you gentlemen that this matter is being followed at the highest levels in Berlin. It was Dr. Goebbels himself who insisted that you be given control of the investigation here in Katyn. He's told me nothing is to be done that interferes in any way with your preeminent role in this matter. My own orders make it quite clear that the German military authorities in Smolensk are to give the Polish Red Cross every assistance."

I smiled to myself and put my hand to my mouth, as if I might belch after swallowing such egregious lies whole—not just the lies Goebbels told, but the lies I'd told myself.

"It may be, however, that these orders need to be heard again, in certain quarters. I can even write it down in the lieutenant's ring file, if you like. Just to make sure that he remembers."

"Thank you," said Archdeacon Jasinski. "You've been most helpful."

I figured he was the person in the Polish Red Cross probably most in fear of the Nazis; according to what Freiherr von Gersdorff had told me, when Jasinski had been the bishop of Lodz, he had been subjected to close home arrest; the governor of the Kalisz-Lodz District, one Friedrich Übelhör, had forced him to sweep the square in front of the cathedral, while his auxiliary bishop, Monsignor Tomczak, had been sent to a concentration camp after suffering a brutal beating. That kind of thing can test a man's faith not just in his fellow men but in God, too. I'd seen the archdeacon crossing himself on the edge of grave number one; he did it with such alacrity that I wondered if he was reminding himself of what he believed, although the evidence of his own eyes ought to have told him that God was not to be found in Katyn Wood and probably nowhere else, either. Even the cathedral felt more like a museum.

I smiled. "Don't thank me yet, Archdeacon. Give me time here.

History teaches that my superiors can always be depended on to entertain me with one disappointment heaped on top of another."

"One more thing," said the count.

"Two," said the archdeacon. "The Szkoła Podchorążych."

"Please." I glanced at my wristwatch. "I think I'm nearing the limit of my usefulness."

"The lieutenant's ring file contains other mistakes that we've tried to bring to his attention," said the count. "He says the trees on the grave are four years old, but this would mean they were planted in 1939, a year before—"

"I think we can all remember what happened in 1939," I said.

"And he says the epaulettes on some of the victims have the initials 'J.P.' when they are actually 'S.P.,' which is the Polish Cadet Officer's School."

"If you'll forgive me, Count, I have to go to the airport and help look after the distinguished medical representatives of twelve countries, not to mention journalists and other Red Cross officials."

"Of course," said the count.

"But rest assured, gentlemen, I promise to speak to Berlin today about those two other matters we discussed. It will give me something to do."

BUHTZ, INES, SLOVENTZIK, AND I WENT in a coach to fetch the experts and their assistants from the airport. I had a peculiar feeling about that coach. Supplied by the SS, it had new windows, and the floor under the carpet was made of thick steel; beneath the hood was a Saurer engine, but it was fitted with a curious gas generator that ran on wood chips—you could smell the huge amounts of carbon monoxide it created long after the thing had gone—because, according to the driver, gasoline was short and all our spare supplies were now being directed north to supply the Ninth Army. That much was true, I knew, but still, I had a peculiar feeling about that coach.

Ines told me she was very excited because the international commission included all of the most distinguished names in the field of forensic medicine outside of Great Britain and the United States, and that she hoped to learn much from these men during their three days in Smolensk. She was as eager as if she'd been a little girl who was going to meet her favorite movie stars. Professor Naville of Geneva and Professor Cortes of Madrid were the two she declared to be specially eminent in her field; the rest were from as far afield as Belgium, Bulgaria, Denmark, Finland, Croatia, Italy, Holland, Bohemia and Moravia, Romania, Slovakia, Hungary, and France. Not officially part of the international commission, Buhtz and Ines were going to present the experts with evidence they had collected from the 908 bodies that had so far been exhumed; but the commission's all-important report was to be compiled without any German participation. Being the ringmaster suited Buhtz just fine; he was tired; since the beginning of April he'd carried out more postmortems than an Etruscan soothsayer and identified almost seven hundred men. Ines had performed several dozen postmortems herself; and when it was all over and done with, I wondered what she'd make of my own entrails.

In truth, none of the great experts were exciting to look at; they were mostly a collection of elderly-looking, pipe-smoking gentlemen wearing gabardine coats with battered briefcases and equally battered felt hats; none of them looked remotely like what this was: a lot of money and a great deal of trouble. And it was perhaps no more a genuine international commission of inquiry than a pathologists' jamboree. What it was—if anyone had stopped and listened to the operetta of silence that had been written by the Nazis—was the most expensive piece of propaganda ever dreamed up by the doctor; with a little help from me, of course. I had my own reasons for that; and if things worked out, then maybe I'd have achieved something important.

When the plane landed and the experts were counted off on

Sloventzik's clipboard, we learned that at the last minute Professor Cortes from Spain had decided not to come and Dr. Agapito Girauta Berruguete, who was a professor of pathological anatomy at Madrid University, had taken his place.

This seemed to be disturbing news to Ines, who was silent all the way from the airport back to Krasny Bor. I asked her about it, but she smiled a sad little smile and said it was nothing in the kind of way that makes you think that there was more in it than she was prepared to tell—the way women do sometimes. It's what makes them mysterious to men and, on occasion, infuriating, too. But they will have their secrets and there's no good worrying at it like a dog with its teeth clenched on a piece of rag; the best thing you can do when that happens is just to let it go.

AFTER LEAVING THE EXPERTS TO GET themselves settled in at Krasny Bor, I drove the short distance back to the castle to send a telegram to the ministry asking them to countermand any local orders about a separate burial for *Volksdeutsche* Polish officers and to correct the numbers of dead in the official broadcasts. Lutz was the signaler on duty. While I was waiting for a reply from the Wilhelmstrasse, I offered him a cigarette and asked what he knew about the call-girl ring that Ribe and Quidde had been running.

"I knew they were working some kind of racket but I didn't know it was girls," he said. "I thought it was army surplus, that kind of thing. Cigarettes, saccharin, a little bit of petrol."

"Captain Hammerschmidt from the Gestapo appears to have been a regular client," I said. "Which would explain why he was so reluctant to follow up on your initial report."

"I see."

"That might also be what got them killed," I added. "Maybe someone thought he wasn't getting his proper cut." I shook my head. "Any ideas?"

"None," admitted Lutz.

"It didn't bother you, for example, that you were being kept out of the action."

"Not enough to kill them," he said calmly. "If that's what you mean."

"It is."

Lutz shrugged and might have said something more but for the fact that the telegraph sprang into action.

"This looks like your reply from Berlin," he said, as he began to decipher the message.

When he'd finished, he turned to the typewriter.

"No need to type it out," I said. "I can read your capital letters."

The message was from Goebbels himself; it read:

TOP SECRET. KATYN INCIDENT HAS TAKEN SENSATIONAL TURN. SOVIETS HAVE BROKEN OFF DIPLOMATIC RELATIONS WITH POLES BECAUSE OF "ATTITUDE OF POLISH GOVERNMENT IN EXILE." REUTERS ISSUED EARLIER REPORT TO THIS EFFECT. AMERICAN PUBLIC OPINION NOW DIVIDED. AM WITHHOLDING NEWS HERE IN GERMANY FOR PRESENT, HOWEVER. POLES ARE BEING BLAMED BY BRITISH GOVT FOR NAIVELY PLAYING INTO OUR HANDS. I AWAIT MORE DEVELOPMENTS TO SEE WHAT I CAN DO WITH THIS NEWS. REPRESENTS A 100 PERCENT VICTORY FOR GERMAN PROPAGANDA. SELDOM IN THIS WAR HAS GERMAN PROPAGANDA REGISTERED SUCH A SUCCESS. WELL DONE TO YOU AND ALL CONCERNED AT KATYN WOOD. HAVE ASKED KEITEL IN CAPACITY AS CHIEF OF OKW TO ORDER VON KLUGE TO COMPLY WITH POLISH RED CROSS REQUEST REGARDING VOLKSDEUTSCHE. GOEBBELS.

"All right," I told Lutz. "Now you can type this out neatly. There are others who need to see this, including the Polish Red Cross."

When Lutz had finished typing out the message I folded it up and placed it carefully in an envelope. As I was leaving the castle I bumped into Alok Dyakov. As usual he was carrying the Mauser Safari rifle that had been a gift from the field marshal. Seeing me, he snatched off his cap respectfully and grinned, almost as if he knew that I knew he was there to see Marusya, the castle kitchen maid with whom he had a romantic attachment.

"Captain Gunther, sir," he said. "How are you, sir? Good to see you again."

"Dyakov," I said. "I've been meaning to ask you something. When we first met, Colonel Ahrens told me you were rescued from an NKVD murder squad that was going to shoot you. Is that right?"

"Not a squad, sir, it was an individual NKVD officer called Mikhail Spiridonovich Krivyenko and his blue-hat driver. German soldiers found me handcuffed to his car after I killed him, sir. He was taking me to prison in Smolensk, sir. Or possibly to execute. I hit him and then couldn't find the key to the manacles. Lieutenant Voss found me sitting at the side of the road beside his body."

"And the NKVD arrested you because you were a German teacher—is that right?"

"Yes, sir." He shrugged. "You are right. Today, if you are not working for NKVD and you speak German is virtually the same as to be a member of fifth column community. How Peshkov stayed out of their hands I don't know. Anyway, after 1941, when Germany attacked Russia, this made me suspicious to the authorities. It is the same as if I had been a Polish-Russian."

"Yes, I know." I gave him a cigarette. "Tell me, did you know any other NKVD officers in Smolensk?"

"You mean other than Krivyenko? No, sir." He shook his head. "Mostly I tried just to keep out of their way. They're easy to recognize, sir. NKVD wear a very distinctive uniform. Names I hear, sometimes. But like I say, I keep away from these men. Is only sensible thing to do."

"What names did you hear?"

Dyakov was thoughtful for a moment and then looked pained. "Yezhov, sir. Yagoda. These were famous names in NKVD. Everyone heard their names. And Beria. Him, of course."

"I meant lower-ranking than those names."

Dyakov shook his head. "It's been a while, sir."

"Rudakov," I said. "Ever hear about him?"

"Everyone in Smolensk knows that name, sir. But which Rudakov do you mean? Lieutenant Rudakov was head of local NKVD station, sir. After he was hurt, his half brother, Oleg, came back to Smolensk to look after him. From where I don't know. But when Germans took Smolensk, he got the job as doorman at Glinka to stay on and keep an eye on his brother, sir. You know what I think, sir? I think he found out that Dr. Batov had told you about what happened here in Katyn. And so he killed Batov and took Arkady away somewhere safe. To protect him. To protect them both, I think."

"You might just be right about that," I said.

Dyakov shrugged. "In life we can't always win, sir."

I smiled. "I'm not sure I ever learned how."

"Is there anything else I can help you with, sir?" asked Dyakov unctuously.

"No, I don't think so."

"You know, sir, now that I come to think about it, there is someone who might know something about Oleg Rudakov: Peshkov. Before he got his job translating for the adjutant at Krasny Bor, Peshkov was translating for the girls at the Hotel Glinka. So that the madam could tell the German boys about how much and how long."

THE EXPERTS IN THE INTERNATIONAL COMMISSION were accommodated in one large hut at Krasny Bor that had been vacated by German officers—most of whom went to live in the GUM department store in Smolensk—and that night, in the absence of half his general staff, Field Marshal von Kluge offered these distinguished professors the hospitality of his mess, which he had not done with the members of the Polish Red Cross. Perhaps this wasn't so strange; of the many countries represented in the international commission, five were friendly to Germany and two were neutral. Besides, the field marshal was keen to speak French—which he did excellently—with Professor Speelers from Ghent and Dr. Costedoat from Paris. I won't say that we were a jolly party. No, I wouldn't have said that. For one thing, Ines absented herself from the dinner, which, for me at any rate, was like someone blowing out a beautifully scented candle. And after Tanya's story about the river Zapadnaya Dvina, I had little stomach for more lamprey pie. But I had no choice but to swallow a dull conversation with Judge Conrad, who had been spending most of his time examining some reluctant Russian witnesses about what had happened at Katyn—which was the last thing I wanted to talk about.

After an excellent brandy and a cigarette from the field marshal's own silver box, I went for a walk around the grounds at Krasny Bor. I hadn't gone very far when Colonel von Gersdorff caught up with me.

"It's a fine night," he said. "Mind if I join you?"

"Be my guest. But I'm not much company tonight."

"Nor am I," he said. "I missed dinner. Somehow I didn't fancy dining with all those forensic scientists. It looked a bit like the aquarium at the Berlin Zoo in there. All those cold fish in their precise little spaces. I was speaking to one of them this afternoon: Professor Berruguete, from Spain. It was like talking to a very unpleasant species of squid. So I went for a walk instead. And now here you are."

Try as I might, it was hard to imagine the colonel holding that bayonet; a dueling saber, maybe—even the broom-handle Mauser—but not a bayonet. He didn't look like someone who could ever have cut someone's throat.

"What did you talk about?" I asked.

"With the professor? He holds some very unpleasant opinions about race and eugenics. Seems to think that Marxists are degenerates and will enfeeble our German race, if we let them live. My God, I swear, some of these Spanish fascists make the Nazis look like models of reason and tolerance."

"And what do you think, Colonel? About Marxists?"

"Oh, please, for God's sake, let's not talk about politics. I might not like the communists but I've never thought of them as subhuman. Misguided, perhaps. But not degenerate or racially corrupt the way he does. Christ, Gunther, what do you take me for?"

"You're not the fool I thought you were, that's for sure."

Von Gersdorff laughed. "Thanks very much."

"By the way, what's the news of von Dohnanyi and Bonhoeffer?"

"They're both in Tegel Military Prison, awaiting trial. But so far we've been very lucky. The judge advocate general appointed to investigate their case is Karl Sack. He's very sympathetic to our cause."

"That is good news."

"Meanwhile, we listened to your tape. Myself and General von Tresckow. And von Schlabrendorff."

"It wasn't my tape," I insisted. "It was Corporal Quidde's tape. Let's get that straight, just in case of any mishap. I don't happen to have any friends who are judge advocate general."

"Yes. All right. I take your point. But the tape certainly confirms what you said about von Kluge. You know, I didn't believe it when you told me, but I could hardly ignore the evidence of that tape. Anyway, it puts a whole new complexion on our conspiracy here in Smolensk. It's very clear we can't trust those we thought we could trust. Henning—I mean von Tresckow—is very upset and angry with the field marshal. They're old friends, after all. At the same time, it now seems that von Kluge may not be the first Prussian Junker that Hitler ever bought off. There have been others, including, I'm afraid to say, Paul von Hindenburg. It may even be that back in 1933 Hitler agreed to drop the Reichstag's 'East-Help' investigation into the misappropriation of parliamentary subsidies by Junker land barons in return for the president's blessing for his becoming chancellor."

I nodded. It was only what many like me had always suspected—a behind-the-scenes deal between the Nazis and the impoverished aristocrats of East Prussia that had let the Nazis to snatch control of the German government.

"Then it seems only fitting that your class should be the one to get rid of Hitler, given it was your lot who landed us with him in the first place."

"Touché," said von Gersdorff. "But look here, you can't say we haven't tried."

"No one could ever say *you* haven't tried," I admitted. "I'm not so sure about the others."

A little sheepishly von Gersdorff looked at his watch. "I'd better be getting along. General von Tresckow is joining me for a drink in a while." He flicked away his cigarette. "By the way, have you heard the news? The Soviets have broken off diplomatic relations in London with the Poles. I got a telegram this morning from the Abwehr. It would seem that the little doctor's plan is working."

"Yes. I'm almost sorry I gave him the idea."

"Did you?"

"I think I did," I said. "Although him being him, he probably thinks it was all his idea."

"Why did you?"

"You have your plans to knock over the heap and so have I. Perhaps my plans will take less courage than yours, Colonel. In fact, I'm sure of it. I aim to be alive when my bomb goes off. Not a real bomb, you understand. But there will be a sort of an explosion, and I hope some serious repercussions."

"Would you care to share those plans with me?"

"Trust doesn't come easily to a Fritz with my background, Colonel. Perhaps if I had an extensive family tree framed on the wall of my big house in East Prussia, I could share them with you. But I'm just a regular boy from Mitte. The only family tree I can remember is a rather sorry-looking linden in the gloomy yard my mother called a garden. Besides, I think you'll do better not knowing what I'm up to. I'm not a hundred percent sure yet I'm even doing the right thing, but when I go through with it—or don't go through with it—I mean to make sure I'm only answerable to my own conscience and no one else's."

"Now I really am intrigued. I had no idea you were so independently minded, Gunther. Or so resourceful. Of course, there is the rather enterprising way you shot Corporal Quidde in the head in Glinka Park. Yes, we mustn't forget what happened there."

"That certainly doesn't make me independently minded, Colonel. Not since Operation Barbarossa. These days everyone is shooting someone in the head. It was necessary to put a tap in the corporal's head, and I just happened to be in the right place at the right time. I've always been lucky that way. No, it's my sense of adventure that's persuaded me to take the course I'm on. That and an overpowering desire to cause trouble for the people who invented it."

"And if it did? What then? What if I were to suggest that whatever you have in mind might also cause trouble for me and my friends? In the same way that you believed Corporal Quidde might cause trouble?"

"Are you threatening me, Colonel?"

"Not at all, Gunther. You mistake me. I'm just trying to point out that there are times when you need a very steady arm when you're taking aim at something. Or someone. Someone like Hitler, for example. And it helps if someone isn't rocking the boat while you're doing it."

"That's a good point. And I'll certainly bear it in mind the next time you're taking aim at him." I made a face. "Whenever that might be."

AFTER VON GERSDORFF LEFT, I walked on my own for a while and smoked another cigarette in the encroaching darkness. I was tempted to go and knock on Ines's door, only I didn't want her to think I couldn't handle a whole evening without her. And I was just about ready to concede that I couldn't handle a whole evening without her when I heard two shots in the distance; there was a short interval and then a large splinter from the birch tree next to my head flew into the air as, a split second later, I heard a third shot. I dropped to the ground and extinguished my cigarette. Someone was trying to kill me. It was a while since anyone had fired a gun at me but absence had not made the experience feel any less personal or unpleasant; bullets don't care who they hit.

I kept my head down for several minutes and then glanced nervously around; all I could see were trees and more trees. My own hut and the officers' mess were on the other side of the health resort; Ines's front door was two or three hundred meters away, but without knowing where the shots had come from, there was no point in making a run for it; I could as easily have run toward the shooter as away from him.

Another minute passed and then another. Two wood pigeons settled on a branch above me and a gust of wind rose and then died away. All was silence now, apart from the beating of my heart. Ignoring the sharp pain in my ribs—I had fallen onto the root of an upturned tree stump—I tried once again to estimate where the shots had come from but without success and, deciding that caution was the better part of valor, I scrambled behind the rest of the stump and tried to get as much of my body underneath it as possible; then I took out my gun, worked the slide quietly, and waited for something to happen. Four long years in the trenches had taught me the wisdom of staying put and doing nothing under fire until it's possible to make out a target. I lay very still, hardly daring to breathe, staring up at the treetops and the twilight sky, assuring myself that one of the guards at Krasny Bor would surely have heard the shots, and asking myself who wanted me dead enough to try to make that happen sooner than later. I could think of any number of people, of course, but mostly they were in Berlin and, gradually, instead of questioning the identity of my assailant, I started questioning the wisdom of the plan I had been reluctant to tell von Gersdorff.

In truth, there wasn't much to it; conceived in the office of the minister of Enlightenment and Propaganda, it certainly wasn't heroic and didn't compare to the bravery of von Gersdorff's attempt on Hitler's life. You might say it was nothing less than an attempt to restore the value of truth in a world that had debased it; because the minute I'd mentioned to Goebbels the idea of inviting foreign journalists to Katyn Wood, I'd realized that the proper thing to do with the military intelligence report I'd found in the frozen boot of Captain Max Schottlander was simply to try to give it to the journalists. If I couldn't destroy the Nazis, I could perhaps acutely embarrass them.

Eight correspondents had arrived from Berlin; of course, the majority were Nazi stooges from Spain, Norway, France, Holland, Belgium, Hungary, and Serbia, and none of these was likely to print a story that proved beyond a shadow of a doubt the criminality of the present German government; but the correspondents from the neutral countries—Jaederlund from *Stockholms Tidningen* and Schnetzer from the Swiss newspaper *Der Bund*—looked like they were still interested in truth: a truth that exposed the most egregious lie of the Second World War—*how the war had started.*

Everyone in Europe had heard about the Gleiwitz Incident. In August 1939, a group of Poles had attacked a German radio station in Gleiwitz, Upper Silesia, a piece of provocation that was used by the Nazis as justification for the invasion of Poland. Even in Germany there were some who did not believe the Nazi version of what had happened; but Max Schottlander's report was the first detailed proof of the perfidy of the Nazis. The report demonstrated unequivocally that prisoners from the Dachau concentration camp had been forced to dress up in Polish uniforms and, led by a Gestapo major named Alfred Naujocks, to mount an assault on German territory. The prisoners were all killed by lethal injection and then riddled with bullets to make it look—when the world's press correspondents were brought in to observe the scene—as though the saboteurs' attack had been beaten off by brave German soldiers.

Goebbels always had his propaganda aims; and now so had I. History was not going to be prevented from knowing what had really happened at Gleiwitz—not if I had anything to do with this.

Speaking to any of the correspondents assembled in Smolensk wasn't going to be easy. They were all accompanied by Secretary Lassler from the Foreign Office, Schippert from the Reich Chancellery press department, and Captain Freudeman, a local army officer who, according to von Gersdorff, was very possibly Gestapo, too. I thought my best chance was to speak to one of the reporters the next day, when they visited the temporary laboratory where all the Katyn documents recovered from grave number one were now exhibited; this was the specially glassed-in veranda of the wooden house where the field police was billeted just outside Smolensk, in Grushtshenki— the temporary lab in Katyn Wood having proved unsuitable because of the overpowering smell of the corpses and the swarm of flies that had descended upon the open grave.

I must have lain under that stump like one of those dead Polish officers for ten or fifteen minutes; and perhaps it was this image that changed my mind about what I was proposing to do. I won't say that I started to see things through the eyes of the dead men in Katyn Wood. Let's just say that lying there, in what was not much less than an open grave, after someone had tried to put a bullet in my head, I began to see things from a different perspective. I started to feel uneasy about what I was planning to do with Captain Schottlander's intelligence report. And I remembered something my father had told me once during the course of a very German argument about Marx and history and "the world's spirit on horseback"—I think that was his phrase. He'd been trying, unsuccessfully, to persuade me not to volunteer for the army in August 1914. "History," he said—with a dismissive inconsequence that stopped me from paying more attention to his words at the time—"is all very well, and perhaps it does progress by learning from its mistakes, but it's people that really matter. Nothing ever matters quite as much as them." And as I stared up at the treetops it began to dawn on me that while it was one thing owing a responsibility to history, it was surely something greater when you owed a responsibility to more than four thousand men. Especially when they had been ignominiously murdered and buried in an unmarked grave. Their story deserved to be told, and in a way that could not be denied—as it surely would be if another egregious Nazi lie was now exposed to the world's press. A genuine effort by the Ministry of Enlightenment and Propaganda to expose the truth of what had really happened at Katyn Wood would certainly be compromised if I revealed the truth of what had really happened at Gleiwitz.

It was dark when I dared to move from the cover of my open grave. By now it was clear that whoever had been shooting at me was long gone, and also that no one else had heard the shots; but for an owl hooting its derision at my own lack of courage, the wood at Krasny Bor was quiet. I might have reported the matter to the field police but I had no wish to waste any more time. So I brushed the earth off my army uniform and went and knocked on her door.

INES GREETED MY APPEARANCE at her door with a mixture of shock and amusement. There was an unlit cigarette in her hand and her boots and medical whites lay on the floor where she had dropped them earlier. She seemed a little less pleased to see me than the previous evening but that might just have been because she was tired.

"You look like you need a drink," she said, ushering me inside. "Correction: you look like you've already had two. What did you do? Exhume a dead body with your bare hands?"

"I was almost a dead body myself. Someone took a shot at me just now."

"Anyone you know?" She closed the door and then looked out the window.

"You don't sound very surprised about it."

"What's another corpse around here, Gunther? I've spent my whole day with them. I never saw so many dead people. You were in the war—the Great War. Was it anything like this?"

"Yes, now you come to mention it."

"Think he's still out there?" She drew the curtain and turned to face me.

"Who? The gunman? No. All the same, I think I'd better stay here tonight. Just in case."

Ines shook her head. "Not tonight, lover. I'm exhausted."

"*Have* you got a drink?"

"I think so. If you don't mind Spanish brandy." She pointed at the bed. "Sit down."

"I don't mind it at all," I said.

Ines opened one of her cases, took out a silver hip flask that was as big as a hot water bottle and poured me one into a teacup. I sat down on the edge of her bed, tipped it into my mouth, and let the stuff chase down my nerves and put them safely under anesthetic for another time.

"Thanks." I nodded at the flask in her hand. "Is there a dog that comes with that thing? To rescue travelers?"

"There should be, shouldn't there? This was a present to my uncle, from the nursing staff at the Charité Hospital in Berlin, when he retired."

"I can see why he had to go. That's quite a drinking habit he must have had."

She was wearing black baggy trousers and a thick tweed jacket over a plaid shirt; her red hair was gathered at the back of her head in a bun and there were black loafers on her feet; she smelled lightly of sweat, and her usually pale flesh was looking just a little flushed—

the way all natural redheads do when they've been doing something strenuous like running or making love.

"You're hurt, do you know that?"

"It's just a scratch. I threw myself on the ground when the shooting started and landed on a tree root."

"Take off your shirt and let me put some iodine on it."

"Yes, Doctor. But I'd rather you saved the shirt, if you could. I didn't bring that many with me and the laundry here is a little slow."

I took off my tie and then my shirt and let her clean the scratch with some lint.

"I think this shirt has had it," she said.

"Which makes it fortunate I own a needle and thread."

"I'm considering asking you to fetch it. Your wound is actually quite deep. But for now we'll see how you manage with a field dressing."

"Yes, Doctor."

Ines tore open a bandage parcel and began to wind a roll around my chest; she worked quickly and expertly, like someone who'd done it many times before, but gently, too, like she wanted to spare me from pain.

"You know, I really don't think there's much wrong with your bedside manner."

"Maybe that's because you're used to sitting on my bed."

"True."

"Help yourself to more brandy."

I poured another cupful but before I could drink it she took it out of my hands and drank it herself.

"Why didn't you come to dinner tonight?"

"I told you, Gunther, I'm exhausted. After we picked up the commission from the airport, Professor Buhtz and I went back to grave number one and did another sixteen autopsies. The last thing I feel like doing is putting on a nice dress and having my hand kissed by so many gallant army officers. It still stinks of the rubber glove it's been wearing."

"Tough day."

"Tough but interesting. As well as having been shot, some of the Poles were stabbed first with a bayonet. Probably because they resisted being dragged to the graveside." She paused and finished tying off the bandage. "Interestingly, many of the bodies we've found aren't in a condition of decomposition at all. They're in the initial phase of desiccation and of formation of adipocere. The internal organs have almost normal color. And the brains are more or less . . . Well, it's interesting to me, anyway." She smiled a sad little smile, stroked my cheek, and added, "There. It's done."

"There's mud on your shoes."

"I went for a walk instead of coming to dinner."

"See anything suspicious?"

"You mean like a man with a gun?"

"Yes."

"The last time I looked there were several by the front gate."

"I meant hiding in the bushes."

"I should really give you a tetanus shot. God only knows what's in the ground around here. Luckily for you I brought some from Breslau. Just in case I cut myself working down here. No, I didn't see anyone like that. If I had I would have roused the sheriff."

She fetched her doctor's bag, found an unpleasant-looking syringe, and filled it from a little vial of tetanus vaccine.

"Was that your uncle's, too?"

"As a matter of fact, it was."

"It looks as if it's going to hurt," I said.

"Yes. It is. So it's best I stick it in your behind. If I put this needle in your arm it'll hurt for days and then you might not be able to do a nice salute and you wouldn't want that. This way only your dignity is affected. Not your Nazism."

When the needle went in it felt like it was going all the way down my leg but of course that was just the cold tetanus vaccine.

"Is my dignity affected if I groan?"

"Of course. Weren't you ever a Boy Scout? They're not supposed to cry out when they're in pain."

I groaned. "I think you're confusing them with the Spartans."

She rubbed on some alcohol and then let me alone. The hypodermic went into a little velvet-lined black leather case with a latch in the front.

"But I wasn't ever a Boy Scout," I said, buttoning my trousers. "And I was never a Nazi."

"Did you consider the possibility that maybe it's why someone was trying to shoot you?"

I left off my shirt and put my tunic back on. "It's not something I generally tell people. So, no."

"I think that's where the problem started, don't you? Too many people keeping quiet about what they really think?" She collected her still unlit cigarette and put a match to it, but nervously, like it was about to go off in her mouth.

"What do you think?"

"Me?" She tossed the match on the floor. "I'm a Nazi through and through, Gunther. SA brown on the outside and Falangist black in the middle. I hate the stab-in-the-back politicians who betrayed Germany in 1918, and I hate the Weimar republican fools who bankrupted the country in 1923. I hate communists and I hate the people who live in Berlin West and I hate the Jews. I hate the bloody British and the goddamned Americans and the traitor Rudolf Hess and the tyrant Joseph Stalin. I hate the French and I hate defeatists. I even hate Charlie Chaplin. Is all that clear enough for you? Now, if you don't mind, let's change the subject. We can talk politics all you like when we're both banged up in a concentration camp."

"You're all right," I said. "I like you a lot, you do know that, don't you?"

Ines frowned. "What do you mean?"

"What do you mean, what do I mean?"

"Yes. I didn't tell you anything about what I think."

"Maybe not then, but just now, when you frowned, your face told me plenty, Doctor. Like you meant not a word of what you said."

We both looked around as somewhere outside in the Krasny Bor forest we heard a police whistle blowing.

"You'd best stay here," I said, reaching for the door handle.

"I should have pushed that needle right down to your hip bone," she said, pushing past me. "Don't you get it? I'm a doctor, not a delicate Meissen figurine."

"We've got plenty of doctors at Krasny Bor," I said, and went after her. "Most of them are ugly and old and quite expendable. But delicate Meissen figurines are in shorter supply."

THE POLICE WHISTLE had stopped blowing but the cops were easy to find; they usually are. There were two field police under-officers standing in the forest: the army-issue flashlights suspended from their greatcoat buttons looked like the eyes of an enormous wolf. At their feet was what looked like a discarded raincoat and a lost homburg hat. In the air was a strong smell of cigarettes—as if someone had just put one out—and little Pez breath mints that nearly every man in the German Army ate when he was going to see a girl or he had nothing better to do but suck on his own thoughts.

"It's Captain Gunther," said one.

"We've found a body, sir," said the other, and shone his flashlight onto a man lying on the ground as other uniformed men arrived with more lights and the scene soon resembled some arcane midsummer night ritual with all of us standing in a circle, and our heads bowed in what might have looked like prayer. But it was too late for the man lying on the ground; no amount of prayer was ever going to bring him back to life. He was about sixty years old; most of the blood had dyed his gray hair red; one of his eyes was closed but his mouth was open and his tongue was hanging out of his bearded mouth as if he was pushing it out to taste something—maybe he'd been sucking a mint, too. It appeared he'd been shot in the head. I didn't recognize him.

"That's Professor Berruguete," said Ines. "From the international commission."

"Jesus. Which country?"

"From Spain. He was professor of forensic medicine at the University of Madrid."

I groaned loudly. "Are you sure?"

"Oh yes," she said. "I'm quite sure."

"This could be the end of everything. The Poles are already in fear of their lives. If the commission gets wind of this, they might never come out of their damned hut."

"Then you'll have to try to contain the situation," she said coolly. "Won't you?"

"That's not going to be easy."

"No, it isn't. But what else can you do?"

"Gentlemen, this is Dr. Kramsta," I said to the field police. "She's been assisting Professor Buhtz at Katyn Wood. Look, you'd best fetch Lieutenant Voss from Grushtshenki right away. And General von Tresckow's adjutant, Lieutenant von Schlabrendorff. The field marshal will have to be told, of course. Next, I shall want the immediate vicinity of this crime scene cordoned off. No one from the international commission is to see or hear about this. No one. You understand?"

"Yes, sir."

"If any of them ask about the police whistle, it was a false alarm. And if anyone asks about the professor, he had to return to Spain unexpectedly."

"Yes, sir."

Ines was kneeling beside the body. She pressed her fingers against the dead man's neck. "Body's still warm," she murmured. "He can't have been dead long—half an hour, perhaps." She bent forward, sniffed at the dead man's mouth, and then pulled a face. "You know, he stinks of garlic."

"Search the area," I told two other field policemen. "See if you can find the murder weapon."

"Maybe," said Ines, "the person who you thought took a shot at you earlier wasn't shooting at you at all. Maybe it was Berruguete he was shooting at."

"Looks like it," I said, although it was not obvious why, if someone had been aiming to shoot Berruguete, they had almost hit me on the opposite side of the forest.

"Or maybe they were aiming at you and hit him instead. Lucky for you. Not so lucky for him."

"Yes, even I can understand that."

"Here," said Ines to one of the field policemen. "Give me your flashlight."

I bent down beside her as she took a closer look at the dead man's body.

"He appears to have been shot through the forehead."

"Right between the eyes," I said. "A good shot."

"That all depends, doesn't it?" she asked.

"On what?"

"On how far away the shooter was when he fired the cannon."

I nodded. "He smells of garlic. You're right."

"But it's not the reason Berruguete wasn't exactly popular with his medical colleagues."

"And what is the reason?"

"He held some rather extreme views," she said.

"That doesn't exactly put him outside of polite society. Not these days. Some of our leading citizens hold views that would embarrass Dr. Mabuse."

Ines shook her head. "From what I heard, Berruguete's views were rather worse than his."

"So maybe one of them shot him," I said. "Professional jealousy. Settling an old score. Why not?"

"They're all of them highly respected doctors, that's why not."

"But this Spanish fellow wasn't highly respected. At least not by you, Dr. Kramsta."

"No. He was—he was—" She shook her head and smiled. "It doesn't really matter what I think about him now, does it? Not now he's dead."

"No, I guess not."

She stood up and looked around. "If I were you, I'd stick to my first instinct—which was to try to cover this up, not investigate it. There's a bigger picture here, right? Those men from the international commission have enough awkward questions of their own without you asking some more."

"All right," I said, and stood up next to her. "There's that way. And then there's my way—the Gunther way."

"Which is?"

"Maybe I can find out who did it without asking anyone any awkward questions. During the course of the past decade I've grown to be quite good at that."

"I'll bet you have."

"Sir," said one of the field policemen. "Over here, sir. We've found a gun."

Ines and I walked toward him. The cop was about seventy or eighty meters away. His flashlight was trained on the ground—it was pointed right at a broom-handle Mauser, very like the one Ines had found in the door pocket in von Gersdorff's car. I might even have said it was the same one because of the red number nine that was burned and painted onto the grip panel to warn the pistol's users not to load it with 7.63 ammunition by mistake but to use only the nine-mill Parabellum cartridge for which the gun had been re-chambered.

"That looks kind of familiar," said Ines. "Doesn't your friend with the 260 own a Mauser exactly like this?"

"Yes, he does."

"Hadn't you better see if he's still got it?"

"I don't see what that will prove."

"I don't know, but it could prove that he did it," she said.

"Yes, I suppose it could."

"You know, I don't see what there is to be so cagey about, Gunther, I was only making a suggestion."

"Do you remember back in your hut just now, I was telling you I might need a tetanus shot, and you were telling me you didn't think it was necessary?"

She frowned. "I didn't say anything of the kind. And nor did you."

"Exactly. You do your job, Doctor, and I'll do mine. Okay?"

She stood up abruptly, momentarily angry; her hands were shaking and it took a moment for her to calm down.

"Is it your job?" she said evenly. "To play detective here? I don't know. I thought you were working with the Ministry of Propaganda in Katyn."

"Actually, it's the Ministry of Enlightenment and Propaganda, and being a detective, enlightenment—which is to say the full comprehension of a situation—is what I'm good at. So maybe I'll just stick to that."

"You manage to make being a detective sound almost religious."

"If praying helped solve crimes, there would be more Christians than there are lions to eat them."

"Spiritual, then."

I borrowed the field cop's flashlight and flicked it over the ground while she talked. Something small caught my eye but for a moment I left it alone.

"Maybe. The ultimate goal of the science of criminal detection is a state of complete understanding and, of course, the liberation of oneself from various states of imprisonment." I shrugged. "Although these days there's only one state of imprisonment that means a damn to anyone."

"Self-preservation, huh?"

"It's generally preferable to ending up like your friend Dr. Berruguete."

"He was no friend of mine," she said. "I didn't even know him."

"That's good. Maybe that makes you the right person to perform an autopsy."

"Maybe," she said stiffly. "In the morning, perhaps. But right now I'm going to bed. So, if you want me, I'll be in my hut."

I watched her walk away into the darkness. I wanted her, all right. I wanted to feel her smooth thighs wrapped around me the way I had the previous night. I wanted to feel my hands squashed under her behind as I nudged deep into her. But it bothered me a bit that she had tried—oh so subtly—to scare me off from behaving like a detective. It bothered me also that she had mentioned the word "cannon" before we'd found the broom-handle Mauser. Of course, she might have been in the habit of describing guns as cannons; some people were; then again, she'd used the name "box cannon" when she'd been handling the gun in von Gersdorff's Mercedes and that was what some people called a Mauser C96. And I knew she could handle a gun. I'd seen her handling the Mauser as comfortably as her Dunhill lighter.

It also bothered me that she'd been so quick to finger him for the murder and that she'd had mud on her shoes when I'd gone to see her in the hut—shoes she had not long changed into after removing her medical whites and boots.

I bent down and retrieved the object I'd seen on the ground: a cigarette end. There was more than enough left on it for a Berlin street vendor to have put it on his tray of half-smoked cigarettes, which was how most people—the poor, anyway—went about supplementing their daily ration of three johnnies. Had she been smoking at the scene of the crime? I couldn't remember.

Then there was the Spanish connection. I had a strong feeling there was a lot more about her time in Spain that Ines wasn't telling me.

Von Gersdorff had a little glass in his fingers; the gramophone was playing something improving only I wasn't improved enough to recognize it. But he wasn't alone: he was with General von Tresckow. They had a carafe of vodka, some caviar, pickles, slices of toast on an engraved silver salver, and some hand-rolled cigarettes. It wasn't the German Club but it still looked pretty exclusive.

"Henning, this is the fellow I was telling you about. This is Bernhard Gunther."

To my surprise, von Tresckow stood up and bowed his bald head politely, which had my eyebrows up on my scalp; I wasn't used to being treated with courtesy by the local flamingos.

"I am delighted to meet you," he said. "We are in your debt, sir. Rudi told me what you did for our cause."

I nodded back at him politely but all the same it irritated me the way he'd talked about "our cause," as if you needed a red stripe down your trouser leg or a gold signet ring with your family crest engraved on the face to want to be rid of Adolf Hitler; von Tresckow and his piss-elegant, aristocratic friends had some airs—that was understandable—but this struck me as the worst air of all.

"You make that sound like a kind of plutarchy, sir," I said. "I had the impression that half the world would like to see the back of that man. With a couple of holes in it."

"Quite right. Quite right." He puffed his cigarette and grinned. "According to Rudi here, you're a bit of a tough guy."

I shrugged. "I was tough last year. And perhaps the year before. But not anymore. Not since I got to Smolensk. I found out how easy it is to wind up dead, in an unmarked grave with a bullet in the back of your head just because there's a *ski* at the end of your name. A tough guy is someone who's hard to kill, that's all. I guess that makes Hitler the toughest guy in Germany right now."

Von Tresckow took that one on the chin.

"You're a Berliner, yes?" he said.

"Yes."

"Good." He made a fist that he held up in front of his face and mine; it was clear he'd been drinking. "*Good.* The ideal of freedom can never be disassociated from real Prussians like us, Gunther. Between rigor and compassion, pride in oneself and consideration for our fellow man, there must exist a balance. Wouldn't you say so?"

I'd never really thought of myself as a Prussian but there's a first time for everything; so I nodded, patiently: like most German generals, von Tresckow was a little too fond of the sound of his own natural leadership.

"Oh, surely," I said. "I'm all in favor of a little balance. Where and when you can find it."

"Will you have some vodka, Gunther?" said von Gersdorff. "A little caviar, perhaps?"

"No, sir. Not for me. I'm here on business."

That sounded provincial and dull—as if I was out of my depth—but I couldn't have cared less what they thought; that's the Berliner in me, not the Prussian.

"Trouble?"

"I'm afraid so. Only, before I get to that I want to tell you, what we talked about earlier this evening, me rocking the boat with my own plans—you can forget what I said. It was a very bad idea. One way or another I get a lot of those. And I realized that I'm not as independently minded as I thought I was."

"Might I ask what those plans were?" asked the general.

Henning von Tresckow was not much more than forty and was one of the youngest generals in the Wehrmacht; that might have had something to do with his wife's uncle, Field Marshal Fedor von Bock, but his many decorations told a more inspiring story. The fact is, he was as bright as a polished cavalry saber and cultured, and everyone seemed to love him—von Kluge was forever asking von Tresckow to recite the poet Rilke in the officers' mess. But there was something ruthless about the man that made me wary. I had the strong feeling he, as with all of his class, disliked Hitler a lot more than he had ever loved the republic and democracy.

"Let's just say that I went for a walk, like Rilke. And I was grasped by what we cannot grasp and which changed me into something else."

Von Tresckow smiled. "You were in the mess, the other night."

"Yes, sir. And I heard your rendition. I thought it was good, too. You make quite a performer. But it so happens I always did like Rilke. He might just be my favorite poet."

"And why is that, d'you think?"

"Trying to say what can't be said seems a very German dilemma. Especially in these anxious, disquieting times. And I've changed my mind about that drink. On account of how things just became a little more disquieting than they were before."

"Oh?" Von Gersdorff poured me one from the carafe. "How so?"

He handed me the drink and I put it away quickly, just to keep things tidy in his small but well-appointed quarters: von Gersdorff's bed had an eiderdown as thick as a cumulus cloud and his furniture looked as if it had all come from home—or at least one of his homes. He poured me another. After the brandy, it was probably a mistake, but since the war I never mind mixing my drinks; my policy on drinking is simply the result of the shortages and what the Austrian school of economics calls praxeology: I accept whatever is offered—mostly—whenever it's offered.

"Someone has murdered the Spanish expert from the international commission. Professor Berruguete. Shot him right between the eyes. It doesn't get much more disquieting than that."

"Here at Krasny Bor?"

I nodded.

"Who did it?" asked von Tresckow.

"That's a good question, sir. I'm afraid I don't know."

"You're right," he said. "That is disquieting."

I nodded. "What's even more disquieting is that they used your gun to do it, Colonel."

"My gun?" He glanced at the crossbelts and holster hanging off the end of his bedstead.

"Not that one. I mean the broom-handle Mauser in the door pocket of your car. I hope you don't mind but I already checked. I'm afraid it's not there."

"Lord, does that make me a suspect?" asked von Gersdorff, smiling wryly.

"How many people knew it was there?" I asked.

"In the door pocket? Any number of people. And I didn't ever lock the car. As doubtless you have just found out. After all, this is supposed to be a secure area here at Krasny Bor."

"Ever use it down here in Smolensk?" I asked.

"In anger? No. It was a backup firearm. Just in case. There's also a machine pistol in the trunk. Well, you can't be too careful on these Russian country roads. You know what they say: keep one gun for show and another to blow someone's head off. The Walther is all right at close range, but the Mauser is as accurate as a carbine when the shoulder stock is attached, and it packs a hell of a punch."

"The shoulder stock is missing, too," I said, "but so far it hasn't been found."

"Damn." Von Gersdorff frowned. "That's a pity. I was fond of that rig. It belonged to my father. He used it when he was in the guards."

He reached under the bed and took out the empty carry case, which was complete with gun oil and several stripper clips, each holding nine bullets.

Von Tresckow ran his hand along the polished wooden surface of the case, admiringly. "Very nice," he said, and then lit a cigarette.

"You see a beautiful German gun like this and you wonder how it is we can be losing the fucking war."

"Pity about that stock," complained von Gersdorff.

"I daresay it will turn up in the morning," I said.

"You must tell me where the gun was found and I'll go and look for it myself," said von Gersdorff.

"Can we forget about your gun for a moment, Colonel?"

I felt myself becoming slightly exasperated with them both; von Gersdorff seemed to care more about the loss of his rifle stock than the death of Dr. Berruguete. Von Tresckow was already looking at his friend's collection of classical records.

"A man is dead. An important man. This could prove to be very awkward for us—for Germany. If the rest of these experts get wind of what's happened, they might all clear off and leave us needing some new laundry."

"It seems you need some new laundry yourself, Gunther," observed the general. "Where's your shirt, for God's sake?"

"I lost it on a horse. Just forget about that. Look, gentlemen, it's very simple. I need to put the brake on this, and quick. In the middle of a war it might sound ridiculous, but ordinarily I'd make a shot at catching the fellow who killed this Spaniard, only right now I figure it's more important not to scare the suspects. By which of course I mean the assembled experts of the international commission."

"Are they suspects?" asked the general.

"We're all suspects," said von Gersdorff. "Isn't that right, Gunther? Anyone could have helped himself to the Mauser in my car. Ergo, we're all of us under suspicion."

I didn't contradict him.

General von Tresckow grinned. "I'll vouch for the colonel, Captain Gunther. He's been here all night, with me."

"I'm afraid the captain knows that isn't true, Henning," said von Gersdorff. "He and I went for a walk in the forest earlier this evening. I suppose I could have done it after that. I'm a pretty good shot, too. At my military school in Breslau I was considered the best marksman in my year."

"In Breslau, you say?" I said.

"Yes. Why do you ask?"

"Only that you seem to be one of several people here in Smolensk who have a Breslau connection. Professor Buhtz, for one—"

"And your friend, the beautiful Dr. Kramsta, for another," added von Gersdorff. "We mustn't forget her. And yes, before you ask, I do know her—sort of. Or at least her family. She's a von Kramsta from Muhrau. My late wife, Renata, was related to her, distantly."

"The von Schwartzenfeldts are related to the von Kramstas?" said the general. "I didn't know that."

This was a lot more than I knew—about Ines, about everything; sometimes I had the strange idea that I knew nothing and no one—certainly no one that the *von*s and the *zu*s would have called anyone.

"Yes," said von Gersdorff. "I believe she and her brother Ulrich came to our wedding, in 1934. Her father was with the Foreign Office. A diplomat. But we lost touch soon after that and haven't seen each other in years. Ulrich became very left-wing—to be honest, I think he was a communist—and regarded me as not much better than a Nazi. He was killed after fighting for the republicans in 1938—murdered by the fascists in some Spanish concentration camp."

"How awful," said the general.

"There *was* something awful about it," admitted von Gersdorff. "Something nasty. I remember that much."

"Sounds like a motive for murder right there," said the general, gallantly fingering Ines Kramsta. "But Captain Gunther is right, Rudi. We need to manage this situation before it gets out of hand." He allowed himself another wry smile. "By Christ, but Goebbels is going to go mad when he finds out about this."

"Yes he is," I said, realizing that I was probably the one who was going to have to tell him. He had only just recovered from being told about the murder of Dr. Batov and the disappearance of the only documentary evidence of precisely what had happened at Katyn.

"And about the only person who's going to be pleased at this turn of events is the field marshal," he added. "He hates all this."

"And the murderer," I said. "We mustn't forget him." I said "him" very firmly for the general's benefit. "I'm sure he's pleased as a snowman with a new carrot."

"Take whatever measures you think are appropriate here, Gunther," said the general. "I'll back you all the way. Speak to my adjutant and tell him you need to make this problem go away. I'll speak to him for you if you like?"

"Please do," I said.

"And perhaps I could contact the Tirpitzufer," said von Gersdorff, "to see if the Abwehr's Spanish section can turn up anything on this dead doctor. What was his name again?"

I wrote it down on a piece of paper for him. "Dr. Agapito Girauta Ignacio Berruguete," I said. "From the University of Madrid."

Von Tresckow yawned and picked up the field telephone. "This is General von Tresckow," he said to the operator. "Find Lieutenant von Schlabrendorff and send him to Colonel von Gersdorff's quarters right away." He paused. "Is he? Well, put him on." He covered the mouthpiece for a moment and turned to von Gersdorff. "For some reason Fabian's down the road, with those ghastly signals people at the castle."

He waited for a moment, tapping his boot impatiently while I wondered why he thought they were ghastly. Was it possible he knew about the call-girl service that had been available through the 537th switchboard? Or were they just ghastly because they weren't barons and knights?

"Fabian? What are you doing over there?" he said eventually. "Oh, I see. Can you really handle that by yourself? He's a big man, you know. Did he? I see. Yes, you had no choice. All right. Look, come and see me in my quarters when you get back here. Look, don't for Christ's sake do anything foolhardy. I'll see if I can send you some help."

Von Tresckow replaced the phone and explained the situation: "Von Kluge's *Putzer* is drunk. Some peasant girl who works at the castle has thrown him over and the ignorant Ivan bastard has been sitting all night beside grave number one with a bottle, getting steadily pissed. Apparently he's got a pistol in his lap and is threatening to shoot anyone who goes near him. Says he wants to kill himself."

"I can think of any number of people here who would like to do it for him," said von Gersdorff. "Me included."

Von Tresckow laughed. "Exactly. It seems that Colonel Ahrens telephoned the field marshal's office, and von Kluge asked poor Fabian to go over there and sort it out. Typical of Clever Hans—to get someone else to do his dirty work. Anyway, that's what Fabian is still trying to do but without success." He shook his head bitterly. "I really don't know why von Kluge keeps that man around. We'd all be a lot better off if he did shoot himself."

"I wouldn't care to disarm Dyakov," observed von Gersdorff. "Not if he's drunk."

"That's what I was thinking," said the general.

"Do you think Fabian's up to it? He's a lawyer, not a soldier."

Von Tresckow shrugged. "I would have told Fabian to leave the Russian and come back here," he said, "because what's happened here at Krasny Bor is obviously more important. But always supposing they don't go straight home tomorrow morning, Gunther's experts will want to see the valley of the Polacks before they see anything. Under the circumstances, the last thing they probably want to meet is a fucking tanked-up Russian with a pistol in his hand."

Von Gersdorff laughed. "Might add to the sense of verisimilitude, sir," he said.

The general allowed himself a smile. "Perhaps it would at that."

"I know you're a general," I said, "but I've got a better idea. How about you try to keep the lid on things here and I go down to Katyn Wood and take care of Dyakov?"

It certainly didn't sound like a better idea; not to me; maybe I was regretting making that little speech about me not being a tough guy; or maybe I just felt like hitting someone and Dyakov looked like he was made for it. What with the Polish Red Cross, someone shooting at me, and the murder of Dr. Berruguete, it had been that kind of day.

"Would you, Gunther? We would both be awfully grateful."

"Take my word for it. I've dealt with drunks before."

"Who better than a Berlin copper to deal with a situation like this, eh?" He clapped me on the back. "You're a good man, Gunther. A real Prussian. Yes, indeed, you can leave things here to me."

Von Gersdorff had buttoned up his tunic and was pouring another drink.

"I'll drive you, Gunther," he said. "I'm going to send that signal off to the Tirpitzufer." He grinned. "You know, I think I'd like to see you take care of Dyakov." He handed me the drink. "Here. I've got a feeling you might need this."

10

THURSDAY, APRIL 29, 1943

It was after midnight when we got to Katyn Wood. I preferred it in the dark. The smell and the flies weren't so bad at night. Things were quieter, too—or at least they ought to have been. We heard Dyakov a long time before we saw him; he was singing a lachrymose song in Russian. Von Gersdorff pulled the car up outside the front door of the castle where Colonel Ahrens was waiting with Lieutenants Voss and von Schlabrendorff and several men from the field police and the 537th. They all ducked at once as a pistol shot rang out in the forest. It was easy to imagine that sound multiplied four thousand times during the early spring of 1940.

"He does that every so often," explained Colonel Ahrens. "He fires his pistol in the air, just to let everyone know he's not bluffing about shooting someone."

I looked at everyone and snorted with derision. Dyakov wasn't the only one with a few drinks inside him.

"It's one drunken Ivan." I sneered. "Can't you just find a marksman and shoot the bastard?"

"This isn't any Ivan," said von Schlabrendorff. "This is the field marshal's own *Putzer*. This is the man who sleeps beside the dog, on his veranda."

"He's right, Gunther," said von Gersdorff. "You shoot Alok Dyakov and von Kluge is very likely to shoot you. He's very attached to that damned *Putzer*."

"You couldn't shoot him even if you wanted to," added Voss. "He's knocked out all the damned spotlights. The ones above grave number one, which is where we think he's sitting. As a result it's hard to make out any kind of a target."

"Yeah, but not for him," said von Schlabrendorff. "That man is like a cat. Drunk or not, I swear he can see in the dark."

"Give me your cosh," I said to one of the field policemen. "He'll be hearing 'Berliner Luft' in the forest theater by the time I've finished stroking his head."

The cop handed over his truncheon and I hefted it in my hand for a moment.

"Wish me luck," I told von Gersdorff. "And while I'm gone, brief Voss about the latest murder. You never know, he might have an idea who did it."

All right, Gunther, I told myself, as I set off up the slope in the direction of the singing Russian, now you're really for it; after all that big talk, now you're going to have to show them some old-fashioned police work.

Of course, it was a long time since I'd done anything as honest as that.

Up until now four great mass graves had been found in Katyn Wood but further test digging had revealed the existence of at least three more. Graves one, two, three, and four were already completely uncovered to a depth of about two meters and the uppermost layer of bodies completely exposed. Most of the bodies so far removed had come from graves two, three, and four. From graves five, six, and seven only a few centimeters of earth had been removed and the graves only partly exposed. All of this meant that the whole area was difficult to navigate even in daylight, and I was obliged to come at Dyakov diagonally, across graves five and six; a couple of times I stumbled and almost gave the game away entirely.

Dyakov was still drinking and singing, and sitting on the shorter arm of the L-shaped grave number one, which was still full of bodies. I knew precisely where he was because I could see the red-hot eye of his cigarette glowing in the dark. I thought I recognized the tune but I wasn't at all sure about the words, which didn't sound like any Russian dialect I had ever heard.

"*Del passat destruïm misèries, esclaus aixequeu vostres cors, la terra serà tota nostra, no hem estat res i ho serem tot.*"

Of course, that was hardly unusual: in Smolensk they spoke not just Russian but White Ruthenian, not to mention Polish, and—until we Germans showed up—Yiddish. I don't suppose there was anyone who still spoke Yiddish—anyone alive, that is.

When I was perhaps less than ten meters away I picked up a length of wood intending to throw it over Dyakov's head but ended up throwing it a lot higher when I discovered it wasn't a stick at all but some human remains; the bone clattered into a grove of birch trees close to where he was sitting. Dyakov cursed and fired a shot into the branches; it was enough of a distraction for me to cover the rest of the ground at a lick and then clout him with the copper's truncheon.

It had been a long time since I'd wielded a cop's thumper. When I was a bull in uniform you would only have taken it away from me if I'd been dead. Patrolling a dark back street in Wedding at two o'clock in the morning, a thumper felt like your best friend. It was useful for knocking on doors, to smack a bar top, to rouse a sleeping drunk, or to curb an unruly dog; there was very little that could stop a brawl faster than a blow from a thumper to the shoulder or the side of the head. It was rubberized but that was only to make it easier to grip in wet weather; inside it was all lead and the effect was literally stunning;

getting hit on the shoulder felt like you'd been hit by a car you didn't see coming; getting hit on the head felt like you'd been run over by a tram. Some skill was needed to place a blow that would render a man unconscious without injuring him more seriously, and in a fight, this was rarely possible. But I was badly out of practice and it was dark. I was aiming for Dyakov's shoulder, only I was off balance because of the uneven ground and instead I caught him on the temple, just above the ear, and harder than I had intended. It sounded like a hundred-meter drive with a good hickory wood off the first tee at the GC Wannsee.

Silently, he toppled over into grave number one like he wasn't coming back up, and I cursed, not because I had hit him too hard but because I knew we were going to have to go among the bodies of all those stinking Poles and pull him out—possibly even take him to the hospital.

I lit a cigarette, found the Walther P38 and the bottle he had been holding when I'd hit him, took a swig, and shouted to Voss and von Schlabrendorff to bring some lights and a stretcher. A few minutes later we had hauled his insensible body out of the grave, and Oberfeldwebel Krimminski, who had some medical training, was kneeling beside him checking his pulse.

"I really am impressed," admitted von Gersdorff, examining Dyakov's P38.

"So's his skull," I told him. "I may have tapped him a little too hard."

"I don't think I would like to take on an armed man in the dark like that," he added kindly. "Look here, the fool had every chance to surrender. There's no need to reproach yourself, Gunther. He fired a shot at you, didn't he? And he had three shots left in the magazine. You could easily have been killed."

"It's not my own opinion I'm worried about," I said. "I can live with that. It's the field marshal's displeasure I'm concerned about."

"Good point. It might be a while before this fellow's able to find his own arsehole, let alone Smolensk's best hunting spots."

"How is he?" I asked Krimminski.

"He's alive," murmured the Oberfeldwebel. "But his breathing is shallow. Of course, that could be the booze. And either way, he's going to have a hell of a headache. Feels like a duck egg on the side of his crown."

"We'd best take him to the hospital and have them keep an eye on him," I said, feeling a little guilty.

"That might be a good idea," said von Schlabrendorff.

"Let me know how he is in the morning," I said. "Would you?"

"Of course. I'll have them telephone the office first thing."

"Don't, for Christ's sake, tell Professor Buhtz about this," I said to no one in particular. "If he finds out that we just trampled through his crime scene to fetch this Ivan out of there, he'll go nuts."

"You manage to upset everyone, don't you, Gunther?" said Colonel Ahrens. "Sooner or later."

"You noticed that, too, eh?"

AT THE CASTLE VON GERSDORFF SENT a telemessage to the Abwehr in Berlin asking for information about Dr. Berruguete. We sat in the neat little sitting room Ahrens had created for officers awaiting a reply, under an Ilya Repin print of Russian men hauling a barge along a bit of coastline. They were making heavy going of it and their hopeless, bearded faces reminded me of the Red Army prisoners we were using to carry the bodies out of the graves. I don't know what it is about Russians, but I can't look at any of them without my soul, and then my back, beginning to ache.

"Quite a night," observed von Gersdorff.

"It is when you've been shot at," I said. "Twice." I told him about the gunshots in Krasny Bor.

"That explains why you're not wearing a shirt," he said, offering me a cigarette. "And why there's dirt on your tunic."

"Yes, but it certainly doesn't explain why I was shot at."

"I wouldn't have thought it was one of life's greatest mysteries. Not from one who is as insubordinate as you, my friend."

"I'm not always insubordinate. It's a little special service I provide everyone with a red stripe on his trouser leg."

"Then how about a case of mistaken identity?" Von Gersdorff lit us both with his lighter and leaned back in his chair; he was the most elegant smoker I ever saw: he held the cigarette between his middle fingers so as to minimize the amount of staining on his well-manicured nails, and consequently everything he said seemed to have a similarly measured aspect to it. "Perhaps the murderer intended shooting you and managed to hit Dr. Berruguete instead. Colonel Ahrens, perhaps. And by the way, what have you done to offend him so egregiously, Gunther? The man seems to have taken a very personal dislike to you that goes well beyond simple insubordination."

"The sleeping dogs outside," I said, nodding at the window. "I rather think he wishes I'd let them lie there."

"Yes. I can imagine. This used to be a nice little post until we started digging it up. Certainly the air was a lot easier to breathe."

"I think it's safe to assume that one of the first two shots accounted for Dr. Berruguete and that only the third was meant for me—or not, given that the shooter missed, perhaps deliberately, perhaps I was just farther away: Berruguete was on the opposite side of the wood, after all. Which is one reason I'm not buying a case of mistaken identity. How accurate is that broom-handle of yours anyway?"

"With the stock attached? It's very accurate to about a hundred meters. But the sights are more optimistic. They say a thousand meters. A hundred meters is about right, in my opinion. But, if you'll forgive me for saying so, why would someone shoot at you intending to miss?"

"Perhaps to make me keep my head down until they'd made their escape."

"Yes, the Mauser is good at that. Keep your trigger tight and it's like a garden hose of bullets."

"Been a while since I used one. And never with nine-mil ammo. Much of a kick to it?"

Von Gersdorff shook his head. "Hardly any at all. Why?"

I shook my head but, being an intelligence officer, von Gersdorff wasn't so easily fobbed off or treated like an idiot. He smiled.

"What you really mean is—could a woman have fired it?"

"Did I say that?"

"No, but it's what you meant. Dammit, Gunther, are you suggesting Dr. Kramsta could have killed Dr. Berruguete?"

"I wasn't suggesting it," I insisted. "I think you were. All I asked was if the C96 has much of a kick on it."

"She's a doctor," he said, ignoring my evasion. "And a lady. Although one could be forgiven for thinking otherwise since, unaccountably, she seems to have singled you out for particular favor."

"I've met some doctors who were as lethal as any Mauser. Those fancy clinics in Wannsee are full of them. Only, there it's the bill that packs a kick, not the ammunition. As for the ladies, Colonel, my policy is simple: if they can bang a door shut to end an argument, they can bang a gun to the same effect."

"So you *do* think she's a suspect?"

"We'll see, won't we?"

Signalman Lutz came into the room bearing a telemessage from Berlin. He delivered a smart Hitler salute and then left us in private, although having decoded the message on the Enigma, he knew the contents well enough.

"It's from Admiral Canaris himself," said von Gersdorff.

I glanced at my watch. "I guess he's one of those admirals who can't sleep on land."

"Not with Himmler breathing down his neck." Von Gersdorff started to read aloud.

"MET BERRUGUETE IN 1936. NOT SURPRISED WAS MURDERED AS B. MAJOR ARCHITECT OF FRANCOIST POST-WAR REPRESSION."

"Yes, of course," he said, breaking off for a moment, "the admiral was stationed in Spain during the civil war, setting up our own spy network down there. Canaris learned to speak fluent Spanish while he was a prisoner in Chile during the last lot. There's no one in the whole Tirpitzufer knows more about the Iberian peninsula than him. It was the admiral who persuaded Hitler to support Franco during the war. Spain has always been his special area of interest."

"That worked out well for everyone," I said.

Von Gersdorff ignored me—he was good at that—and continued reading the telemessage:

"B. STUDIED MEDICINE AT UNIV. VALLADOLID AND ANTHRO-
POLOGY AT KAISER WILHELM INSTITUTE IN BERLIN WHERE IN-
FLUENCED BY OTMAR FREIHERR VON VERSCHUER AND PROF
VON DOHNA-SCHLODIEN WHO ARGUED CASE FOR STERILIZING
MENTALLY DISABLED. TAUGHT GENETICS AT CIEMPOZUELOS
MILITARY CLINIC. 1938 SET UP RESEARCH BUREAU OF INSPEC-
TION OF POWS IN CONCENTRATION CAMPS NEAR SAN PEDRO DE
CARDENA. CARRIED OUT EXPERIMENTS ON INTERNATIONAL
BRIGADE POWS TO ESTABLISH EXISTENCE OF A RED GENE BE-
LIEVING ALL MARXISTS WERE GENETIC RETARDS. PROVIDED
FRANCO WITH SCIENTIFIC ARGUMENTS TO JUSTIFY FASCIST
VIEWS ON SUBHUMAN NATURE OF RED ADVERSARIES. CARRIED
OUT FORENSIC WORK ON MANY SPANISH COMMUNISTS LOOK-
ING FOR EVIDENCE OF SMALLER BRAINS. PROB RESPONSIBLE
FOR SPANISH STERILIZATION PROGRAM AND REMOVAL OF
30,000 CHILDREN FROM RED FAMILIES. BELIEVES ALL REDS
ARE DEGENERATE AND IF ALLOWED TO BREED WILL ENFEEBLE
SPANISH RACE. NONSENSE, OF COURSE, SO GOOD RIDDANCE.
COMMUNISTS JUST WRONG NOT EVIL. ROSA LUXEMBURG THE
MOST INTELLIGENT WOMAN I EVER MET. CANARIS."

Von Gersdorff took a last puff on his cigarette before extinguishing it. "Jesus," he said.

"No relation, I suppose?" I said cruelly. "Von Verschuer and Professor von Dohna-Schlodien?"

Von Gersdorff frowned. "I believe I met a von Dohna-Schlodien who commanded a Freikorps in the Silesian uprisings. He was a navy man, not a doctor. Perhaps it's his son to whom Canaris was referring. But I strongly object to the implied suggestion that my family in any way condones the sterilization of mentally disabled people."

"Take it easy, Bismarck. I'm not suggesting anything that would get you drummed out of the club."

"Really, Gunther, I wonder how it is that you can have stayed alive for so long. Especially under the current government."

"I like the way you say that," I told him. "Like you think there's another government just around the corner."

"It's very simple. When we get rid of Hitler, we'll have a government that's worthy of the name."

"You mean a government of the barons. Or even the restoration of the monarchy."

"Would that be so bad? Tell me. I'm interested in your opinion."

"No you're not. You just think you are. And I'm more interested in your opinion about what's going on in Germany right now and not what might happen in the future. You're in the Abwehr. You're supposed to know more than most about what is going on. Do you suppose it's possible there are German doctors conducting similar experiments?"

"Frankly? I think the Nazis are capable of just about anything. After Borisov—"

"Borisov?"

"It's a city in the Minsk Voblast. In early 1942 we learned that six death camps were in operation around Borisov, where more than thirty thousand Jews have been systematically killed. Since then we have learned of the existence of many larger camps: Sobibor, Chelmno, Auschwitz-Birkenau, Treblinka. I don't doubt for a minute that there are things going on in these places that would horrify any decent German. It's equally certain that the mentally weak are already being murdered in special clinics throughout the Reich."

"I thought as much."

Both of us were silent for a moment before von Gersdorff brandished the plaintext in his hand. "Well, there's your motive," he said. "Quite clearly this Dr. Berruguete was a bastard. And deserved to be murdered."

"With an attitude like that, I don't think you have much of a future as a policeman, Colonel."

"No, perhaps not."

"Didn't you say that Dr. Kramsta had a brother, Ulrich, who was murdered in a Spanish concentration camp?"

"Yes, I did. Only I don't know if Berruguete had anything to do with it."

"But she might."

"She might at that."

"Dr. Kramsta was very quiet on the bus from the airport after it was revealed that Dr. Cortes had been replaced by Dr. Berruguete. She seemed to have recognized his name right away. There's that and the fact that she knew where your Mauser was. By her own admission, she knew how to use it. I wouldn't be surprised if she could put a bullet through a buttonhole at a hundred meters."

"Anything else before you telephone the field police?"

"There was a cigarette near the Mauser. A Caruso. Dr. Kramsta smokes Caruso. And there was mud on her shoes when I went to see her earlier on this evening."

Von Gersdorff glanced down at his own handmade boots. "There's mud on my boots, too, Gunther, but I haven't murdered anyone." He shook his head. "Still, it just might help explain why the shooter missed when they shot at you. Although, frankly, I'm beginning to think that was a mistake. I hate to think how you treat your enemies if this is how you treat your friends."

I stubbed out my own cigarette and grinned patiently.

"I didn't say I was going to send her over," I said. "I just want to know who did it, that's all. In case there are any more experts from the international commission she decides to murder. Look here, we might get away with one—although the jury is out on that until breakfast—but I can't see them all staying on at Krasny Bor and calmly carrying out their investigations while some modern Medea conducts a personal vendetta against the European forensic profession."

"No, perhaps not," admitted von Gersdorff. "Although it seems unlikely Dr. Kramsta would have a motive to kill any of them."

"I don't know. That Frenchman, Dr. Costedoat, looks pretty tempting to me."

Von Gersdorff laughed. "Yes, a German never needs much encouragement to shoot a Frenchman. So what are you going to do? Have it out with her? Pistol-whip a confession from her before the day is through? You are welcome to borrow my spotlight."

"I'm not sure." I shrugged. "It's still a hell of a shot with a broomhandle—to shoot at me and aim to miss. That bullet missed me by only a few centimeters."

"Yes, I do see what you mean," he said. "I think."

"What I mean is, it could so very easily have hit me after all. That's the bit I find hardest to understand—if it *was* her who shot Berruguete."

"She likes you too much to risk killing you, is that it?"

"Something like that."

"Maybe she's an even better shot than you think."

"I thought you were on her side."

"I am on her side. I just enjoy watching you entertain the notion that someone you clearly like a lot was perhaps prepared to kill you in pursuit of her revenge."

"Yes, it sounds very amusing when you put it like that. I wonder that you don't have the score to read while you're enjoying the show. Just so you can keep a couple of bars ahead of what's happening."

"That's what a good intelligence officer would do."

"Mm-hmm. You know, I read scores, too, Colonel. They're not leather-bound and printed by Bernhard Schott, and I don't think you'd find them very amusing but they do keep me entertained. The one on my lap right now is an opera with not just one murder but several. It's even possible they're all connected by the same leitmotif, only my ear isn't sufficiently skilled to pick out what that is yet. I'm tone-deaf, you see."

"Remind me. About the other murders."

"The two signalers, Ribe and Greiss, Dr. Batov and his daughter, and now Dr. Berruguete."

"Let's not forget the murder of poor Martin Quidde. We do at least know who killed him."

"Yes, we do. And you know? I'm getting kind of tired of hearing you mention it since I had the stupid idea I killed him to keep your chestnuts out of the horse's nosebag. Yours and half the general staff in Smolensk."

"Don't think I'm not grateful. I am. So is General von Tresckow. Or weren't you listening?"

"Maybe I don't hear so good after I've been shot at."

"But those others. You can't possibly think Dr. Kramsta killed them, too?"

"No, of course I don't. On account of the fact that she wasn't even here when those other murders took place. I'm just reminding myself that I'm not much of a detective since no one has yet been apprehended for any of them. Which may actually be the best reason I can think of to persuade me that Dr. Kramsta is innocent, after all."

"Yes, you're right. So far you make a much more effective murderer than anything else you've been tasked with."

"I wish I could pay you the same compliment, Colonel."

· · ·

I ROSE EARLY AND MADE MY WAY to the mess. Breakfast was always the best meal of the day at Krasny Bor. There was coffee—real coffee, von Kluge wouldn't have tolerated anything less—cheese, rye-wheat and whole grain breads, salted butter, cinnamon rolls, coffee cake, and of course plenty of wurst. Life was very different for enlisted men, of course, and nobody at Group HQ asked too many questions about what they had for breakfast; nobody asked too many questions about the wurst, either, and it was generally held that it was horsemeat; but there were also tins of real Löwensenf from Düsseldorf on the table to make your sausage taste more like the kind of real pork sausage you ate at home. The schnapps decanter was always left conspicuously on the table for those who liked to start the day with nothing more than an extra brick in the wall. Generally speaking, I went for everything—including the schnapps—as I had little time for lunch and even less time for the coffee and apple cake that would magically appear in the mess at around four o'clock. Some German officers actually managed to put on weight while they were in Smolensk; unlike the people of Smolensk, of course—not to mention our POWs: there was no chance of any of them putting on weight.

In spite of my late night I was up before any of the international commission had arrived in the mess. So was the field marshal, and as soon as he saw me, von Kluge came to my table, kicked a chair out impatiently, and sat down. His granite gray face was a study of snarling fury, like a gargoyle on an old German church.

"I understand from Colonel Ahrens that it was you who thought it fit to batter my man Dyakov over the head with a truncheon last night," he said through clenched yellow teeth. It was clear he would have bitten me if had he not been an officer and a gentleman.

"Sir, with respect, he was drunk and he was shooting at people," I said.

"Rubbish. I might have understood your actions, Gunther, if he'd been on a tram, or in a crowded building. But no—he was in the middle of a fucking forest. At night. I should have thought everyone with a brain in his head would have realized he was well out of harm's way. It seems to me that the only people he was in danger of shooting were a few thousand of your beloved dead Polacks."

Suddenly they were my dead Polacks.

"That's not how it seemed at the time, sir. General von Tresckow asked me to assist his adjutant and—"

"Was anyone injured? No, of course they weren't. But like some stupid, heavy-handed Berlin goon, you had to crack his skull. Probably enjoyed it, too. That's the reputation of the Berlin police, isn't it? Crack skulls, ask questions later? You should have left him alone to sleep it off. You should have waited until the morning. By now he'd have been quite manageable instead of fucking insensible."

"Yes, sir."

"I just had a call from the hospital. He's still unconscious. And there's a lump on his head that's the size of your fucking brain."

Von Kluge leaned forward and extended a long, thin forefinger toward the center of my face. There was a slight smell of alcohol on his breath and I wondered if he'd already had a nip from the schnapps decanter. I knew that as soon as he was gone I was going to have one myself; there are better starts to a man's day than being chewed out by an irate field marshal.

"I tell you this, my blue-eyed Nazi friend. You had better fucking pray that my man recovers. If Alok Dyakov dies, I'll court-martial you and then I'll tie a rope under your ear myself. D'you hear? I'll hang you for murder. Just like I hanged those two bastards from the Third Panzergrenadiers. And don't think I can't. You're a long way from the protection of the RSHA and the so-called Ministry for Enlightenment now. I run the show down here in Smolensk, not Goebbels or anyone else. I'm in command here."

"Yes, sir."

"Arse."

He stood up abruptly, knocking over the chair he had been sitting on, turned, kicked it out of his way, and stomped out of the mess, leaving me in need of some clean underwear. I'd suffered a verbal barrage before, only none quite as public or perhaps as threatening, and von Kluge was right about one thing—I was a long way from the relative safety of Berlin. A German field marshal—especially one whose loyalty had been expensively bought by Hitler—could do more or less what he liked with a whole army at his back.

Not that the ministry looked like it would be of much help to me anyway as, soon after the field marshal had left, an orderly presented me with a teletype message from State Secretary Otto Dietrich at the ministry informing me that if the international commission left Smolensk before completing its work, then neither Sloventzik nor myself should even bother coming home. It was—the message informed me—our joint responsibility to make sure the death of Dr. Berruguete remained a secret, at all costs. I tossed a second glass of schnapps at the back of my head since it seemed unlikely that I could feel any worse than I did right then.

"It's a little early for that, isn't it?"

Ines Kramsta was standing behind me with a cup of coffee, a cinnamon roll, and a cigarette. She was wearing the same combination of trousers, blouse, and jacket she'd been wearing the previous night but she still looked better than most women.

"That all depends on whether I went to bed or not."

"Did you?"

"Yes, eventually, but I couldn't sleep. I had too much to think about." I took the cigarette from her mouth and puffed at it for a second while ushering her to a spare table. We sat down.

"I'm quite sure schnapps won't help you think any better than you can manage normally."

"Well, that's the whole point of it. Too much thinking is bad for me. I get ideas when I'm thinking. Crazy ideas like I know what I'm doing down here."

"Would some of those crazy ideas include me?"

"After last night? They just might. Then again, that's hardly a surprise. It seems you're a woman of many parts."

"I had formed the impression that there was only one part that really interested you. Are you sulking because I didn't let you sleep with me last night?"

"No. It's just that even as I think I might be getting to know you, I find I don't know you at all."

"Do you think it's because I'm smarter than you?"

"It's that or everything I've discovered about you, Doctor."

She didn't flinch. I had to hand it to her, if she had killed Dr. Berruguete, she was a cool one.

"Oh? Like what, for instance?"

"For one thing, I found out that you and Colonel Rudolf Freiherr von Gersdorff are related."

Ines frowned. "I could have told you that."

"Yes, and I wonder why you didn't when you suggested I should arrest him for Dr. Berruguete's murder. That was very cute of you." I stubbed out the cigarette in an ashtray before quietly pocketing the stub.

She smiled a sly smile and then stopped it up with the cinnamon roll; it certainly didn't stop her from being cute—not in my eyes.

"We're not exactly close, Rudolf and me. Not anymore."

"He told me that himself."

"What else did he tell you?"

"That you used to be a communist."

"That kind of thing is called history, Gunther. It's a favorite subject for Germans. Especially rather backward Prussians like Rudolf."

I sighed. "Family feud, huh?"

"Not really. Tolstoy says that every unhappy family is unhappy in its own way. But it's simply not true. With any family, it's always the same reasons that cause trouble for everyone: politics, money, sex. That's how it was for us. I think that's how it is for everyone."

I sighed. "I don't think any of those cover the kind of trouble I'm in right now."

"Your trouble is that you persist in seeing yourself as an individual in a systematized collectivist world. Trouble is what defines you, Gunther. Without trouble you have no meaning. You might think about that sometime."

"It will be a real comfort to me when I'm hanged to know that I really didn't have any choice but to do what I did."

"You really are in trouble, aren't you?" She touched my arm solicitously. "What's wrong?"

"The field marshal tells me he's going to hang me if his Russian *Putzer* dies."

"Nonsense."

"He means it."

"But what's that got to do with you?"

"After you went to bed I tried to knock some sense into the fellow. He was drunk and threatening to shoot people. German people."

"And you knocked a little too hard, is that it?"

"You understand everything, Doctor."

"Where is he now?"

"In the state hospital. Unconscious. Maybe worse than that. I'm not so sure there's anyone there who knows the difference anymore."

"Is that where they took Berruguete's body last night?"

"Yes."

"Then why don't we look in on him before I carry out the autopsy?"

"Professor Buhtz can spare you?"

"Autopsies are a bit like making love, Gunther. Sometimes there's no need to make a meal of it."

I smiled at her candor. "Well then, bon appétit, Doctor."

"I'll get my bag."

AT THE SSMA we found Alok Dyakov in a busy ward full of Russians in which the beds were only a few centimeters apart; unlike German wards in the hospital, this one was noisy and understaffed. Wearing a threadbare white gown that had the effect of making him seem abnormally clean and a bandage on his head, Dyakov was sitting up in bed, largely recovered and full of penitence for his behavior of the previous night. The ward nurse turned out to be Tanya; she met my eyes warily a couple of times while she had a brief conversation with Ines and then left the three of us alone. I didn't say anything to either of them about what I knew of Tanya's past; now that I'd seen the conditions she was working in, I was almost sorry that I'd helped Lieutenant Voss to put an end to her other source of income.

"Sir," said Dyakov, grasping my hand—he would have kissed it, I think, if I hadn't pulled it away, "I am very sorry for what happened last night. I am a stupid *Pyanitsa*."

"Don't apologize," I said. "It was me who hit you."

"Was it? I don't remember. I don't remember nothing. *Ya sebya prativen.*" Instinctively he touched the side of his skull carefully and winced. "You hit me pretty good, sir. *Bashka bolit.* I don't know which gives me the biggest headache now—the vodka or whatever you hit me with. But I deserved it. And thank you, sir. Thank you very much."

"For what?"

"For not shooting me, of course." He pulled a face. "Red Army, NKVD, they would have shot drunken man with gun for sure, sir. No hesitation. I make sure it won't happen again. I apologize for making so much trouble. I will tell this to Colonel Ahrens, too."

"Marusya," I said. "The kitchen maid at the castle. She was worried about you, Dyakov. And so was the field marshal."

"Yes? The field marshal, too? *Pizdato*. He will give me my job back? As his *Putzer*? There's hope for me?"

"I'd say there's a very good chance, yes."

Dyakov breathed a loud sigh of relief that made me glad I wasn't about to light a cigarette. Then he laughed loudly. "Then I am very lucky fellow."

"This is Dr. Kramsta," I told him. "She's going to take a look at you and see that you're all right."

"Really, he should have a radiograph," she murmured. "The machine is working all right but according to the nurse there are no plates to make an image on."

"Head as hard as that?" I grinned. "I doubt a radiograph would get through the bone."

Dyakov thought that was funny. "Dyakov—he's not so easy to kill, eh?"

Ines sat down on the edge of Dyakov's bed and inspected his skull and then his eyes, ears, and nose before testing his reflexes and then pronouncing him to be in no immediate danger.

"Does that mean I can leave this place?" asked Dyakov.

"If it was anyone and anywhere else, I'd advise them to stay in bed and rest for a few days. But here." She smiled thinly and glanced around as a man down the ward started to shout very loudly. "Yes, you can leave. I think things would be a lot more congenial for you at Krasny Bor."

Dyakov kissed her hand, and when we left him he was still thanking us.

"You sure he's all right?" I asked.

"Are you asking as someone who's worried about him or yourself?"

"Myself, of course."

"I think your neck is safe enough for the moment," she told me.

"Well, that's a relief."

We went down to the basement, to the hospital morgue where Dr. Berruguete's body, still fully clothed and occupying the same grimy, bloodstained stretcher that had been used to carry him out of the wood at Krasny Bor, was lying upon the floor. There were other bodies, too, and these were stacked on some cheap wooden shelves like so many cans of beans. When we arrived in the room, she held us quiet for a moment with a hand near my mouth.

"Oh, my God," she murmured slowly.

There was a porcelain dissecting table, heavily stained and looking as if it had been recently occupied, with a length of rubber hose attached to a tap, and a drain. The room was congealed with artificial light that turned green on the cracked wall tiles and glinted on Ines Kramsta's surgical instruments as, shaking her head, she laid them out methodically like so many cards in a lethal game of patience. The place stank like an abattoir—with each breath you felt you were inhaling something hazardous, an effect that was enhanced by the buzz of the occasional airborne insect and the humidity that you could feel underfoot.

"They haven't even washed the body," she said dismissively. "What kind of a damned hospital is this, anyway?"

"The Russian kind," I said. "The doing-its-best-in-a-war kind. The no-one-really-gives-a-damn kind. Take your pick."

"I thought I saw some dreadful hospitals in Spain during the civil war," she said. "That ward upstairs was a zoo. But this—this really is the reptile house."

"You were in Spain?" I asked innocently. "During the civil war?"

"It would seem that I'm going to need your help. At least to get him on the table." Ignoring my question, Ines put on her gown and gloves and then dabbed at her beautiful nostrils with perfume. "Want some?"

"Please."

She dabbed it on me, crossing the stuff on my forehead for the comedy of it, and then we lifted the stiff body onto the table, where in just a few seconds she cut the clothes away with a razor-sharp knife. Her sleeves were rolled up and the area between the edge of the gown and her glove revealed a muscular arm that rippled powerfully as she wielded the knife. For a moment I thought I loved her, but before I was sure, I knew I would first have to answer the question that remained at the back of my mind like an awkward collar stud. Had she killed Berruguete?

"I take it this isn't your first autopsy," she said.

"No."

I might fairly have added that it was, however, my first autopsy at which the chief suspect was performing the procedure, but I was interested to see if Ines Kramsta would say anything that might reveal guilt; it wasn't much of a plan, and the whole thing made me uneasy because it wasn't anything other than a low trick designed to exact some sort of emotional response from a woman I admired; after all, if Berruguete was half the bastard Canaris had said he was and Ines was guilty of murdering him, then she was to be commended, not deceived into yielding a tacit admission of her own culpability. But there was little emotion to be seen on her face and not much in her hands or in her tone.

"I was in Barcelona for a while, in 'thirty-seven," she said, finally answering my earlier question. Her voice was even and uninflected and quite without expression, as if most of her concentration was directed through the knife that was scoring a pink-gray line along the center of the dead man's torso. "I spent ten months working in a clinic for the Popular Front. During which time I saw some things that will stay with me for the rest of my life. And atrocities that were committed on both sides. That cured me of politics forever. You might tell Rudolf that the next time you're gossiping about me."

"Why don't you tell him yourself?"

"Oh no." She sounded momentarily wary. "Too much water has

flowed down the mountain since then for that to happen. We were lovers briefly. Did he tell you that?"

"No. No, he didn't. Only that your brother met an unfortunate end. In Spain."

"That's one way of describing it." She allowed herself a quiet smile. "I wouldn't be so quick to rule him out for this if I were you. Rudi's much more ruthless than he seems."

"Oh, I know. He can be explosive. And who said I was ruling him out?"

"Only that you seemed touchy about this when I mentioned it last night. Dr. Berruguete was at Rudolf's wedding, you know. In 1934. Berruguete was finishing his studies in Germany and I believe he knew Renata's family. The Kracker von Schwartzenfeldts."

"According to him, you were also at his wedding."

"True, but I didn't invite Berruguete." She smiled again. "Small world, isn't it?"

"It would seem so." I paused. "At least that's how it must look from up there. I imagine it's pretty crowded on that high mountaintop that you and the *vons* and *zus* are pleased to share with each other."

"It bothers you, doesn't it? The idea of a German aristocracy."

"I imagine it must have bothered you, too. Or else why the youthful Bolshevism?"

"It did. But there seems to be so much more to be bothered about now than a simple matter of inherited wealth and privilege. Wouldn't you agree?"

"Can't argue with that. What happened to her anyway? His wife."

"Renata? God, she was a lovely woman. The loveliest woman I ever knew. She died last year, didn't she? She was just twenty-nine, I think. I forget what it was, exactly. Complications after childbirth, perhaps, I don't remember."

She worked quickly and without hesitation, revealing first of all that Berruguete had been shot twice—through the head and the heart—before digging a bullet out of his chest and, in the absence of a petri dish, laying it in an ashtray but only after throwing away the ash and the spent matches. Her hands were quite steady—steady enough to have fired a broom-handle Mauser and hit what she was aiming at.

"Well, that was a surprise," she murmured.

"What was?"

"I had supposed he was only shot in the head."

"Maybe not a surprise to me. I heard three shots last night. Only one of those bullets came my way."

"There's the second gunshot wound and the fact that he even had a heart."

"You sound like you knew him. From the wedding, perhaps."

"No," she said. "I never spoke to him. I told you. But I knew *of* him, of course. His reputation went before him. As I said before, he held some rather extreme views on racial hygiene. On everything, probably." She took a closer look at the chest bullet now in her forceps. "Ballistics is not my thing, I'm afraid. Can't tell if that's from a broom-handle Mauser or not. You should give the slug to Professor Buhtz. See what he makes of it. He's the expert on ballistics."

"So I believe."

"Probably tell you what batch of ammunition it came out of, knowing him."

"Yes. I expect so."

"One through the heart, one plumb between the eyes. Whoever shot this man must have been a marksman. That Mauser they found was at least seventy-five meters from the body. Assuming he dropped it at the spot where he fired from, that's good shooting in failing light, isn't it?"

"With the stock on? I don't know."

"I don't think I could have made a shot like that. Besides, the stock wasn't on the gun when they found it."

"It wasn't in the car, either," I said. "I expect he disassembled the rig, meaning to fit the gun back inside the stock, and then panicked, dropped the gun, and simply threw the stock away."

"The shooter doesn't sound to me like the kind of person to panic. He steals the gun from von Gersdorff's car, and then calmly shoots Berruguete inside a secure area that is patrolled by Wehrmacht soldiers. You need quite a cool head to do something like that. He even manages to get off a third shot in your direction before making his escape."

"Only, that one wasn't accurate."

"That all depends, doesn't it?" she said. "On whether he was trying to hit you or not."

"Yes, good point. I didn't think of that."

"Sure you did. It's been scratching your ear ever since it happened."

Ines lifted Berruguete's head by the hair. The plum-sized exit wound at the back of the skull was clear enough. "I don't suppose there's much point in carrying out a brain obduction," she said. "The bullet that hit him in the head is obviously gone. We're not going to find out anything other than the fact that he was shot."

"No, I suppose not."

She dropped his head back onto the table with a thud, as if she didn't much care what happened to it; he was dead, of course, and it couldn't have mattered less to Berruguete, but all the same I was used to seeing pathologists treat their cadavers with just a little more respect.

"Makes a change, I suppose," she said.

"How's that?"

"Everybody in Katyn Wood was shot in the back of the head, with a commensurate exit wound in the forehead. This is the other way around."

"I guess you find a novelty where you can."

"Sure," she said grimly. "You could call it that, if you want. You know, either one of these bullets would have been enough to have killed him."

"Impossible to say which was first, I suppose. The head shot or the chest shot."

She shook her head. "Impossible. Anyway, it would seem the shooter wanted to make sure of his victim."

She rinsed off her rubber gloves with the length of rubber tube and peeled them off, although Berruguete's chest cavity was still open. It looked like a small volcano had erupted out of his insides.

"Isn't it customary to put some of the liver and bacon back in and sew him up again?" I said.

"Yes," she said, coldly lighting a cigarette. "But what would be the point of that here? It's not like his family are going to see him. There's no way they're ever going to send him all the way back to Spain from Smolensk. No, I should have thought they'll box him up and bury him, don't you? In which case, sewing him up is just a waste of my time."

I shrugged. "I suppose you're right."

"Of course I'm right."

"All the same, it seems just a shade disrespectful. To him."

"Maybe I didn't make it quite clear to you, Gunther, but this was not a good man. In fact, I'd go so far as to say this man was a monster."

"I can't disagree with that description. Forced sterilization is about as bad as it gets."

"You could be forgiven for thinking so," she said. "But if I said that this man had republican people shot so that he could carry out autopsies to see if there was anything peculiar about their brains— what would you say to that? Would you still want me to sew him back up neatly out of respect for his cadaver?"

"I think maybe I would. I'm the old-fashioned type, I suppose. I like to do things by the book if I can. You know? The proper way.

The way things were done before 1933. Sometimes I think I'm the only truly honest man I know."

"I'd no idea you were quite so particular, Gunther."

"Yes, that's true—more and more so, I think—while everyone else, it seems, becomes rather less so. These days I don't even cheat at solitaire if I can help it. Last week I reported myself to the adjutant for having a second helping at dinner."

Ines sighed. "Oh, very well."

She tossed her cigarette onto the floor and searched her forensic wallet before producing a large curving needle that looked like it could have stitched a sail on the *Kruzenshtern*. She threaded some suture through the eye of the needle with expert speed and held it aloft for my inspection.

"Will this do?"

I nodded my approval.

She gathered herself over the table for a moment and then went to work, stitching Berruguete up again until he looked like an elongated football. It wasn't the neatest work I'd seen but at least they wouldn't be using him for a display in the local butcher's shop window.

"You won't ever work for a tailor," I said. "Not with stitching like that."

She tutted loudly. "I never was very good at putting in sutures. Anyway, that's the best I can do for him, I'm afraid. It's more than he did for his victims, I can tell you."

"So I heard." I lit a cigarette and watched as she rinsed her gloves again and then her instruments. "How did you get into this business anyway?"

"Forensic medicine? I told you before, didn't I? I haven't got the patience for all the aches and pains and imaginary ills of the living patient. I much prefer working with the dead."

"That sounds suitably cynical," I said. "I mean, for this day and age. But really, what was it? I'd like to know."

"Would you, now?"

She took the cigarette from my mouth, puffed it thoughtfully for a second, and then patted my cheek.

"Thank you," she said.

"For what?"

"For asking me. Because I'd almost forgotten the real reason why I started to work with the dead. And you're right, it wasn't for the reason I told you just now. That's just a silly story I made up so that I could avoid telling people the truth. The thing is, I've repeated that lie so often I've almost started to believe it myself. Like a real Nazi, you might say. Almost as if I was someone else entirely. And you may think what I'm going to tell you is pompous, even a little pretentious, but I mean it, every word.

"The sole aim in forensic medicine is the pursuit of truth, and in case you hadn't noticed, there's precious little of that around in Germany these days. But especially in the medical profession, where what is true and what is right matter for very little beside *what is German*. Theory and opinion have no place beside the dissecting table, however—no more do politics and crackpot ideas about biology and race. Forensic medicine requires only the quiet assembly of genuine scientific evidence and the construction of reasonable inferences based on honest observation, which means that it's about the one facet of the practice of medicine that hasn't been hijacked by the Nazis and by fascists like him." She flicked her ash at Berruguete's corpse before returning the cigarette to my lips. "Does that answer your question?"

I nodded. "Did Dr. Berruguete have something to do with your brother's death, perhaps?"

"What makes you say so?"

"Nothing at all other than the fact you just used him as your ashtray."

"Maybe. I can't be sure. Ulrich and about fifty Russian members of the international brigades were captured and imprisoned in the concentration camp at San Pedro de Cardeña, a former monastery near the city of Burgos. I don't think anyone who was not in Spain can have any real idea of the level of barbarism to which that country descended during the war. Of the cruelties that were inflicted by both sides, but more particularly by the fascists. My brother and his comrades were being used as slave labor when Berruguete—whose model, incidentally, was the Holy Inquisition and who once wrote a paper arguing in favor of the castration of criminals—received permission from General Franco to pathologize left-wing ideas. Of course, the military was delighted that science was being used to justify their opinion that all of the republicans were animals. So Berruguete was given a senior military rank and the prisoners, including my poor brother, were transferred to a clinic in Ciempozuelos, which was headed by another criminal called Antonio Vallejo Nágera. None of them were ever seen again but it's certain that's where my brother died. And if Berruguete didn't kill him, Vallejo did. By all accounts he was just as bad."

"I'm sorry," I said.

She snatched the cigarette from my mouth again and this time she kept it.

"So while I regret that the work of the international commission has been jeopardized, I'm not in the least bit sorry that Berruguete's dead. There are plenty of good men and women in Spain who will cheer and give thanks to God when they hear that justice caught up with him at last. If anyone deserved a bullet in the head around here, it was him."

"All right," I said. "Fair enough."

I put my hand on her soft cheek and she leaned in to my palm and then kissed it, fondly. She began to cry a little, and I put my other arm around her shoulders and drew her close to me. She didn't say another word but she didn't need to; my earlier suspicion was now gone; I'm a little slow making up my mind about these things and full of a cop's caution, which stops me from behaving like any normal man, but I was certain now that Ines Kramsta had not shot Berruguete. After ten years at the Alex, you get to recognize when someone is a killer and when they're not. I had looked into her eyes and seen the truth, and the truth was that this was a woman with principles who believed in things, and those things did not include subterfuge and cold-blooded murder, even if it was someone who deserved to be murdered.

I had seen another truth, too, which was just as important, and this was that I thought I loved her.

"Come on," I said. "Let's get the hell out of here."

At the front door of the hospital, the nurse Tanya caught up with me.

"Herr Gunther," she said. "Are you going to Krasny Bor?"

"Yes."

"Could you please return these things to Alok Dyakov?" she asked, handing me a large brown envelope. "He left about ten minutes ago—caught a ride back to Krasny Bor with some grenadiers who were also discharged—before I had time to return his personal possessions: his wristwatch, his glasses, his ring, some money. It's standard hospital policy to remove the contents of a patient's pockets when they're brought in, to keep them safe." She shrugged. "There's a lot of theft in here, you understand."

"Certainly." I looked at Ines. "Is that where you want to go? Back to Krasny Bor?"

She glanced at her watch and shook her head. "Professor Buhtz will probably be at Grushtshenki by now, with the commission," she said. "Perhaps you could take me there?"

I nodded. "Of course. Anywhere you like."

"You can give him the bullet we dug out of Berruguete's heart then, if you like," she added helpfully. "And see what he makes of it. Not that I think there's going to be much doubt that it came from that red nine you found."

"That's all right," I said. "I'm going to take another look at the

376

crime scene first. See if there's anything I've missed. And maybe find that missing shoulder stock."

So I drove her to Grushtshenki, the headquarters of the local field police, where all of the Katyn documents recovered from grave number one were now exhibited in an especially glassed-in veranda of the wooden house.

When we arrived it was plain that the international commission was already on the scene and that both Buhtz and Sloventzik—easily distinguishable in their field gray uniforms—were surrounded with the experts. Most of these men were in their sixties, many of them bearded, carrying briefcases and making notes while Sloventzik patiently translated Professor Buhtz's remarks. Official photographers were taking pictures and there was a buzz in the air that wasn't just pertinent questions; the air was full of mosquitoes. It looked more like Zadneprovsky Market on Bazarnaya Square than an international commission of forensic inquiry.

I pulled up next to Colonel von Gersdorff, who was leaning on the hood of his Mercedes and smoking a cigarette.

He nodded at me as we stepped out of the Tatra and then, rather more warily, at Ines. "How are you, Ines?" he asked.

"Well, Rudolf."

"Good God, haven't you arrested this woman yet, Gunther?" he added. "Didn't Siegfried's wounds flow fresh with blood when the guilty Hagen stood beside the corpse, so to speak?" He grinned. "I thought she was well in the frame for the doctor's murder when last we talked about things. Motive, opportunity, the whole Dorothy L. Sayers. And don't forget, the beautiful Bolsheviks are the most dangerous, you know."

He laughed again, and of course what he said was meant to be a joke, but Ines Kramsta didn't quite see it that way. And in view of what happened next, nor did I.

For a moment she stared at me without a word but when her jaw dropped it was plain to see she felt that I had betrayed her.

"Oh, I see," she said quietly. "That explains why—"

Ines blinked with obvious astonishment and started to turn away but I took a step after her and grabbed her arm.

"Please, Ines," I said. "It's not like that. He didn't mean it. Did you, von Gersdorff? Tell her you were just joking. I never had any intention of arresting you."

Von Gersdorff chucked away his cigarette and straightened. "Er, yes. I was just joking, of course. My dear Ines, none of us thought for a minute that you actually shot the doctor. Well, I certainly didn't. Not for a moment."

This admission was no less clubfooted than his joke, and it was plain from her face that the damage was well and truly done. I felt as if someone had just kicked away the stool I had been standing on and I was now hanging by the neck on a very thin length of cord.

"It seems obvious now," she said, wresting her arm out of my grip. "All those interested questions about Spain and my brother. You were trying to find out if I shot Dr. Berruguete, weren't you?" Her nostrils flared a little and her eyes filled with tears, again. "It actually crossed your mind that— To think that you thought I could have carried out an autopsy on a man I had murdered."

"Ines, please believe me," I said. "I never had any intention of arresting you."

"But you still considered the possibility that I might have killed him, didn't you?"

She was right, of course, and I felt a certain shame about that, which—of course—she was able to read in my eyes and on my face.

"Oh, Bernie," she said.

"Perhaps for just a minute," I said, fumbling for some words that might satisfy her. I felt my feet desperately reaching to touch the stool I had been standing on but already it was too late. "But not anymore." I shook my head. "Not anymore, do you hear?"

Her disappointment in me—her dismay that I could ever have suspected her of murder—was already turning to anger. Her face flushed and the muscles in her jaws stiffened as, biting her lip, she regarded me with new contempt.

"I really thought that there was something special between us," she said. "I can see now I was terribly mistaken about that."

"Honestly, Ines," said von Gersdorff, putting his polished jackboot in it again. "You're making a mountain out of a molehill with this. You really are. The poor fellow was only doing his job. He is a policeman, after all. It's his job to suspect people like you and me of things we didn't do. And you must admit, for a while there you made a pretty reasonable suspect."

"Shut up, Rudi," she said. "Just for once know when you should say nothing."

"Ines, we do have something special," I told her. "We do. I feel that, too."

But Ines was shaking her head. "Perhaps we did. At least for a moment or two."

Her voice was husky with emotion and it made me acutely aware of just how much I wanted to comfort her and look after her, and but for the fact that it was me who had caused her hurt, I might have done so, too.

"Yes, we were a good pair, Gunther. From the first time I was with you it really felt that we were more than just one man and one woman. But none of that matters a damn when one of the two decides to play cop on the other, as you just did with me."

"Really, Ines," muttered von Gersdorff.

But she was already walking away, toward Buhtz and the international commission, not looking back, and out of my life, forever.

"I'm sorry, Gunther. I didn't mean that to happen. You know, I really should have remembered. Like a lot of lefties, Ines has never had much of a sense of humor." He smiled. "But look, I expect she'll get over it. I'll speak to her. Put things right. Obtain a reprieve for you. You'll see."

I shook my head because I knew no reprieve would ever arrive.

"I don't think that's going to be possible, Colonel," I said. "In fact, I'm certain of it."

"I should like to try," he said. "Honestly, I feel terrible." He shook his head. "I had no idea that you and she—had become quite so close. It was—it was careless of me."

There was very little I could say to that. Von Gersdorff was right about it being careless of him, although I might have added that it was typically careless of him and all Prussian aristocrats. They were just careless people, careless because they didn't really care about anyone other than themselves. It was their carelessness that had allowed Hitler to take possession of the country in 1933; and through their carelessness, they had failed to remove him now, some ten years later. They were careless and then other people had to sort it out, or deal with the mess they had made.

Or not.

I walked away. I smoked a couple of cigarettes on my own and stared up at the blue sky through newly minted leaves in the tops of the tall, shifting silver birch trees and realized how, in that part of the world especially, all human life is grotesquely fragile. And feeling glimpses of raw Russian sunlight on my face—which, after all, was much more than the poor ghosts of four thousand Poles could ever have done, I eventually managed to recover a few blackened, ash-covered fragments of my earlier composure.

A little later on I found a nervous-looking Lieutenant Voss on the edge of the crowd. Several field policemen were doing their best to distinguish those who had a reason to be there from those who did not, which wasn't easy as many off-duty German soldiers and locals had come to see what all the fuss was about.

"What a fucking circus." Voss slapped his neck irritably. "Christ only knows what will happen if Russian partisans choose today for an attack."

"I think malaria or old age is more likely to take down some of these fellows than a Russian hand grenade," I said, and slapped my own cheek, hard. "I almost wish it was cold again so we might be free of the plague of these fucking insects."

Voss grunted his agreement.

"By the way, how's that Russian bastard you clouted with the truncheon last night? Dyakov? Good job, by the way, sir. If anyone needed a thump on the head it's the field marshal's pet Ivan."

"Alive, thank God. And on his way back to Krasny Bor and his master."

"Yes, I heard Clever Hans tore a strip off your face this morning. Makes you wonder what Dyakov has got on the field marshal to make him behave like that."

"Yes, it does, doesn't it?"

I led Voss a short distance away to ask if the late Dr. Berruguete's sudden absence had caused any alarm among our distinguished guests.

"Not at all," said Voss. "On the contrary. Several of them seemed quite relieved to hear he'd had to return to Spain. That's what Sloventzik has told them, anyway. A family tragedy that required his immediate return during the night."

"After what I learned about him today, I'm hardly surprised they're glad to see the back of that man. Nor am I surprised that someone put a bullet in him. Two, actually. According to the autopsy I just attended, he was shot once in the head and once in the chest."

"Could one of them have done it?" asked Voss, glancing over at the commission.

I pulled a face. "I don't think so, do you? Look at them. There's none of them that looks like he could hit a vein with a needle, let alone fire a broom-handle Mauser and actually hit anything."

"But if not one of them, who?"

"I don't know. Find that shoulder stock yet?"

"No. To be honest, I can't spare the men to look for it. We have our hands full keeping people away from this place and Katyn Wood."

"That's all right. I'm just on my way back to Krasny Bor now. I'll take a look for the stock myself."

BACK IN THE WOODS AT KRASNY BOR all of the wildflowers were in bloom and it was hard to believe there was a war on. Von Kluge's huge staff car was parked in front of his villa but almost everywhere else there was no clue that the place was anything other than the health resort it had once been. Behind the neat curtains of the wooden huts where Russians had previously stayed to take the sulphurous spring waters to move their bowels, nothing moved. There were just the trees whispering to each other in the breeze and some birds punctuating the silence with their bright exclamations that spring had truly arrived at last.

I drove through the gates and, leaving my car, walked to the place where the field police had found the murder weapon, which was marked with a little field police flag. I began to search the long grass and the bushes. I did this in ever-increasing circles, walking around the spot like the hands on a clock until, after about an hour, I found the paddle-shaped polished-oak Mauser stock resting against a tree. It was immediately obvious that this was the spot from which the gunman had shot Berruguete for, tied to the branch of the tree at about head height, was a length of rope through which anyone seeking to steady his aim might have pushed the Mauser's ten-centimeter barrel and then secured it tightly with a couple of quick turns. The place where Dr. Berruguete's body had been found was almost a hundred meters away and unimpeded by any trees or bushes. Less obvious, however, was how the gunman could have used the same length of rope to shoot at me in the opposite direction; he would need to have turned more than a hundred and fifty degrees to his right, which would have left the barrel of the Mauser knocking against another branch of the same tree. In other words, to have shot at me from this same spot using the tie was impossible. This left me puzzled and wondering if there might have been a second gunman.

I pocketed the length of rope and spent the next thirty minutes carefully searching the grass until I'd found two brass bullet casings. I didn't bother to look for a third as it was immediately apparent that these could not have been fired from the same gun: one was a nine-millimeter Mauser casing, but the other was something bigger—most likely a rifle bullet.

In Krasny Bor the spring silence endured; but inside my head there was now a riot of noise. Finally, one clear voice asserted itself against the clamor. Had there been one gunman or two? Or perhaps one gunman with two different weapons—a pistol and a rifle? Certainly it made sense to shoot at me with a rifle—I had been the more distant target. But why not shoot Berruguete with the rifle, too—unless the reason had been to use the borrowed Mauser to point the finger of blame elsewhere.

I walked over to the upturned stump under which I had sought to bury myself to escape my putative assassin and glanced around, looking for the standing tree that the third bullet had hit instead of me and, when I found it, I spent the next few minutes gouging it out with my lock-knife.

Lying on the palm of my hand were two misshapen pieces of metal, one of which—the one gouged from the tree—was larger than the other taken from my pocket and, before that, from Berruguete's chest.

WHEN THE INTERNATIONAL COMMISSION arrived back from their morning's inspection of documents at Grushtshenki and went along to the Krasny Bor officers' mess for lunch, I sought out Professor Buhtz.

Ines, who came into the mess with him, ignored me as if I had been invisible, and continued into the dining room.

I motioned Buhtz to follow me. "Doubtless you've already heard something of the events of last night. The unfortunate death of Dr. Berruguete."

"Yes," said Buhtz. "Lieutenant Sloventzik has put me in the picture about that and the overriding need for discretion. What happened, exactly? All Sloventzik told me was that Berruguete had been found murdered in the woods."

"He was shot in the woods with a Mauser C96," I said. "I only know that because we found the weapon on the ground not very far from the body."

"A broom-handle, eh? Fine pistol. Can't think why we stopped using them. Good stopping power."

"More importantly, how were our guests? Did they believe the story—that Berruguete was suddenly obliged to return home to Spain?"

"Yes, I think so. None of them has commented on it, although Professor Naville said he was glad to see the back of him. There's no love lost there, that's for sure. Under the circumstances, it has been a very satisfactory morning. The display of Polish documents recovered from grave number one is most effective. And persuasive. The smell, or rather lack of it, at Grushtshenki means that we have been able to take our time with the papers. To have read them in Katyn Wood would have proved difficult, I think. The inspection of the graves and the autopsies are an ordeal yet to come, of course. François Naville is perhaps the best of the experts, with the most searching questions—especially since he seems to detest the Nazis so much. I imagine it's for this reason that he's refused to take any payment from Berlin, unlike some of the others. Several of them are rather less principled than Naville, which makes the Swiss's opinion all the more valuable, of course. He speaks reasonable Russian, which is useful, as he intends to interview several local people himself—the ones Judge Conrad has deposed. And he's quite free with his opinions concerning politics and the rights of man. Several times this morning he's told me in no uncertain terms what he thinks of 'Herr Hitler' and his Jewish policies. I didn't know what to say. Yes, he's proving to be a very highly awkward fellow is our Professor François Naville."

"There's a possibility that the death of Dr. Berruguete is somehow connected with the death of Signalman Martin Quidde," I told him. "You remember, earlier this month? What happened there? You were able to determine from the ballistics tests you carried out that it wasn't a suicide but a murder."

"Yes, that's right. Quidde was shot with a Walther that wasn't the one we found in his own hand. A police pistol, I would suspect. Some fool assuming we'd simply accept the most obvious explanation."

I nodded, doing a very good impersonation, I thought, of someone who was entirely innocent of this foolish crime.

"And you gave me until the end of the month to find his killer before informing the Gestapo. In order that we might avoid any unnecessary action against the local population."

"Very principled of you." Buhtz nodded. "Hadn't forgotten. Wondered if you had, though."

"This is one of the bullets that killed Berruguete," I said, handing him the spent bullet and its casing. "Your charming assistant, Dr. Kramsta, dug it out of his chest first thing this morning when she carried out the autopsy."

"Good girl, Ines Kramsta. First-rate pathologist."

"The casing I found later on when I searched the area." I paused, and then added, "Yes, she is."

"Not had the best of luck, though. Her brother was killed in Spain. And her parents were killed in a bombing raid just a year ago."

"I didn't know."

Buhtz looked at the metal on his palm and nodded. "Nine milli-meter, by the look of it. Quidde was shot with a Walther, however. Not a Mauser. A PPK."

"Yes, I know. Look, sir, I need to know more of what only the author of *Metal Traces in Bullet Wounds* can tell me."

"Of course. I am at your service."

"There were three shots fired in Krasny Bor last night. Two at Berruguete and a third at someone else."

"I didn't hear a thing," admitted the professor. "But then, I did have more than one schnapps last night. Then again, I've noticed that the trees and the ground sort of deaden the sound around here. It's a noticeable phenomenon. The NKVD picked a good spot to murder those Polacks."

"I know there were three shots," I continued, "because the third shot was fired at me."

"Really? How do you know?"

"Because fortunately it missed me and hit a tree from which this was dug out just a few minutes ago." I handed him the bullet and the second brass casing.

Buhtz smiled with an almost boyish enthusiasm. "This begins to be interesting," he said, "since clearly this third shot you describe was fired not from a red nine but from a rifle."

I nodded.

"You need to know more about that rifle," he said.

"Anything you can tell me would be useful."

Buhtz glanced at the bullets in his hand and across the hall, where commission members were now seating themselves at the various ta-bles and reading lunch menus with rather obvious pleasure: for most of the forensic scientists who'd come to Smolensk the officers' mess at Krasny Bor provided the best meal they'd had in a long time.

"Well, now you come to mention it, I would rather like to escape from these fellows for a short while. Besides, it's lamprey pie again. I'm never all that keen on lampreys, are you? Nasty things. That peculiar spiral-toothed mouth those creatures have. Horrible. Yes, why not, Captain? Let's go to my hut and we'll take a closer look at what you've found."

In his neat little hut Buhtz took off his military belt, opened the top button of his tunic, sat down, collected a magnifying glass off his table, switched on a desk light, and scrutinized the bottom of the brass rifle casing I'd found near the abandoned Mauser stock.

"On the face of it," he said, "I should have said this came from a standard infantryman's M98. It's a fairly ordinary eight-millimeter round, by the look of it. Except for one thing. The M98 uses a rimless bottlenecked rifle cartridge and this is rimmed, which leads me to think of a different rifle and to suppose that the cartridges were loaded with something a little different—something a little heavier and more suitable for game shooting. A Brenneke rifle bullet, perhaps. Yes. Why not?"

He took the bullet and placed it under the lens of his microscope, where he stared at it for several minutes.

"I thought as much," he murmured eventually. "A TUG. A torpedo-tail deformation bullet with a hard core for bigger game, like deer. Developed in 1935. That's what you have here." He looked up and grinned. "You're lucky to be here, you know. You were shot at with a decent hunting rifle. If this had hit you, Gunther, you'd be missing a large part of your head. When I have more time I can probably tell you what metal this is—maybe a bit more than that, like where this ammo came from."

"You've already told me a great deal," I said, wondering how he knew that the shooter had aimed at my head—although, perhaps it was just a reasonable assumption. "But what kind of a hunting rifle?"

"Oh well, Mauser have been making excellent hunting rifles for fifty years. I would have said a Mauser 1898. But given the fact that I almost mistook this bullet, I might almost say a Mauser Oberndorf Model B or a Safari." Buhtz frowned. "Oh, I just had a thought. You know who has a pair of Obendorfs, don't you? Here? At Krasny Bor."

"Yes," I said grimly. "I already had the same thought myself."

"Tricky one, that."

I lit a cigarette. "Look, I hate to ask you this again, sir, but would you mind keeping this quiet for now? The field marshal already dislikes me—his *Putzer* got drunk last night and started waving a gun around so I had to rubber-stamp his head."

"Yes, I heard about that from Voss this morning. It's not like Dyakov. When you get to know him, Dyakov isn't a bad fellow. For an Ivan."

"The field marshal isn't going to like me any better if it gets around the camp that we think one of his favorite hunting rifles might have been used to murder me."

"Of course," said Buhtz. "You have my word. But look here, I owe a great deal to the field marshal—I owe my commission to him. But for him I'd still be languishing in Breslau, so I should hate it to get around that it was me who identified this bullet as coming from a rifle like his."

I nodded. "I certainly won't say anything about it," I told him. "For now."

"But you don't seriously think for a moment that it was Günther von Kluge who tried to kill you?" he asked. "Do you?"

"No," I said. "I think if the field marshal actually wanted me dead, he could find a much better way of doing it than to shoot me himself."

"Yes. He could." Buhtz smiled grimly. "Then again, you could just stay here. If you wait in Smolensk long enough, the Russians will be in your lap."

I SKIPPED LUNCH. After seeing Berruguete's autopsy I wasn't that hungry; the only meal I wanted to have was in the schnapps bottle on the mess table but that would have meant enduring Ines Kramsta's stony indifference to my existence. That hurt more than it ought to have done. So I went back to the car thinking I might drive to the castle and send a signal to the ministry telling them that the members of the commission had already forgotten about Berruguete, and that their work was proceeding as hoped. Sometimes it's useful to have duties in which you can take refuge.

I drove out of the gates and east, along the main Smolensk road. About halfway there I saw Peshkov again, his coat flapping in the stiffening breeze. I didn't stop to offer him another ride. I wasn't in the mood to drive Hitler's doppelgänger anywhere. I didn't go to the castle, either. Instead I kept on going. I suppose you might say that I was distracted, although that would have been an understatement. I had the distinct feeling that I'd lost so much more than the regard of a lovely woman—that in losing her good opinion of me I'd also lost the slightly better opinion that lately I'd formed of myself; but her good opinion was more important, not to mention her smell and her touch and the sound of her voice.

I had half an idea to go to the Zadneprovsky Market on Bazarnaya Square and buy another bottle, like the *chekuschka* that I'd shared with Dr. Batov, although I would have been just as satisfied with the more lethal brewski he had warned me about—possibly more so; complete and lasting oblivion sounded just fine to me. But a few blocks before the market, the field police had closed Schlachthofstrasse to all traffic—a security alert, they said; a suspected terrorist who was holed up in a railway shed near the main station—and so I turned the car around, drove a few meters west again, pulled up and just sat there, smoking another cigarette before it dawned on me that I was right outside the Hotel Glinka. And after a while I went inside because I knew they always had vodka in there and sometimes even schnapps and a lot of other ways to take a man's mind off what is troubling him.

Without a doorman since the Rudakov brothers had left Smolensk, the Glinka's madam was now in charge of the temple entrance as well as the girls inside; she was little more than a babushka with a rather obvious wig possessed of long, Versailles-style locks. Gap-toothed with too much lipstick and a cheap black peignoir, she had the face and *faux demure* manner of a corrupted milkmaid and was about as greedy as a hungry fox, but she spoke good German. She told me they weren't open yet but let me in all the same when she saw my money.

Inside, the place was decorated like The Blue Angel with lots of tall mirrors and chipped mahogany and a little stage where a bespec-tacled girl wearing just a *Stahlhelm* was seated on a beer barrel pumping out a tune on a piano accordion that covered her rather obvious nakedness, or at least just about. I didn't recognize the tune, but I could see she had nice legs. Over the fireplace there was a large portrait of Glinka lying on a sofa with a pencil in his hand and a score on his lap. From the dark and painful expression on his face I guessed he'd disappointed a woman he was keen on and she'd told him it was over between them; either that or it was his music being squeezed to death on the accordion.

The madam led me to a high-ceilinged corner room with a view of the street and an evil-smelling bed with a green button-back head-board and a little tin cup for tips. There was a green carpet on the wooden floor, pink sheets on the bed, and some chocolate-brown wallpaper that was almost hanging on the wall. The chandelier on the ceiling was made of barley-sugar glass with a shard missing, as if someone had tried taking a bite out of it. The room was every bit as depressing as I needed it to be. I handed the madam a fistful of oc-cupation marks and told her to send me up a bottle, some company, and a pair of sunglasses. Then I took off my tunic and put the only German record on the gramophone player—Evelyn Künneke was always a local favorite on account of all the concerts she gave for soldiers on the Eastern Front. I pressed my face against the grimy windowpane and stared outside. Half of me was wondering why I was there but it was not the half of me that I was listening to at that moment, so I unlaced my shoes, lay down, and lit a cigarette.

A few minutes later three Polish girls arrived with vodka, took off their clothes—without being asked, I might add—and lay close beside me on the bed. Two lay on either side of me like a pair of sidearms; the third lay between my legs with her head on my stomach. Her name was Pauline, I think. She had a nice body and so did the others but I didn't do very much and nor did they. They just stroked my hair, and shared my cigarettes and watched me drink—too much—and generally despise myself. After a while one of them—Pauline—tried to unbutton my trousers but I swatted her hand away. There was sufficient comfort in their idle nakedness, which felt natural and like one of those old paintings of some stiff scene invoking pastoral poetry or a stupid bit of mythology, the way old paintings sometimes do. Besides, if you drink enough it provokes only the desire to sleep and takes the edge off any thoughts that might prevent this from happening; that was the general idea, anyway. Thinking I was playing some sort of coy game, Pauline laughed and tried to unbutton me again and so I held her hand and told her in my halting Russian—for a moment I forgot that she was Polish and she spoke German—that her company and that of her friends was quite enough for me.

"What are you doing in Smolensk?" she asked when she realized I was quite serious about being serious.

"Oppressing the Russians," I told her. "Taking what doesn't belong to Germany. Committing a crime of truly historic proportions. Killing Jews, on an industrial scale. That is what we're doing in Smolensk. Not to mention everywhere else."

"Yes, but you personally. What do you do? What is your job?"

"I am investigating the deaths of four thousand of your countrymen," I told her. "Polish officers who were captured by the Russians as a result of an unholy alliance between Germany and Russia and then murdered in the Katyn Wood. Shot one after another and piled into a mass grave, one on top of the other, like so many sardines. No, not like sardines. More like a horrible lasagne, with layers and layers of pasta and something darker and slimier in between. Sometimes I have this nightmare that I'm part of that lasagne. That I'm lying in a pool of fat between two decaying human strata."

They were silent for a moment; then Pauline said, "That's what we heard," she said. "That there were thousands of bodies. Some of the soldiers who come here say the whole area smells like a plague."

"But is it true?" asked another. "Only we hear a lot of rumors about what is happening over at Katyn Wood and it's difficult to know what to believe. Soldiers are such liars. They're always trying to scare us."

"It's true," I said. "Hand over heart. Just for once the Germans aren't lying about something. The Russians murdered four thousand Polish officers here in the spring of 1940. And many others besides in several other places we don't yet know about. Perhaps as many as fifteen or twenty thousand men. Time will tell. But right now my government is rather hoping to tell the world about it first."

"My elder brother was in the Polish Army," said Pauline. "I haven't seen him since September 1939. I don't even know if he's alive or dead. For all I know he could be one of those men in the forest."

I sat up and took her face in my hands. "Was he an officer?" I asked.

"No. A sergeant. In an Uhlan regiment. The Eighteenth Lancers. You should have seen him on his horse. Very handsome."

"Then I sincerely doubt he's one of these men."

This was a lie but I meant it kindly; by now we knew that as many as three thousand of the bodies found in the mass graves at Katyn were those of Polish NCOs, but it didn't seem right to tell her that, not while she was lying beside me. Three thousand NCOs seemed like a lot to me—perhaps as many NCOs as there were in the whole Polish Army. It wasn't that I thought she would get up and leave, merely that I didn't have the stomach for the truth. And, after all, what was one more lie now when so many lies had been and probably would still be told about what had really happened in Katyn Wood?

"And we certainly didn't find any horses," I added by way of corroboration.

Pauline breathed a sigh of relief and laid her head back on my stomach. The weight of her head was almost too much for me.

"Well, that's a relief," she said. "To know that he isn't one of them. I wouldn't like to think of him lying up there and me lying down here."

"No, indeed," I said quietly.

"But it would be ironic, don't you think, Pauline?" said one of the others beside me. "Both of you eight hundred kilometers from home, in a foreign country, lying on your backs, all day and all night."

Pauline shot her friend a look. "You know, you don't seem like the other Germans," she said, changing the subject.

"No, you're so wrong," I insisted. "I'm just like them. I'm every bit as bad. And don't ever make the mistake of thinking that there's any one of us who's decent. We're not worth a damn. None of us is worth a damn. Take my word for it."

Pauline laughed. "Why don't you let me help you to forget about all that?"

"No, listen to me, it's true. You know it's true, too. You've seen the bodies hanged on street corners as an example to the rest of the local population."

I drank some more and tried to lasso a stray thought that was running around my head like a loose horse. That image and the picture of six Russians hanged by the Gestapo rope was very much in my mind. I didn't know why. Perhaps it was the length of rope in my tunic pocket that I'd untied from the shooter's tree at Krasny Bor. And the certainty that I'd seen something since then that seemed relevant to all that.

I drank some more and we just lay there on the bed and someone played the only German record again and I dreamed a terrible waking allegory of poetry and music and forensic pathology and dead Poles. It was always dead Poles and I was one of them, lying stiffly in the ground with two bodies pressed close beside me and one on top of me, so that I could not move my arms or my legs; and then the earthmover started up its engine and started to fill in the grave with tons of soil and sand, and the trees and the sky gradually disappeared, and all was suffocating darkness, without end, amen.

11

FRIDAY, APRIL 30, 1943

When eventually I awoke with a start my eyes and my skin were leaking with fear at the idea of being buried alive. Or dead. Either one seemed an intolerable idea. My dreams always seemed designed to warn me about death, and they swiftly turned into nightmares when it appeared that the warning had come too late. Fueled by alcohol and depression, this one had been no different from the worst of them.

The three girls were gone and everything was bathed in a urine-colored moonlight that seemed to add an extra loathsomeness to the already sordid room. Outside the window a dog was barking and a locomotive was moving in the distant railway yards like a large wheezing animal that couldn't make up its mind which way to go. Through the floor I could hear the sound of music and men's voices and women's laughter. I felt as if one of the uneven bedsprings was twisting its way through my stomach.

An armored car on Schlachthofstrasse came past the window, shaking the dirty glass in the damp casement. I glanced at my wristwatch and saw that it was well after midnight, which meant that it was time to leave and straighten myself. A delegation of French, including Fernand de Brinon, the Vichy secretary of state, had flown in the previous afternoon, and later this morning several German officers including me were supposed to escort them to the graves of those bodies already exhumed from Katyn Wood—among them two Polish generals, Mieczyslaw Smorawiński and Bronislaw Bohatyrewicz.

When I got up from the bed an empty bottle of vodka and an ashtray that had been balanced on my chest fell onto the floor. Ignoring an overwhelming feeling of nausea, I found my boots and my tunic and when I put my hands in my pockets and found the length of rope I'd untied from the tree at Krasny Bor, I remembered what it was that I'd been trying to recall before the drink had claimed me.

Peshkov's coat. When I'd driven past him on the road from Krasny Bor to the castle, his coat—normally tied around the waist with a length of rope—had been loose. Had he lost the rope? Was that rope now in my pocket? And if it was, had Peshkov been the gunman who'd murdered Berruguete and taken a shot at me?

I went downstairs and then—following a sincere and lengthy thank-you to the madam for letting me sleep—I stepped out into the night air of Smolensk, retched into the gutter, and walked back to the car, congratulating myself that the other thing—the thing I had tried to forget—was now forgotten. Now if I could only remember my name.

By the time I was on the road to Vitebsk I had started to feel well enough to think of my duties again, and I stopped at the castle and sent the message to Goebbels as I had originally intended doing. Lieutenant Hodt, the duty signals officer, was manning the radio himself because several of his men—including Lutz—were sick with fever.

"It's this damned place," he said. "The men keep getting bitten by insects."

I nodded at the livid red lump on the side of his neck.

"Looks like you've been bitten yourself."

He shook his head. "No, that was one of the colonel's bees. Hurts like bloody blazes."

I offered him a cigarette.

"Given up," he said, shaking his head.

"You should start again," I told him. "Insects don't like the smoke. I haven't been bitten since I got here."

"That's not what I heard." Hodt grinned. "The word is von Kluge bit you pretty hard, Gunther. They say your head is still lying on the floor of the officers' mess."

I tried a grin—my first for a while; it almost worked, I think. "He'll get over it," I said. "Now that his *Putzer* is out of the hospital."

"In my opinion, you didn't hit him hard enough."

"Given the field marshal's threat to hang me," I said, "I'll take that as a compliment."

Rope again; I was going to have to find Peshkov and return his belt and keep a close eye on his expression as I did so.

"Yes, you should," said Hodt. "The man's a damned nuisance. He's always in here. Acts like he owns the place. Only no one wants to irritate the field marshal by telling him to clear off."

"Maybe this incident will have brought Dyakov to his senses," I said. "I'm sure the field marshal will have a word with him."

"I wish I shared your confidence in the field marshal."

Back in the car, I thought some more about Peshkov and remembered his familiarity with the history of the NKVD—the way he'd known about Yagoda and Yezhov and Beria. Was there more to his knowledge than just an interest in politics and current affairs? I unlocked the glove box and was stuffing the rope inside when I noticed a brown envelope and remembered I still had Alok Dyakov's things from the hospital. I placed the envelope on the seat beside me so as not to forget to return them and drove off. I hadn't gone very far when an animal shot out of the bushes and across my path and instinctively I braked hard. A wolf, perhaps? I wasn't sure but now that we'd opened the graves, the smell of the bodies had been drawing them in and the sentries had reported seeing several at night. I glanced down at the passenger seat and saw that the contents of the envelope had spilled to the floor of the car, and I risked the wrath of the sentry who was enforcing the blackout by turning on the map light to pick them up. As nurse Tanya had said, there was a watch, a gold ring, a pair of spectacles, some occupation money, a key, and a simple piece of thin brass about ten centimeters long.

And suddenly all thoughts of the rope in the glove box and Peshkov were gone.

I was looking at an empty brass stripper clip from an automatic weapon; it worked like this: you would fit the stripper clip of nine bullets, arranged one on top of the other, into the top of the pistol and then push them straight down into the magazine, leaving the strip standing proud of the gun; when you removed the stripper clip, the bolt would fall on the first round in the chamber and the weapon was ready to fire. Mauser was the only manufacturer that used a loading mechanism like that. The stripper clip for an M98 held five rounds and was shorter; this was the stripper clip for a broom-handle Mauser, and from the amount of polish on the clip it was almost certain that this was one of the stripper clips that had been in the door pocket of von Gersdorff's Mercedes and, before that, in his father's immaculate wooden presentation case.

They were useful and you tended not to throw one away. Unless it was prima facie evidence of a murder, in which case you ought to have thrown it away as soon as you had loaded the gun and certainly not kept it in your pocket out of habit, no doubt. The one I was holding was as clear a piece of evidence of murder as I'd seen in a long time, and had it not been for my hangover I might have cheered. But a moment's further reflection persuaded me that there was still considerable reason for caution; a simple stripper clip in the Russian's pocket would hardly have persuaded a man like Field Marshal von Kluge that his *Putzer* had murdered Dr. Berruguete; I was going to have to find out why he murdered him; and to do that I was going to have to find out a lot more about Alok Dyakov before I took what I had learned to his master.

It was then that I remembered the bayonet in von Gersdorff's car; if Dyakov had murdered Berruguete with von Gersdorff's gun, was it possible he might have used the Abwehr officer's razor-sharp bayonet to do a bit of throat-cutting, too?

I switched off the map light and sat in the darkness of Katyn Wood for a moment before returning at last to the only reasonable explanation—an explanation that took account of the field marshal's strange loyalty to his own *Putzer*. Everything was exactly as I had supposed from the very beginning, and the call-girl business that Ribe had been running from the castle switchboard had been nothing more than herring smoke that had got in my eyes.

Von Kluge knew the telephone on his desk was not working properly; I remembered him complaining to an operator about it when I was in his office. He must have realized—too late—that his compromising conversation with Adolf Hitler could have been overheard by the two signalers from the 537th manning the switchboard at the castle; it would have been a relatively simple matter for Alok Dyakov—who was often in and out of the castle to see his girlfriend Marusya—to check the duty roster and see who had been running the telephones during the Leader's visit to Smolensk and—on his master's orders—to have killed them, unaware that one of them had already thought to record the conversation on tape. Naturally, von Kluge would have correctly assumed that the Leader would have approved of Dyakov's actions.

If any of this was true, I would have to move even more carefully with an investigation into Alok Dyakov than could ever have been supposed.

I switched on the map light again and took another look at the key from the brown envelope. It was the key for a BMW motorcycle.

Everything was starting to make sense now; on the night of their murder, Ribe and Greiss would hardly have been on their guard meeting a figure as familiar to them as Dyakov outside the Hotel Glinka; and the sound of a German motorcycle heard by the SS sergeant who had disturbed their killer was now explained: Dyakov had access to a BMW. It certainly explained why their killer had chosen to escape along the Vitebsk road; he was heading home to Krasny Bor.

And if he had murdered Ribe and Greiss, then why not Dr. Batov and his daughter, too? Here, the motive was harder to fathom, although the killer's penchant for using a knife looked persuasive; Dyakov could easily have learned about their existence from von Kluge after I had petitioned the field marshal to give the two Russians asylum in Berlin—a petition he had resisted. Was it possible the field marshal was sufficiently against the idea of their being granted the right to go and live in Berlin that he had ordered his *Putzer* to kill them, too?

But if he had just shot and killed Dr. Berruguete, why had Dyakov gone to Katyn Wood and got drunk? To celebrate the death of a war criminal, perhaps? Or was the reason more prosaic—that by drawing attention to himself in Katyn Wood, he was simply trying to establish an alibi for what had happened at Krasny Bor? After all, who would have suspected a drunken man who was threatening to shoot himself of the cold and calculated murder of the Spanish doctor? And had I helped with that alibi by rendering him insensible?

But I was getting ahead of myself. First there was some elementary detective work to complete—work I ought to have done weeks ago.

I drove back to Krasny Bor and parked next to von Gersdorff's Mercedes. As usual his car door was not locked and, sitting in the passenger seat, I searched the glove box for the bayonet, intending to give it to Professor Buhtz in the hope that he might be able to find traces of human blood on the blade, but it wasn't there. I checked the door pocket, too, and under the seat, but it wasn't there, either.

"Looking for something?"

Von Gersdorff was standing immediately by the car, with a gun in his hand. The gun was pointed at me. I sat up sharply.

"Oh," he said. "Gunther, it's you. What the hell do you think you're doing in my car at nearly one in the morning?"

"Looking for your bayonet."

"What on earth for?"

"Because I think that it was used to murder those two signalers. Just like your Mauser was used to murder Dr. Berruguete. By the way, I found your shoulder stock."

"Did you? Good. Look, I can easily see why I might make a better suspect than Ines Kramsta. Her legs are better than mine."

"I didn't say you were a suspect, Colonel," I said. "After all, I hardly think you'd have been so careless to use your own Mauser. No, I think someone else used a gun and a bayonet that he knew were in this car—quite possibly with the intention of compromising you at some later stage, or perhaps they were just convenient for him, I don't know."

Von Gersdorff holstered his Walther and went around to the back of the car, where he unlocked the trunk. "The bayonet is in here," he said, fetching it out. "And when you say 'someone,' Gunther, I assume you don't mean Dr. Kramsta."

"No," I said.

"Funny thing about this bayonet," said von Gersdorff, handing it to me. "When I fetched it from the glove box the other day I thought for a minute it wasn't mine."

"Why?" I pulled the bayonet out of the scabbard and the blade gleamed in the moonlight.

"Oh, it was mine. I just thought it wasn't. That's why I put it away in the trunk."

"Yes, but why did you think it wasn't yours?"

"It's the same bayonet, all right, just a different scabbard. Mine was loose. This one is a close fit." He shrugged. "Bit of a mystery, really. I mean, they don't repair themselves, do they?"

"No, they don't," I agreed. "And I think you just answered my question."

I told him about the bayonet and the pieces of broken scabbard found in the snow near the bodies of Ribe and Greiss.

"So you think that was my scabbard probably?" said von Gersdorff.

"Yes. I do."

"Christ."

Then I told him about the stripper clip I'd found among Alok Dyakov's belongings; and how Alok Dyakov was now my best suspect for the murders of Ribe and Greiss.

"We're going to have to be very careful how we proceed with this," he said.

"We?"

"Yes. You don't think I'm going to let you do this alone, do you? Besides, I'd love to see the back of that Russian bastard."

"And von Kluge?"

Von Gersdorff shook his head. "I don't think you've got much chance of hurting him with this," he said. "Not without that tape."

"What do you mean?"

"I gave it to General von Tresckow," said von Gersdorff. "He judged it too dangerous to use and destroyed it."

"That's a pity," I said, but I could hardly fault the general for thinking, as I had done, that a tape recording of the Leader offering to buy the loyalty of one of his top field marshals with a substantial check was much too dangerous to keep.

"You'll remember that von Dohnanyi and Bonhoeffer were arrested. At the time we were more worried about the Gestapo than we were about Günther von Kluge. And I'm afraid it will take a lot more than a tape recording of a compromising conversation to bring down Hitler."

I nodded and handed him back his bayonet.

"So what's the next step?" he asked. "I mean, we are going after Dyakov, aren't we?"

"We need to speak to Lieutenant Voss," I said. "After all, it was him who first encountered Alok Dyakov. The Russian told me his version of what happened on the road, much of which I've forgotten. I was distracted by the arrival of the members of the international commission when he told me. We need the whole story from Voss, I think."

BEFORE I WENT TO BED I RETURNED the envelope containing his belongings to Dyakov; his light was on in his hut and so I was obliged to knock on his door and give him a story that I suspected he only half believed.

"The nurse gave me the envelope to return to you," I said, "and then I'm afraid I forgot all about it. Your stuff's been in my car all afternoon."

"I went back to the hospital to fetch it," he said. "And then I was looking for you, sir. Nobody knew where you were."

Had he remembered that the stripper clip was in his pocket?

"Sorry about that," I said. "But something came up. How's your head, by the way?"

"Not as bad as yours, perhaps," he said.

"Oh, is it that obvious?"

"Only to a boozer like myself, perhaps."

I shrugged. "Got some bad news, that's all. But I'm fine now." I clapped him on the shoulder. "Glad to see you're fine, too, old fellow. No hard feelings, eh?"

"No hard feelings, sir."

AT THE POLISH GRAVESIDES LATER that morning there were twenty of us, of whom at least half were French, including de Brinon, two senior army officers, and three reporters who wore berets and smoked pungent French cigarettes and generally looked like characters from *Pépé le Moko*. De Brinon was a fiftysomething figure wearing a fawn-colored raincoat and an officer's cap that made him look a bit like Hitler and seemed an affectation given that he was merely a lawyer. Von Gersdorff—who knew about these things—informed me that de Brinon was an aristocrat, a marquis, no less, and that he also had a Jewish wife whom the Paris Gestapo had been persuaded to ignore. Which might have explained why he was so keen to look like a Nazi. The French were making a big deal out of coming to Katyn Wood because it seemed that prior to the Polish-Soviet War of 1920, the French had sent four hundred army officers to help train the Polish Army, and many of these—including the two generals now in Katyn—had stayed on as part of the Fifth Chasseurs Polonais to fight Marshal Tukhachevsky's Red Army. All of which meant that Voss, Conrad, Sloventzik, von Gersdorff, and I endured a wasted morning answering endless questions and apologizing for the smell, the rather makeshift wooden crosses on the graves, and the sudden change in the weather. Even Buhtz put in an appearance, having left the international commission in the hands of the Polish Red Cross to conduct their own autopsies exactly as they saw fit. Someone took a picture of us: Voss is pictured explaining Russia's "worst war crime" to de Brinon, who looks at him uncomfortably, as if fully aware of the fact that he, too, would be shot by the French for war crimes in April 1947 while the two French generals do what French generals always do best: look smart.

There was no priest; the Poles had already conducted a proper burial service, and no one thought it important to pray again for the dead. Religion was the last thing on anyone's mind.

After we'd disposed of the French—something that never takes very long for Germans—von Gersdorff and I took Voss aside and asked him to sit with us for a while in the Abwehr colonel's car. In his long field policeman's coat and cunt cap, the tall military policeman—he had been the tallest of any man standing beside the graves—cut a handsome figure; slimmer men look good wearing a cunt cap, and when they're German officers they look businesslike, as if they have no time for appearances and formalities. There was just a hint of Heydrich about his canine features and in the way he bore himself and, for a moment, I wondered what the former Reichsprotektor of Bohemia would have made of my efforts in Katyn. Not much, probably.

Von Gersdorff handed out cigarettes and we were soon enclosed in a fug of tobacco smoke that made a very pleasant change to the rank air of Katyn Wood.

"Tell us about Alok Dyakov," said the colonel, coming straight to the point.

"Dyakov?" Voss shook his head. "He's a fox, that one. You know, for a former schoolteacher, he's an excellent shot with a rifle. The other week one of the motorcycle lads who outride the field marshal's car told me that he saw Dyakov take a dog down at seven hundred and fifty meters. Apparently they thought it was a wolf but it turned out to be some poor fucking farmer's mutt. Dyakov was very upset about it, too. Loves dogs, he said. Loves dogs, hates reds. True, he's got a telescopic sight on that rifle—same as the field marshal—but whatever he was teaching, I don't think it was Latin and history."

"What kind of a sight?" I asked.

"Zeiss. ZF42. But that rifle isn't really designed to have a sight. The rifle has to be machined by a skilled armorer."

"That's right," said von Gersdorff. "I have one like that myself."

"What, here in Smolensk?"

"Yes. Here in Smolensk. Should I speak to a lawyer?"

Seeing Voss frown at that, I put him squarely in the picture and then prodded him for some more information about the Russian *Putzer*.

"It was probably early September 1941," said Voss. "My boys were on the southeast of the city, inside the Yelnya salient."

"That was a fifty-kilometer front that our Fourth Army had extended from the city to form a staging area for a continued offensive toward Vyazma," explained von Gersdorff. "The Russians attempted an encirclement that failed, thanks to our air superiority. But it only just failed. It was the most substantial reverse our armies suffered, until Stalingrad."

"We were operating on the flanks of the salient," continued Voss. "About ten kilometers along the Mscislau Road and charged with mopping up any last pockets of resistance. Partisans, a few deserters from the 106th Mechanized Rifle Division and the 24th Army, some NKVD units. Our orders were simple." He shrugged, and began to look evasive. "Anyone still resisting was to be shot, of course. Also anyone who had surrendered who fell within the guidelines issued by General Müller that we were still enforcing back then. Until they were canceled in June last year."

Voss was talking about Hitler's Commissar Order demanding that prisoners who were active representatives of Bolshevism—which certainly included NKVD—should be shot summarily.

"We'd already shot a lot," he said. "It was payback for what we'd been through. The Geneva Convention doesn't seem to count for a lot the farther you get from Berlin. Anyway, we came across this open-topped GAZ that had gone off the road near a farm."

The GAZ was a Russian four-wheel-drive vehicle—the equivalent of a Tatra.

"There were three people sitting in it. Two of them were wearing NKVD uniforms—the driver and one of the men in the back. They were dead. The third man, Dyakov, was dressed as a civilian. He was only half conscious and still handcuffed to the side rail in the back of the GAZ and seemed very pleased to see us when he came around a bit. He claimed he'd been arrested by the NKVD and that he was being taken to prison, or worse, by the other two, whom he'd attacked when the road in front of the car had been strafed by a Stuka.

"We found the keys to the manacles and fixed him up—he'd been banged about a bit when the car came off the road and possibly also by the two NKVD when they arrested him. He spoke good German, and when we interrogated him he told us he was a German language teacher at the school in Vitebsk, which was why he'd been arrested in the first place, although by then he was making his living as a poacher. According to him, speaking German automatically brought you under suspicion from the secret police, but we later formed the impression that the real reason he'd been arrested was probably more to do with him being a poacher than anything else."

"What papers did Dyakov have on him?" I asked.

"Just his *propiska*," said Voss. "That's a residency permit and migration recording document."

"No internal passport?"

"He said that had already been confiscated by the NKVD on a previous security check. It's what the NKVD termed 'open arrest' since there is very little you can do in Soviet Russia without an internal passport."

"That's convenient. And the NKVD men? What papers did they have?"

"The usual NKVD clothbound identity booklets. And in the driver's case his license, his Komsomol Party ID book, some transit coupons, and a certificate for carrying a gun."

"I hope you kept those documents," I said.

"I'm afraid the originals were destroyed in a fire with a lot of other documents," said Voss. "I think one of the officers was called Krivyenko."

"Destroyed?"

"Yes," said Voss. "Not long after we moved into our billet at Grushtshenki there was a mortar attack by partisans."

"I see. That was very convenient, too. For Dyakov."

"I expect I have photographs of those at the Abwehr offices in Smolensk," said von Gersdorff. "It's standard practice for the Abwehr to keep a photographic record of all captured NKVD documentation."

"Does Dyakov know that?"

"I doubt it."

"No time like the present," I said. "Shall we take a look?"

On the drive to the Army Kommandatura I had some more questions about Dyakov.

"How did he come to meet the field marshal, for God's sake?" I asked.

Von Gersdorff cleared his throat uncomfortably. "I'm afraid that's my fault," he said. "You see, I handled the interrogation. I questioned him to see what he could tell us about the NKVD. The trouble with that Commissar Order was that we never got any good intelligence, and to have one of their own prisoners was about the next best thing. He was actually very helpful. Or so it seemed at the time. During the course of this interview Dyakov and I got talking about what kind of game there is to hunt around here."

"Of course," I said lightly.

"I was hoping for some deer but Dyakov told me that all of the deer had been killed by local hunters for food the previous winter but that there were still plenty of wild boar about and if I was interested he could show me where all the best spots were and even organize a drive for us. I happened to mention this to von Kluge, who, as you know, is a very keen hunter—and he got very excited at the prospect of shooting wild boar in Russia. At his estate in Prussia there are several drives like that a year. I hadn't seen him quite so happy since we captured Smolensk. A boar hunt was duly organized, for several guns—the field marshal, the general, myself, von Boeselager, von Schlabrendorff, and other senior officers—and I have to say, it was very successful. I think we got three or four. The field marshal was delighted and almost immediately he ordered another drive, which was equally successful. After that he decided to make Dyakov his *Putzer,* and since then there have been more shoots, although lately the wild boar seem to have disappeared—I think we shot them all, quite frankly—which is why the field marshal now goes after wolves, not to mention hare and rabbit and pheasant. Dyakov seems to know where all the good spots are. Voss is right—I think it's much more likely the fellow was a local poacher."

"Not to mention a murderer," I said.

Von Gersdorff looked sheepish. "I could hardly have known something like that would happen. In many ways Dyakov is a very affable sort of chap. It's just that since the field marshal took him under his wing, he's become a law unto himself and insufferably arrogant—as you witnessed for yourself the other night."

"Not to mention a murderer," I repeated.

"Yes, yes, you've made your point."

"To you," I said. "But if it's going to stick, I'm going to need more than a damned stripper clip. So let's hope we find something in the Abwehr files."

The Abwehr office in the Smolensk Kommandatura overlooked a small garden that was planted with vegetables and faced onto the windows of the local German foreign ministry; beyond that you could see the jagged crenellations on top of the eastern Kremlin. On the wall of the office was a map of the Smolensk Oblast and a larger one of Russia, with the front clearly marked in red and uncomfortably nearer than I had previously supposed: Kursk—which was where German armor was now grouped before the Red Army—was only five hundred kilometers to the southwest of us; if Russian tanks broke through our lines, they could reach Smolensk in just ten days.

A young duty officer with an accent so astonishingly upper class that I almost laughed—where did they get these people? I wondered—was on the telephone and quickly concluded his conversation when we appeared in the door; he stood up and saluted smartly. Von Gersdorff, whose manners were normally impeccable, went straight to the filing cabinets without bothering to introduce us and started to hunt through the drawers.

"What was that you were saying about the uprising in the Warsaw ghetto, Lieutenant Nass?" he murmured.

"The reports from Brigadier Stroop indicate that all resistance has ended, sir."

"We've heard that before," he said. "I'm amazed the resistance has lasted so long. Women and small boys fighting the furious might of the SS. Mark my words, gentlemen, this won't be the last we hear of it. In a month's time the yids will still be coming up from their crypts and their cellars."

Finally, he found the file he was looking for and laid it on a map table by the window.

He showed me the photographs of the documents found on the dead NKVD men and on Alok Dyakov.

"The *propiska* found on Dyakov tells us nothing," I said. "There's no photograph and it could belong to anyone," I said. "At least anyone called Alok Dyakov."

I spent the next few minutes staring closely at the pictures of the two NKVD identity cards—one in the name of Major Mikhail Spiridonovich Krivyenko and the other in the name of Sergeant Nikolai Nikolayevich Yushko, an NKVD driver.

"Well, what do you think?" asked von Gersdorff.

"This one," I said, showing the two men the picture of Krivyenko's identity card. "I'm not sure about this one."

"Why?" asked Voss.

"The right-hand page is clear enough," I remarked. "It's not so easy to be sure without the original document in my hands, but the stamp on the picture page on the left looks suspiciously faint on the bottom right-hand-corner photograph. Almost as if it's been taken off something else and stuck on. Plus the circumference of the stamp seems slightly out of line."

"Yes, you're right," said Voss. "I hadn't noticed that before."

"It would have been better if you had noticed it at the time," I said pointedly.

"So what are you saying, Gunther?" asked von Gersdorff.

"That maybe Dyakov is really Mikhail Spiridonovich Krivyenko?" I shrugged. "I don't know. But just think about it for a minute. You're a major in an NKVD car with a prisoner when you realize that the Germans are probably just a few kilometers down the road—that you're going to be captured at any moment, which means an automatic death sentence for NKVD officers. Don't forget that Commissar Order. So what do you do? Perhaps you shoot your own driver and then force your prisoner—the real Alok Dyakov—to undress and put on your NKVD uniform. Then you put on his clothes and murder him, too. You take the picture from Dyakov's internal passport—and use it to replace the one on your own NKVD identity card. They were found near a farm, so maybe he could have used some egg white to stick the picture down. Or maybe some grease off the axle, I don't know. Then you destroy your own picture and the real Dyakov's internal passport—you can maybe get away with one fake document but not two. Next you drive the GAZ off the road and make things look like an accident. Your last action is to handcuff yourself to the handrail and wait for rescue as Alok Dyakov. What German could argue with a man who had been such an obvious prisoner of the NKVD? Especially a man who speaks good German. Almost automatically you would be less suspicious of him."

"That's right," said Voss, who was still smarting from my earlier comment. "We didn't suspect him at all. Well, you don't, do you, when you find a man who's a prisoner of the reds? You just assume—Besides, my men were tired. We'd been on the go for days."

"That's all right, Lieutenant," I told him. "Better men than you have fallen for Russian tricks like that. Our government has been treating the Protocols of the Elders of Zion as if it was gospel ever since the 1920s."

"The way you tell that story, Gunther," said von Gersdorff, "it sounds obvious, but it would take a hell of a lot of nerve to pull it off."

I turned to Voss. "About how many so-called commissars did your unit execute, Lieutenant?"

Voss shrugged. "Lost count. Forty or fifty at least. Eventually it was like shooting rabbits, quite frankly."

"Then Dyakov—let's call him that for now, shall we?—he had nothing to lose, I'd have thought. Shot summarily, or shot after a game attempt at remaining alive."

"Yes, but having deceived us," asked von Gersdorff, "why not just slip away back to your own lines, one night?"

"And give up a nice little berth here in Smolensk? The field marshal's confidence? Three meals a day? As much booze and cigarettes as you can handle? Not to mention an excellent opportunity to spy on us—perhaps even carry out some small acts of sabotage and murder? No, I should say he's well set here. Besides, his own lines are hundreds of kilometers away. At any time on that road he could be arrested and then shot by the field police. And if ever he did get back to his own lines, then what? It's generally held that Stalin doesn't trust men who've been in German custody. Chances are he'd end up with a bullet in the back of the head and a shallow grave just like those fucking Polacks."

"You're very persuasive," admitted Lieutenant Voss. "If this was any Ivan but Dyakov, you could have him in jail by now. But all this is just a theory, isn't it? None of this proves anything."

"He's right," agreed von Gersdorff. "Without those original identity papers, you've still got nothing."

I thought for a moment. "What you were saying just a moment ago, about the Jews of the Warsaw ghetto. Coming up from their crypts and their cellars."

"One has to admire courage like that. And to deplore the kind of treatment that brings about a situation where the German military behaves like an army of condottieri from the Middle Ages. I know I do and many others besides me."

Von Gersdorff bit his lip for a moment and shook his head bitterly. I tried to interrupt with an idea I'd just had but, seeing the colonel had hardly finished, I kicked the door shut in case anyone heard our raised voices; even after Stalingrad, there were plenty of men serving with the Wehrmacht in Smolensk who still worshipped Adolf Hitler.

"This whole exercise in Katyn Wood—aren't the reds awful? This is the kind of Bolshevik barbarism that Germany is fighting against—it's all bullshit while we're busy blowing up synagogues and firing tank rounds at schoolboys with Molotov cocktails. What, do we think the world hasn't noticed what we're doing in Warsaw? Do we honestly believe that public opinion is going to ignore heroism like that? Are we really expecting that the Americans are ever going to come over to our side after we've murdered thousands of lightly armed Jews in Poland on the strength of what we're uncovering here in Smolensk?" He made a fist and held it in front of his face for a moment, as if wishing he could hit someone with it—me, probably. "This Warsaw ghetto uprising has been going on since January eighteenth, long before anyone found a human bone in Katyn Wood, and it's the scandal of Europe. What kind of a propaganda minister is it who thinks that the corpses of thirteen thousand Jewish insurgents can be hidden away or ignored while we bring the world's reporters here to show them the bodies of four thousand dead Polacks? That's what I'd like to know."

"When you put it like that," I said, "it does sound ridiculous."

"Ridiculous?" Von Gersdorff laughed. "It's the most stupendously fatuous piece of public relations nonsense I've ever heard. And thanks to you, Gunther, my name will forever be associated with it as the man who found the first body in Katyn Wood."

"Then tell him that," I suggested. "Joey the Crip. Tell him that next time you see him."

"I can hardly be the only person who thinks the same way. My God, I expect there are lots of Nazis who recognize the obvious truth of what I'm saying, so perhaps I will."

"And what good would that do? Seriously. Look, Colonel, I'm too old to lie to myself, but I'm not so stupid that I can't lie to others.

I've had a rotten feeling in my stomach every morning for the last ten years. There's hardly been one day when I haven't asked myself if I could live under a regime I neither understood nor desired. But what am I supposed to do? For the present, I just want to pinch a man for the murders of three—possibly five—people. That's not much, I'll agree. And even if I do succeed in pinching him, I won't get much satisfaction from it. For now, being a policeman seems like the only right thing I can do. I'm not sure that makes sense to a man with a keen sense of honor like you. But it's all I've got. So. What you were saying just a moment ago, about the Jews of the Warsaw ghetto. Coming up from their crypts and their cellars. That's given me an idea for what to do about Dyakov."

THE ENTRANCE TO SMOLENSK CATHEDRAL was up a series of wide steps under a great white vault that was as big as a circus tent. The outer corridors with their low roofs and frescoes of rather fey-looking angels were more like fairy grottoes. Inside, the gold icon stasis resembled a couple of stalls in a street full of jewelers' shops and framed a Fabergé egg of a central shrine and a copy of a Madonna—the original having been destroyed during the battle for Smolensk—who looked out from the window of her gleaming home with a mixture of pique and embarrassment. Light from the hundreds of flickering candles that burned in several tall brass chandeliers added an ancient, pagan touch to the cathedral interior and, instead of the Christian Madonna, I would not have been surprised to see a vestal virgin maintaining the sacred fire of the many candles or weaving a straw figure to throw into the Tiber. All religion seems like something hermetic to me.

Preceded by a sergeant of panzer engineers, who was an expert in hidden bomb removal—by von Gersdorff's account, Sergeant Schlächter had removed more than twenty mines left by the reds on the two remaining bridges across the Dnieper and, as a result, was a twice-decorated pioneer—the colonel and I stepped carefully down a long and narrow winding stone staircase that led into the cathedral crypt. There was a small elevator but that had stopped working and no one cared to try to fix it just in case that was booby-trapped, too.

A strong smell of damp and decay filled our nostrils, as if we were going so deep into the dark bowels of the earth that we might find the river Styx itself; but as Schlächter informed us, the crypt and the church were really not all that old:

"The story goes that during the great siege of Smolensk in 1611 the city's defenders locked themselves down here and then set fire to the ammunition depot to stop it from falling into Polish hands. There was an explosion and everything in the crypt—including the Ivans themselves—was destroyed or killed. That's probably true. Anyway, the place fell into complete disrepair and had to be demolished in 1674. But it was 1772 before the rebuilding was finished because the first attempt fell down, and so when Napoleon turned up and told everyone how marvelous he thought the cathedral was, it could only have been about thirty or forty years old. Down here is damp only because they didn't build proper drainage for the foundations—it's right next to an underground spring, see? Which is why those original defenders thought it a good place to barricade in the first place—because of the access to fresh water. But it's not so damp that an explosive charge won't go off.

"We removed the main explosive charges when we captured the cathedral," he explained. "At least the ordnance that was meant to blow the place right up to heaven when the Ivans cleared out of Smolensk. Now, that's what I call a bloody assumption. The Red Army had filled the whole fucking crypt with explosive, just like they did in 1611, and they thought to detonate it with radio-controlled fuses from several hundred kilometers away, the same as in Kiev, only this time they forgot that the signal couldn't travel underground, so the charges didn't go off. We were walking around upstairs for days before we found the stuff down here. It could have blown us up at any time."

"Are you sure you want to do this?" I asked von Gersdorff. "I don't see any point in us both risking our lives. This was my crazy idea, not yours."

"You forget," said von Gersdorff, "I've armed and disarmed antipersonnel mines before. Or had you forgotten the Arsenal? Besides, I speak much better Russian than you, and more to the point, I read it, too. Even if you do manage to open one of the NKVD's filing cabinets without getting your head blown off, you don't really know what the hell it is you're looking for."

"You have a point there," I admitted. "Although I'm not even sure that what we're looking for is down here."

"No, of course not. But like you, I think it's certainly worth a shot. I've been longing to get a chance to come down here, and now you've given me a good reason. Anyway, two of us can get the job done much more quickly than one."

At the foot of the stairs Schlächter unlocked a heavy oak door and switched on a light to illuminate a long and windowless basement that was full of filing cabinets and bookshelves and religious paraphernalia, including some precious-looking silver icons and a couple of spare chandeliers. A large marker sign of a yellow skull and crossbones hung on a length of wire that extended across the width of the room, and here and there—on walls and cupboards—were some red chalk marks.

"Right, gentlemen," said Schlächter. "Pay attention, please. I'm going to tell you what I would tell anyone who joins the panzer engineers. I apologize if any of this sounds like basic training but it's the basics that will help to keep you alive.

"What we have down here is the handiwork of a real joker of an Ivan. He must have had days down here setting up practical jokes for us. Funny for the enemy, no doubt, but not, I can assure you, for us.

You pull something open and find that whatever it is you're pulling—a drawer, a cabinet door, a box file off a shelf—is linked by a short length of det cord to a half kilo of plastic explosive that goes off before your arm has stopped moving. I've had one man lose his face and another lose his hand, and frankly I just don't have the men to spare for a job like this right now—not when there's still so much to clear up top. The SS have offered me some Russian POWs to clear this room but I'm the old-fashioned type—I don't believe in that sort of thing. Besides, it would defeat the object if the hidden bomb clearance resulted in the destruction of the very thing that makes hand clearance of this kind of ordnance necessary in the first place.

"So here's how it works: you get to find them. That's the hard part—which is to say it's hard finding them without getting a nasty surprise. Then I'll come along and do the business. Now, the first thing is to understand your adversary. The aim of using a hidden bomb is not to inflict casualties and damage. That is merely a means to an end. The main thing is to create an attitude of uncertainty and suspicion in your enemy's mind. This lowers morale and creates a degree of caution that slows up his movement. Maybe so. But there's nothing wrong with a bit of uncertainty in here.

"Please put out of your mind any preconceptions you might have about Russians because I can tell you that the man or men who made these devices had a keen understanding of the essence of hidden bombing, which is low cunning and variety, not to mention human psychology. While you are in here, continual vigilance is essential. It must become second nature. Keen eyesight and a suspicious mind will keep you alive in this room, gentlemen. You must look for signs of unusual activity, which will warn you of potential hazards. Spend a good while looking at something before you think to touch it.

"And the following clues may indicate the presence of a trap: anything valuable or curious that might make a good souvenir—apparently harmless but incongruous objects. On other occasions elsewhere I have found bombs in the most unlikely objects: a flashlight filled with ball bearings and explosive, a water bottle, a table knife, a clothes peg, underneath the butt of an abandoned rifle—if it can be moved or picked up, it can also explode, gentlemen."

He pointed at one of the icons leaning against the crypt wall. It had a valuable-looking silver frame. On the wall immediately beside the icon was a red chalk mark.

"Take that icon, for instance," he said. "That's just the sort of thing some light-fingered Fritz might steal. But underneath the frame is a piece of paper covering a hole in the floorboards and a release switch connected to five hundred grams of plastic explosive. Enough to take a man's foot off. Maybe his whole leg. The chandeliers are wired, so don't touch them, either. And in case you were wondering about it, the remains of the filing cabinet that you see at the head of the room ought to be eloquent proof of the risk you're running."

He pointed at a blackened wooden filing cabinet that had once contained three drawers and been the height of a small man: the top drawer was hanging at an angle off its rails and the contents looked like the remains of a bonfire; on the wooden floor immediately below was a dark brown stain that might have been blood.

"Take a long hard look at it. That drawer was hiding just two hundred grams of plastic but it was enough to take a man's face off and blind him. From time to time, take another look at it and ask yourself—do I want to be right in front of a hidden bomb like that when it goes off?

"Other things to look out for are nails, electric leads—or pieces of wire—loose floorboards, recent brickwork, any attempt at concealment—new paint or marks that don't seem to fit in with the surroundings. But frankly, there is no end to this kind of list so it's best to tell you of the three principal methods of operating a hidden bomb that you will find in this room. These are the pull method, the pressure method, or the release method. Also be aware that an obvious trap may be used to disguise the presence of another, and always remember this: the more dummies we find, the more your vigilance is likely to be reduced. So keep paying attention. Safe procedure is to do everything slowly. If you encounter the least bit of resistance, stop what you're doing. Don't let go but call me and I will take a closer look. With most of these devices there's a safety pinhole. To neutralize the device, I will use a nail or a pin or a piece of strong wire and put it in the safety pinhole, after which the device will be safe to handle."

The sergeant of engineers rubbed his stubbled face and thought for a moment. The stubble that covered his face wasn't so very different from his eyebrows or the stubble that covered his head. His head looked like a rock covered with dry moss. His voice was no less rugged and laconic and the accent Low Saxon, probably—as if he was about to tell a Little Ernie joke. Around his neck was a small crucifix on a chain, which we soon discovered was the most important part of his disposal kit.

"What else? Oh yes." From a haversack that was slung over his shoulder he handed us each a dental mirror, a penknife, a piece of green chalk, and a small flashlight. "Your protective equipment. These three things will help to keep you alive, gentlemen. Right, then. Let's get started."

Von Gersdorff consulted his notebook. "According to our records, we believe the case files to be on the shelves while the NKVD's own personnel files are probably in those cabinets marked with the People's Commissariat's symbol, which is a hammer and sickle on top of a sword and a red banner featuring the Cyrillic symbols НКВД. None of the drawers appear to be alphabetically marked—although there is a little slot, so possibly the marker cards were removed. Fortunately, Krivyenko starts with the Cyrillic letter к, which is an easy one to spot for someone like you who doesn't read Russian. Unfortunately, there are thirty-three letters in the Cyrillic alphabet. Here— I've written out an alphabet for you, so you'll have a better idea of what you're looking at. I'll work down the cabinets on the left side of the room and you, Gunther—you take the right-hand side."

"And I'll take a look at what's on the shelves," said Sergeant Schlächter. "If the drawer is safe, put a green cross on it. And don't, for Christ's sake, slam them shut when you've finished."

I went to the first filing cabinet and scrutinized it for a long minute before turning my attention to the bottom drawer.

"Pay attention to the bottom of the drawer as well as to the top," said Schlächter. "Look out for a wire or a piece of cord. If the drawer opens safely and it happens to be the drawer you're looking for, don't pull a file out without observing the same precautions that apply to everything else here."

Kneeling down, I drew the heavy wooden drawer out only two or three centimeters and shone my flashlight carefully into the space I had made. Observing nothing suspicious, I gently pulled the drawer out a bit more until I was sure there were no wires or hidden bombs and then looked inside; the files were all headed with the letter к. Briefly I paused and began to examine the outside of the drawer immediately above; I knew there was nothing on the underside so once again I drew it out a couple of centimeters and scrutinized the narrow gap; this drawer was also harmless and contained files beginning with the letter π, so I stood up and began to look at the last drawer in the cabinet; and when at last I was satisfied that it, too, was safe— like the two others before, it contained к files—I put a cross on all three drawers with my chalk and let out a long breath as I stood back. I glanced at my wristwatch and I clasped my hands together for a moment in order to stop them from shaking. Checking one filing cabinet and pronouncing it clear of hidden bombs had taken me ten minutes.

I glanced around. Schlächter was between two high sets of metal shelves that were filled with papers and box files; von Gersdorff was checking the underside of a drawer with his dental mirror.

"At this rate it will take us all day," I said.

"You're doing fine," said the sergeant. "Clearing a room like this might take as long as a week."

"There's a thought," murmured von Gersdorff. He placed a green cross on the drawer in front of him and moved on to the next cabinet a meter or so behind me.

This went on—the three of us working at a snail's pace—for another fifteen or twenty minutes; and it was von Gersdorff who found the first device.

"Hello," he said calmly. "I think I've found something, Sergeant."

"Hold on. I'll come and take a look. Herr Gunther? Stop working, sir, and go to the door. I'd rather you didn't find another device while I'm assisting the colonel."

"Besides," added von Gersdorff, "there's no point in three of us getting it if the file is active, so to speak."

This was good advice and, as instructed, I went back to the door. I lit a cigarette and waited.

Sergeant Schlächter came and stood by von Gersdorff and took a long hard look at the drawer the colonel was still holding partly open, but not before he had kissed the little gold crucifix on the chain around his neck and placed it in his mouth.

"Oh yes," he said with the crucifix between his teeth. "There's a paper clip hooked over the lip of the drawer. It's attached to a length of wire. There's slack on the wire so I think we can be sure it's not a tension device but a bomb that's designed to go off when a firing pin is pulled out. If you don't mind, sir, perhaps you could gently pull the drawer back another few centimeters until I tell you to stop."

"Very well," said the colonel.

"Stop," said the sergeant. "Now, keep it steady, sir."

Schlächter pushed his hands through the narrow space and into the drawer.

"Plastic explosive," he said. "About half a kilo, I think. More than enough to kill us both. An electric dry-cell battery and two metal contacts. It's a simple device, but no less deadly for that. You keep pulling the drawer, you pull one plate toward the other, you make contact, the battery sends a signal to the detonator, and ka-boom. Battery might well be dead after all this time but there's no point in risking it. If you could hand me a small chunk of modeling clay, sir."

Von Gersdorff searched in the sergeant's haversack and took out a chunk of clay.

"If you wouldn't mind just handing that to me inside the drawer, sir."

The colonel pushed his hand into the drawer alongside Schlächter's and then withdrew it gently.

"I'll put some clay around the metal contacts, to prevent a circuit from being made," said the sergeant. "And then we can—pull out the detonator."

A long minute later, Schlächter was showing us the plastic explosive and the detonator it had contained. About the size of a tennis ball, the explosive was green and looked just like the same plasteline modeling clay Schlächter had used to isolate the metal contact strips. He tore the wires off the detonator and then tested the one-and-a-half-volt AFA battery with a couple of wires of his own that were attached to a small bicycle lamp. The bulb lit up brightly.

"German battery." He grinned. "That's why it still works, I suppose."

"I'm glad that amuses you," remarked von Gersdorff. "I don't think I like the idea of being blown up by our own equipment."

"Happens all the time. Ivan bombers are nothing if not resource-ful." Schlächter sniffed the explosive. "Almonds," he added. "This stuff is ours, too. Nobel 808. Bit too much, in my opinion. Half as much would achieve the same result. Still, waste not want not." His grin widened. "I'll probably use this when it's my turn to set some traps for the Ivans."

"Well, that's certainly a comfort," I said.

"They fuck with us," said Schlächter, "we fuck with them."

The afternoon passed, safely, with three more hidden bombs discovered and neutralized before we found what we were looking for: the People's Commissariat for Internal Affairs personnel files that started with the Cyrillic letter к.

"I've found them," I said. "The к files."

Von Gersdorff and the sergeant appeared behind me. Minutes later he had identified the file we were looking for.

"Mikhail Spiridonovich Krivyenko," said von Gersdorff. "Looks like your idea paid off, Gunther."

The drawer appeared to be clear but the sergeant reminded me not to pull out the file until we were quite sure it was safe to do so, and he checked this himself, again with the crucifix in his mouth.

"Does that work?" asked von Gersdorff.

"I'm still here, aren't I? Not only that but I know for sure that this is solid gold. Anything else would be sucked to nothing by now." He handed von Gersdorff Major Krivyenko's file, which was at least five centimeters thick. "Best take it outside," he added, "while I close up in here."

"Delighted to," said von Gersdorff. "My heart feels like it's about to burst through my tunic."

"Mine, too," I admitted, and followed the Abwehr colonel out of the door of the crypt. "I haven't been such a bag of nerves since the last time the RAF came to Berlin."

At the door the colonel opened the file excitedly and looked at the photograph of the man on the first page who, unlike Dyakov, was clean shaven. Von Gersdorff covered the lower half of the man's face with his hand and glanced at me.

"What do you think?" he asked. "It's not the best photograph."

"Yes, it could be him," I said. "The eyebrows look much the same."

"But either we draw a beard on the picture and ruin it or we'll have to persuade Dyakov to see the barber."

"Perhaps we can get a copy made," I suggested. "Either way, the picture in this file is nothing like the one on the photograph you have of Major Krivyenko's identity card. It's a different man. The real Dyakov, I expect."

"Yes, it looks like you were right about that."

"If my nerves weren't shredded already from being in here, I'd suggest looking for Dyakov's case file. I bet there's something about him on those shelves, eh, Sergeant?"

"I'll be with you in a minute, gentlemen," said Sergeant Schlächter. "I'm just going to make a quick note on the record of where all of the devices today were found."

Von Gersdorff nodded thoughtfully. "Page one—personnel record of Major Mikhail Spiridonovich Krivyenko in the NKVD Police Department of the Smolensk Oblast, hand-signed by the then deputy chief of the NKVD, one Lavrenty Beria, no less, in Minsk. Dneprostroy Badge—that means he was an NKVD officer who once supervised forced labor in a prison camp. Merited NKVD Worker medal—I suppose that's what you would expect of a major. Voroshilov Marksman badge for shooting, on the left breast of his tunic—well, that certainly fits with what we already know about the man, all right. That he can shoot. But shooting what? I wonder. Wild boar? Wolves? Enemies of the state? Fascinating. But look, there's more work to do on this file before we can put it in front of the field marshal. I can see I'm not going to get much sleep tonight while I translate what's in here."

"All right," said the sergeant, "I'm coming." But we never saw him again. Not alive, anyway.

Afterward we could only tell Major Ondra, his furious commanding officer—Sergeant Schlächter had been his most experienced man in Smolensk—that we hadn't a clue what had happened.

He himself thought there had been a deliberately loosened floorboard near the door in the safe area on the near side of the warning sign; the space immediately underneath the wooden board had already been checked for a pressure switch and was perfectly safe, but each time someone stood on one end of the board an exposed nail on the opposite end had been lifted several millimeters near another nail on the wall; we—and others besides us—must have walked across that part of the floor many times before finally it made contact and completed the circuit, which exploded several kilos of gelignite that was hidden behind a piece of dummy plasterwork in the wall. The blast knocked both the colonel and myself off our feet; if we had been standing in the room beside the sergeant, we, too, would probably have been killed; but it wasn't the explosion itself that killed the sergeant but the bicycle ball bearings that were pressed into the plastic explosive like several handfuls of sweets; the combined effect of those was like a sawn-off shotgun and took the man's head off as cleanly as a cavalryman's saber.

"I hope you think it was worth it," said Major Ondra. "Eighteen months we've left that crypt alone, and for a damned good reason. It's a fucking death trap. And all for what? Some fucking file that's probably out of date by now, anyway. It's a bloody shame, that's what it is, gentlemen. It's a bloody shame."

We went to the sergeant's funeral that same evening. His comrades buried him in the soldiers' cemetery at Okopnaja Church, on Gertnereistrasse near the Panzergrenadiers' billet in Nowosselki, just west of Smolensk. Afterward the colonel and I walked up to the banks of the Dnieper and looked back across the city at the cathedral where Schlächter had met his death just a few hours before. The cathedral seemed to hover above the hill on which it was built as if, like Christ's assumption, it was physically being taken up into heaven, which was, I suppose, the desired effect. But neither of us felt there was much consolation in that particular story. Or truth. Even von Gersdorff, who was a Roman Catholic, confessed that these days he crossed himself largely out of habit.

When we drove back to Krasny Bor I noticed that von Gersdorff's glove box now contained all of the Nobel 808 explosive that Sergeant Schlächter had made safe in the crypt—at least a couple kilos of the stuff.

"I'm sure I can find a proper use for it," he said quietly.

12

SATURDAY, MAY 1, 1943

The international commission headed by Professor Naville was returning to Berlin to draft the report for Dr. Conti, the head of the Reich Health Department, leaving the Polish Red Cross—from the beginning the Poles had worked separately from the international commission—still in Katyn. Gregor Sloventzik and I escorted the members of the commission to the airport in the coach, and understandably they were glad to be leaving—the Red Army was getting closer every day and no one wanted to be around when finally they arrived in Smolensk.

I was glad to see the back of them, and yet it was a journey that left me feeling pretty hollow as—her work with Professor Buhtz now concluded—Ines Kramsta had chosen to fly back to Berlin with the commission. She comprehensively ignored me all the way to the airport, choosing to stare out the window as if I didn't exist. I helped to carry her luggage to the waiting Focke-Wulf—Goebbels sent his own plane, of course—and hoped to say something by way of atonement for having suspected her of Dr. Berruguete's murder; but saying sorry didn't seem equal to the task, and when she turned on her elegant patent heel and disappeared through the door of the plane without uttering a single word, I almost cried out with pain.

I could have told her the truth—that maybe she was looking for too much from a man—instead I left it alone. For the few weeks while she'd been in Smolensk, my life had seemed like it mattered to someone more than it did to me; and now that she was going, I was back to not caring about it very much one way or the other. Sometimes that's just how it is between a man and a woman; something gets in the way of it, like real life and human nature and a whole lot of other stuff that isn't good for two people who think they're attracted to each other. Of course, you can save yourself a lot of pain and trouble by thinking twice before you get into anything, but a lot of life can pass you by like that. Especially in a war. I didn't regret what had happened—how could I?—only that she was going to live the rest of her life in complete and total ignorance of the rest of my life.

After this poignant little scene, Sloventzik and I got back into the coach.

We rode the coach back to the wood, where we found a scene of great excitement: the Russian POWs, working under the supervision of the field police and Alok Dyakov, had found another grave. This one—number eight—was more than a hundred meters to the southwest of all the others and much nearer the Dnieper, but I paid little attention to this news until Count Casimir Skarzynski, the secretary general of the Polish Red Cross, informed me during lunch that none of the bodies in grave eight were dressed for winter; moreover, their pockets contained letters, identification cards, and newspaper clippings that seemed to indicate they had met their deaths a whole month after the other Poles we had found. A discussion ensued between Skarzynski, Professor Buhtz, and Lieutenant Sloventzik about the Russian internment camp from which the men had been removed; but I kept out of it, and as soon as I was able I went back to my hut and tried to contain my impatience while Colonel von Gersdorff stayed in his own hut translating the file we had recovered from the crypt at the Assumption Cathedral. It was a very long afternoon.

So I did a little smoking and a little drinking and read a little Tolstoy, which is like a lot of something else and almost a contradiction in terms.

To avoid the field marshal, I ate an early dinner and then went for a walk. When I got back to my hut, an anonymous note under the door read as follows:

I UNDERSTAND YOU ARE LOOKING FOR MORE INFORMATION ABOUT ALOK DYAKOV—THE REAL ALOK DYAKOV THAT IS AND NOT THE ILLITERATE PEASANT WHO PRETENDS TO BE THIS MAN. I WILL SELL YOU HIS GESTAPO/NKVD CASE FILE FOR 50 MARKS. COME ALONE TO THE SVIRSKAYA CHURCH IN SMO-LENSK BETWEEN TEN AND ELEVEN O'CLOCK TONIGHT AND I WILL GIVE YOU ALL YOU NEED TO DESTROY HIM FOREVER.

The paper and the envelope were good quality: I held the paper up to the light to see the watermark. Nathan Brothers on Unter den Linden had been one of Berlin's most expensive stationer's until the Jewish boycott had forced its closure. Which begged the question why someone who once had been able to afford expensive stationery was asking fifty marks for a file? I read the note again and considered the wording carefully. Fifty marks was nearly all the cash I had and not to be given away lightly, but worth every penny if indeed the file proved to be the real thing. Of course, as a detective in Berlin I'd used many informers and the request for fifty marks presented me with a more reliable motive for betrayal: if you're going to give a man away, you might as well get paid for it. I could understand that. But why had the author used the words "Gestapo/NKVD case file"? Was it possible that the Gestapo knew much more about Alok Dyakov than I had considered? Was it possible that they already had a file on Dyakov? Even so, ten o'clock at night was not the sort of time I like to be in a remote part of a city in enemy country. And you can call it super-stitious of me, but I decided to take two guns along with me, just for luck: the Walther PPK I always carried, and—with its neat shoulder stock and handy carrying strap—the broom-handle Mauser that I had yet to return to von Gersdorff. Since the war started, I've always believed that two guns are better than one. I loaded both automatic pistols and went out to the car.

The road east into Smolensk just north of the Peter and Paul bridge across the Dnieper was blocked as usual with a field police patrol and—as usual—I talked with them for a little while before driving on. The only way to the Svirskaya Church—without incurring a fifty-kilometer diversion to the west—was across this bridge in the center of Smolensk, and I thought that talking to the fellows at the roadblock might give me some clue as to the identity of my new informer. You can learn a lot from field policemen if you treat them with respect.

"Tell me, boys," I said—they knew me, of course, but like every-one else I had to show them my papers, anyway—"what other traffic has been along here in the last hour?"

"A troop transport," said one of the cops, a sergeant. "Some lads from the 56th Panzer Corps who've been stationed in Vitebsk and are now ordered north. They were heading to the railway station. They say they're on their way to a place called Kursk and that there's a big battle brewing up there. Then there were some fellows from the 537th Signalers who were going to the Glinka for a bit of a night out."

He made a "night out" at the Glinka sound like something as innocent as a trip to the cinema.

"Naturally, you took their names," I said.

"Yes, sir, of course."

"I'd like to see those names if I could."

The sergeant went to fetch a clipboard and, although it was an-other brightly moonlit night, he showed me a list under the flashlight attached to his coat. "Anything wrong?" he asked.

"No, Sergeant," I said, casting my eye down the list. None of the names meant anything to me. "I'm just being nosy."

"That's the job, isn't it? People don't understand. But where would any of us be without a few nosy cops to keep us safe?"

The church was in an isolated and quiet part of the city west of the Kremlin wall and well away from any civilian houses or military outposts. Built of pink stone with just the one cupola, it was positioned at the top of a gentle grassy knoll and looked like a smaller version of the Assumption Cathedral; there was even a surrounding wall made of white stucco with an octagonal bell tower and a large green wooden gate through which entrance to the church and its grounds could be gained. There were no lights on inside the church, and although the gate was open, the place looked as if even the bats in the bell tower had taken the night off to go somewhere more lively.

I parked at the bottom of a small path that led up to the gate and helped myself to a handful of broom-handle; the automatic felt comfortingly large in my hand and easy against my shoulder, and while the old box cannon might have been hard to clean—one reason it was superseded by the Walther—it was a reassuringly solid weapon to point and fire. Especially at night when the longish barrel made it easier to aim and the shoulder stock made it look altogether more substantial. It wasn't that I was expecting trouble, but it's best to be ready for it if it shows up with a gun in its hand.

I advanced slowly through the gate of the bell tower, which was almost as high as the cupola of the church itself and occupied a corner position on the wall, affording it an excellent view of at least two-thirds of the church grounds. Before entering the church, I walked once around it—clockwise for good luck—just to see if anyone was waiting around the back to ambush me. Nobody was. But when I went to go inside the church, I found the door was locked.

I knocked and waited without answer. I knocked again and it sounded as hollow inside the church as the beating of the heart in my own chest. It was obvious that there was no one inside. I ought to have left there and then. But working on the assumption there was possibly a different entrance I might have missed, I took another walk around the church. This time I went counterclockwise, which, in retrospect, was probably a mistake. There wasn't another entrance—at least not one that was open—and thinking now that the whole thing had been a wild-goose chase, I started down the slope toward the gate in the bell tower. I hadn't gone very far when I stopped in my tracks, for it took only a split second to see that someone had closed the gate; it was at the same moment equally obvious that from the octagonal-shaped bell tower the same someone probably had an uninterrupted sight of me. My nose twitched: I was like a rabbit in no-man's-land. It twitched again but it was much too late. I was a fool and I knew I was a fool and nothing about that could be altered now.

In the other half of that same split second a loud gunshot hit the polished oak shoulder stock I was holding against my chest; but for that I would certainly have been killed, and as it was, the impact knocked me backward off my feet and sent me sprawling onto the grass. But I knew better than to crawl for cover; for one thing there wasn't any I could have reached in time, and for another whoever had shot me had worked the bolt and pushed another bullet into the breech and was probably already staring at me down his rifle sights; on a night like this one a mole with one eye could have put a bullet in my head. My best chance was to play dead—after all, the gunman had hit me dead center and he wasn't to know that his rifle bullet had actually struck a piece of hardened wood.

My chest hurt and the back of my head as well and I wanted to groan and then to cough but I lay as still as I could and held what was left of the breath inside my body, waiting either for the almost welcome oblivion that would be provided by another shot, or the sound of my assailant's footsteps walking toward me as, almost inevitably, he came to see where his bullet had struck me. I'd never yet met a man who didn't like to check on the accuracy of his marksmanship if he could. It was several minutes before I heard footsteps on some stairs, and then a door opening inside the gate, and I enjoyed a worm's-eye view of a man coming across the churchyard in the moonlight.

The Mauser—minus the shoulder stock, which, split in two, now lay on the ground on either side of my body—was still in my hand and seeing this demanded that he ought to have pumped another shot into me just to make sure. Instead he shouldered his rifle on a strap and walked over to me, paused for a moment, and lit a cigarette with a lighter—I didn't see his face but I had an excellent view of his well-polished jackboots. Like his expensive notepaper and cigarettes, *the man was German*. He inhaled loudly and then kicked at the gun in my hand with the toe cap of his German jackboot. That was my cue. The next moment I was on my knee, ignoring the pain in my sternum and leveling the long barrel of the broom-handle at the man with the rifle and pulling the trigger without much thought for where the shot would hit him as long as it took him down. He cursed and reached for the carrying strap and dropped his cigarette but it was all too late. The shot turned him sharply to one side and I knew without doubt that I had hit him in the left shoulder.

He was wearing an officer's leather coat and a *Stahlhelm*; a pair of goggles sat up on the front of the helmet and a pair of thick motor-cyclist's gauntlets were tucked under his belt. He looked like a German but the beard was unmistakable. It was or had been Alok Dyakov, whom I now knew a little better as Major Krivyenko. He bit his lip and writhed on the ground from side to side, as if trying to get comfortable. I ought to have shot him again but I didn't. Something stopped me from pulling the trigger a second time, although I badly wanted to.

This was just enough hesitation for him to come back at me with a bayonet in his hand.

I was up on my toes in a second and twisting around in an almost complete circle to avoid the sharp point of the blade; if I'd been the great Juan Belmonte with a cape in my hand I couldn't have done it better. Then I shot him again. The second shot was as lucky for him as it was for me: the bullet went through the back of the hand holding the bayonet, and this time he went down, clutching his hand and looking altogether incapable of mounting a third attack, but I kicked the side of his head anyway, just for good measure; I get upset when people try to shoot and then stab me within the space of a few minutes.

I let out a breath and gulped down some air.

After that the only problem I had was how to get Krivyenko to the prison in Kiewerstrasse; I didn't have any manacles and the Tatra didn't have a trunk I could throw him in and the field radio that had been in the back of the car was now back at the castle; kicking him in the head hadn't helped much, either, since that had merely rendered him unconscious—I was already regretting that. After a while I removed the leather shoulder strap from his rifle and used it and my necktie to bind his arms together behind his back; then I smoked a cigarette while I waited for him to come round. I decided it was best to question him before I took him into custody, and to do that properly I needed to have him to myself for a while.

Finally, he sat up and groaned. I lit another cigarette, puffed it gratefully, and then pushed it between his bloodied lips.

"That was a good shot," I said. "Dead center. In case you were wondering, the bullet hit the Mauser's shoulder stock. This is the same Mauser you used to shoot Dr. Berruguete."

"I was wondering how you survived that, *pizda zhopo glaza.*"

"I'm just a lucky man, I guess."

"*Pozhivyom uvidim,*" he muttered. "If you say so. You know, you should thank me, Gunther. I could have killed you before and didn't. At Krasny Bor."

"Yes, I can't figure that. You must have had me plumb in your sights. Like tonight."

"At the time, I just wanted you out of the way, not dead. Big mistake, huh?" He puffed hard on the cigarette and nodded. "Thanks for the smoke but I'm done with it now."

I took it out of his mouth and flicked it away.

"The quality notepaper was a nice touch," I said. "I was ready to believe the author was a German. I presume it's the field marshal's personal notepaper you used. And asking for fifty marks. That was good, too. You don't expect a man who's asked you for money really just wants to shoot you." I glanced around. "I have to hand it to you. This place—it's inspired. Quiet, out of the way, nobody to hear the shot. I walk in, like a rat into a trap, and you're up there in the tower with an excellent field of fire. Well, mostly. Tell me, what would have happened if I'd gone behind the church?"

"You'd never have got that far," he said. "I don't usually need a second shot."

"No, I guess not."

"I don't suppose you've got a drink on you, comrade?"

"Matter of fact, I have." I took out a little hip flask—it was full of schnapps I'd stolen from the mess—and let him take a bite off it before taking one myself. I needed it almost as much as him; my chest felt like an elephant had stamped on it.

"Thanks." He shook his head. "I thought if I only killed Berruguete, you krauts would try to cover it up, for the sake of your international commission. Von Kluge hates all these fucking foreigners, anyway. He just wanted them away from Krasny Bor as soon as possible. But you being an officer and all—even though he hates you, too—well, he'd have felt obliged to order the field police to conduct an investigation. Not that Voss could find his own prick in his trousers but still, on top of everything else, I didn't need that shit. So I put one just past your skull to make you keep your head down until I could make my getaway."

"All right. I owe you. But why did you shoot Berruguete? I can't figure that out. What did you care about him?"

"You don't know anything, do you?" He grinned painfully. "It's comical really, how much you don't know after all this time. Give me another drink and I'll tell you."

I let him have some more schnapps. He nodded, smacked his lips, and then licked them.

"Before the war I was a political commissar with the international brigades in Spain. I loved that place. Barcelona. Best time of my life. I heard all about that fascist doctor then, what he did to some of my comrades. Experiments on the brains of living men because they were communists, that kind of thing. I took an oath then that if I ever got the chance, I'd kill him. So, when he turned up here in Smolensk, I couldn't fucking believe it. And I knew I'd never get another opportunity so I did it and I don't regret it for a moment. I'd do it again in ten seconds."

"But why'd you use the Mauser and not the rifle?"

"Sentiment. All my life I've been in love with guns."

"Yes, I saw from your NKVD file you'd won the Voroshilov Marksman badge."

He didn't acknowledge that—just kept on talking: "When I was in Catalonia I carried a Mauser, the same as that one in your hand. I loved that gun. Best gun you krauts ever made, in my opinion. The Walther is all right—good stopping power and all right for a coat pocket and it doesn't jam, I'll say that for it—but in the field you can't beat the Mauser, not least because it has a ten-shot magazine. They used that gun to shoot the tsar, you know. When I saw that Colonel von Gersdorff had one, I was dying to have a go with it. So I borrowed it and used it to kill the doctor."

"You're a damned liar," I said. "You were quite well aware that Professor Buhtz is an expert in ballistics. You just wanted to throw us off your scent. The same way the rope you used to steady your aim—that was what Peshkov had been using to tie his coat up, wasn't it? Just to help point the blame somewhere else."

Krivyenko grinned again.

"You guessed that if you used your rifle, we would give Professor

Buhtz the bullet and he would tell us the kind of rifle that was used. Your rifle. So you borrowed von Gersdorff's gun. You knew it was in the door pocket of his car the same way you knew there was a bayonet in the glove box—the same bayonet you used to kill Dr. Batov and his daughter and, before them, very likely the two signalmen at the Hotel Glinka. I suppose von Kluge put you up to that."

"Maybe he did and maybe he didn't, but that's my insurance policy, isn't it? Because what you know, you could put in a fucking matchbox. And what you can prove to the field marshal wouldn't butter a crust of bread."

"I don't know that I have to prove anything, do I? Your word against a German officer's? Soon as we've shaved your beard off in the prison hospital we can match you with the photograph in your NKVD file and prove to anyone's satisfaction that you're a major in the People's Commissariat. I doubt even the field marshal will want to help you once we've demonstrated that."

"Maybe he'll think he has to help me. To keep my mouth shut. Have you thought of that? Besides, why would I kill Dr. Batov? Or maybe you think he put me up to that, too. Have you thought of that?"

"My guess is that you had something to do with what happened in Katyn Wood—maybe you were even one of the team of murderers who executed all those Polacks. When you heard from the field marshal that I'd asked for asylum in Germany for Batov and his daughter, you asked him a few questions, and von Kluge told you what I'd told him: that Batov had documentary evidence of what happened back there in Katyn Wood. So you tortured and killed them both and took the ledgers and photographs from Batov's apartment. I suppose Batov must have given away Rudakov and possibly you killed him, too. His brother, the doorman at the Hotel Glinka—well, maybe he just put two and two together and ran, or maybe you killed him, too, just in case. Besides, that's what you do best, isn't it? You're good at killing wild boar and wolves but you're even better at killing people. As I almost discovered to my cost."

"Not that good. If I was any good like you say, Captain, I would have put another round in your head before coming down from the tower."

"You may not be glad you didn't kill me. But I'm delighted you're still alive, my friend. You're going to be a very useful witness in Germany. You're going to be famous."

"*Idl ti nafig.*" Krivyenko shook his head. "*Chto za chepukha,*" he said. "The boss isn't going to allow any of that."

"Oh, he'll have to allow it," I said. "You see, it's not just me who'll be there to convince him that he has to. There's Colonel von Gersdorff, too. And even if von Kluge doesn't want to believe you were part of what happened to Batov and at Katyn, he'll have to believe it if someone of his own noble class tells him."

Krivyenko grinned. "Better for you that you should let me go. Better for you and better for me. It will be embarrassing for him and he won't appreciate that. *Ya tebya o-chen proshu.* Let me go and you'll never see me again. I'll just disappear." He nodded to his right. "The river is that way. I'll just walk over there and disappear. But there will be hell to pay—for us both—if you try to make this stick."

"You think I'm going to let you go just because it might cause some embarrassment for von Kluge?"

"He will let me go if you don't. Just to avoid the possibility of any scandal."

"I reckon that if it comes to you accusing him of inciting the murders of the signalmen, it'll be your word—the word of an NKVD major—against the word of a German field marshal. Nobody will believe anything you say. The minute you're in custody, my guess is that von Kluge will try to put as much distance between him and you as possible." I frowned. "By the way, how did you get through the checkpoint on the bridge without your name appearing in the field police records? You didn't swim, so how did you do it? Every boat between here and Vitebsk was requisitioned last summer."

"Trouble with you Germans, you think there's only one way to skin a cat."

"From what I've heard, most people use a knife."

"I'll tell you for another drink," he said, "as I suppose even you will manage to find out, sooner or later."

I put the flask to his lips and tipped some into his mouth.

"*Spasiba.*" He shrugged. "About five hundred meters upriver from here, there's a simple wooden raft. Some lady friends made it for me. You've probably seen them—in the river, binding logs together to transport stuff up and down the river. And I had a long stick with which I just pushed it across. Nothing more complicated than that. You'll find a motorcycle hidden in some bushes on the other bank. Look, if you're not going to let me go, then I'd like to see a doctor. My shoulder aches and I'm bleeding. You mentioned something about a prison hospital?"

"I ought to kill you right here."

"Maybe you should."

I grabbed him by the collar and hauled him to his feet. "Get moving."

"What if I don't want to walk?"

"Then I can shoot you again. You should know, there are lots of ways to do it without injuring you too badly." I grabbed his ear and pushed the barrel of the Mauser inside it. "Or I could shoot your greasy fucking ears off, one at a time. I don't think anyone but you and the hangman will mind very much if your head is minus a couple of spoons."

I DROVE BACK TO THE PETER AND PAUL BRIDGE and kicked my prisoner out of the passenger seat and onto the ground. I told the field police to take Krivyenko to the prison on Kiewerstrasse and, after the doctor had treated his wounds, to lock him up in solitary for the night.

"I'll be there with a list of charges first thing in the morning," I said, "just as soon as I've spoken with Colonel von Gersdorff."

"But this is Dyakov, sir," they said. "The field marshal's *Putzer.*"

"No, it's not," I said. "The real Dyakov is dead. This man is an NKVD major called Krivyenko. He's the one who murdered those two German signalers." I didn't mention the Russians he'd murdered, or the Spaniard; Germans weren't much concerned about people from a country other than Germany. "And he's still dangerous, so treat him with care, do you hear? He's a fox, that one. He just tried to shoot me, too. And almost succeeded. But for a rifle stock that got in the way, I'd be a dead man."

My chest was still hurting so I unbuttoned my shirt to take a look, and under the kennel hound's flashlight I saw a bruise that was the size and color of a Friesian tattoo.

Back at Krasny Bor, I noticed straightaway that the colonel's Mercedes was gone, and when I knocked on the door of his hut to tell him that Krivyenko had now revealed his hand, there was no reply and none of the lights were burning.

I went to the officers' mess in search of some information as to his whereabouts.

"Didn't you see the notice?" asked the mess sergeant—a Berliner who was a bit on the warm side, I thought.

"What notice?"

"Most of the officers of the High Command are dining tonight in the mess at the department store, in Smolensk, as guests of the local army commandant."

So I put a note under von Gersdorff's door telling him to wake me up the minute he arrived back in Krasny Bor.

Then I went to bed.

13

SUNDAY, MAY 2, 1943

I was awoken by a banging on my door, which was louder than seemed reasonable, even for a man who might have spent the whole evening drinking with the commander of the town garrison. I switched on the light, and still wearing my pajamas, I swung out of bed, took a step toward the door—it wasn't a very big hut—and opened it. Instead of Colonel von Gersdorff there were three soldiers— a corporal and two privates—standing outside. They were carrying machine pistols and from their expressions they looked like they meant to do a lot more than draw my attention to a blue moon.

"Captain Gunther?" said the corporal in charge.

I glanced at my watch. "It's two A.M.," I said. "Don't you people ever sleep? Get out of here."

"Come with us, please, sir. You're under arrest."

My yawn turned to surprise. "What the hell for?"

"Just come with us, please, sir."

"On whose orders am I being arrested? What's the charge?"

"Please do as you're told, sir. We haven't got all night."

I paused for a moment and considered my options, which didn't take that long after I noticed that one of the privates had his finger on the trigger of his MP40; like a lot of soldiers in that part of the world, he looked like he was itching to shoot someone.

"Can I put on some clothes or is this strictly come as you are?"

"My orders are that you're to come with us immediately, sir."

"All right. If that's the way you want it."

I picked up my greatcoat and was about to put it on when the corporal took it away from me and started to search the pockets, which was when I remembered the Walther that was there, only he got there first.

"Funny guy, huh?"

I felt myself grin sheepishly. "I was about to mention that, Corporal."

"Sure you were," said the corporal. "When it was in your hand, maybe, and pointed at my gut. I don't like that you were trying to bring a gun along on my arrest detail." He took a step nearer—near enough for me to smell the sweat on his shirt and the dinner on his breath. "You know, in my book, that counts as resisting arrest."

"No, Corporal, I was just putting on my coat. It's late and I forgot the gun was in the pocket."

"Like hell you did," said the corporal.

"We don't like people resisting arrest," said the soldier with the itchy trigger finger.

"Really, I'm not resisting arrest," I said. "The gun was an oversight."

"They all say that," said the corporal.

"They? Who's they? You sound like you arrest people all the time when it's plain you haven't the least fucking clue what you're doing. Now give me my coat back and let's go wherever it is we're going so we can get this nonsense cleared up."

He handed me back my greatcoat and, putting it on, I followed them outside; they marched me not to the mess, or to the adjutant's office—or even to the field marshal's quarters—but to a waiting bucket wagon.

"Where are we going?"

"Get in. You'll find out soon enough."

"Although clearly that's not the case," I said, getting into the backseat, "since soon enough would be right now."

"Why don't you shut up, sir?" the corporal said, and climbed into the wagon.

" 'Sir.' I like that. It's funny how respectful people sound when they're just aching to bang you over the head."

He didn't contradict me so I kept quiet for a few minutes; but it didn't last long. Not after we drove out of the main gate and toward the city. I was liking my situation less and less. The farther away from Krasny Bor we got, the longer it was going to take to have a senior officer solve my predicament; and not just that: I was easier to kill, too. I knew what these men were capable of. In spite of the very best efforts of people like Judge Goldsche, the Wehrmacht was as cruel and indifferent to human life and suffering as our enemy. On the first days of Barbarossa, I'd seen soldiers on the road into Russia machine-gunning civilians for the sheer hell of it.

"Look," I said, "if this is something to do with that damned Russian fool Dyakov, then I'd count it as a favor if you would go and find Colonel von Gersdorff—from the Abwehr?—and inform him of my situation. He'll vouch for me. So will Lieutenant Voss of the field police."

None of them said a word—they just stared straight ahead at the deserted country road as if I didn't exist.

"You know, I'd count it an even bigger favor if you would take that MP40 out of my ear. If we hit a bump in the road, I might end up with a serious hearing problem."

"I think you've already got a hearing problem," insisted the corporal. "Didn't you hear me telling you to shut up?"

I folded my arms and shook my head. "You know, we are on the same side, Corporal. In this war. I may not enjoy the confidence of the Leader but the minister of Propaganda will take it very amiss if

I'm not available to show our important foreign guests around Katyn Wood later on this morning. It will render all of his careful work meaningless. I don't think it would be a presumption to say that the doctor will be very angry when he finds out that I've been arrested. I'm certainly going to make a point of finding out who you are and informing him that you were most unhelpful."

I hated myself for saying all that but in truth I was scared; I'd been arrested before, of course, but life seemed to count for very little so far from home, and after what I'd seen in Katyn Wood, it seemed all too easy that mine could end abruptly in some ditch, shot in the back of the head by some grumpy army corporal.

"I'm just obeying my orders," said the corporal. "And I don't give a fuck who you know. Someone like me—someone at the bottom of the heap—none of that bullshit matters a damn. I just do what I'm told, see? And that's the end of it. An officer says 'shoot that bastard,' then I shoot that fucking bastard. So why don't you save your fucking breath, Captain Gunther? I'm dog tired. All I want to do is finish my fucking shift and go to bed and get a couple of hours' sleep before I have to get up and do what I'm told all over again. So fuck you and fuck your little friend in the ministry."

"You certainly have a way with words, Corporal."

I checked my mouth and retreated into the warmth of my coat collar. We reached the outskirts of Smolensk and the checkpoint at the Peter and Paul bridge again. The same boys from the field police were on duty. And it was them who filled in some of the blanks while the corporal showed them our signed orders.

"Do you know what's going on here?" I asked the kennel hounds.

"Sorry, sir," said one—the man I'd spoken to before—"but we did like you said. We were on our way down to the prison with the prisoner, but when we stopped at the checkpoint near the Kommandatura the field marshal—who was in a passing car—saw us and, more importantly, he saw his *Putzer*, Dyakov. Dyakov told him some story about how you'd tortured him in retaliation for the field marshal tearing a strip off you in the officers' mess the other day. At least that's what I think he said. Anyway, the field marshal believed him and he was absolutely furious about it. Never seen him look so pissed off. Turned the color of beetroot. I'm afraid he countermanded your orders and made his escort drive Dyakov straight to the SSMA. Then he asked where you were. We told him you'd gone back to Krasny Bor, and he said that if we saw you before he did we were to place you under immediate close arrest and take you to the Luchinskaya Tower."

"Where the hell's that?" I asked.

"It's in the wall of the local Kremlin, sir. Not a very nice place at all. The Gestapo use it sometimes to soften up their prisoners. Sorry, sir."

"Tell Voss," I said. "Tell Voss that I think that's where I'm being taken to now."

One of the other field policemen handed back our orders and waved us on our way.

A few minutes later we arrived at a round corner tower made of red brick. From the outside it was a forbidding sort of place; inside, the forbidden had become downright proscription: damp and smelly, and that was just the entrance hall. The cell where I was to spend what remained of the night was through a heavy wooden trapdoor in the floor and down a series of slippery stone steps. It was like descending into a story by E. T. A. Hoffmann. At the bottom of the steps I realized I was on my own, and when I turned around I saw the corporal's boots exiting through the trapdoor. It was the last thing I saw. The next moment the trapdoor dropped with a loud bang that was like a meteorite hitting a mountaintop and I was plunged into darkness I could have cut with a knife.

With eyes straining to see if there was something more than my own poor self, and with hands outstretched in front of me lest I come upon some wall or door, I looked one way and then the other, but there was only darkness visible. Plucking up what remained of my sorely tested courage, I gulped down some of the cold damp air and called out. "Hallo," I said. "Is there anyone down here?"

No answer came.

I was alone. I had never felt more alone. Death itself could not have felt much worse. If the purpose of my incarceration was—as the kennel hound on the bridge had put it—to soften me up, then I was already feeling pretty soft. I couldn't have felt softer if I had been made of cream cheese.

I sat down and waited patiently for someone to come and say what was to become of me. But it wasn't any use. Nobody came.

14

They released me a couple of hours before the court proceedings, so I might wash and eat something and put on my uniform and consult with Judge Johannes Conrad, who had kindly agreed to defend me. We met in an office at the Army Kommandatura, where Conrad informed me that I was charged with the attempted murder of Alok Dyakov, who was also the principal witness; that von Schlabrendorff was to prosecute; and that Field Marshal von Kluge was presiding over the court by himself.

"Can he do that?" I asked Conrad. "He's hardly impartial."

"He's a field marshal," said Conrad. "He can pretty much do whatever the hell he wants in this theater. The Kaiser had rather less power than von Kluge commands in the Smolensk Oblast."

"Doesn't he need two other judges?"

"Not really," said Conrad. "There's no legal requirement that there should be two other judges. And even if there were, they'd only do what he told them anyway." He shook his head. "It doesn't look good, you know. I think he really means to hang you. In fact, he almost seems to be in an indecent hurry to do so."

"I'm not really worried about that," I said. "There's too much

447

evidence against his *Putzer*, Dyakov. As soon as that comes out, this whole thing will collapse like a paper house."

I told Conrad what I had learned about who Dyakov really was and that Colonel von Gersdorff and the NKVD file on Major Krivyenko he had spent all of Saturday translating would prove everything I said.

"The colonel and I have been working pretty closely on this one," I said. "He's just as keen to prove Dyakov is really Major Krivyenko as I am. There's no love lost between those two."

Conrad looked pained. "That's all very well," he said. "But Colonel von Gersdorff hasn't been seen since the commandant's dinner in the officers' mess at the department store on Saturday evening. And no one seems to know where he is."

"What?"

"He received a message while he was at the dinner, got up and left and hasn't been seen since. His car is gone, too."

I swallowed uncomfortably. Was it possible that Krivyenko had already murdered the colonel when he'd tried to shoot me? That would certainly have explained why he was so confident of remaining at liberty.

"See if you can find out an exact time that the colonel left the department store dinner," I said.

Johannes Conrad nodded.

"Then I need you to send an urgent message to the Ministry of Propaganda."

"I already did that," explained Conrad. "Dr. Goebbels is in Dortmund right now. Unfortunately communications and rail links there have been disrupted because of an RAF bombing raid the other night. The heaviest since Cologne, apparently. And our own local communications have been disrupted by a new Russian offensive, in the Kuban and Novorossik sectors."

"I'm beginning to understand von Kluge's indecent haste," I said.

"What about the War Crimes Bureau? What about Judge Goldsche? Did you manage to contact him?"

"Yes. But there's not much consolation there, either."

"Oh?"

"I'm afraid Judge Goldsche's hands are tied," said Conrad. "As you know, the bureau is just a section within the legal department of the military High Command. He takes his orders from the international law section of the OKW and Maximilian Wagner. And Wagner—who's been ill anyway—well, he takes his orders from Dr. Rudolf Lehmann. And I'm sorry to tell you this but Lehmann is unlikely to do anything at all. The politics are delicate here, I'm afraid, Gunther."

"So's my neck."

"You see, recently Lehmann wrote a memo to the Foreign Office arguing that the perpetrators of French war crimes against German soldiers should be a matter left to the French courts. He also ordered a stay of all executions in France, in order to improve relations with the French government. Neither of these went down very well with some of our more senior generals in Berlin, who felt that Lehmann had overstepped himself and that these were matters for local army commanders, most of whom dislike lawyers at the best of times. And that's not all. Rudolf Lehmann's from Posen, just like von Kluge. He's an East Prussian who's a close friend of the field marshal and owes his advancement as colonel general of the armed forces legal department to none other than Günther von Kluge. There's no way on earth Dr. Lehmann's going to try to interfere with the way von Kluge runs things at Army Group Center. Not without losing his power base and main patron." Conrad sighed. "I'm sorry, Gunther, but that's just how it is."

I nodded and lit one of Conrad's cigarettes. Outside, it was the warmest day of the year; everyone—even the Russians—had a smile on his face, as if summer was truly here at last. Everyone except me, that is.

"General von Tresckow," I said. "Speak to him, will you, please?

He owes me a favor. A big Magnetophon-sized favor. You might remind him of that. And you might use those exact words. He'll know what it means."

"The general is out of town since yesterday," said Conrad. "As you might know, there's a major offensive being planned north of here at a place called Kursk, and as chief operations officer of AGC, he's up there discussing logistical support with Field Marshal von Manstein and General Model. He won't be back in Smolensk until Thursday."

"By which time I will have been hanged." I grinned. "Yes, I do begin to see the full extent of my predicament."

"I also spoke to Lieutenant Voss," said Conrad. "He's is prepared to testify on your behalf."

"Well, that's a relief."

"Reluctantly."

"He's afraid of angering the field marshal."

"Of course. The field marshal has been very supportive of the field police in this theater. It was the field marshal who gave Voss his infantry assault badge. And who made sure that the field police were given what is considered to be a very comfortable billet at Grushtshenki." He shrugged. "Under the circumstances, he's not likely to make a very convincing witness."

"I don't seem to have many friends, do I?"

"There's another thing," said Conrad.

"Yes?"

"Professor Buhtz—who also owes his current position to Field Marshal von Kluge, one might even go so far as to say his rehabilitation—has carried out some forensic tests on your personal Walther PPK. He's not absolutely certain—due to a lack of proper equipment here in Smolensk, the tests have been inconclusive—but it seems there's a possibility that your gun was used to murder Signal Corporal Quidde. It's been suggested—by Professor Buhtz—that you might have shot Quidde."

I shrugged. "Well, I don't see that the fact that it was my gun proves anything," I said. "Von Gersdorff's broom-handle Mauser was used to murder Dr. Berruguete. Very likely Krivyenko is trying to frame me for Quidde, in the same way that he tried to frame Colonel von Gersdorff."

"Yes, I do see that, Captain," said Conrad. "Unfortunately, Krivyenko is not the one who is on trial here. You are. And you might like to consider this, as well. That Mauser was found in your hut, not Dyakov's. Sorry, I mean Krivyenko's."

I smiled. "You have to admire someone's housekeeping," I said. "Hanging me is an excellent way of sweeping a lot of our unsolved crime into the nearest mouse hole."

"Frankly, I think your only real chance is to admit that you made an error of judgment," said Conrad. "To throw yourself on the mercy of the court and admit that while you did indeed shoot Alok Dyakov, you did not mean to kill him. I don't see any other alternative."

"That's my best defense?"

"I think so." He shrugged. "Then we'll see about getting you off the other charges. Perhaps by then the colonel will have turned up back in Smolensk."

"Yes, perhaps."

"Look, I believe what you say. But without any evidence to support your story, proving it to the satisfaction of this court as it is convened is going to be almost impossible. It can't be denied that there's an element of bad timing in all of this."

"Not just an element." I let out a breath. "It's the whole periodic table."

I rubbed my neck nervously. "They say that the prospect of being hanged concentrates a man's mind wonderfully. I'm not sure I'd have used the word 'wonderfully.' But there's certainly no doubt about the concentration. Especially when you've seen a few hangings yourself."

"You're talking about Hermichen and Kuhr."

"Who else?" I pulled my tunic collar away from my neck—it was tight—and took a long, steady breath. "You might as well tell me.

That window-frame gallows in the prison yard at Kiewerstrasse. Have they erected it again?"

"I really don't know," said Conrad.

Since he'd just come from interviewing a potential Katyn witness at the prison at Kiewerstrasse, I knew he was lying.

For a moment I had a nightmare vision of myself strangling on the gallows at Kiewerstrasse, my feet swinging loose like a flap, one shoulder reaching for the sky, my tongue hanging out of my mouth like a mollusk leaving its shell. And my heart missed a beat, and then another.

"Do me a favor," I told Conrad. "I'm going to write a letter for Dr. Kramsta. If I really do swing for this, will you see that she gets it?"

MY COURT-MARTIAL BEGAN IN the Army Kommandatura at ten A.M., in the very same room where Hermichen and Kuhr had been tried back in March before being hanged, of course; after my conversation with Field Marshal von Kluge, that had seemed a foregone conclusion—to me and to him. No doubt he was feeling the same way about these latest proceedings. I was sure of that as he entered the room with a scowl and avoided my eye altogether. I've sat through enough criminal trials to know that's not a good sign. He looked at his wristwatch; that wasn't a good sign, either. Presumably he was hoping to find me guilty so that I could be hanged before lunch.

Of course, I could perhaps have said one thing to disrupt my trial, although I thought it would actually do very little to save my life. My unsubstantiated allegation—the tape was now destroyed, of course—that Adolf Hitler had paid a substantial bribe in return for von Kluge's loyalty was hardly likely to endear me to my judge, and the chances were very strong that he would have ordered my immediate execution anyway; especially as there also remained his probable involvement in the murders of the two signalers from the castle who might have overheard his conversation with the Leader; surely this was the very thing he was in a hurry to cover up. Would my mentioning any of this in court actually change anything? Who among the Prussian knights and barons of the Wehrmacht would believe a peasant like me, instead of a fellow aristocrat?

No, Judge Conrad was right. My only real chance was to admit a terrible mistake—to throw myself on the mercy of the military court and to confess that, while I had indeed shot Alok Dyakov, twice, I had not actually meant to kill him. That much was true, at least. And surely even a field marshal could not order the execution of a German officer for merely wounding a Russian *Putzer*. Rape and murder was one thing; a simple case of bodily harm on an Ivan was another.

But it was soon clear that I was wrong. In spite of my plea, von Kluge still intended to hear all of the evidence, which could only mean one thing: that he meant to hang me anyway but needed to justify it with his *Putzer*'s evidence—the Russian's story that I had actually meant to kill him.

Krivyenko, his left arm heavily bandaged and in a sling but otherwise looking none the worse for wear, was, I have to say, a very convincing witness—as you might have expected of a man who was a major in the NKVD. From the way he talked, I had the strong impression that mine wasn't the first show trial he had attended or given evidence in: he spoke with a show of probity that would have convinced the Inquisition. He even managed to look like he regretted having to tell the court how I had threatened and tortured him with one gunshot and then another. At one stage real tears rolled down his face as he told the court how he had genuinely feared for his life. Even I was convinced of my own guilt.

The Russian had almost finished giving his evidence when, to my everlasting relief, the door at the back of the courtroom opened and Colonel von Gersdorff walked in. His entrance caused quite a stir—not because he was late but because he was accompanied by a small man in the uniform of a German admiral; admirals were hardly common in that landlocked part of Russia. The man had white hair, a sailor's ruddy complexion, bushy eyebrows, and round shoulders. The only decoration on his rather shabby tunic was an Iron Cross, First Class—as if that was really all that was needed. I guessed immediately who it was, even if I didn't recognize him myself; von Kluge had no such problem, and he and the rest of the court stood up immediately, for the man was the head of the Abwehr after all—none other than Admiral Wilhelm Canaris. He himself was accompanied by two wire-haired dachshunds that stayed loyally at the heels of shoes that had seen better days.

"Gentlemen, please forgive this interruption," Canaris said quietly. He glanced around the room, which was now, to a man, standing at attention, and smiled gently. "Easy, gentlemen, easy."

The court relaxed. Everyone except Field Marshal von Kluge, that is, who looked thoroughly bewildered by the arrival of Germany's spymaster.

"Wilhelm," stammered von Kluge. "What a surprise. I wasn't informed. No one— I had no idea that you were coming to Smolensk."

"Nor had I," said Canaris. "And to be quite frank with you, I nearly didn't get here. My plane had to turn back to Minsk with engine trouble, and Colonel von Gersdorff here was obliged to come and fetch me in his car, which is a six-hundred-kilometer round-trip. But we made it, somehow. I can't answer for the poor baron, but I'm very pleased to be here."

"I'm fine, sir," von Gersdorff said, and winked at me. "And after all, it's a beautiful day."

"Yes, now that I'm here. I'm very glad I came," continued Canaris. "For I can see that I'm not too late to play a useful part in these proceedings."

"You have the advantage of me, Wilhelm," said von Kluge.

"Not for long, old fellow. Not for long." He pointed at a chair. "May I sit down?"

"My dear Wilhelm, of course. Although if you have just traveled all that way by road, then perhaps it would be better to adjourn, so that you may refresh yourself, after which you and I can talk in private."

"No, no." Canaris removed his naval officer's cap, sat down, and lit a small, pungent cigar. "And with all due respect, it's not you I came to see, nor Colonel von Gersdorff, nor indeed this impudent fellow." Canaris pointed at me. "About whom I have heard a great deal during my journey."

Von Kluge shook his head irritably. "He is more than impudent, sir. He is a bare-faced liar, an unmitigated scoundrel who stands accused of trying to murder an innocent man, and a disgrace to the uniform of a German officer."

"In which case, he should certainly be severely punished," said Canaris. "And you should proceed with this trial immediately. So, please, don't stop on my account."

"I'm glad you agree, Wilhelm," said von Kluge, sitting down again. "Thank you." He glanced over at von Schlabrendorff and nodded at him to carry on examining his witness, but it seemed that Canaris was not yet finished speaking. Indeed, he had hardly started.

"But I should, however, like to know who it is that Captain Gunther tried to kill."

"My Russian *Putzer*, sir," said von Kluge. "He is the man with his arm in a sling now giving evidence. His name is Alok Dyakov."

Canaris shook his head. "No, sir. That man's name is not Alok Dyakov. And he could never be described as an innocent man. Not in this life. Nor perhaps the next." He puffed his cigar patiently.

The Russian stood up and seemed about to do something until he saw that von Gersdorff was now pointing a gun at him.

"What on earth is going on here?" spluttered von Kluge. "Colonel von Gersdorff? Explain yourself."

"All in good time, sir."

"I think at this stage," said Canaris, "it might be better if we cleared the court of everyone who is not immediately germane to these legal proceedings. There are things I am going to say that perhaps not everyone needs to hear, old friend."

Von Kluge nodded curtly and stood up. "These proceedings are suspended," he said. "While, er . . . Admiral Canaris . . . and I . . ."

"You and I can stay, naturally," Canaris told the field marshal, as men started to troop out of the room. "Colonel von Gersdorff, Captain Gunther, Judge Conrad—you had better stay, as well, since you are somewhat pivotal to this whole matter. And you, of course, Herr Dyakov. Yes, I think you had better stay for now, don't you? After all, you're why I came here."

When the court was empty of all who had not been named by the admiral, von Kluge lit a cigarette and tried to look as if he was still in control of a court-martial; but in truth, everyone now knew who had the whip hand. For a moment Canaris played with the ear of one of the dachshunds before proceeding.

"I think you should prepare yourself for a shock, Günther," Canaris told von Kluge. "You see, that man—the man you know as Alok Dyakov, your *Putzer*—is an NKVD officer, and I recognized him the moment I came into this court-martial."

"What?" said von Kluge. "Nonsense. He used to be a schoolteacher."

"This man and I have met at least once before," said Canaris. "As you may know, during the Spanish Civil War I was in and out of Spain on several occasions, setting up a German intelligence network that survives to this day and continues to serve us very well. Occasionally it amused me to test myself and my fluency in Spanish by working among the reds. And it was in Madrid that I met the man I now see in this court, although he might remember me rather better as Señor Guillermo, an Argentine businessman posing as a communist sympathizer. I went to the Soviet Embassy in Madrid in January 1937 to have a meeting with him when he was Military Attaché Mikhail Spiridonovich Krivyenko. He was in Spain to help set up the international brigades on the republican side, although it's fair to say that, as a political commissar in Barcelona and Málaga, he succeeded in shooting as many of them as he did of the people on the side of the Falangists. Isn't that right, Mikhail? Anarchists. Trotskyites. The POUM. Anyone who wasn't a Stalinist, really. You've killed all sorts."

Krivyenko stayed silent.

"I don't believe it," said von Kluge. "It's fantastic."

"Oh, I can assure you, it's quite true," said Canaris. "The colonel has Krivyenko's NKVD file to prove it. I imagine that's why he tried to murder Captain Gunther. Because he realized that the captain was onto him. And he certainly murdered the unfortunate Dr. Berruguete, because of what he'd learned about him while he'd been a commissar in Spain. I believe he may also have murdered several others, as well, since we Germans captured Smolensk. Isn't that true, Mikhail?"

Now, Krivyenko's eyes were on the exit. But von Gersdorff's Walther pistol was in his way.

"And before these latest crimes, he and another man called Blokhin were often in Smolensk with a team of NKVD executioners, murdering the enemies of the revolution and the Union of Soviet Socialist Republics. Including, I'll hazard, several thousand Polish officers in the spring of 1940. That's what Krivyenko is best at: murder. Always has been. Oh, he's very clever. For one thing, he's an excellent linguist: speaks Russian, Spanish, German, even Catalan—that's a very hard language for anyone to learn. I never did. But murder is Krivyenko's specialty. You see, he failed in Spain, and failure is very hard to explain to a tyrant like Stalin—to all tyrants, really. Which explains why he's just a major now when he was a colonel back in 1937. I expect he's had to carry out an awful lot of murders to make up for his failings in Spain. Isn't that right, Mikhail? You were almost shot upon your return to Russia, were you not?"

Krivyenko said nothing but it was plain from his expression that he knew the game was up.

"As soon as Colonel von Gersdorff told me about Krivyenko,

I knew it had to be the same fellow. Which meant that I simply had to come down here to Smolensk and, shall we say, pay my respects? You see, what none of you can know is that Colonel Krivyenko was directly responsible for the death of one of my best agents in Spain—a man by the name of Eberhard Funk. Funk was shot, but not before he had been relentlessly and brutally tortured by this man before us. With a knife. That's how he prefers to kill. Oh, he'll use a gun, if he has to. But Krivyenko likes to feel his victim's last breath on his face." Canaris puffed his cigar again. "He was a good man, Funk. A distant relation of our Reich Minister of Economic Affairs, you know. I honestly never thought that I'd be able to tell Walther Funk that the man who tortured and killed Eberhard had finally been caught."

Von Kluge had turned a quiet shade of gray and his cigarette remained unsmoked in its ashtray. His hands were thrust deep into his pockets and he looked like a schoolboy whose favorite toy had been confiscated.

"The question, of course," said Canaris, "is what has Krivyenko been doing while he's been here in Smolensk working for you, old fellow? What has he been up to while he's been your *Putzer*?"

"We went hunting a lot," said von Kluge, dully. "That's all. Hunting."

"I'm sure you did. By Rudi's account, Krivyenko organized a successful wild boar hunt for you. Yes, that must have been a lot of fun. No harm in that. But Rudi has some opinions about what else Mikhail's been up to, don't you, Rudi?"

"Yes, sir," said von Gersdorff. "It's clear from his NKVD file that Krivyenko was never a trained spy. His expertise was as a policeman and executioner—as the admiral has already said. Since the Germans arrived in Smolensk, he's been lying low, gaining our confidence. Your confidence, Field Marshal. Waiting for the right opportunity to start sending information about our plans to the Ivans. I hold myself partly responsible for that—after all, I introduced the two of you."

"Yes, yes, you did," said von Kluge, as if he hoped that might make things look better back in Berlin.

"Things have been quiet during the winter, of course, so there's been little for Krivyenko to do except interfere with the smooth running of Captain Gunther's investigations into the Katyn Wood massacre. It's probable that it was Krivyenko who helped to spirit away or possibly even murder another NKVD officer called Rudakov, who was also involved in the Katyn massacre, and that he murdered a local doctor called Batov, who might have provided us with invaluable documentary evidence of what actually happened to all those poor Polish officers."

"Evidence like that would have been quite irrefutable," added Canaris. "As things stand, the Kremlin is already arguing that this whole Katyn investigation has been a put-up job, a piece of cynical black propaganda by the Abwehr to drive a wedge deep into the enemy coalition. It's obvious to anyone that these Poles were murdered by the Russians, although that won't stop the Russians from saying different. Of course, once we get Major Krivyenko into the witness box in Berlin, they'll find that lie much harder to maintain. Certainly they'll still argue that we coerced him, or some such nonsense. Lies are what Bolsheviks are good at. But in spite of all that, Krivyenko represents a unique opportunity to present the world with one inarguable truth in this war. I'm sure you appreciate that fact as much as I, Field Marshal."

Von Kluge grunted quietly.

"Now that our new offensive in Kursk is only weeks away, Krivyenko's become more active," said von Gersdorff. "It's almost certain that he murdered the two signalers from the 537th because they discovered he'd been eavesdropping on your own private conversations with the Leader, probably about the new offensive, and using the radio at the castle to send messages to his contact in Soviet military intelligence—the GRU. And that he also murdered a third signaler—Corporal Quidde—when the man discovered irrefutable evidence that Krivyenko had murdered his two comrades."

None of this was true, of course. Von Gersdorff would certainly have told Canaris about the tape recording of Hitler's conversation with von Kluge and the bribe, but Canaris was much too clever to tell von Kluge that he knew this was the real reason why the signalers had been murdered. Embarrassing a field marshal was clearly not on the Abwehr's agenda. It was certainly not on mine, and I judged it better to follow the admiral's canny lead and keep my mouth shut about what I knew.

"At least that's what I'm going to write in my report, Günther," commented Canaris.

"I see," von Kluge said quietly.

"Don't be too hard on yourself, old fellow," said Canaris. "There are spies everywhere. It's all too easy for officers to be caught out like this, during a war. Even a field marshal. Why, just last year it was revealed that a man on my own staff—a Major Thummel—was spying for the Czechs."

He dropped the cigar onto the wooden floor and ground it out under his shoe before picking up one of the dogs and laying it on his lap.

"Look at it this way," said Canaris. "You have helped apprehend an important witness to what happened here in Katyn. Someone who was directly involved in the murders of those poor Polish officers. It's not as good as having pictures and ledgers, but it is the next best thing. And I'm absolutely certain you're going to come out of this very well."

Von Kluge was nodding thoughtfully.

All this time Krivyenko had remained more or less silent, calmly smoking a cigarette and watching the automatic in von Gersdorff's hand like a cat awaiting an opportunity to sprint for a gap in a slowly closing door; he might have had one arm in a sling but he was still dangerous. From time to time, however, he smiled or shook his head and muttered something in Russian, and it was clear that at some future stage—perhaps in Berlin—he intended to dispute the admiral's version of events; the field marshal saw that, too. He wasn't called Clever Hans for nothing.

Finally, when Canaris appeared to have finished speaking, the Russian stood up slowly and, turning his back on his former master, bowed in the little admiral's direction.

"May I say something?" he asked politely. "Admiral."

"Yes," said Canaris.

"Thank you," Krivyenko said, and stubbed out his cigarette.

He looked not in the least bit afraid. There was, I thought, a surprising amount of defiance in his demeanor, although he must have known that there was likely to be a rough time ahead for him in Berlin.

"Then I should like to say that I did indeed kill all the people you mentioned, Herr Admiral—Dr. Berruguete, Dr. Batov and his daughter. The Rudakov brothers are floating down the Dnieper. I don't deny any of it for one minute. However, you might like to know that the real reason I killed the two signalers was not exactly as you have described. There was another—"

The sound of the gunshot made us all jump—everyone except Krivyenko; the bullet hit him squarely in the back of the head and he collapsed facedown onto the floor like an overburdened coat stand. For a brief moment I thought von Gersdorff must have shot him until I saw the Walther in the field marshal's outstretched hand.

"You didn't actually think for a minute I was going to permit that bastard to embarrass me in front of everyone in Berlin, did you, Wilhelm?" he said coldly.

"No, I suppose not," said Canaris.

Von Kluge made the automatic safe, laid it down on the table in front of him, and walked steadily out of the room; there was just enough time for Canaris to pick up von Kluge's gun and lay it carefully on the floor beside Krivyenko's body before everyone who'd been asked to leave earlier came rushing back in.

I had to hand it to the admiral; he had remarkable presence of mind. It really did look as if Krivyenko might have placed the gun to the back of his own head and pulled the trigger. Not that I suppose it would have mattered; no one was likely to accuse the field marshal of murder, not in Smolensk.

"This Russian fellow has shot himself," Canaris announced for the benefit of everyone now present. "With the field marshal's own pistol." He added quietly, "Like a scene from a play by Chekhov. What do you think, Rudi?"

"Yes, sir. That's exactly what I was thinking. *Ivanov*, I should say."

I walked over to Krivyenko's motionless body and pushed it with the toe cap of my boot. The man was without breath and there was so much blood on the floor that I hardly needed to bend down and look for a pulse, although it would have been easy enough to have taken hold of his wrist. It was curious the way he had fallen on his face, with one of his hands slightly behind his back, almost as if it had been tied there. Death had been caused by a single shot in the head. The bullet had struck the man just above the nape of his neck, piercing the occipital bone, close to the lower part of the skull; the point of exit was in the lower part of the forehead. The shot had been fired from a German-made pistol with a capacity of less than eight millimeters. The shot in the victim's head looked as if it had been the work of an experienced man. I thought it much more than likely that the body would end up in a shallow grave—unmarked and unmourned.

"Curious, but it seems as if you're not to have your witness to the Katyn massacre after all, Bernie," said von Gersdorff.

"No," I said. "No, I'm not. But perhaps, in a very small way, the dead have had some justice."

AUTHOR'S NOTE

The International Medical Commission delivered its report on the Katyn Forest Massacre in Berlin, in early May 1943; the work of the members of the commission was honorary; no one was paid or given any other form of compensation. The commission concluded that the Polish officers found in Katyn had indeed been murdered by Soviet forces.

The Soviet Union continued to deny responsibility for the Katyn murders until 1991, when the Russian Federation confirmed Soviet responsibility for the massacre of more than 14,500 men; however, the Communist Party of the Russian Federation continues to deny Soviet guilt in the face of what is by now overwhelming evidence.

Following its defeat at the Battle of Kursk in July 1943, the German Army fell back on Smolensk; the second Battle for Smolensk lasted two months (August–October 1943), and Germany was defeated there, too.

The liquidation of the Vitebsk ghetto took place as described in the novel.

The Wehrmacht War Crimes Bureau continued to exist until 1945. Anyone who wishes to know more about its work should consult the excellent book of the same name by Alfred M. de Zayas, published by the University of Nebraska Press in 1979.

Hans von Dohnanyi was sent to Sachsenhausen concentration camp in 1944; on Hitler's orders he was executed on or after April 6, 1945, at the same time and place as Dietrich Bonhoeffer and Karl Sack.

Colonel Rudolf Freiherr von Gersdorff supplied Claus von Stauffenberg with the explosives to use in an unsuccessful attempt on Hitler's life in July 1944. He survived the war and dedicated his exemplary life to charity. A riding accident in 1967 left him paraplegic for the last twelve years of his life. He died in Munich in 1980 at the age of seventy-four.

Like several other senior members of the Wehrmacht, including Hindenburg himself, Field Marshal Günther von Kluge's loyalty to Hitler was secured by large bribes. Nevertheless, he continued to flirt with conspiracy; he committed suicide in Metz in August 1944, believing that the SS intended arresting him following the failure of the July 20 Stauffenberg plot.

Professor Gerhard Buhtz was—according to the official version—run over and killed by a train while making his escape from Minsk in June 1944; others have suggested he was murdered by the SS around the same time for desertion.

General Henning von Tresckow was a key conspirator in the Stauffenberg plot; he committed suicide near Bialystok on July 21, 1944.

Fabian von Schlabrendorff was arrested on July 20, 1944, following the failure of Colonel Stauffenberg's plot to kill Hitler, and he was brought before the infamous People's Court of Roland Freisler; he was tortured but refused to talk and was sent to a concentration camp; he survived the war and died in 1980.

Admiral Wilhelm Canaris was an active conspirator against Hitler and was involved in as many as ten to fifteen plots to kill him; he was arrested after the July plot and executed on April 9, 1945, at

Flossenburg concentration camp just a few weeks before the end of the war in Europe.

Philip von Boeselager was one of the few July 20 conspirators to survive the war; his role went undetected and he died in 2008.

The chief executioner at Katyn, one Major Vasili Mikhailovich Blokhin, died insane and an alcoholic in 1955.

The fates of Judge Goldsche, Lieutenant Voss, and Gregor Sloventzik are unknown to the author.

There really was a demonstration in Rosenstrasse organized by the wives of the last Jews in Berlin in March 1943; there is a Litfass column there today that commemorates the event, and a piece of sculpture named *Block der Frauen* in a park not far from the site of the protest.

Medical experiments on communists really were carried out by fascist doctors in Spain following the republican defeat in 1939 at a clinic in Ciempozuelos, which was headed by another criminal called Dr. Antonio Vallejo Nágera. Those who are interested should read Paul Preston's excellent book *The Spanish Holocaust* for more information.

The Jewish Hospital in Berlin was liberated by the Russians in 1945 and eight hundred Jews were found alive.